"A TRIUMPH . . . A SUPERB COMIC NOVEL . . . FULL OF GOOD THINGS. . . . There is mortal profundity to Heller's humor. Even as he provokes your laughter, he will be engaging your deepest emotions."—*Sun-Times* (Chicago)

"BRAVO! . . . ORIGINAL, SAD, WILDLY FUNNY, AND FILLED WITH ROARING. . . . Mr. Heller's King David, a splendid creation, is not so much a man for all seasons as man in all his seasons. . . . It is unlikely we will see a more ambitious or enjoyable novel about God and man in this season."

—*The New York Times Book Review*

"SO INSPIRED AND FUNNY. . . . It exceeds the achievement of Heller's *Catch-22.*"

—Mark Harris, *Chicago Tribune*

"AN AUDACIOUS GAMBLE THAT [HELLER] PULLS OFF WITH VERVE AND PANACHE. . . . Nearly every page of this rambunctious narrative has a laugh-out-loud sequence . . . but beneath the banter, Heller is also asking existential questions. . . . Under the mordant humor is a story with modern implications and Heller tells it with comic genius."—*Publishers Weekly*

GOD
KNOWS

JOSEPH HELLER

A DELL BOOK

Published by
Dell Publishing Co., Inc.
1 Dag Hammarskjold Plaza
New York, New York 10017

Dell ® TM 681510, Dell Publishing Co., Inc.

ISBN: 0-440-13185-5

Reprinted by arrangement with Alfred A. Knopf, Inc.
Printed in the United States of America
First Dell printing—October 1985

But how can one be warm alone?

1

ABISHAG
THE
SHUNAMMITE

Abishag the Shunammite washes her hands, powders her arms, removes her robe, and approaches my bed to lie down on top of me. I know even as she takes gentle possession of me with her small arms and legs and with her tiny plump belly and fragrant mouth that it will do no good. My shivering will continue, and she will fear she has failed me again. The chills that rack me grow from within. Abishag is beautiful. They tell me the child is a virgin. So what? I've had beautiful virgins before and felt I'd wasted my time. Both women I've loved most in my life were married when I met them and had learned how to please me through living with their first husbands. Both times I was lucky, for their husbands died at just the right time for me. Abishag the Shunammite is a comely, tidy girl of a yielding and obedient nature and quiet, graceful motions. She bathes each morning, each afternoon, and each evening. She rinses her hands and washes her feet more often than that and scrupulously cleans and perfumes beneath her arms each time before she draws near to feed me, cover me, or lie with me. She is slight and delicate in body and very young, with a smooth and dusky complexion, glossy, straight black hair combed back and downward and rolling outward at her shoulders into an even curl, and very large, meek inviting eyes with huge whites and dark irises that are almost the shade of ebony.

Even so, I would rather have my wife, who asks to see me now at least twice a day. But she comes only in anxious concern for her life and for the safety and future high station of her son after, so to speak, I am no longer among the quick. She does not care about me and probably never really did. She wants her son to be king. Fat chance. He's my son too, of course; but I have others—more, I think, than I have memory left to name should I ever try to list them. The older I get, the less interest I take in my children and,

11

for that matter, in everyone and everything else. Who gives a damn for the country? My wife, large and wide-hipped, is a breathing contrast to Abishag in almost every vital respect. Unlike Abishag, she habitually has an unfriendly stare for everyone, and her eyes are blue, small, and keen. Her skin is fair, and she still dyes her hair yellow with that mixture of saffron and loosestrife she perfected eons back after decades of trying. Tall, brazen, selfish, and formidable, she is more than a match for the shy servant girl and subjects her frequently to rude looks of inspection. With the native instinct of the born connoisseur, her scornful eye asserts confidently that she was always more knowledgeable than Abishag when it came to men. Probably she still is. And probably she always will be. But she has long since given all that up.

As usual, my wife knows what she wants and is unashamed to ask for it. As usual, she wants everything and wants it now. With guilty gaze shifting nervously from mine, she feigns detachment from any ulterior motive and alludes, with an air of innocent and fluttering distraction, to promises we both know I never made. And as usual, she has concentrated on her objective with an intensity so single-minded as to allow no consideration to any subtle strategy that might actually assist in its fulfillment. She cannot make herself believe, for example, that I still might really love and want her. I continue to ask her to lie beside me. She feels we are both now too old. I don't. So to warm and minister to me instead, I have Abishag the Shunammite, who has oiled her arms and lovely young brown breasts with sweet-smelling lotions and scented her neck, ears, and hair. Abishag will try her best without succeeding, and when she rises from my bed, I will be just as cold as before, and just as forlorn.

All day long the light in my room is dreary, as though densely clouded with too many invisible motes. The flames in my oil lamps flicker dimly. My eyes often close without my sensing that I am again drifting off into another brief sleep. They usually feel gritty, inflamed.

"Are my eyes red?" I will inquire of Abishag.

She tells me they are very red and soothes them with trickles of cool water and glycerine squeezed from strips of white wool. The weirdest silence prevails under my roof and outside my windows in the streets and seems to hold and muffle all the jarring noises of the city in a deadening grip. About my halls, my watchmen and servants go on tiptoe and speculate in whispers. Perhaps they are making bets. Jerusalem is prospering as never before, but the populace is astir with rumors and alarming expectations. The atmosphere is rife with suspense and increasing dread, with mounting displays of ambition, deceit, and hungering opportunism. None of this upsets me anymore. The people are splitting into opposing camps. Let them. The threat of a bloodbath is already quivering electrically in the nightly sea breeze. Who cares? My children are waiting for me to die. Who can blame them? I've led a full, long life, haven't I? You can look it up. Samuel I and II. Kings. Chronicles also, but that's a prissy whitewash in which the juiciest parts of my life are discarded as unimportant or unworthy. Therefore, I hate Chronicles. In Chronicles I am a pious bore, as dull as dishwater and as preachy and insipid as that self-righteous Joan of Arc, and God knows I was never anything like that. God knows I fucked and fought plenty and had a rousing good time doing both until the time I fell in love and the baby died. Everything took a turn for the worse after that.

And God certainly knows I was always a vigorous, courageous, and enterprising soul, overflowing with all the lusty emotions and desires of life until the day I waxed faint in warfare on the field at Gob, was succored by my nephew Abishai, and grasped beyond all possibilities of continued self-deception that I had passed my physical peak and could never again be counted on to defend myself in battle. Between sunrise and sunset, I had aged forty years. In the morning I was feeling like an indestructible young man, and in the afternoon I knew I was an elderly one.

I don't like to boast—I know I boast a bit when I say I don't have to boast—but I honestly think I've got the best story in the Bible. Where's the competition? Job? Forget him. Genesis? The cosmology is for kids, an old-wives' tale, a fey fantasy spun by a nodding grandmother already dozing off into satisfied boredom. Old Sarah's fun—she laughed and lied to God, and I still get a big treat out of that. Sarah is almost real in her generous, high-spirited good nature and rivalrous female jealousy, and Abraham, of course, is ever up to the mark, obedient, fair, judicious, and brave, always the perfect gentleman and intelligent patriarch. But where's the action once you get past Isaac and Hagar? Jacob stands up as narrative in a primitive way, and Joseph is pretty lively as the pampered, late-born, bratty favorite of his doting father. But he

13

drops out kind of suddenly as a grown-up, doesn't he? One minute he's dispensing corn and land in Egypt as the pre-eminent agent of the Pharaoh, and just a few paragraphs later he's on his deathbed, breathing his last wish that his bones be carried up from Egypt someday into the land of Canaan. Another headache for Moses, four hundred years later.

Now Moses isn't bad, I have to admit, but he's very, very long, and there's a crying need for variation after the exodus from Egypt. The story goes on and on with all those laws. Who could listen to so many laws, even in forty years? Go remember them. Who could write them down? When did he have time for anything else? And he had to pass them on. Keep in mind that Moses was slow of speech. No wonder it took so long. Michelangelo made statues of us both. The one of Moses is better. Mine doesn't look like me at all. Moses has the Ten Commandments, it's true, but I've got much better lines. I've got the poetry and passion, savage violence and the plain raw civilizing grief of human heartbreak. "The beauty of Israel is slain upon thy high places." That sentence is mine and so is "They were swifter than eagles, they were stronger than lions." My psalms last. I could live forever on my famous elegy alone, if I wasn't already dying of old age. I've got wars and ecstatic religious experiences, obscene dances, ghosts, murders, hair-raising escapes, and exciting chase scenes. There were children who died early. "I shall go to him, but he shall not return to me." That's for the one who died in infancy, because of me or God or both—take your pick. I know where I place the blame. On Him. "My son, my son" was for another, who was struck down in the prime of young manhood. Where in Moses can you find stuff like that? And then, of course, my favorite, that crowning jewel of a triumphal paean that made me grin from ear to ear the first few times I heard it swell to greet me as I strutted along in my youthful exuberance and naïveté. That pleasure soured quickly. Soon I was cringing in fright at the sound of the first of those lovely syllables and glancing over my shoulder in horror as though to evade a blow from some lethal weapon descending upon me from behind. How I grew to fear that rousing tribute to me. But as soon as the first of my mortal enemies had been killed, I found myself shamelessly cherishing again that unique accolade. And even now, in my shivering decrepitude, I am disposed to glow with pride and thrill with sexual thoughts at the picture of all those barelegged girls and women in their tossing skirts of brilliant scarlet, blue, and purple, kicking up their sun-browned knees as they streamed out jubilantly from one hillside village and city after the next to meet us with tabrets and other instruments of music as we trooped back victorious once more, hailing us gloriously again and again with that exultant, beguiling refrain:

> *Saul hath slain his thousands,*
> *and David his ten thousands.*

In the original it's even better:

הִכָּה שָׁאוּל בַּאֲלָפָו
וְדָוִד בְּרִבְבֹתָיו:

Imagine how Saul took to that one. I didn't imagine, and the next thing I knew I was dodging javelins to save my ass and running for my life. You think you've had problems with in-laws? I had a father-in-law who wanted to kill me. Why? Only because I was too good, that's why. Those were the days when butter wouldn't melt in my mouth. I couldn't do a single thing wrong if I tried, I couldn't make a bad impression on anyone if I wanted to—on anyone but Saul. Even his daughter took a shine to me, and turned out a bitter shrew as the first of my thirteen, fourteen, or fifteen wives. Michal saved my life once, it's true, but that hardly justified all the vicious nagging I was subjected to afterward.

Wherever Saul sent me to fight, I went. And the better I was able to serve him in war against the Philistines, the greater grew his envious and furious suspicions that I was slated to replace him and was scheming already to do so. Was that fair? Was it my fault people liked me?

By that time, of course, Saul had been repudiated by Samuel and subjected by God to one of those vast and terrible metaphysical silences that only someone truly almighty and as indispensable as the Lord has the power to inflict. Here I can speak from personal experience: I no longer talk to Him, and He no longer talks to me.

Even my own heart melted with compassion at news of Saul's affecting plaint at Endor on the eve of his death that God would answer him no more. And this was long after I had been anointed

privately by Samuel in my father's house in Bethlehem and told—
for whatever the intelligence was worth—that I had been chosen
by the Lord to be His king in Israel someday. I had a vested
interest in his death, certainly, but I swear I was sometimes sorry
for him and that my hands were always clean. Never was I engaged in anything more sinister than trying to enlarge the affection
and admiration with which he had first welcomed me into his fold
on the day of my killing of Goliath. But his swings of mood were
unpredictable and extreme, and there was seldom a clue beforehand as to when our noble, tortured general and first king would
change into a raving lunatic once more and try to take my life.
There were times, it seemed, when he wanted to kill just about
everyone, everyone, even his natural son Jonathan.

Now there's a problem for you, isn't it? A father-in-law who
spends the better part of his time and strength seeking your death,
who sends assassins to your home at night to murder you in the
morning and leads armies of thousands of his best soldiers into the
wilderness to run you to earth, instead of using them to drive
Philistines back down to the coastal plains where they belonged.
He offered his daughter to me only in the furtive hope I would be
killed collecting the grotesquely low price he set for her. One hundred Philistine foreskins! Saul suffered the paranoid's delusion that
even his daughter and his son were in sympathy with me, and he
was thoroughly correct. I learned from this a fact applying to everyone that is probably of no practical use to anyone: there is
wisdom in madness and strong probability of truth in all accusations, for people are complete, and everybody is capable of everything. There were spooky, tempestuous spells in which killing me
was just about the only thing Saul had on his rabid and demented
mind, the poor fucking nut. Go figure him out.

I've got all those wars and conquests and rebellions and chases
to talk about. I built an empire the size of Maine, and I led the
people of Israel out of the Bronze Age and into the Iron Age.

I've got a love story and a sex story, with the same woman no
less, and both are great, and I've got this ongoing, open-ended
Mexican standoff with God, even though He might now be dead.
Whether God is dead or not hardly matters, for we would use Him
no differently anyway. He owes me an apology, but God won't
budge so I won't budge. I have my faults, God knows, and I may

even be among the first to admit them, but to this very day I know in my bones that I'm a much better person than He is.

Although I never actually *walked* with God, I did talk with Him a lot and got along with Him in perfect rapport until I offended Him the first time; then He offended me, and later we offended each other. Even then He promised to protect me. And He has. But protect me from what? Old age? The deaths of my children and the rape of my daughter? God gave me long life and many sons to continue my name—although all of them have names of their own—but it's hot as hell today, and muggy as well, and I can't get warm; I get no heat, even with Abishag the Shunammite fondling and licking me and covering me with her sinuous, lithe, beautiful little body. Abishag my Shunammite has a good-sized shapely ass for someone who is small and built on so delicate a scale.

Guess what—I was a hunted criminal once, with the "man wanted" sign out for me all over Judah, and not many people talk about that. I was a fugitive outlaw, with a motley crew of six hundred weather-beaten crooks and roughnecks at my command. Do you know what an organized band of six hundred battle-hardened men amounts to? A formidable, disciplined striking force any army would welcome, including Achish and his Philistines of Gath as they mobilized for war against Israel and invited us to ally ourselves with them. Blame Saul that we accepted and really did march off to war against Israel; not many people know about that, either, but there we were on the side of the Philistines as they massed for the battle of Gilboa, where Saul was killed. Lucky for me we were sent away by the Philistines before the fighting began.

If ever I stole, plundered, or extorted, with Judeans or Israelites as the victims—and I'm not admitting I did—Saul left me no alternative. How else was I expected to survive after he drove me away from him and turned nearly the whole country against me? The people of Ziph informed against me, the people of Maon told him where I had come to rest. And meanwhile all I longed for was to go on loving him. I thought of Saul as a father.

"My father," I called from an undergrowth of thickets on the rocky hillside after I'd come upon him sleeping on the floor in the cave of Engedi and had cut a strip from the skirt of his robe to prove I'd been there. "See, I killed thee not."

"Is this thy voice, my son David?" he answered me, and wept. "I will seek no more to do thee harm." The promises of maniacs, like those of women, are not safely relied upon.

Later, the Philistines cut off his head when they found him dead, and nailed what was left of him to the walls of the city of Bethshan.

Gory deeds? I've got more than enough for every taste. I have suicide, regicide, patricide, homicide, fratricide, infanticide, adultery, incest, hanging, and more decapitations than just Saul's. Listen.

I had sons.

I had concubines.

I had a son who went in unto my concubines in broad daylight on the roof of my palace.

I had a star named after me—in London, England, yet—in 1898. Whoever heard of a star of Samuel?

One of my sons murdered another of my sons, and what was I supposed to do about that? Cain and Abel? That was then and this is now. God dealt with Cain himself: "Start walking," he said.

So Cain took to the road and Adam was off the hook. But I had the whole jam-packed city of Jerusalem watching to see what I was going to do after Absalom killed Amnon.

And now the same thing is about to happen again, and I get to pick which will reign and which will die. Adonijah or Solomon. A painful decision? Only if I still cared about my children or the future of my country. But the truth is, I don't. I hate God and I hate life. And the closer I come to death, the more I hate life.

I'm far too old, I feel, to be a father anymore, although I'm not too old to be a husband, and I want my wife Bathsheba back in bed with me. I think I may have been the first grown man in the world to fall truly, passionately, sexually, romantically, and sentimentally in love. I practically invented it. Jacob took to Rachel the first time he laid eyes on her at the well in Haran, but Jacob was a boy, and that was puppy love compared to mine. He worked seven years to get her, then worked seven more when her weak-eyed sister was fobbed off on him in her place on his wedding night. I had Bathsheba the first day I saw her. I had fucking from her that made my brain spin in those few great years I enjoyed with her in which, one day after the next, I could think of nothing better I wanted to do morning, noon, evening, and night than fly back to her side and lock my hands and my mouth and my groin and my soul to her flesh once more. Oh, boy, did I cleave to her! We loved to kiss and talk. We trysted secretly, embraced on the way to the couch, made giddy jokes and laughed excessively, and enjoyed every other kind of cozy, intimate hilarity together until the day the roof caved in with the news she was pregnant.

"Holy shit!" were the words that sprang to my lips.

I don't know whose idea it was to recall her husband, Uriah the Hittite, from the siege at Rabbah-Ammon to legitimatize the fruits of my adulterous intercourse with his wife as the appropriate issue of his own. But I know it didn't work.

"Uriah, go home," I enticed him handsomely, and sent a mess of meat and other victuals to his house to help fuel the licentious marathon Bathsheba and I had mapped out for him. "Enjoy yourself. You have brought me good news of the campaign."

He elected instead to sleep like my servants on the floor of my palace, in quixotic and telepathic solidarity with his comrades-in-arms still encamped in the open fields of Ammon, and in frustrating obedience to our Mosaic laws respecting cleanliness and combat. You could not go into holy battle for at least three days after lying with a woman. Or with a man either, for that matter, or even with a sheep, a goat, or a turkey. People wishing to evade military service commonly lie with their wives, their concubines, or their turkeys just before a call-up. We call this conscientious objection. But Uriah was not even a Jew. Go reason with a Hittite.

"Uriah, go home," I proposed, suggested, commanded, beseeched him frantically all the second day. "Go home, Uriah, please go home. Probably your wife is expecting you. Your wife is a luscious woman, I'm told. Stick it to her. Go give her a boff or two. *Shtup* her. You've earned the pleasure."

Again he slept on my floor instead. Did the bastard know something? I felt myself going mad. I don't know whose idea it was to send him back into battle to be killed. Let's call that one hers.

The widow Bathsheba moved into my palace as my eighth wife as soon as she finished mourning her dead husband.

And immediately she asked to be queen. We had no queens. Would that stop my darling from continuing to ask? Within an hour of arriving in my palace she had examined the apartments, closets, and cosmetic pots of all my other wives and demanded that her own be better and more. The ballsy baby was my favorite from the start. I took more delight in my love for Bathsheba than I did even in my love for Abigail, my elegant lady of quality and refinement who fed me the best lentil soup, barley bread, and leeks I ever ate in my whole life and would be content to cook for me now if she were still among the living. Bathsheba, when I met her, would not put her hands into dishwater if there were any way to avoid it, and she never had to do so again once I took her as wife.

Now she comes to see me daily only in a subversive effort to insure her safety. Her native selfishness is fascinating still; it's heartening to perceive that some things never change. Didn't I once observe that there is nothing new under the sun? She knows much about making love but not much about men, or what can lie in our hearts. She hardly concerns herself with what might lie in mine. Instead she keeps asking that I make Solomon king.

"No way," I started telling her laughingly the day he was born. "There's a dozen ahead of him."

Now there is only Adonijah.

"It's not myself I'm thinking about," she says, "but the future of the people and the country."

She's thinking only of herself. She cares no more about the future than I do. She insists that I've given her my word.

"I'm sure you must have made that promise to me sometime," she says. "I could never make something like that up."

Bathsheba could always make up any lie she chose and instantly believe it true. Her duplicity is transparent. But never underestimate the power of a woman. See what happens in Kings I. I'm the best there, too. Solomon may have more space, but is there anything in his whole life to compare with any portion of mine? The only smart line he ever spoke—the one directing Benaiah to kill Joab in the tabernacle—he got from me. All of the good ones in Proverbs are mine, and so are the best in the Song of Solomon. Study my last charges. They're marvelous, witty, dramatic, climactic. With Shimei I'm merely ingenious. I'm infinitely more decisive with my kinsman Joab, loyal lifelong companion and courageous military captain over all my host for almost my entire career. Not once has he wavered in his allegiance to me and even now, in ripe old age, he has committed his hardy arm and forceful authority to safeguarding the remainder of my rule and securing the orderly transfer of my throne to the only heir with a legitimate claim to receive it.

For sturdy, loyal, valiant Joab, I decreed: "Kill him! Waste him! Blow the bastard away!"

I was always full of surprises, wasn't I? And I was smart enough to appreciate that for Solomon you had to spell everything out. I'll let you in on a secret about my son Solomon: he was dead serious when he proposed cutting the baby in half, that *putz*. I swear to God. The dumb son of a bitch was trying to be fair, not shrewd.

"Do you understand what I'm saying to you about Joab?" I asked him with a look of intent scrutiny and waited for his leaden nod before I added for stress, "Do not let his hoar head go peacefully down to the grave."

Solomon lifted his eyes from the clay tablet on which he was scratching his notes and asked, "What's a hoar head?"

"Abishag!"

Abishag showed him the door and petted my heaving chest until she felt my exasperation abate. Then she washed and dried herself, perfumed her wrists and armpits, and removed her robe to stand before me a moment in all her wonderful virginal nakedness before raising a leg gracefully to enter my bed on one of her biscuit-brown knees to lie down with me again. Naturally, it did no good. I got no heat then, either. I wanted my wife. I want my wife now. Bathsheba does not believe this and would not let it make a difference if she did.

"I don't do things like that anymore," Bathsheba responds firmly each time I ask, and, if out of sorts, adds, "I am sick of love."

She lost her lust when she found her vocations. Her first was to be a queen. Too bad that we had no queens. The next was to be a queen mother, the first in our history, the widowed mother of a reigning sovereign. I refuse to trade and I refuse to grovel. I could order her into my bed with a single cursory command, of course, and she certainly would be here. But that would be begging, wouldn't it? I am David the king, and I must try not to beg. But God knows that, by one means or another, I am going to lie with her at least one more time before I give up the ghost and bring my fantastic story to an end.

2

OF THE
MAKING OF
BOOKS

Of the making of books there is no end and the longer I reflect on this tale of mine, the stronger grows my conviction that killing Goliath was just about the biggest goddamn mistake I ever made. Saul drafted me into his army that same day and I have been living under the sword almost all my life since. Fucking Bathsheba, then fucking her again, then again and again and again, and holding her in my arms until I almost could not hold her longer, and could not bear separating from her—that could have been my second biggest mistake. Nathan really got on my ass about that one, and the next thing I knew there was a dead baby. Love is potent stuff, isn't it? My love for Bathsheba back then was as terrible as an army of banners, as pale as the moon in its heartache, as clear as the sun in its joy. God and I had a pretty good relationship until He killed the kid; after that I kept my distance. I'm sure He's noticed by now, for it's been almost thirty years.

One time even before that, in an access of pride during a lull between conquests, I decided to construct a spectacular edifice to myself and call it a temple of the Lord; but God said no. God knew my inward reason. Vanity of vanities, said the Preacher, all is vanity. God had no need for Ecclesiastes to acquaint Him with vanity.

Nor did I from my youth, for I knew even better than my three infuriated older brothers at the battlefront that I was afire with conceit and bursting with a zeal to show off when I found myself with the chance to fight Goliath one on one. There was no way I was going to let that opportunity pass.

I paid no attention when my brothers ordered me to go back to Bethlehem after I had delivered the foodstuffs sent them by my father for their maintenance in battle. Instead, with the dauntless effrontery for which I was already unpopular in my family, I bounded deftly from outpost to outpost on my mission of crafty

25

instigation, exciting curiosity all along the battle line with my reckless impudence and bold candor. Who could resist wanting to learn more about the brash and fresh-faced lad from the hinterlands of backward Judah who had arrived in their midst so providentially and appeared so willing?

Not Saul. Certainly not Saul, who, with resolute and uncustomary good sense, was striving to create a standing professional army in place of the unwieldy voluntary musters of tradition, in which individual families like my own, or separate clans and tribes, chose to participate or not each time a military crisis arose. Saul was centralizing a government. He had beaten the Ammonites at Jabesh-gilead, whipped, with a good deal of indispensable help from his son Jonathan, the asses of the Philistines at Michmash, and overrun the Amelekites in the desert to the south. It was in the course of assaulting the Amelekites that he had alienated Samuel for all time by taking the king for ransom and the best of the cattle for booty: his commission from Samuel, speaking for God, was explicitly to destroy all, slaying both man and woman, infant and suckling, ox and sheep, and camel and ass. Saul was too uncomplicated in intellect to produce the only lie that might have placated our raging holy man: "I forgot." He gambled instead on the clumsy excuse of having taken the cattle for sacrifice.

"To obey is better than to sacrifice" was the gruff rebuke from the saturnine figure who was benefactor to both of us sequentially. "Because thou hast rejected the word of the Lord, He hath rejected thee as king."

I could have told Saul it wouldn't work. Samuel hewed the Amelekite king, Agag, to pieces, left in a sulk for his home in Ramah, and came no more to see Saul until the day of his death. For Saul, this rupture with Samuel meant a burden of mental distress he was not always able to bear, as well as a tangle of quandaries from which he was never able to extricate himself completely. For me, it was a break.

I was familiar with Saul's methods of recruiting. Every time he saw a strong man, or a valiant man, he took him unto himself for his permanent fighting force as a mercenary to be well rewarded for his prowess and enthusiasm with liberal shares of the spoils. When, after the duel, I was back with the head, the sword, and the armor of Goliath—it would have needed more strength than you think to lug all that crap back up the hill without help—Saul took me to him that same day and would let me go no more home to the house of my father.

I have to confess that living under the sword was not always that disagreeable when we were robustly smiting away at Philistines, Ammonites, Moabites, and Syrians and trouncing them with such predictable regularity that winning seemed easy and bravery normal. But war with Abner, Sheba, Amasa, Absalom, and even Saul were conflicts of a different sort entirely. These were countrymen. Some were blood relations. Amasa was a nephew, Absalom my son. I meant what I said when I said, "Absalom, O my son Absalom, would God I had died for thee!" but neither God nor Joab afforded me the chance. Destroying your own son for some slight and pardonable infraction—as Saul wished to do to Jonathan— might appear an intoxicating treat to some fathers. Not to this one. I could hardly ever bring myself even to scold any of mine. I think I spoiled them all by sparing the rod—most of them did vile or foolish things, even my favorites. Especially my favorites. And when Absalom was dead, I cried as though my heart must surely break.

I cried even longer when my infant child lay very sick and slowly died. For seven days I grieved with my face to the ground. I ate no bread. Nebuchadnezzar went mad and ate from the ground like an ox. I was sane and did almost the same thing, hoping by my fasting and weeping to move God to be merciful. Fat chance. I could better have moved a mountain.

That was one flaw in my makeup—I felt for my children, at least for my sons. I took no account of my daughters. That was another flaw, and I paid for it dearly in ways still too intricate to unravel fully. When my lovely daughter Tamar was raped by her half brother Amnon, I was upset, naturally. Mainly, though, I was annoyed that I had been put in an awkward situation which I hoped somehow would resolve itself. I took no action. I counted on the matter to blow over, as indeed it seemed to. And two years later I was mourning the violent death of Amnon and the exile of avenging Absalom, who fled into Geshur after staging his slaughter.

Three years passed before Joab coaxed me to permit his return. Two years more before I allowed Absalom into the palace to see my face. Absalom bowed. I kissed him. In no time at all he was

27

launching his armed rebellion that forced me to abandon my city of Jerusalem and flee to the other side of the Jordan.

"Remember the curse?" reminded Nathan, almost with glee, as we picked our way on foot from the back of the city toward brook Kidron. The victory of Absalom was all but absolute. A streak of lightning gives more warning. And I a puissant king. I left ten concubines behind to keep my palace clean.

Of course I remembered the judgment of God relayed to me through Nathan that he now chose to call a curse. Whatever possessed me to suppose I could go unpunished for sending Uriah the Hittite to his death? That I knew I should not escape punishment was evident in my spontaneous accord with the impoverished man in the parable invented for the instance by Nathan—the man who was deprived of his one lamb by the rich man who owned many.

"As the Lord liveth," I declared with an anger greatly kindled against the haughty culprit, "the man that hath done this will surely die."

"Thou," declared Nathan, and clapped his hands with a squeal of happiness at the success of his ploy, "art the man."

The bastard had me dead to rights. And the litany of reprisal he recited did indeed have much of the flavor of a curse.

"Three ways there are to humble thee with repentance," he began. "No, make that four. Yea, four things there are that know no surcease of sorrow." Nathan moralizing is as vinegar to my teeth, as smoke to my eyes. Compared to Nathan, Polonius was as silent as the Sphinx. Now, however, my mood of apprehension gradually lifted while he spoke.

That the sword would never depart from my house caused me scarcely any concern; since when, before or after, has there been much peace for anyone dwelling in this Fertile Crescent between Asia and Africa and between the Arabian desert and the Mediterranean Sea? Or anywhere else in the world that we know of? I could settle for that, and my attention was in danger of meandering as he started to dilate on section two of my Olympian sentence, which proved no more alarming.

Evil would rise up against me in my own house. So what? This was an eventuality taken for granted by every Jewish parent. What father is ever spared all kinds of trouble from his children? Our Judges were no better off. Samuel's sons took bribes; those of his predecessor, Eli, lay with women at the tabernacle of the congregation. And I had more children than I could count. Do any of them ever know the meaning of gratitude? It's so much sharper than a serpent's tooth to have a thankless child.

Part three was rather remote: because I had lain with another man's wife, shame of like kind would come to me through mine from a neighbor. That seemed fair enough if it ever occurred. But who could foretell from Nathan's enigmatic words that a son of mine would be the "neighbor" to enact with my wives in the sight of the sun what I had performed with Uriah's wife in shadows and stealth? Who would have guessed that Amnon would rape and degrade his half sister? Where is there even one clue in Nathan's lengthy enumeration of the punishments awaiting me that he was talking not of separate penalties but of interrelated consequences that would fuse into a comprehensible whole with the sudden insurrection of my son Absalom?

Nathan rambled on with so much Delphic obscurity that even had I been concentrating, I probably would have missed in his prognostication any glimpse of Absalom as the principal agent of its fulfillment. God was canny in selecting an addlepate like Nathan. He knew I'd be listening with one deaf ear; otherwise I might have averted it all. I would know the means, find the safeguards. I am David, not Oedipus, and I would have broken destiny to bits. To save my children then, I would have drawn thunder from the sky. But God, that sneak, didn't want me to know. It was one of the few times He has been able to outsmart me.

In time it all came true, didn't it, even part three in that obscure bundle of punishments, although they were concubines rather than wives who were violated after I abandoned the city. But I never thought of my son as a neighbor or of any of my concubines as my wives. To tell you the truth, I never even thought of most of my wives as wives. Michal, Abigail, and Bathsheba were women of special importance to me at different stages of my life, as is Abishag now. This black-haired girl is phenomenally beautiful naked, particularly at the black-haired juncture of her thighs—even Bathsheba says so—and I am thinking of making her my wife if we go on seeing each other much longer on my deathbed. But that's neither here nor there. I remember how grateful I felt for a moment when Nathan surprisingly injected into his monologue a cheery note that seemed to presage a satisfactory finish.

"Don't worry, don't worry," he assured me with a consoling

shrug. "The Lord hath lifted the sin from thee." That was good. "No harm will come to you." That was even better. And then came the zinger. "But the child," said Nathan, "shall surely die."

Trust in the Lord for a twist like that.

I lost my God and my infant in the same instant.

Until HE LIFTED my sin from me and placed it on my baby, God and I were as friendly as anyone could imagine. I inquired for guidance whenever I wished to. He could always be counted on to respond. Our talks were sociable and precise. No words were wasted.

"Should I go down to Keilah and save the city?" I asked while still a fugitive in Judah.

"Go down to Keilah and save the city," He answered helpfully.

"Should I go up into Hebron in Judah and allow the elders to crown me king?" I asked after receiving news of Saul's death and completing my famous elegy.

"Why not?" God obliged me in reply.

Without fail, the answers I received from Him were those I wanted most to hear; and it often seemed I was talking just to myself. I suffered none of that volcanic bullying with which the life of Moses was blighted from the day God entered it, or even one second of agony from that profound and bleak unbroken silence that drove Saul at length to the forbidden witch of Endor to commune in desperation with the spirit of Samuel, the man more responsible than any other human for the deteriorated condition of his mind. When Samuel broke with Saul and cast him adrift in our harrowing world with just his own flimsy resources to rely upon, he took all hope of God away from Saul permanently. There was never again a word or signal for Saul that anyone above was watching or that anyone cared. Burnt offerings could just as well have been used for chopped meat.

Propelled by his miserable need, Saul went to the witch of Endor to learn from the ghost of Samuel the outcome of the battle of Gilboa, which the armies of the Philistines and the Hebrews were preparing to fight the following day. And Samuel let him have it, right between the eyes: Saul would die on the morrow, Jonathan would die, two other of his sons would also die, and the Israelites would be routed thoroughly and scattered from their houses and their tents.

Saul needed that knowledge like a hole in the head. His morale was low enough. A larger nature than Samuel's might have pressed good counsel upon him. What would it have hurt Samuel to tell Saul, don't fight? *Let* them move through the valley of Jezreel. How far can they go? Hammer them from the hills. Harass and skirmish, procrastinate and postpone. Slash them from the rear, smite them on the flanks. Aggravate them, aggravate them. How long can they last?

But Saul's day was drawing to a close, and mine was destined to dawn. Destiny is a good thing to accept when it's going your way. When it isn't, don't call it destiny; call it injustice, treachery, or simple bad luck.

And now my day is drawing to a close, while Adonijah and Solomon jockey for position and Bathsheba, lobbying for her son, visits me with devious and transparent intent, coached in the background by Nathan, who rightly presumes himself on very tenuous ground. If I die tomorrow, Nathan will not outlive me by much. And God seems to be keeping out of things these days. Miracles are past.

For Bathsheba, all show of interest in the well-being of other people is an effort of the will that she is able to exert for about a minute and a half. Inhibition is not natural to her, tact is foreign. She shows me her newest underwear; she still designs those things on occasion to keep busy. If Abishag is ministering to me, she will watch dully and make critical suggestions casually, like a retired veteran giving pointers from the sidelines.

"He never liked that," she might tell the willing servant girl, with her drowsy face resting on her hand and her lids half lowered in boredom. "That way used to be better with him. Why don't you moisten your fingertips with something slippery, dear? Honey is good. Olive oil is the best. Good olive oil."

"You do it," I've suggested.

Now that she is the mother of a grown man—one, as she repeats, fit to be king—the very idea of sexual contact with me is abhorrent. She did not used to find it abhorrent.

She is terribly perturbed because the rival Adonijah, advised by Joab, has come to me with a request to be allowed to give a public luncheon at which he will function as both host and heir apparent.

Adonijah *is* the heir apparent. He believes he will succeed me, and I have done nothing to discourage his assumptions. Adonijah is more gullible than diplomatic and not deeply intelligent. I would hate to have to be the one to do him in. On the other hand, I perversely treasure the possibility of seeing anyone on either side commit an irreversible blunder. Adonijah is already coming close. But so are Bathsheba and Solomon.

If I allow Adonijah his feast, he would be honored to have me attend. Why shouldn't he be? Bathsheba tries to beguile me with a counteroffer.

"Solomon would like to have a small dinner for you right here in the palace instead. That would be easier for you and much less extravagant. Solomon hates extravagance. Let me bring him in to tell you about it."

"Don't bring him in!" I warn sharply. "If I see him I'll hate him, and I'll leave him nothing. Abishag! Abishag!"

Abishag the Shunammite soothed me with touches and sweet kisses after she had shown Bathsheba the door and we were again alone. Bathsheba forgets I have pride and a temper. Remember: it was I who stopped talking to God, not He to me. It was I who broke up that friendship. God was never displeased with me in direct discourse, never brusque or enraged, as He tended to be with Moses. Cross words and criticism from Him came to me only through my prophets, and I always took them with a grain of salt. I cannot help wondering what would happen if I tried speaking directly to God once more. Would He hear me? Will He reply? I have a notion He might if I promised to forgive Him. I'm afraid that He won't.

Unlike me, poor muddled Moses felt the full brunt of God's furious ill humor within moments of hearing from the voice in the burning bush of the astounding mission for which he had just been tapped.

"W-w-w-why me?" was the sensible question posed by this simple and unprepossessing man in the Midian desert to the voice in the bush declaring itself to be the God of his father, the God of Abraham, the God of Isaac, and the God of Jacob. "I st-st-st-stammer."

The anger of God was kindled against Moses right then and there by the implication that He perhaps had erred and gotten the wrong party and that the force that could lay the foundations of the earth and draw out leviathan with a hook might be deterred by something so trivial as a minor speech impediment. He would give Moses a brother named Aaron into whose mouth words could be put. Moses was stunned by the swiftness and intransigence of these tyrannical prescriptions. There was not much room for compromise. Now the man Moses was very meek, and he could raise only pitiful objections to the summary treatment he was encountering.

"Whoever said I was supposed to be nice?" challenged God. "Where is it written that I have to be kind?"

"Aren't You a good God?"

"Where does it say that I have to be good? Isn't it enough that I'm God? Don't waste your time daydreaming, Moses. I ordered Abraham to be circumcised when he was already a grown man. Was that the act of someone who's kind?"

"I'm not c-c-c-circumcised," Moses suddenly recalled, shaking.

"Just wait," said the Lord, laughing.

In practically no time at all, Zipporah, his Midianite wife, was upon him with a sharp stone, haranguing him fiercely for the life of their child. He let her do it. I would never have allowed any one of my wives to draw that near to my privates with a knife, not even Abigail, and especially not Michal. Zipporah cut off his foreskin and cast it at his feet. It's doubtful he could have comprehended much in the tirade of condemnation with which she followed up this action.

"Surely a bloody husband art thou to me," she let our Moses know. "A bloody husband thou art, because of the circumcision."

"It h-h-hurts," whimpered Moses.

"Whoever said that there wouldn't be pain?" asked the Lord. "Where is it written that there shouldn't be pain?"

"It's a hard life You gave us."

"Why should it be soft?" spake the Lord.

"And a very tough world."

"Why should it be easy?"

"Why should we love and worship You?"

"I'm God. I AM THAT I AM."

"Will it make things better for us if we do?"

"Will it make things worse? Go into Egypt now and say to the children of Israel that the God of their fathers wants you to gather them around you and lead them all out."

Moses, ever unassuming, was pessimistic about his chances.

"Why should they believe me? Why should they follow me? What should I say to them when they ask me Your name?"

"I AM THAT I AM."

"I AM THAT I AM?"

"I AM THAT I AM."

"You want me to tell them You're I AM THAT I AM?"

"I AM THAT I AM," repeated God. "And from the Pharaoh," He went on, "I charge you to get permission to journey into the wilderness for three days to make sacrifices to Me. Tell him to let your people go."

"Let my people go?"

"Let my people go," spake the Lord.

"Will he let my people go?"

"I will harden his heart."

"So he won't let my people go?"

"Now you've got it. I want to show what I can do. I want to trot out my stuff for the children of Israel."

"It won't work," insisted Moses in a voice laden with gloom. "They'll never believe me."

"They'll believe you, they'll believe you," promised the Lord. "Why shouldn't they believe you?"

The children of Israel believed, and boy—were they sorry. To some, the petition for three days in the wilderness might have seemed a legitimate request. To the Pharaoh, it was proof that the Jews had spare time and were entertaining foolish ideas.

"Ye are idle, ye are idle," the Pharaoh reproved them. "That's why you have time for sacrifice. Let more work be laid upon the men."

"We are worse off than before," groaned those children of Israel beneath the increased work load and the beatings. There was menace in the sullen eyes with which they regarded Moses. "Why did you ever start in with us?"

Moses, in bafflement, returned to the Lord to complain. "Why are You being so evil to the people? Is this why You sent me to them? You haven't made things any easier, and neither have they been delivered from the Pharaoh."

"I am hardening his heart."

"Again You're hardening his heart? Why must his heart be so hard?"

"To allow Me to demonstrate powers that are greater than those of all his magicians and of all other gods. And to impress upon the world forever that you are the people I have chosen as favorites."

"Will that make much difference?"

"No difference at all."

"Then where is the sense?"

"Whoever said I was going to make sense?" answered God. "Show Me where it says I have to make sense. I never promised sense. Sense, he wants yet. I'll give milk, I'll give honey. Not sense. Oh, Moses, Moses, why talk of sense? Your name is Greek and there hasn't even been a Greece yet. And you want sense. If you want to have sense, you can't have a religion."

"We don't have a religion."

"I'll give you a religion," said God. "I've got laws to give you that have never been heard before. I will bring you out of slavery in Egypt into a good land, a land of brooks of water, of fountains and springs, flowing forth in valleys and hills, a land of wheat and barley, of vines and fig trees and pomegranates, a land of olive trees and honey, a land in which you will eat bread without scarcity."

That's what He promised and that's all that He gave us, along with a complicated set of restrictive dietary laws that have not made life easier. To the *goyim* He gives bacon, sweet pork, juicy sirloin, and rare prime ribs of beef. To us He gives a pastrami. In Egypt we get the fat of the land. In Leviticus He prohibits us from eating it. A perpetual statute He makes it yet, that we eat neither the fat nor the blood. The blood contained the spirit of life and therefore belonged only to Him. The fat was bad for our gall bladders.

And so much trouble. Hardly had Moses made good the exodus from Egypt into the wilderness of Sinai than the people were murmuring against him in hunger and thirst and were ready to stone him. Moses and me—each of us faced death by stoning from followers soon to exalt us. With God yakking away at him from one side for forty years and the people groaning and threatening on the other, it's no wonder he looks so old in that statue in Rome and went to his grave at only a hundred and twenty.

K EEP IN MIND that by the day of my battle with Goliath, I had already been to see Saul once, to sing and play for him after his troubled soul was afflicted by the first of the visitations of acute and profound depression from which he was to suffer the rest of his life. By one of those extraordinary coincidences giving rise to a belief in mystical and extrasensory phenomena, the evil spirit fell upon Saul in Gibeah the day Samuel appeared in my home in Bethlehem. Samuel, afraid Saul would kill him if the purpose of his coming were guessed, arrived with a red heifer on a rope, as though journeying on a mission of sacrifice. He anointed me from a horn of olive oil hanging from a long leather strap around his neck. In Gibeah at just about that same moment, Saul went into the doldrums. He would not come from his room.

"Comfort him with apples" was the suggestion of Abner, captain of all Saul's host. "Stay him with flagons."

When apples and flagons failed to work, someone in attendance suggested music as a remedy known to have charms to soothe a savage breast.

"No shit?" said Abner, and agreed to give it a try.

Thereupon one in the group recommended me as a youth cunning with the harp, and valiant, prudent, and comely besides, a son of the worthy family of Jesse in Bethlehem. I'd never had doubt that my skill with stringed instruments and my remarkable talent for verse would someday open doors for me.

Yes, we did have music then, and a love for dancing, and we liked clothes also; the gaudier the colors, the livelier our delight. The tunic I wore for my fight with Goliath was of fine bleached linen with hyacinth-blue jagged vertical streaks woven down my skirt and with the same heavenly blue at all of the borders and seams. Around my waist was a vermilion girdle of dyed kidskin. As soon as the Phoenicians had perfected a mordant for gold, I put my dye factory at Dirjath-sepher to work producing thread and yarn in that color for ornamental contrast in the garments of different reds and greens and blues so popular with men and women and with the murex purple from Tyre that had given the land of Canaan its name. We liked smart clothes in many colors and always had. Samson gambled for shirts, and Joseph swaggered about in his coat of many colors and nearly forfeited his life to the jealousy of his ten older half brothers. Lucky for all of us they sold him into slavery in Egypt instead.

We had jewelry also—rings, pendants, brooches, and bells. Women wore some too. I was thrilled with the crown and arm bracelet brought me by the wandering Amelekite who'd come upon Saul mortally wounded. And I took another crown from the king of Rabbah-Ammon when the city fell. Apart from helmets for battle, these crowns were just about the only headgear around. We had no hats in Palestine but had no problem about going into temple without them, because we had no temples either.

I liked my women in yellow, blue, and crimson, and I loved the scarlet lipstick, azure eye shadow, and dark mascara that came into use as our economy moved us into an era of luxury, leisure, and decadence. All of my wives, thank God, were concerned with being beautiful and spent most of their hours with attire, cosmetics, combs, mirrors, and hair curlers. Only Bathsheba was ambitious for more. Always an acquisitive clotheshorse—she invented bloomers, you know, as one in a number of careers to which she successively applied herself for a short while—her preferences in style ran toward the daring and unorthodox. While the rest of my wives were tinting their hair red, Bathsheba was experimenting with yellow and gold compounds and often looked like hell when the dyes did not stain or remain fast uniformly. She was the first woman I know to wear false eyelashes and fingernails and black kohl on her eyelids, and she designed the caftan and the miniskirt, along with her bloomers. Abishag the Shunammite enchants me with her lovely scarves and headbands and with her clinging robes. Each day I grow more pleased with her; I may be falling in love with Abishag. At my age too, and in my condition. But Abishag, it strikes me suddenly, must think I'm a fag because I haven't been able to get it up with her yet, and because she's probably heard all those ancient and unfounded rumors about me and Jonathan.

First impressions die slowly, bad impressions take even longer. Most likely it was that line about Jonathan, love, and women near the end of my famous elegy that is more to blame than anything else for the malicious gossip about the two of us that lingers on in smutty repetitions by small-minded people seeking to find fault with me. Nobody ever talks about the phrase just ahead in which I assert unequivocally that I think of him merely as a brother. I was writing serious poetry, I was not abasing myself with scandalous public confessions. I am David the king, not Oscar Wilde; and I probably would use those same words today if I could not improve upon them, even with foreknowledge of the spate of derogatory and sniggering tales they would spawn. *Vita brevis, ars longa.*

Another trait in all my wives, and nearly all my concubines, for which I certainly do pay homage to God or good luck is their compulsive predilection for excessive applications of powerful perfumes and colognes, and of rouges, body ointments, and skin and air fresheners of fragrant nature as well. A harem in a warm climate is not an easy thing to keep in mint condition. And the stench in other parts of my palace and in the noisy streets outside was no bracing improvement. I had endeavored without results to enlist the efforts of Adonijah and Solomon in wrestling with the challenging problems of garbage removal and sewage disposal. Adonijah remained dedicated to his social life, Solomon to his pornographic amulets, and the administrative awareness of each was restricted to the sources of royal revenues and to the cultivation of the good will of our military leaders, Joab and Benaiah, respectively. I had hoped for my beloved city of Jerusalem to flower into the sparkling showplace of the Middle East, comparable in beauty and significance to such distinguished capitals as Copenhagen, Prague, Vienna, and Budapest; instead, as Michal was quick to point out, it was turning into another Coney Island. Michal, that bride of my youth who never ceased invoking her royal pedigree, was on balance a royal pain in the ass and lived, unfortunately, to a ripe old age. I will never forget the cry of joy that soared from my lips when they brought me the news she was dying.

It was indeed a mixed and colorfully diverse neighborhood in which we found ourselves living after Joshua led us across the Jordan and leveled the walled city of Jericho to start the conquest of Canaan. In the main, Hebrews, Canaanites, and Philistines got along rather well with each other when not engaged in war. From the friendly Phoenicians in Tyre we acquired the dyes and the knowledge of handling fabrics that enabled us, in time, to establish our own famous garment center. From Hiram king of Tyre I got the cedar trees, carpenters, and stone-squarers to construct my palace, after I had taken Jerusalem from the Jebusites. Just about the only thing missing in the entire area was an Arab, and no one was looking for one. By the time I was born, we were already using tools of iron bought from the Philistines, and from the people in Canaan we had learned how to farm and to live sedentary lives in houses built of mud brick with wooden beams and rafters. We had pastures, groves, vineyards, tillable acres for barley and wheat, and our own towns and cities. The homes were small, of course, without any privacy for sex, but vastly preferable to the goatskin tents of our nomadic past and infinitely more comfortable and refined than sleeping outdoors rolled up in our woolen cloaks, as we did when traveling. And that was another practice of Solomon's that was widely regarded as mean and grasping: if he took a man's cloak as a pledge in the morning, he would not always return it to him by nightfall.

People with means still keep tents in the country for the summer months; others erect them on the roofs of their houses to catch the refreshing evening breezes from the sea. There is always more space and seclusion above than indoors below. In fact, it was during a meditative and solitary stroll on the roof of my palace, taken to insulate myself against another querulous diatribe from Michal, that my eye first lit upon the exquisite spectacle of Bathsheba taking her bath on the roof of her house. I stopped in my tracks. Up spoke the Devil. I lusted, sent for her, and had her that same day. And the next morning, and the evening following, and the next, and the next, and the next. I could not stop touching her once I began. I could not help staring at her. I could not end wanting her. This was love. I soaked her up—I could not stop breathing her in. I can't stop looking at her now. I wanted to fuck her every day. I want to fuck her now. We arranged after that first night that she would bathe on her roof each morning and each evening on days I could not have her with me but would be free to watch her. Her motions were lascivious when she knew I was staring.

Lewdness was always more openly important to the Canaanites and Philistines than to us, and when we came upon them, their fertile ways proved a hearty catalyst for the close commercial, cultural, and sexual intercourse soon flourishing among us all. Moses and his men had never seen so much pussy as they were offered by the women of Moab on their tortuous trek from Egypt into the land of Canaan. We had the wine, wool, grain, and fruit once we settled here. The Canaanites had the pork and their religious idols and temple prostitutes; the Philistines had the seafood and beer and a monopoly on the secrets of ironworking, which they guarded ruthlessly. They sold us the tools but would not teach us to sharpen them or allow us weapons of iron. Travel was safe in peacetime, trade brisk, relations friendly. Now and then, I'll admit, we might run into a little anti-Semitism from the Philistines, but this seemed to be more a recognition of parochial distinctions than anything else. And we, in turn, had our term of disparagement for them: they were uncircumcised, and we would never let them forget it.

More typically, relations were mutually profitable and interdependent, and familiar to us all since childhood was the sight of the Philistine workingman trudging into view with his grinding wheel strapped to his back, arriving to sharpen the kitchen knives and scissors of the women and the goads and plowshares of the men of the field. And we would go down to Gaza, Gath, or Askelon with wares to sell or coulters, mattocks, and axes of iron to be filed, or sometimes just for a pleasant evening of fish and beer. On the way there or back, or both, we might break our journey at a Canaanite temple to participate with the reverent in their religious practices of temple prostitution and contribute that way to the general welfare of the community. It still is touch and go whether humping a single or married woman on the grounds of a temple does indeed enhance the fertility of our fields and our flocks. But the Canaanites knew more about agriculture than we did. And it certainly couldn't hurt.

We had our Jehovah and our purification rites, and the Canaanites and Philistines had a nifty little deity in their goddess Astarte, who was always portrayed with her ample breasts bare, and with her thighs deep and her heavy hips rounding almost into full circles. Sometimes in all that hurly-burly, things got a little mixed up and we got the pork and the idols and they got our laws and our purification rites. As with Uriah, a Hittite, who would have felt himself unclean for battle had he lain with Bathsheba when I wanted him to. That was one of those laws God gave Moses that did not make things easier for us. A man lying with a woman was unclean. A man lying with another man was even more unclean: an abomination. And a man who lay with a beast, said the Lord, would surely die. And if he doesn't lie with a beast, I would have countered, he won't die?

Naturally, intermarriage was commonplace in this melting pot and always had been. Bathsheba had her gentile husband, Joseph married an Egyptian, Moses had his Cushite and his Midianite, and girl-crazy Samson was a natural pushover for Philistine twat and feminine Philistine wiles. Even my own great-grandmother on my father's side was not Jewish: she was that same Moabite woman, the widow Ruth, who followed Naomi back into Judah, choosing our God and our people, and who married my great-grandfather Boaz. And that hairy man Esau took two Hittite women for wives, a grief to both Isaac and Rebekah, who doubtless had fixed their hopes on a big Jewish wedding party. We had wedding parties, though we had no such thing as a wedding or a marriage and no words for either. The man simply paid the price of the woman to her father and took her home as a wife. There might or might not be a celebration. I know I danced and drank at the festivities attending my taking of Michal with a gusto my new wife, the princess, strongly deplored and assured me was gross. I still feel I lost much on Michal, though she cost but the symbolic hundred Philistine foreskins Saul had requested for her. I threw in an extra hundred just to show I was a sport. Michal turned out a snob and a common scold and wasn't worth even one Philistine foreskin.

The thing about Philistines is that they were more cultured than we were and had a higher form of civilization when we first ran into them. Everyone we met then had a higher civilization. No sooner did Joshua move us across to the west bank of the Jordan to conquer the Canaanites and learn from them how to farm and fuck and build houses than we found with dismay that the Philistines were really the dominant military forces in the area, and this was especially so back in the days of Samson, that goon, that troglodyte, that hairy ape. Oh, that Samson. Such a dope he was, a *yold*, an overgrown ignorant country rube stupidly tempting the savage wrath of the Philistines again and again with the headstrong misdeeds of an erring half-wit. Who could handle him? A Judge they named him yet! One day he's falling in love with a Philistine girl and playing games of riddles with her neighbors for thirty changes of sheets, pillowcases, and shirts, the next he's killing a bunch of them wholesale and setting their fields, vineyards, and olive groves ablaze with firebrands tied to the tails of three hundred foxes. *Oy vey.* He couldn't think of an easier way? A hundred times the people of Judah pleaded with him to behave.

"Samson, Samson, what are you trying to do to us?" the elders argued with him. "Don't you know the Philistines are rulers over us and can make us servants as of yore?"

They were talking to a wall. A hundred times they wanted to tie him up and deliver him bound to the Philistines. At last he let them; then, just when they seemed to be rid of him once and for all, he burst his cords amid his Philistine captors and slew a thousand more of them with the jawbone of an ass. And the next thing you knew, before anyone could blink an eye, there he was again, already in love with Delilah, another Philistine chippie, spilling his precious secret to her, and losing his hair, his strength, and his eyes in return. Milton was a mile off the mark in his *Samson Agonistes*. The Samson we remember was too coarse and obtuse to define himself as "eyeless in Gaza, at the mill with slaves" or to picture himself dying with "all passion spent." Although his own last words aren't bad with his "strengthen me, I pray thee, only this once, O God, that I may be at once avenged of the Philistines for my two eyes."

Though John Milton is frequently imperfect—the first of his two "Tetrachordon" sonnets is contemptible and the second is not excellent—I beg the same indulgence for him that I occasionally require for myself. Our art comes first. He and I are poets, not historians or journalists, and his *Samson Agonistes* should be looked at in the same fair light as my famous elegy on the deaths of Saul and Jonathan, along with my psalms and proverbs and other outstanding works. Adore them as poems. Look to us for our beauty rather than factual accuracy. A striking case in point can be found in my notable "Tell it not in Gath, publish it not in the streets of Askelon, lest the daughters of the Philistines rejoice." If literal truth and common sense were factors, there would be no way to account for the enduring popularity of this mellifluous statement, for the people in Gath and Askelon knew about Saul's defeat and death at Gilboa a good two and a half weeks before I did. Such departures from reality may generally be explained on aesthetic grounds. Milton was a man of considerable ability. Who knows—who can say for certain that his works will not last as long as mine have and perhaps enjoy someday a readership as large as does my famous elegy?

What a merry dirge I was able to produce under pressure on the spur of the moment! Considered objectively, my famous elegy is really as high-spirited as an ode to victory and joy. The death of Saul did open doors to me and clear a path. How lively my humor when I saw what I had written and concluded as my own severest critic that I would have to change not a word and delete not a line. At times since, I'll admit, I have regretted that I did not look longer at my "Jonathan: very pleasant hast thou been unto me: thy love to me was wonderful, passing the love of women." Now that's the troubling statement that gave birth to all the unsavory and unfounded speculations by people seeking to deprecate me or wishing to supply impressive justification for their own deviate inclinations. What's wrong with it? My meaning is as clear and frank and wholesome to me now as it was when I wrote it. John Milton might have said the same thing if he'd thought of it first.

But Milton was a grave Puritan in a cold climate, while we were a raunchy and polygamous lot in a warm and teeming locale. So we reveled in intermarriage, inbreeding, and outbreeding, and always had, even in the days of Abraham, first father to us all. And here's something else. We started out with short beards and straight noses—you can look at the wall paintings—and who knows? With a slightly different genetic break in our wanderings and couplings, we might all be as blond and gorgeous today as Danish schoolchildren. No wonder our moral philosophers then and since have tended to be glum, censorious, and ascetic. Milton was a prude and a pedagogue and made his daughters learn Hebrew; I never made mine learn English. And I think I had a nobler subject in Saul and Jonathan than he did in Samson, that crude, blundering jackass who bullied his parents into arranging marriages they disapproved of and couldn't keep his cock out of Philistine harlots. A *naar* like him they make a Judge, while I don't even have one book in the Bible named after me. What really gets my goat is that Samuel has I and II, even though he dies in I and doesn't get a single mention in II, not one. Is that fair? And those two books of Samuel should be named for me, not for him. What's so great about Samuel?

"Whoever said I was going to be fair?" I can just see God replying if ever I should ask. "Where does it say I have to be fair?"

"Do You always know what You're doing now?" I believe I might say if I ever could swallow my pride and speak to Him again.

"What difference would it make?" I can hear Him retort with indestructible aplomb.

For cynicism like that, who needs Gods like Him? Am I blind? More than fifty years ago I could perceive for myself that the race is not always to the swift nor the battle to the strong, but that time and chance happen to us all. The sun ariseth and the sun goeth down and the same things come alike to the righteous and the wicked. Bread does not always come to the wise, nor riches to men of understanding, nor favor to men of skill, but one event happens to us all. The wise man dies no better or more wisely than the fool. In what way, then, is the wise man wise? Therefore, I began to hate life and came to the conclusion that a man has no better thing to do under the sun than to eat and to drink and to be merry, although that isn't always the easiest thing to do when all you've got is a pastrami. Just the forequarters of a cow and sheep He gives us to eat. What are we supposed to do with the rest?

But Samson did want those shirts, Joseph treasured his coat, and I delighted in my crowns and bracelet. The daughters of Israel rejoiced in their clothing of scarlet, together with other delights, and in their ornaments of gold. I don't know where those descendants of ours from eastern Europe ever got the idea that somber black hats with wide brims and gloomy long alpaca or gabardine coats without decoration were part of our tradition or that the drab hues of mourning were especially appropriate for prayer. Probably from the lamentations of Isaiah and Jeremiah, the invasions and destruction of Israel by the Assyrians, Babylonians, Greeks, and Romans, the Diaspora, the medieval European persecutions, the pogroms of Poland and Russia, and Adolf Hitler.

To this day just about anyone can tickle me with the gift of an exotic bauble or a flashy blanket, robe, or skirt, or with presents of clothing or jewelry to my servant Abishag. There is no hypocrisy or greed in the pleasure with which she receives them. Bathsheba was acquisitive, Abishag is not. I love to watch Abishag preening herself in something delightfully new. I like the way our women today mince along coquettishly, with roving, flirtatious eyes reflecting from the glass of their hand mirrors. I like their glittering headbands, earrings, bonnets, wimples, and crisping pins, the rings on their fingers and the bells on their ankles, their bracelets, chains, mantles, hoods, and veils. I love women, and I always have, and I enjoy their ambitious and exhausting efforts to make themselves attractive. They've got jewels coming out of their noses. And we've got our own Savonarolas too; we no sooner attain some stage at which we can relax a little and start enjoying the fruits of our progress than others begin foretelling our destruction for doing so —people who don't like our pleasures and entertainments at all and insist on prophesying our doom.

"Instead of sweet smell," goes the familiar street saying, "there shall be stink. And instead of a girdle, a rent. And instead of well-set hair, baldness. And instead of a stomacher, a girding of sackcloth. And burning instead of beauty."

Nevertheless, we've decided to take our chances. Who gives up opulence voluntarily?

ALSO KEEP IN mind that I had already been chosen by Samuel to succeed Saul as king by the time I traveled from Bethlehem to Shochoh with my carriage of cheeses, loaves, and parched corn on the day of my fight with Goliath, and I was therefore even more certain than formerly that I no longer had to take shit from my brothers or sisters, or, for that matter, from my father or mother, although they were never much bother to me. Consequently, it was in rather buoyant spirits that I gave the finger to my brothers Eliab, Abinadab, and Shammah when they commanded me to return home without delay after I had delivered the provisions for them and their captain. There was just no way in the world I was going to turn my back on that glorious spectacle of the two armies facing each other across the valley of Elah, or discard the chance to be a hero once I spied it beckoning to me.

Leading his red heifer on a rope to outwit Saul's informers, Samuel had appeared at our house without notice and directed without waste of time that each of the sons be brought before him in order of descending age. I wondered about that red heifer as soon as I was told about it. The rest is much like the Cinderella story, for I, the youngest and least significant of the boys in that family, was out keeping the sheep and not in the forefront of anybody's thoughts on that historic day.

"Come in," said my father hospitably to the unsmiling and determined traveler who had walked with his red cow from Ramah to Bethlehem on instructions from the Lord. "Take off your sandals and come inside. Wash your feet. Sit yourself down on the floor and have a bite to eat. Would you like to go up on the roof and rest awhile?"

Samuel was prepared to settle right off for Eliab, the firstborn. But God was speaking my language when He told Samuel a book must not be judged by its cover or a man by his countenance or height. All of my brothers were taller than I. Abinadab and Shammah were passed over in turn. It was the same way right down the line with the rest of the seven.

"No more?" Samuel was disgruntled. "Is this all thy children?" They sent to fetch me.

The tall, thin, gloomy man I found waiting for me when I arrived back home certainly was hairy. If you believe that Esau was a hairy man, you should have had a look at Samuel in his long robe, with all that black and graying hair drooping out from almost every visible inch of him. Apart from sunken dark eyes that were fervid and sad and a narrow patch of forehead that was wrinkled and yellow, it was impossible to tell where the flesh and bone of his face left off and the stringy growth from his scalp and cheeks began. He was not so disagreeable a sight to me once I came to know him better, although I was never at ease in his company and I cannot say I really liked him. His mother, Hannah, mumbling like a drunkard at the altar of the tabernacle of Eli, had vowed that no razor would come upon the head of her son if God ever allowed her to bear one. You could bet without risk that the promise had been kept.

His manner that day was arbitrary and short-tempered, his voice was dry, and there was nothing remotely like exultation in the manner in which he greeted me as the person he had been sent to find and anoint. The words with which he explained himself were uttered tonelessly. He did not seem at all the sort of traveler who might enjoy a good joke or take a moment for friendliness or small talk.

"The Lord hath repented Himself of having chosen Saul king," he said, uncorking his horn of oil, "for he hath not always followed all His words and performed His commandments. This day He hath rent the kingdom from Saul and given it to a neighbor who is better than he and who is more after His own heart. That neighbor is you."

You'll be interested to know I was flattered. But Samuel was already leaving. I ran to catch up.

"Does that mean," I cried, "that I don't have to keep the sheep anymore or let myself be bossed around by my family? Does it mean that you and everyone else have to do whatever I command?"

"It means," came the tart retort, "that you and everyone else always have to do whatever *I* and the Lord command. For the Lord and I are more powerful than anything on earth, more powerful than all of the armed might of Saul. Saul has not always obeyed every command. Therefore, we have rejected Saul and chosen thee."

I was struck suddenly by the presence of his red cow. "The heifer, the heifer," I blurted out in a rash heresy typical of my audacious personality. "Your red cow. What did you need it for? How come you and the Lord are so frightened of Saul if you've really got all that power?"

"Don't mix in," Samuel answered in a rasping voice. "Do you want to be king of Israel or don't you?"

Well, you know the answer I gave to that one. "When can I start? How soon does it happen?"

"When it happens."

"Can I tell people?"

"Tell nobody," he cautioned, turning pale. "Your words will put us both in danger."

I told everybody.

"If you don't stop talking about it," came the threat from my brothers, "we'll put you down a well and sell you into slavery in Egypt."

Even illiterates like my brothers and sisters knew a little bit about the story of Joseph and that epochal journey down into Egypt and could espy the similarities in situation between me and the central character.

And a constant threat I endured through childhood was to have done to me what was done to Joseph if I didn't mind my sheep and my manners and go to bed when told and make no noise about the house when anybody else was trying to sleep. They sure did hate the sound of my playing and singing when they were trying to rest. Neither my brothers nor my sisters took any interest in my music or writing and, to the last days of each, were unanimously unimpressed by my famous elegy and impervious to the virtue and stately beauty of the many psalms and sayings with which I am rightly credited. Like Joseph, I was the glittering prodigy in a large family of older, primitive, unappreciating boors. To call them Philistines would be a slander—against the Philistines, who were really quite advanced. Uncircumcised, but advanced. Doubtless the vanity and snobbishness characteristic of Joseph and me were continual incitements to the animosity of the others; but I was never as bratty as he, and I believe I had more than a coat of many colors and a good way with interpreting dreams on which to base my early presumption of superiority.

Still, Joseph is a collateral ancestor with whom I can easily identify and sympathize, even at his infantile worst, although he certainly put them all through the wringer, didn't he, once they journeyed down into Egypt during the famine to buy food and he found himself with their lives in his hands. He recognized them; they did not identify him. But revenge was not that sweet for him. Hope deferred makes the heart grow sick, but I don't think he knew that.

Fighting tender emotions he could not always contain, he tantalized his brothers with a fine drawn-out cruelty before disclosing himself in the end as their long-lost brother and affording them haven in Egypt. What was the point? He didn't enjoy it. If you keep in mind how long it took those days to go down to Egypt from Canaan by foot, and then trudge back and forth again, you realize he must have kept them sweating on tenterhooks for almost half a year with his bewildering frame-ups for theft and spurious accusations of reconnoitering and with his unnerving demands. More than anything else in the world, he wanted to feast his eyes on Jacob again, and see, kiss, and embrace Benjamin, his younger full brother. By prolonging the suspense and terror, he was needlessly delaying the reconciliation he himself was yearning so dearly to consummate. Where were the laughs? After each new frightening setback he engineered for them, he went flying away with his eyes bathed in tears to cry by himself in his chambers. Even that same aged father he revered he subjected to an agony of heartbreak and dread, and he came close to bringing his gray hairs with sorrow down into the grave by asking for Benjamin as a hostage.

"Joseph is not," Jacob had warned with foreboding when left with no alternative but to send Benjamin down into Egypt with the others, "and my son is left alone to me of my marriage with Rachel. If I am bereaved of my children, I am bereaved, and my gray hairs with sorrow soon will be brought down into the grave."

With humble integrity, Judah offered himself as prisoner instead, describing to Joseph the danger to their father. Listening, Joseph's heart broke. He could maintain the deception no longer and he kissed all his brethren and wept upon them. At Jacob's death Joseph had him embalmed, and how the eyes of those rustic

GOD KNOWS

nomads must have opened at their first exposure to that Egyptian practice! For Joseph, it was already familiar stuff.

What goes on in families that they perpetrate such heartless deeds upon each other? God knows I've been guilty of much in my time, but I've never been guilty of anything like that. And my children have been just as bad as Jacob's, with the things they've done to each other and to me. It could be that the spoiled child in all of us never grows up and that the feelings of Joseph for his father and his brothers were no less confused and confusing than were Saul's to me, or toward his real son Jonathan. Or than mine for Saul. Or mine for God, and His for me: we can't seem to make up our minds. I was sorry for Saul all the way and I am sorry for him now. I worshipped and idolized Saul, for he allowed me at last, for a little while, to be able to love myself unembarrassedly to the fullest, until he began to hate me unfairly with that malignant and psychotic mistrust and I was finally forced to run from his murderous anger. My drive was to excel rather than to subvert, and I don't believe I deliberately ever said or did a single thing to weaken his position.

And I know I certainly never went nearly as far against any of my brothers as Joseph did against all of his; but mine, of course, never went that far with me. They mocked, they growled, they ordered, they nagged, criticized, and interfered. But they never seized me with the intent to kill me, imprisoned me in a well, and sold me instead into slavery to a caravan of traders crossing down through Canaan from Gilead into Egypt. They did not come with my bloodied coat to my thunderstruck father and report I had been eaten by an animal. That part was ugly. I was young when I killed Goliath, and after that I was no longer in their power and they were in mine. I gave them all what protection I could when they dispersed in panic from Bethlehem at the rumors that Saul was planning a blood feud against my whole family, and they made their way as best they could to the headquarters I had established in the cave at Adullam. My mother and father I placed in the keeping of the king of Moab on the other side of the Jordan. All the rest in the families of my brothers and my sisters I took with my two new wives and my six hundred fighting men and their full households when I crossed over into Gath in the service of King Achish and his Philistines.

49

"You worked and fought for the Philistines?" people to this day will be aghast to recall.

"You're goddamned right I did," I could reply in warm temper. "And my men would have stoned me to death if I hadn't."

Now that's another good part of my struggles with Saul that you aren't likely to find in Chronicles, are you? They bowdlerized us both. What difference does it make now? I came through when it counted, didn't I? So did Joseph and Moses, and God should give thanks to all three of us for helping Him make good on His promises to Abraham. I did it with the sword. Joseph did it by translating a confounding dream of the Pharaoh's about stalks of corn and fat cows and skinny cows into a familiar two-word precept that might have earned him a stinting accolade from Sigmund Freud and ignited a flash of esteem in the eye of every trader in commodity futures. The interpretation?

"Buy corn," said Joseph.

"Buy corn?" said the Pharaoh.

"The dream," said Joseph. "The dream wants you to buy corn."

When the famine struck, only the storehouses of the Pharaoh were full. Hungry people came with money from round about the lands of Egypt and Palestine to buy the food they needed in order to live. When the money failed, they paid with cattle, horses, and asses. When the livestock was gone, they paid with their land, and then with themselves. The Pharaoh owned it all, except for the land of the priests. Joseph decided on a fifth for the Pharaoh of everything produced, and lo—among the other amazements of their civilization, the Egyptians had also devised feudalism and sharecropping.

A fifth? Not even I could get away with that much, or ever wanted to. Solomon did want to, but had to settle for a twelfth and brought the kingdom to the brink of collapse with his reckless and vainglorious expenditures. He reached for everything and lavished all on himself, and his imbecilic heir gave the shattering blow to all hopes of restored national amity with a jeering public utterance as soon as he took possession of the throne following Solomon's death.

"My little finger shall be thicker than my father's loins," said the princely Rehoboam fatuously to a populace already restive from exploitation. "My father made your yoke heavy, and I will add to your yoke. My father chastised you with whips, but I will chastise you with scorpions."

With scorpions yet, that moron. As smart as Samson he was, and half as civil. Who did he think he was talking to? Overnight, the work of Joseph, Moses, God, and me had disintegrated into explosive chaos and ruin. Civil war again, and the empire I had created was once more split in two separate countries.

Moses got nothing but abuse from every side for all his trouble. Joseph, at least, got permission from the Pharaoh for everyone in the families of the sons of Jacob to move down into Egypt, where all of the good of the country awaited them. But these shaggy tent-dwellers from Canaan were in for another discouraging surprise when they arrived with their cattle and perceived at once that assimilation into this cultivated society was going to be impossible. They were an abomination. Egyptians wouldn't eat with them. Not because they were Jewish, mind you—they themselves hardly understood that. All they knew was that they were the sons of Jacob. They were shunned because they were cattlemen, shepherds. To the polished Egyptians, every sheepherder was an abomination, every nomad. Thus, there could be no room for them at any of the inns of Egypt until Joseph requested and secured from the Pharaoh pleasant pastures in the land of Goshen upon which the sons of Jacob, who was now also called Israel, could settle with their wives and their little ones and their tents and animals, and eat, as a grateful Pharaoh gave assurance, the fat of the land. The genius of Joseph for oneiromancy had saved the country from starvation and enriched the Pharaoh beyond his wildest fantasies.

Four hundred years later there arose up a new Pharaoh over Egypt who knew not Joseph. The Egyptians had short memories, didn't they? He cast the descendants of the children of Israel into slavery under hard taskmasters and it fell upon Moses, poor soul, to lead us out. He never asked for the job and he got no pleasure from it.

"Take off your shoes," was the first he heard of it from the burning bush. "You're standing on holy ground."

There went the rest of his life. To talk the Pharaoh into releasing the Hebrews from Egypt was going to be hard enough. To organize a harmonious resistance movement and persuade the Hebrews to follow him out was not going to be much easier. To follow? Maybe.

Without argument and faultfinding? Impossible. Like striving for the wind.

"Who-who-who-who—"

"Stop that, Moses," said the Lord. "I fixed your stammer, didn't I?"

"—am I that they should continue to believe me? How-how-how—"

"Moses!"

"—shall I answer when they ask for a name?"

"I AM THAT I AM."

Moses stepped back with a look of pain. "Again I AM THAT I AM?"

"Why not?"

"They look darkly at me now and mutter curses already. What-what-what—"

"Will you stop that?"

"What will they say when the hardships increase?"

"Vey is mir" is what they did say when the hardships increased, which translated means "Woe is me." The Pharaoh bore down harder as they toiled in the field and labored with mortar and brick.

"I'm still hardening his heart," the Lord replied when Moses objected. "And don't you dare tell Me again that it makes no sense. That's a commandment. I'll take care of the Pharaoh, you take care of the people. I think you're going to have your hands full."

That was no lie. What would have happened had Moses said no?

As though taking note of the volume of conversation that necessarily lay ahead, God did give Moses a brother named Aaron into whose mouth they could put words, then a sister named Miriam to pitch in as a prophet. Otherwise, with Moses slow of speech, the ten plagues could have amounted to twenty and the forty years of wandering to four hundred.

In departing from Egypt, they wisely avoided the way of the land of the Philistines and headed southward through the way of the wilderness of the Red Sea. Moses took the bones of Joseph with him. The grumbling and kibitzing he deplored were aggravating him from the start, along with that peculiar ironical statement, shaped in the form of a rhetorical question, which we Jews invented and with which we have been identified since the day Cain responded: "Am I my brother's keeper?"

"What's the matter?" was the snarling recrimination with which the crowds descended upon Moses when they saw the Egyptian chariots racing after them. "Are there no graves in Egypt that you had to lead us away to die in the wilderness?" That was another good one.

By the middle of the second month the whole congregation was murmuring in hunger against Moses and Aaron and missing the good old days of bondage in Egypt where they sat by the fleshpots and ate bread to the full. Moses was defensive. The Lord sent manna. They preferred the fleshpots and bread. God gave them some quail. And poisoned them for eating it.

And He spake. And He spake and He spake and He spake a lot to Moses, and then He spake and spake to Moses some more. There was so much spaking it's a wonder Moses had time to walk. And not one word of thanks or praise, not one word ever. And never anything to anyone afterward about missing him when he was gone. The good Lord just never seemed to tire of speaking to Moses, blowing up over one thing or another with his threats of mass annihilation and laying down the laws one day after the next all through Exodus, Leviticus, Numbers, and Deuteronomy. He wrote them on stone with his finger; for him that was easy, but Moses was the one who had to bear the heavy tablets down the mountain. And that time that he smashed them when he saw the golden calf, he had to go all the way back up the mountain for another set. Forty years this went on, with God wrathful and fulminating and the people recalcitrant, stiff-necked, and disobedient. Till that day arrived when—weary enough to want to wash his hands of it all, I'd bet—he hiked up Mount Nebo to the top of Pisgah for his look across the Jordan at the Promised Land he was barred from entering for some undisclosed trespass neither I nor anyone else has been able to figure out. And shortly thereafter, though his eye was not dim nor his natural force lessened, Moses died, and no one even to this day knows the place of his sepulchre.

Some Promised Land. The honey was there, but the milk we brought in with our goats. To people in California, God gives a magnificent coastline, a movie industry, and Beverly Hills. To us He gives sand. To Cannes He gives a plush film festival. We get the PLO. Our winters are rainy, our summers hot. To people who didn't know how to wind a wristwatch He gives underground oceans of oil. To us He gives hernia, piles, and anti-Semitism.

Those leery spies returning from Canaan after their first look described the place as a land that eats up its people, a land inhabited wholly by giants. The reports were false but not altogether off the mark. True, there were figs, pomegranates, and clusters of grapes so heavy they could be borne back only on a thick staff shouldered between two men. But the land does tend to eat up its people. Still, it's the best that's been offered us, and we want to hold on to it.

Only Joshua and Caleb of the twenty-four taking part in that first exploration had confidence enough in the destiny proclaimed by the Deity to wish to move forward. The people balked at the black picture painted by the others.

"Push on, push on," the Lord sought to rouse them when He found them mired in consternation. "I will send hornets before thee. I promise. The dukes of Edom will be amazed, the mighty men of Moab will tremble, the inhabitants of Canaan will melt away. Fear and dread shall fall upon them and they'll all be still as stone. You'll drive out the Hivite, the Canaanite, and the Hittites, and the Perizzites and Jebusites too. They'll turn their backs and run. Nothing can stop you. I give you My word."

Nobody budged. The Lord resolved to strike them dead on the spot. He was livid, He was wroth.

"I'll kill them all!" He roared to Moses. "You think I'm joking? How much more do you think I'm going to be provoked by these people and do nothing? How many more signs do I have to show them before they begin to believe? I did it before, once with a flood, once with fire and brimstone. Stand back, Moses."

"Can't we reason together?" Moses began trying earnestly to deter Him, emphasizing that God would become a laughingstock to the Egyptians for destroying His chosen people after taking them so far and promising them so much. "And they will tell the people of other lands, who will laugh at You also and no longer fear You. They will say we were killed because You were unable to lead us in, not because we were unable to follow. They will believe You failed, not us."

"All right," relented God, who did not wish to become a laughingstock in Egypt. But He aimed his thumb over His shoulder in a jerking motion and commanded, "Start walking. Hit the road."

And back into the wilderness of Paran near Kadesh-barnea they went for another thirty-eight years, until all who had murmured against God then had given up the ghost and one generation had passed away and another generation had come. If God is ever remembered, it certainly won't be for His patience and human kindness, will it? Of all who had traveled from Egypt, Joshua and Caleb were the only ones allowed to enter the Promised Land. When the Lord said, "Hear, O Israel, thou art to pass over Jordan this day," Joshua and Caleb led their forces across the Jordan to Jericho and embarked upon the conquest of Palestine that nobody till me was able to complete. The land of Palestine is still a vigorous place of diverse and mutually enriching cultures. The difference now is that all of it is mine.

But don't ever get the idea He made things easy for me. Life as one of God's chosen has never been a bed of roses. Ask Adam, ask Eve. Give a look at what He did to Moses, at what happened to Saul. God might have set things up for my encounter with Goliath, but I still was the one who had to kill him. I had to work and suffer like a dog almost all my life. I was nearly forty years old before I reigned in Jerusalem, and everything I got I earned by the sweat of my brow.

Joseph sheltered and preserved us, Moses brought us to the border, and Joshua took us in. But I'm the one who finished God's job. And God knows, I think, that He owes me at least something for the part I played in helping Him reach His goal.

Imagine how He would rate today if we'd never even got here or been exterminated after we did. And He also knows I expect to be rewarded before I die, not after. He owes me an apology too—at the very least. I'm not saying I shouldn't have been punished for those sins I committed. I'm saying that the punishments He chose were inhuman. I wonder what favor I'd want. I think I may be afraid to ask for it. I'm afraid He won't grant it. I'm more afraid that He will. Wouldn't it be tragic to find out that He really has been here all this time?

God does have this self-serving habit of putting all blame for His own mistakes upon other people, doesn't he? He picks someone arbitrarily, unbidden, right out of the blue, so to speak, and levies upon him tasks of monumental difficulty for which we don't always measure up in every particular, and then charges *us* for *His* error in selecting imperfectly. He tends to forget that we are no more infallible than He is. He did that with Moses. He did it with me. He was gravely disappointed in Saul. But He sure guessed right with Abraham, didn't He, our first patriarch.

Now Abraham was a prize, and I am proud to be his descendant, for reasons having little to do with his covenant with God or his being the first of our patriarchs. He himself did little bragging about either. Sarah, his wife, is a favorite of mine too, for her laugh and her lie. Abraham laughed also. Abraham laughed so hard he fell down on his face upon hearing from God that Sarah would bear a son, for she was already past ninety, and it had long ceased to be with her after the manner of women. Sarah lied to God when He asked her why she'd laughed and she reminds me of Bathsheba at her best with her laughter and her lie, her penchant for mirth and her fondness for lively deceit. A convivial beauty in youth, Sarah was a hellcat with other women when it came to protecting her own. Bathsheba was that way too, and I would like to put my arms about her waist again and cling with my head resting upon her.

Abraham dumbfounds me still for having performed with apparent ease a feat of incredible difficulty. He circumcised himself. Now this is not an easy thing to do—try it sometime and see. As you surely must know, I speak with extensive, irrefutable knowledge of some of the mechanics of circumcision, acquired in the days of my betrothal to Michal, when I went merrily sauntering down from the hills with my nephew Joab and a band of stouthearted singing volunteers to collect those hundred Philistine foreskins to pay to Saul in exchange for her. It takes six strong Israelites, we figured, to circumcise one live Philistine. The job turned easier after I finally got used to the idea of killing the Philistines first. It did not cross my uncomplicated mind that Saul was setting a snare for me. It did not occur to him I might survive. Each of us had underrated the other, and he was more wary of me than ever after that. I had a wife and he had the big advantage: he knew he wanted to kill me, and I did not.

Even with the passage of so many years, and even with the knowledge that she helped me escape the blades of Saul's assassins, I am unable to retrieve a single fond recollection from my long marriage to Michal. Instead, welling up within me each time I remember her name is the same vindictive resentment I experienced for her the day she marred my triumph after I had finally brought the ark of the covenant into Jerusalem in a national and holy celebration about which everyone in Israel but her felt glorious jubilation. What a festival that was! What a parade I led! But she was a baneful person who spoiled my good days and rejoiced in my bad and who would never allow herself to extol or admire me or to view me as most others did in the mythic dimensions of a hero king, or as a huge, monumental figure immortalized on a great pedestal of white marble, and that's another thing that pisses me off about that Michelangelo statue of me in Florence. He's got me standing there uncircumcised! Who the fuck did he think I was?

If anything, the Michelangelo statue of Moses in Rome looks more like me in my prime than the one in Florence does of me at any phase of my life. Everybody says so. I wasn't that large, naturally, and I'm not made of marble. I have no scar on my shin or horns jutting from my head. But I had that same superior and sublimely articulated physique and that same unquestionable aura of immortal greatness and strength until I began to lessen with age and they would let me go no more out to battle.

My weight has shrunken since. My hair is thinner and my beard is white, and my fingers palpitate with these recurring freezing seizures that often make my jaws chatter and that even Abishag the Shunammite, in all her virginal, firm, congenial loveliness, is powerless to alleviate while they run their raging course inside me, though she blankets me tenderly with all her body and rubs me everywhere with her hands and soft face. I wonder if she is old enough to know how majestic and virile I used to appear before my muscles wasted and I began to wither with age. Beneath the lotions scented with calamus and cassia with which she freshens herself and the fragrance of aloes and cinnamon with which my servants perfume my bed, I can smell the coarse magnetic secretions of the natural human woman, and I want her. I want her, yet I don't get hard. The heat from her pores does not suffuse into mine. Her compact female form is shaped perfectly, her breasts so fresh and full, with long, dark nipples, her flesh shimmering and smooth in the flickering light from my oil lamps and utterly without a mark. Where did they find for me so remarkable a skin lacking even the tiniest mole and faintest freckle? Abishag. Abishag. Abishag?

"Abishag!"

Lately, I have taken to calling her to lie with me even when I'm not cold. I feel better with someone than I do alone. Now that I've grown used to her, I am starting to notice things. Certainly her kisses are sweet. Her mouth is flavored with honey. Against my knee, then upon my thigh, which I struggle to brace in order to increase the sensation, I can feel those bristling, black hairs in her neatly trimmed pubic mound, all of them crisp, curling, and springy. I love the healthy swell of her belly. Recently, just once, and for the very first time, I put my arm out to touch her. I spread my hand at last on the curve of her hip. She is smooth. There is not one ounce of superfluous flesh. All is as firm and silken as I supposed. Bathsheba, changing normally with time, is heavier now and shaped with less definition in face and body than when younger. She still proudly has all her front teeth, which are small, crooked and crowded upon each other, and chipped slightly at some of the corners. She was a child, unfortunately, before we Jews took so naturally to orthodontia. It would not matter to me if she lacked some front teeth, for I am in love with Bathsheba and desire her love more than wine, as much as ever before. Bathsheba could still warm me, bring heat to my veins with a healing rush of blood. Bathsheba could excite me most easily if she wished to, but she doesn't believe so and doesn't want to. She may not want to because she doesn't know she can. If I am seventy, she is somewhere between fifty-two and sixty, according to which one of the lies she habitually told was true. With the circumscribed and subjective vision of a self-centered courtesan, she cannot believe for a second that I would want to fuck her when I can have Abishag the Shunammite. The truth is that I can't fuck Abishag the Shunammite and probably can fuck her. I get my rudimentary stirrings of an erection only when she is with me or when I find myself hoping she is on the way to plead for her life again in her indirect manner and will sit for a while with her head slightly lowered in make-believe deference while she tries to think of things to say to prolong her visit. I aid her at times with teasing bits of information when I see her at a loss. She bites her lip, she bites the side of her finger. Often, I do want her to stay longer. It was I, for example, who first let her know, with a concealed spasm of malicious delight, of Adonijah's idea for his public feast. Slouching listlessly on her cushioned bench, with her long, slender legs sprawling outward in different directions and her finger absently winding her yellow hair, she pricked up her ears at that, improved her posture a bit, and concentrated tensely. The wicked flee when no man pursueth, the cynical see only cynicism in others, the guileful find guile when there is no guile.

We both take it for granted that my death, though approaching, will not come without warning or without leaving me sufficient time for final announcements. It is much to her advantage to keep me alive until I change my mind. Her long hair is golden again this week and deepens almost daily a shade closer to the ash gray that is her natural color and that she will abruptly decide to obliterate by bleaching her whole head bright again. Not for my Bathsheba the wily tinting or delicate touching up with gossamer brushes. For three or four days there might be no word from her. Then she will come breezing in a flaring blonde again, the only one in all Christendom. The thin-spun hairs on her forearms she must color to invisibility too. The hair on her legs she removes with hardened coatings of melted wax. She uses scissors under her arms.

She is as cuckoo and self-seeking as ever, and I am in love with her still. I don't believe now that she was ever in love with me, although she used to say she was, and I do believe she thought she was. Always, I believe, she was more in love with the idea of being in love, and especially, of course, with the idea of being in love with David the king. That much she admitted when she disclosed that her bathing each dusk on her roof in a place observable from my own had the premeditated goal of evoking my fancy and having me send for her. She hit the bull's-eye, that girl, the first time I laid eyes on her.

We certainly did have a rousing good time of it together those first three wild years, the ghastly bad blending incredibly with the carefree and tempestuous good until Uriah and my baby were both dead and she gave birth to Solomon. Then it was over. Her lasciviousness cooled. And she found instead the purpose of her life she had long been seeking, the career for which she had been hunting and unknowingly preparing herself.

"Let's name him King," she actually did suggest, when delivered successfully of our second child, a bouncing baby boy.

God had relented and forgiven us. But I have not relented and forgiven Him.

M Y E I G H T H W I F E, Bathsheba, was the first of the only two people I have ever known who were able to assimilate the terminologies of love into their normal vocabularies with such fluency that even the most mawkish banalities and lurid obscenities rapidly acquired an appreciating verbal currency of shared and precious meaning. I was the second. Bathsheba shamelessly taught me how. She taught me to say things, to make disclosures, to whisper and sigh adoringly and even rhapsodically of responses I was enjoying for the first time, and to ask questions freely about womanly things that have always been mysterious and forbidden and wrapped in darkest secrecy. She proved I could learn to do what I would have staked my life was beyond my masculine capacity to do, that I could someday learn to say "I love you" without hesitating and to say it without quailing or smirking, without feeling so faint my knees might knock, and that, without feeling effeminate, I would *want* to say "I love you" to her and be able to say "I love you" to her without faltering with embarrassment, fright, humiliation, or shame.

"I love you, Bathsheba," I can remember saying to her in utter sincerity shortly after we began, as we lay one afternoon recuperating in each other's arms, "and I so much wish that I didn't."

"That's good." She smiled, a tutor proud of all benchmarks of progress.

"I love you, Bathsheba," I was telling her but a murmur or two later, "and I'm so glad that I do."

"That's better," she judged, rewarding me richly with the beam of pleasure in her bright blue eyes.

Recollections of that sort warm my heart and bones more fervently than Abishag the Shunammite has been able to do yet with all her flourishing beauty and soft caresses. Thank God my burly nephew Joab was never present to hear me say "I love you" to Bathsheba and is not in possession of knowledge like that to add to the belittling surmises about me implanted first in his mind by my devotion to music when we were boys growing up together in Bethlehem, and furthered by my companionship with Jonathan and the assortment of smutty fabrications surrounding that friendship of ours like a polluted garden of rank weeds. But I simply do have to kill Joab, don't I? He has never thought as highly of me as I have thought of myself. That would be reason enough, for the knowledge that he doesn't is more than a king should bear and has gnawed at my vitals for almost a lifetime. And what about Nathan? Nathan, that hypocrite, that prophet, must have known from the outset that I was after Bathsheba's ass and getting it every morning, noon, and night, but never said a word to dissuade me until after her husband was killed and he found he had something real on me. Jerusalem is a very small town. And Bathsheba was a very loud woman. Maybe even Uriah knew.

By releasing me from inhibition and forcing me to say pretty things, Bathsheba uncovered in me a dormant aptitude for romantic eloquence that I applied successfully for years afterward to bewitch and seduce even her after she had resolved she would no longer allow me to. I gloried in doing it once she taught me how. I would use words—pure, poetic, rapturous words—to turn even Bathsheba's head, overcoming attitudes of rigid objection without conceding anything practical she wanted in return. I enjoyed exploiting her old weaknesses unscrupulously with the talents she had given me. I would talk in torrents, use words in flowing cascades, to dissolve and overcome her forthright determination to hold me at arm's length and her passions to herself.

"Now just one minute, David, keep back, you just keep back," she would command with severity, in that manner she had learned to adopt upon fixing her sights resolutely on some meaningful compact she had illusions of arranging with me. "You're going to have to come across with something concrete if you want me to love you. I want a genuine commitment."

"Amethyst?"

"I want Solomon to be king."

"This is my beloved," I would answer, going on the attack by talking to her as fast as I could. My hands on her shoulders would meanwhile be urging her backward. "She feedeth among the lilies," I might say. "My beloved is mine, and I am hers. Your breasts are like two young roes that are twins. Your hair is like a flock of goats, your teeth like sheep that are even shorn. Thou art fair, my love, behold thou art fair. Oooooh, you bastard. Oooooh, oooh, ooooh, you bastard." All I did was let myself speak the truth.

"Oh, David, David," she would sigh loudly in an astonishment of ecstasy, melting backward willingly to the couch with her eyes already skewing about in their sockets. "Where do you get words like that?"

"I make them up."

"Do you want to stick it in?"

Bathsheba was the only one of my wives and concubines who came. With what I know now, Abishag will be the second, if I'm ever lucky enough to put together the will and the stamina. Abigail enjoyed having me near and blossomed in that surcease from lone-liness, fear, and solitude against which my large hands around her back were as a dependable and protective wall. Michelangelo was right in giving me enormous hands. Abigail would have welcomed my sleeping with her every night but was too considerate a human ever to ask. Abigail was the one woman in my life who really did love me. I miss her now. Each dawn now, I find myself missing her more than I did the daybreak before. Mornings are my very worst hours. Abigail would have been distraught to know how poorly I sleep and how isolated I feel. She would seek some way to relieve that wordless melancholy with which I am afflicted when I can't sleep or when I do sleep and awake from dull and dimly remem-bered dreams in which nothing untoward occurs but which leave me despairing nonetheless. Bathsheba, of my three real wives, would explode in bed like a Canaanite or a howling monkey, or like one of those lustful Moabite or Midianite women Moses found impossible to keep distant from his encampment. I was alarmed the first few times by those unexpected paroxysms of cresting noise and unchecked heaving and writhing. "Ooooh, ooh, ooooh, you bastard!" was a blissful and poetic expression I first heard from her.

"Where did you learn how to do things like that?" I asked in my innocence.

"Some of my earliest girlfriends were whores."

There is nothing at all like jealousy in Bathsheba now if she is present while Abishag is ministering to me. Nor ever any of that spontaneous vim with which Sarah, childless, volunteered her ser-vant girl to Abraham for the propagation of his offspring and rooted them both on to fruition from without the tent. A giving nature is not Bathsheba's. A taking nature is. This wife of mine is proud of that and so am I. When one is infatuated, faults are endearing that in others would be heinous. Someone else might wish to strike her dead for her dispassionate attitude toward me. Someone else would not understand her as I do, or treasure her as fully.

"Are you feeling warmer today?" is just about as much as she can bring herself to say about my enfeebled condition. "You seem to be getting thinner. I don't think anything she can do is going to help. What have you said about that feast those people want to give? Is there anything new? What's it all for, anyway?"

GOD KNOWS

This is a different woman from the feverishly possessive one I took into my palace. I wish she were still as jealous. In keeping with custom, Bathsheba offered the daintiest of her servant girls for me to lie with and keep as a concubine when she settled in, but added, with an aspect of serious purpose and grim determination, that she would cut my balls off if I accepted.

"I'm not going to have *her* gloating at me."

I was equally pleased each time she was successful in intercepting me on my way past her apartment in search of someone different in my harem who might capture my fancy for the moment. Arms akimbo, gorgeous head cocked, she would bring me to a halt at her doorway with a despotic voice that compelled respect.

"And just where do you think you're going?" she was likely to demand. "You come in here right this minute. Get your skirt up."

And there we would be once more in a matter of seconds, at it again on her mattress with our skirts up around our necks in thrashing copulation, making the frenzied beast with two backs.

Now she gives tips to Abishag. When she watched me put my hand on Abishag, I spied a flicker of attention move through her, and she leaned an inch nearer to stare with a keener intentness than she had shown in either me or my virginal consort before. In a dull, sleepy voice, she has since occasionally questioned the girl briefly about her thoughts and her past to satisfy some faint glimmer of curiosity.

Abishag is in awe of Bathsheba and regards her at all times with the wide-open, respectful gaze of idolatry befitting a legend. She is so dark, she answers, because of the sun, for she was made by her mother to keep the vineyards of the family in her home in Shunem. More than anything, she wishes to be pleasing to everyone here and tries as hard as she can to be liked by all. Trying hard to be pleasing to others, my wife dryly remarks without raising her cheek from her hand, is not the best way to succeed in becoming so.

"What do you want with an old woman like me," were the words with which Bathsheba refused me the last time I propositioned her, "when you have a pretty girl like her?"

For as long as I've known her, she has been fashioning sequences of plans too convoluted to materialize and timetables for achievement too far-reaching to be met. Definitely, she lacks the discipline of mind needed to impose some consistency on the lies she tells. I

63

have a better memory for her duplicities than she has. Bathsheba lied about everything and told the truth about everything. Her lily-white face would flood a vivid scarlet whenever I caught her in one of those ruinous discrepancies into which I would guilefully conduct her; and then, inevitably, she would laugh from her whole torso, without trace of misgiving, reminding me again in that impenitent and admirable way of the image I keep of Abraham's feisty Sarah, although Bathsheba has never been as plucky or as good-natured.

Sarah had much the better spirit. Sarah, barren, gave Hagar to Abraham for procreation. Hagar, with child, despised her mistress and flaunted her pregnancy over her. She picked the wrong party. Sarah flew upon the uppity servant girl and drove her off into the desert. Not until the Lord appeared with assurances did weeping Hagar dare return. That was Sarah for you, our first Jewish mother, of whom I am so fond and proud.

And Abraham too was remarkable. A father of many nations, God said He would make him, and kings would come out of him. His seed would be as numerous as all of the stars in the heaven and would possess the gates of his enemies. He forgot to add it would take much time. Gracious and peaceful by nature, Abraham took up arms to rescue his nephew Lot from abductors and debated persuasively with God to spare even this one just man in the destruction of Sodom rather than to destroy the righteous with the wicked. He was already rich in cattle and silver and gold when the Lord appeared to him in the form of three strangers in the plains of Mamre as he sat in the door of his tent in the heat of the day. Had they been but passing bedouins, he doubtless would have responded with the same instinctive hospitality, and he was the essence of gentility and etiquette when he invited them to wash their feet.

"Rest yourselves beneath that tree. I'll have some water fetched."

He hurried inside the tent with instructions for Sarah.

"Make ready quickly three measures of fine meal, knead it, and make cakes of bread upon the hearth."

Then he ran to his herd and chose a tender calf to be dressed and served with butter and milk. At that time, it was still okay to eat our meat with butter and milk. Abraham stood by them while they ate in the shade of the oak tree. Wiping their mouths when finishing, they repeated to Abraham the information given to him once before that Sarah would bear him a son. Abraham was contemplative. Listening in the tent door, Sarah heard the prophecy. She laughed. God knew.

"Wherefore did Sarah laugh?" asked God.

"I didn't laugh," Sarah lied.

"You did so," insisted God. "I know you did. What's the matter? Do you think that anything is too hard for Me to do?"

Abraham and Sarah are the only ones I know of who ever got a laugh out of a conversation with God.

Christ knows I could have used one often. I could use one now. But I know more than anyone that I'm not anywhere near the person Abraham was, or so willing and obedient a servant. Abraham was saintly, I guess. Or stupid. He was prepared to go all the way along with God when tested with the order to bring his young boy Isaac up a mountain, build an altar, and sacrifice the child upon it.

"My father," said Isaac, carrying the wood. "Behold, we have the fire and the wood. But where is the lamb to be sacrificed for the burnt offering?"

And Abraham said, "My son, God will provide Himself a lamb for a burnt offering. Let us go together."

Abraham built an altar. He laid the wood on the altar. And he stretched out his hand for the knife with which to slay his bound son. Only then did the angel of the Lord call to him out of heaven and reveal the ram caught in a thicket by his horns that was to be substituted for the boy in the sacrifice. Now God knows I would not have done that, covenant or no covenant. When the notion arose in His head to kill my infant, He had to do the whole job Himself. He knew I would not lift a finger to help. I did all the praying and fasting I could to influence Him to desist. There was no changing His mind. I lacked the genius to sway Him that was congenital in Moses and Abraham. But Moses and Abraham were pious men who were devoted to Him fully. And I was never pious or devoted. I'm not devoted to Him now. God will have to make the first move if He wants to end this tension between us. I have my principles; and I too have a long memory.

They named their baby Isaac, which means "he laughs." With Rebekah as wife, Isaac sired twins. Isaac favored Esau. But Rebekah advanced Jacob, and I doubt Isaac laughed much when, dim of vision with cataracts but with a lip-smacking yen for savory venison, he recognized he'd been hoodwinked into giving the blessing reserved for Esau to Jacob, who had disguised himself in goatskins as his hairier brother. Isaac then had to hear Esau's cry of universal despair that seems to me must pierce almost every human heart.

"Bless me, even me also, O my father," Esau begged bitterly and lifted up his voice and wept. "Hast thou no blessing left for me? Hast thou but one blessing? O my father, bless me, even me also."

So many times those same words could have been my own.

Esau raged aloud against Jacob, swore to kill him. "I'll crush his feet. I'll break his bones."

Instead, when next they met, this artless man embraced with tears of love and unweakened family longing the brother who had appropriated his birthright and his blessing. This was after Jacob, with immense trepidation, had sent ahead his four families and remained all night by himself on the safe side of the brook, where he wrestled to a draw until daylight with a cryptic angel who left him with a damaged hip and told him, upon leaving, that his name would no more be Jacob but Israel.

We still call him Jacob.

And I strongly doubt that Jacob, who was as smooth a man as Esau was a hairy one, did much laughing either when he awoke after his wedding night and discovered that the girl inside the bridal veil and nightgown with whom he'd lain in the nuptial bed was not the Rachel he had toiled seven years to obtain but the soreeyed sister Leah. Rachel was beautiful and well formed and Jacob had loved her from the day of their first meeting at the well. Leah had pinkeye. Seven more years of indentured servitude to Uncle Laban were necessary before Jacob could have his Rachel too.

Leah bore children quickly. Rachel had none, and it was a little like the Sarah-Hagar story all over again. Consumed with envy, Rachel thrust her handmaid Bilhah onto the mat with Jacob to conceive children as her surrogate. Leah counterattacked with *her* maid Zilpah, giving her to Jacob as a wife. With so many women playing such active roles in this orgiastic contest of childbearing whipped up by these competing, hot-blooded sisters of Haran, the poor patriarch found himself being screwed silly four times a day, and it's a wonder his brains didn't go soft. At long, long last, Rachel produced Joseph, then Benjamin. By the time they left off, the tired old man found himself with twelve sons and a daughter by four women. Embalming Jacob was the only existing way to honor his sacred request that his remains be carried back into Canaan and laid to rest with his fathers in the cave of Machpelah before Mamre in Hebron. Sleeping already in the cave of Machpelah were Abraham and Sarah, Isaac and Rebekah, and Leah. Missing now from these first families is only the adored Rachel, who died in the desert giving birth to Benjamin and was wrapped in strips of linen and buried in sand.

Joseph, the late-born favorite of his father, was already seventeen when presented with the coat of many colors, and old enough to know better than to go showing it off to his sweating older brothers, who were already resentful of the maddening partiality of which he was the spoiled and insufferable recipient. And Joseph had a dream. They were all binding sheaves. His stood upright in the center and those of the others bent to it in obeisance. I've had worse dreams. And he dreamed yet another dream, in which the sun and the moon of his parents and the eleven drab stars representing his brothers all dipped in the sky to bow down to him in homage. Another nice dream. But he was a dumbbell for crowing about it. I would have wanted to kill him too. And—presto! They stuck him down a well. And abracadabra! All of a sudden, give a look: he was a grand vizier, and the Pharaoh had made him ruler over all the lands of Egypt.

So it all somehow came to pass, didn't it? It was almost as though God knew what He was doing: only because they *had* sold him into slavery was he there in Egypt with the means to save them.

Coming into his days, Joseph too asked that his bones be carried up out of Egypt to the land sworn by God to Abraham, Isaac, and Jacob. Moses saw that it was done. And Joseph also was embalmed when he died at a hundred and ten in the very last sentence of Genesis. Embalming was not then a transgression of the Mosaic code, because we had no Mosaic code for another four hundred years. All we had was a covenant with God that every century gave indication of having been from the beginning a very bad deal. Abraham kept his part of the bargain.

But God made no tangible move to satisfy His end of the contract until the day He summoned Moses to the burning bush and told him:

"Take off your shoes."

Moses was standing on hallowed ground.

Now there is the man I want most in all history to speak with. My affinity to Joseph is as nothing to the empathy, awe, and reverential admiration I feel for Moses. "W-w-w-why me?" was precisely the right question to issue from this startled, unassuming fugitive in the Midian desert. But Moses held them together and remained in God's good graces, didn't he, for forty years, against every hardship and obstacle imaginable. God was provoked repeatedly by the people He had chosen. They moaned and muttered against Moses; the priests charged him with arrogating too high a station to himself, the sinners fornicated and worshipped idols, and his sister and brother disputed his authority because of the Ethiopian woman whom he had married. As a matter of record, the marriage of Moses to the Ethiopian woman proved a compatible one, and just about the only time she ever raised her voice to call him a dirty Jew was after he had raised his voice to call her a nigger.

Such tumult in that desert. Hardly had the Red Sea closed behind them upon the Pharaoh's chariots than they began to forget the stern taskmasters in Egypt who'd made them serve with such rigor and had turned their lives bitter with such hard bondage. They remembered the fleshpots and the bread they'd eaten to the full, the leeks, melons, and cucumbers. In Rephidim the people murmured against Moses because there was no water.

"Is this what you brought us up out of Egypt for?" they berated him. "To kill us and our children and our cattle with thirst?"

God led them to water. He provided manna from heaven, an omer a day for every man, the tenth part of an ephah, but after forty years of an omer a day of manna, the people were murmuring again and clamoring for more than just manna.

"There is nothing at all but this manna," they cried. "We remember the fish, which we had freely in Egypt, and the cucumbers, and the melons, and the leeks, and the onions, and the garlic. Who can eat so much manna? Is this what you brought us up out of Egypt for?"

God supplied them again with quail, then poisoned the flesh while it was yet between their teeth, in a very great plague. Go figure Him out. Build this, build that, use this kind of wood for one thing, and that kind of wood for another, and don't seethe a kid in the milk of its mother. Why? He isn't saying. Spitework, if you ask me. Ask Him. The people were as naked as pagans when they danced about the golden calf. An old man was stoned to death for collecting sticks on the Sabbath. Korah rebelled with his family of Levites for a larger stake in the priestly duties; they wanted the right to light the incense. The Reubenites rebelled. Many of the children of Israel turned again and again to the worship of other gods. A man brought a Midianitish woman right into the midst of the congregation to lie with her in his tent, and both were thrust through the belly by Phineas the son of Eleazar, the son of Aaron the priest, who thereby mercifully averted still another plague. Miriam died, Aaron died. But Moses pulled them through. He was as nearly perfect as it is possible for a human to be. He asked nothing for himself, and nothing is what he got. I am arrogant enough to wish I were as modest as he, and modest enough to know that this is arrogance. His face was aglow when he descended the mountain after seeing God, and the people feared to come near. He talked back plenty too, and even once lost his temper with God when he heard the people weeping for food throughout their families because they were hungry, every man in the door of his tent.

And the anger of Moses was kindled and he demanded of the Lord: "God damn it, where am I supposed to get the flesh to feed them? Why are You doing this to me? What have I ever done wrong that You lay the burden of all these people on me? Who needs it? They're not my children, are they, that I have to be responsible for them and listen to them crying when they have no food. Where do I shine in? How much longer is it going to take?"

"I told you I would do it little by little," God reminded, "until thou be increased, lest the land become desolate because the bugs and the beasts of the field multiply against you. I warned you I would do it not in one year."

"But twenty, thirty, forty?" Moses protested with disbelief. "I just don't care anymore. It's too much, just too much for me to bear. Forgive us and deliver us this minute, and if not, blot me, I pray Thee, out of Thy book which Thou hast written. I'd rather be dead than go on this way. If ever I've found favor in Your sight, then kill me right now out of hand instead of letting me see any more of this wretchedness."

"Give it to Him, Moses!" I want to cheer him on whenever I recall his words. "That's giving it to Him good!"

And the Lord repented of the evil which He thought to do unto His people. But it was in response to this outburst by Moses that God sent quail until it was coming out of their nostrils, then followed it up with disease while the meat was still unchewed. Who won? Who was right?

I need some answers.

I want to talk to Moses. I would like to make him understand that just because I don't like my statue in Florence doesn't mean I don't like his in Rome or that I blame him for mine. His is great. I could use his advice. I would like some tips from him on how to get along better with God, how to end this long silence between me and the heavens without sacrificing my dignity. Once, in utmost secrecy, recalling how Saul had succeeded through the witch of Endor in speaking with the spirit of Samuel on the eve of the battle of Gilboa, I decided to have a go with the spirit of Moses. What could I lose? I knew I would be violating laws and breaking commandments in a-whoring after wizards and witches and others trafficking with familiar spirits. But I was a king. I was desolate, I no longer had my God, and I felt I was losing my grip. Without a God, you turn to things like witchcraft and religion.

So I went to the necromancer, swallowed the powders, did the dervish, and crept into the cave. I repeated the magic words. Just one lamp burned. I put on the funny hat. I drew my hood close about my face as instructed and called upon the spirit of Moses. I got Samuel instead.

"Oh, Christ," I exclaimed in disgust. "What are you doing here?"

"You sent for me?" said Samuel, with the hollows of his eyes upon me. He was no less wintry in spirit than he had been in the flesh.

"I sent for Moses. Don't butt in."

"Wouldn't you like me to tell you what's going to happen?"

"I'll stop up my ears," I warned. "I won't listen to a word. Get me Moses. I don't want you."

"He's resting. He's still very tired."

"Tell him I have to talk to him. I bet he knows who I am."

"He's deaf as a stone."

"Can't he read lips?"

"He's almost blind now."

"His eye wasn't dim when he died."

"Death sometimes changes people for the worse," said Samuel funereally. "His stutter is back, and bad as ever."

"Tell me this," I requested, hanging on the answer before I'd even put the question. "Where is he?"

"Sitting on a rock."

"Is he in heaven? Is he in hell?"

"There is no heaven. There is no hell."

"There is no heaven? There is no hell?"

"That's all in your mind."

"He's really dead?"

"As nail in door."

"Then where is the rock?" I asked, springing cannily to trap him. "Where did you come from just now? Where do you stay when you're not up here?"

"Don't ask foolish questions," answered Samuel. "Do you want me to tell you what's going to happen to you or don't you?"

"I swear I won't listen."

"I've never been wrong."

"In my ears I'll put cotton. I won't hear a word. You told Saul he'd be killed at Gilboa, didn't you? And that Jonathan and his two other sons there would also be killed, and that the men of Israel would be scattered and forsake the cities and flee from them."

Samuel gave a croupy chuckle. "It all came true, didn't it?"

"It's why I won't listen to you. Why did he go down and fight after hearing you? Why didn't he wait them out in the hills and hit them from there? We're good at guerrilla work. He must have had a death wish."

"It was his destiny, David."

"That's bullshit, Samuel," I told him. "We're Jews, not Greeks. Tell us another flood is coming and we'll learn how to live under water. Character is destiny."

Friedrich Nietzsche would have understood. If character is destiny, the good are damned. In such wisdom is much grief. If I'd known in my youth how I'd feel in old age, I think I might have given the Philistine champion Goliath a very wide berth that day, instead of killing the big bastard and embarking so airily on the high road to success that has carried me in the end to this low state of mind in which I find myself today. The past has no value unless the present's as good.

3

ON THE DAY OF MY KILLING OF GOLIATH

Who could believe it? Who would believe the good fortune I found awaiting me in the valley of Elah when I walked into Shochoh that day with my ass, my family servant, and the small wagon of provisions from my father in Bethlehem and saw what was happening? Not I. Not by a long shot. Not in one million years would I believe it for a minute had I not been the one it was happening to. Someone brilliant must have set the stage for my climactic arrival.

When I appeared on the scene, I came with loaves and parched corn for my three brothers and with ten cheeses for their captain of a thousand, who was in command of about fifty-two volunteers from northern Judah. The valley of Elah is in northern Judah, and this time our families had elected to send people from our cities and towns to assist Saul in attempting to repel the newest incursion by the Philistines. There on our side that day, constituting the main strength in our line of resistance, were hundreds upon hundreds of those vaunted Benjamites, and not one of them spied the opening I did. But Benjamites have not been famous for their brains. Instead, they have been notorious for their madness, savagery, and fierce tempers and passions. Didn't they once rape to death the concubine of that wayfaring Levite passing through?

"Benjamin," old Jacob had forecast in what goes down with us today as part of a rather long-winded and most peculiar deathbed blessing, "shall ravin as a wolf. In the morning he shall devour the prey, and at night he shall divide the spoil."

And wasn't Saul, that kook, my king and future father-in-law, a Benjamite?

Is it any wonder I soon felt both impudence and scorn for all those Israelites and Judeans I saw hugging the ground as though facing annihilation at the mere sight of Goliath or at the sound of

JOSEPH HELLER

his voice? In almost no time at all I had been able to analyze the nature of the impasse that had fixed both armies in place for precisely forty days. With almost equal swiftness I then hit instinctively upon a probable means for its favorable resolution. From that point, there was no holding me back. I have not always been a perfect judge of human character, but I have never failed to recognize a golden opportunity when offered one on a silver platter or to go for the main chance when I found it close at hand. You could have knocked me over with a feather when I began to perceive how simple it was all going to be.

"What will the king do," I could not help exclaiming to my brothers when the thought hit me that I might be the person singled out by destiny to defeat Goliath, "for the one who fights and kills this Philistine?"

"What's it your business?" replied the eldest of my brothers, Eliab, and ordered me to go back home. He was an asshole. And the other two with him were no bargains, either.

Instead of complying, I returned to the carriage for a cloak of wool and slept the night on the ground in a secluded place above a small troop of men from Gad huddling in a natural passage behind an outcropping of yellow rock jutting from the hillside. It cheered me exceedingly to hear in the wary conversation of these men how sore afraid they were. The situation surrounding me seemed just what the doctor ordered. Greater and greater grew my faith that the morrow was going to be my lucky day, and I began to wonder if there might not be some cosmological validity after all to the startling prophecy of Samuel two years earlier, after his peculiar trek to Bethlehem with his red heifer on a rope to smear his scented olive oil on my face and tell me God had chosen me king. "Saul is out and you are in," he said when anointing me. Even with the supplement of herbs, Samuel's olive oil smelled faintly rancid. Nothing much had happened to me since.

The weather the next morning, on that day of my killing of Goliath, was, of course, warm and dry and brilliantly clear. The harvests of winter were in. Trees were putting forth green figs and the vines gave off a good smell. Another year had expired and it was again that gorgeous, balmy time when kings go forth to battle. I have always had this flair for nature writing, and it emerges sensuously in that well-known hymeneal song cycle of mine mistakenly ascribed to my drab sluggard of a son Solomon. The rain

76

was over and gone, the singing of the birds was come. How is that for descriptive excellence? The flowers had appeared on the earth. Our bed was green. Could Solomon have constructed images like those? Never my phlegmatic son Solomon, who couldn't tell a roe from a young hart if his life depended on it. One difference between us is that he is without feeling and I have always had too much. The first time I laid eyes on Abigail—I was girded for battle and thirsting for vengeance as I marched along the road to Carmel—my member grew hard as hickory and I sheepishly and modestly veiled it from her notice with a folded newspaper.

Oh, how my ears would prick up each spring when the muddy, chill winter was over and the voice of the turtle was heard in the land, signaling the approach of another new time for battle. There is no palliative like war—or a fervent immersion in dogmas of any kind—for the terrors of loneliness that our inner lives ordain for us. Believe me, I know. The problem with the loneliness I suffer is that the company of others has never been a cure for it. Being at war, however, always has been.

Keep in mind that never in my long and strenuous career have I lost a war or suffered a wound. I do not know the meaning of defeat. Find one scratch on my body from an enemy and I'll give you a barley field or a couple of my wives. That epochal morning, I awoke early and crept eagerly to the edge of a small precipice to ponder in closer detail all of the factors in this improbable stalemate. Everything I apprehended confirmed the soundness of my inspiration of the afternoon before; I could behold no flaws.

The spectacle itself beggared description. The Philistines in great number had pitched their camps at the base of the foothills of the mountains at the far side of the valley. Saul had set his men of Israel and Judah against them higher in the foothills of the mountains of the other side. The sandy plain of the valley below was divided almost equally by a shallow brook lying almost as a measuring line.

Suspense was building by the minute with the spreading light and growing heat of the new day. All on our side were waiting for Goliath to appear again. The air was incandescent with flashes from the encampments of the Philistines. They were accustomed to armor and we were not, and the glare of the rising sun was soon reflecting magically from what appeared at moments to be an enchanted, molten lake of all that burnished metal they had brought to wear, brandish, and ride in. So much burnished metal you wouldn't believe, so much iron and brass they had. It was with good reason we had arrayed ourselves for battle farther up in the hills than they: we were scared to death of them, for those were still the days when the people of Israel could not drive out of the valleys or the plains any of the inhabitants owning chariots of iron.

There, in fiery and intimidating abundance, were the chariots of iron. There were the ranks upon ranks of Philistine archers. There were the heralds with their purple banners and their magnificent trumpets of silver of a whole piece. It was all just as I had always pictured war to be, and the amplitude of splendor brought a tingle of excitement to my youthful cheeks. I gazed in marveling expectation at the gleaming formations of Philistine foot soldiers of a natural height superior to all other peoples in Palestine, formidable as deities with their double-edged straight swords of iron that could splinter in a single swipe our clubs and axes and maces and our curved swords of bronze, all mounted on shafts of brittle wood. Some luck we had, right? Some wisdom. With all our legendary aptitudes and common sense, with all the useful tips from God to Abraham, Moses, and Joshua, we still had to learn from bitter experience with the Philistines that iron was harder than bronze and that a double-edged straight sword with a point was superior to our short hook-shaped ones sharpened on just the outside. That's the main reason you find us doing so much smiting all through the Pentateuch, and so little thrusting, hurling, and shooting. Smiting is just about all you can do with an axe or a club or a curved sword molded like a sickle with just the exterior edge whetted. The only spears and javelins we possessed were the several captured in small brushes with the Philistines or discarded in their disorderly retreat after Saul's triumphant assault at Michmash. What a battle that must have been! But who knew how to use such weapons? Saul missed me with his javelin all three times he sought to kill me, and I was seated off guard no more than twenty feet away. He missed Jonathan too from across the royal dinner table the night Jonathan took my part against him and tried to intercede. Maybe somewhere inside him some small core of sanity persisted and his heart was not really set on killing us, or on killing us that way himself. Once I was king, I know I always preferred to have others do my killing for me.

No doubt we were outclassed that day in the valley of Elah. But the Philistines had no true history in hill fighting and no plans for attacking us with any probability of success. Their chariots were worthless on anything but level ground. We were protected against their archers by the natural shelter of the rocks and caves we had found in which to station ourselves. Had they foolishly tried to move up against us with their chariots, archers, and armor, we would have pounced upon them like leopards. That dumb they were not.

But we were powerless too, because they did have those chariots and archers and suits of armor, and until me, no Israelite could win a pitched battle on low ground without employing some clandestine or psychological device or receiving supernatural assistance in the form of some rare aberration of nature.

So they could not come up. And we could not go down. And each morning, therefore, and each afternoon they sent forth their mightiest warrior, Goliath, to bait us anew with his flaunting call to a single combat. When I saw him the first time, I could not believe my eyes. His stride was tremendous, his lumbering walk was swaggering and impatient. Moving too rapidly for his overburdened shield carrier to keep pace, he marched from his army's tents to a position beyond the brook and lifted back his head to repeat his humiliating dare. The heat was dry and remorseless, yet he came in a helmet of brass and a coat of brass mail that itself must have weighed about five thousand shekels. He had greaves of brass on his legs and a buckler of brass on his shoulders, and he looked more like a Greek warrior at Troy than a settler in the marshy coastal lowlands of southern Palestine, not far from Sinai. The staff of his spear was like a weaver's beam and had a huge head of iron. He stood about six cubits tall, I estimated—maybe even six cubits and a span, I granted, giving him the benefit of the doubt.

What were we to do with him? Saul and his general staff had been huddling over that one for forty days. Our archers might have driven him back, killing or wounding him if he did not withdraw, but we had no archers. Even then I could detect that it is extremely difficult to employ bowmen with maximum tactical efficiency when you have no bowmen. Had we the bowmen, they would have been useless, because we had no bows and arrows. Had we bows and arrows, we would not have known how to use them. I promised myself right then, you know, to teach my men the use of the bow and arrow someday, if ever I had any men and ever we found ourselves with bows and arrows. You can find that written in the book of Jasher—if you can ever find the book of Jasher. Another resolution I made that day dealt with Philistine iron: I wanted it. Why did I want Philistine iron? I'll tell you why. Do you know what happened every time Philistine iron came up against smart Jewish brains? Jewish brains were spilled, that's what happened. You can find that written too in the book of Jasher, if ever you do find that book of Jasher.

When Goliath finally drew to a halt and spoke, his voice traveled clearly through the dramatic hush that had fallen over all the valley from the moment he first came forth, and his words could be heard distinctly. At the edge of the bluff in the place I had found for myself, I heard him repeat with no alteration of vocabulary what I had heard him say the late afternoon before. My respect for him diminished considerably when I realized he had committed his speech to memory and had no penchant for extemporizing. But what can you look for from a Philistine? Does one find taste in the white of an egg?

"Why are ye come out to set your battle in array against the Philistines?" were the scornful words he thundered, and went on again with the same declaration he had been delivering without variation each morning and afternoon for those previous forty days. All in the army of Israelites were dismayed and greatly afraid. And all they could think to do was lie on the ground, and shrink deeper into their holes and trenches, and clutch at the earth as though in peril of falling off. "Am not I a Philistine and ye servants to Saul?" he taunted with a voice that went booming like explosions through the gullies of the mountains behind us, and would doubtless have precipitated avalanches of snow in the Alps or the Himalayas were we Europeans or Asiatics joining for battle in one of those frozen climes. "Choose you a man for you, and let him come down to me. If he be able to fight with me, and to kill me, then will we be your servants. But if I prevail against him and kill him, then shall ye be our servants and serve us. I defy the armies of Israel this day. Give me a man, that we may fight together. Or else go back to your caves and your tents and your huts and allow us to pass where we please."

The heavy breathing of a grasshopper was just about the loudest noise to be heard in the silence that followed. I must admit my

GOD KNOWS

heart skipped a beat when I saw him the first time. When I saw him the second, it was all I could do not to laugh out loud.

For here in the hills on our side of the valley were close to seven hundred picked ambidextrous Benjamites, all of them slingers who could throw with deadly accuracy as easily with the left hand as the right. And here by the thousand were those patronizing, anti-Judean smart-asses from Ephraim, who, with all their inflated pride in their vineyards and their élite pretensions of superiority, still probably would not be able to pronounce the word *shibboleth* without hissing if their lives again were at stake. There were men of Manasseh, and hundreds upon hundreds more from all our other clans and tribes in the north and west who had this time heeded the summons of Saul. There we were, God's chosen people, if you can believe it, every one of us descended at least in part from canny Sarah and able Abraham. But something rotten in the genes must have contaminated the thinking processes of everyone present but me, for in no other brain but mine did the obvious consideration arise that Goliath might be successfully met in single combat on conditions different from those implied in his own preparations for the fray.

Frankly, the way I saw it, Goliath didn't stand a chance. The poor fucker was a goner. With either hand, every one of those chosen men of Benjamin could sling stones at a hairbreadth fifty yards away and never miss. Skimming flat ones with jagged edges, they could drop clusters of grapes from the vine at the stem. I myself could sever a pomegranate from a bush at thirty paces nine times out of ten. I could blast the pomegranate itself to a splashing pulp just about every time I tried. And the face of Goliath was larger than a pomegranate. Between the brass of his chest and the brass of his helmet, from his neck to his hairline, was exposed an area of bare flesh as large as a good-sized Persian melon. What I shortly was to find myself saying to Saul in the flat-roofed tent of goatskin in which he made his headquarters was almost entirely true: I really had killed a lion, a small one, making off with a lamb when I was out keeping my father's sheep, after crippling it first with a shot from my sling, and I had stunned—not killed—a bear. With the bear I fibbed a little.

Like cunnilingus, tending sheep is dark and lonely work; but someone has to do it. Away from home with my flocks for weeks at a time, I would spend hours on end with a blade of grass between

81

my teeth or a dandelion green on my tongue, practicing on my lyre, composing songs, and slinging stones at broken clay flasks placed atop a wooden fence as standing targets, or at rusty tin cans. I would even sling stones at other stones. Apart from gathering back errant sheep, with which our goats, more intelligent than sheep, were instinctively helpful, there's really little more to shepherding than driving away wild beasts and dividing the sheep and the goats into their separate folds at nightfall before eating a cold dinner and bedding down on the ground in a cloak near a brush fire. It was from this end-of-day activity, incidentally, that I drew my widely quoted "separating the sheep from the goats, and the men from the boys," which stands out so prominently in one of my lesser-known psalms, I think, or perhaps in one of those proverbs of mine for which authorship is often credited to Solomon or someone else. I know beyond doubt that my "separating the sheep from the goats" is used in more than one of the works by that overrated hack William Shakespeare of England, whose chief genius lay in looting the best thoughts and lines from the works of Kit Marlowe, Thomas Kyd, Plutarch, Raphael Holinshed, and me. The idea for *King Lear,* of course, he got from me and Absalom. Are you going to tell me no? Who else but me was every inch a king? Do you think the unscrupulous plagiarist could have written *Macbeth* had he never heard of Saul?

For sheer popularity in coinage, though, nothing in the world by anyone else can hold a candle to my "The Lord is my shepherd," a fortuitous turn of phrase, I can confess now, that was haphazardly tossed off by my Bathsheba in that abbreviated period after she had tired of macramé and crewelwork and before she threw herself wholeheartedly into inventing bloomers. She actually thought she could write better lyrics than I did!

Who can tell why the work endures?

For the Lord, of course, is not a shepherd, not mine or anyone else's. And naming Him one is what I describe as a figure of speech. Anyone luckless enough to have worked as a shepherd would know that calling the Lord a shepherd is not a tribute but a blasphemy. Why would the Lord be a shepherd? Half the day you're walking in sheep shit. Sheepshearing is dismal toil, filthy, soaking drudgery, and it's no wonder that there's such a huge party afterward. It was to just such a celebration that my son Absalom lured my other son Amnon to kill him. If God is indeed a shepherd, I'm sure He suffers even more intensely from the monotony than I did and is probably as good a shot with the sling. Tending sheep is not a vocation for an active mind. I myself preferred the corrupting life of the town to the bucolic diversions of the pasture. At night you were cold, in the daytime you sought shelter from the scorching sun. Where could you go for a good time? What was there in common between me and the other shepherds? They had little or no interest in music and frequently would throw garbage at me when I tried to sing to them.

Is it any wonder I was unhappy? I would spend whole mornings and afternoons practicing with my sling in order to help the time go faster. I knew I was good. I knew I was brash. I knew I was brave. And with Goliath that day, I knew that if I could get within twenty-five paces of the big son of a bitch, I could sling a stone the size of a pig's knuckle down his throat with enough velocity to penetrate the back of his neck and kill him, and I also knew something else: I knew if I was wrong about that, I could turn and run like a motherfucker and dodge my way back up the hill to safety without much risk from anyone chasing me in all that armor.

It took a good deal of intriguing on my part to get that far that morning once I had decided to make my move. I left my carriage in the hands of the keeper and went back into the emplacement of the Judeans, bursting right in and speaking out boldly in a way to command the attention of everyone there instantly. I knew the impression I hoped to make, the kind of comment I wanted to incite. I wanted to startle, gall, and taunt, and to set people buzzing about me all the way down the line until reports of my presence could not fail to be brought to Saul. "What will the king do," I advertised in a trumpeting voice that I hoped would carry even to people in the post abutting, "for the man who fights and kills this Philistine and takes away this reproach from Israel?"

"Don't ask," said my brother Shammah, looking ill.

"I told you yesterday to go back home," my brother Eliab answered me angrily.

"Sure, he told you yesterday to go back home," said Abinadab. "Who is tending those few poor sheep of yours in the wilderness while you are idle here?"

I affected hurt feelings. "All I did was ask a simple question."

"Never mind your simple questions," chimed in my brother Shammah. "We know all about your simple questions."

"I'll give you simple questions," Eliab told me, glaring. "I knew you'd be back here, showing off. Go home, go home, thou vain and naughty boy."

"Can't you see we've got trouble enough?" said Shammah, gesturing toward Goliath.

"Maybe I can help," said I.

"Don't make me laugh," retorted Eliab through gritted teeth. "You just want to hang around and watch the battle, don't you? We know your pride and the naughtiness of your heart."

"What pride?" I answered proudly. "What naughtiness of heart? I've got no pride. I've got no naughtiness of heart. All I did is ask what will the king do for the man who fights and kills this Philistine and takes away this reproach from all Israel?"

"What will the king do?" responded the captain of a thousand incredulously, and at last the information I was after was given me. "What will the king *do?*" the good-natured fellow exclaimed a second time as he chewed on his morning ration of fresh dates and raw onion. My mouth watered at the succulent combination. "What *won't* the king do, better you should ask. Probably the king will enrich him with great riches, give him one of his daughters as a wife, and make his father's house in Israel tax free."

Of course I was elated.

"No shit?" I asked.

"No shit," he assured me.

"Then how is it," I inquired in a carefree and flamboyant manner, "that none will go down to meet him, for who is this uncircumcised Philistine that he should defy the armies of the living God?"

At this, Eliab, Abinadab, and Shammah spun toward me with clenched fists and demanded I quit the battle scene at once for my house in Bethlehem.

It was then that I gave them the finger and was off like a bouncing ray of light on my mischievous business in other emplacements, shooting my mouth off almost without stop. How confusing I found it, I professed with the same pink-cheeked, lighthearted gallantry to one group of fighting men after another, that none in the Israelite army had sufficient faith in the prowess of the living God to assay his strength and cunning against this uncircumcised enemy, invincible though he appeared. What was an unworldly young man from the country like me to believe? Oh, I was irritating and provocative, I aroused curiosity. I moved down our battle line like a spirit of the air. Those were the days when every one of us young could go leaping over the mountains and come skipping over the hills with an agility incredible to the heavyset, slow-footed Philistines, who bulled their way up into our villages to spoil our tender grapes and then strove in vain to fend us off. In one place after the next, I spoke in the same manner. The men of Manasseh conducted me into the camp of the men of Ephraim, who led me in turn to the men of Benjamin to a captain of a hundred, who was in command of twenty-four.

"What shall be done by the king," was again my question, of which by now I myself was beginning to grow tired, "to the man that killeth this Philistine and taketh away the reproach from Israel? For who is this uncircumcised Philistine that he should defy the armies of the living God?"

"Who the fuck are you?" was the response I received from the surly men of Benjamin, who, by reputation, would as soon rape a person, man or woman, as kill one, and on occasion did both.

My answer was discreet. "I am the son of the king's servant Jesse the Ephrathite of Bethlehem in Judah."

"Judah," they snickered.

"It's the reason I'm asking," I responded, pouting. "And why I'm having so much trouble figuring things out. You know how dull-witted we are in Judah. What will the king do for the one who kills this man, and how is it that none will go forth against this Philistine and take away this reproach to Israel?"

"Can't you see how big he is?" asked their captain. "Would you go down to fight a man like that?"

"Why not?" I answered. "He hath defied the armies of the living God, hasn't he?"

"Bring the kid to Saul."

"Let no man's heart fail because of me," I called back over my shoulder. Privately, I was already congratulating myself on having attained even that much.

Saul gave no sign of ever having seen me before. And tactfully I betrayed no memory of any earlier meeting. He had aged very badly in the two years since I'd been brought from Bethlehem to play for him. His face was deeply seamed, his curly hair and short square beard were prematurely gray. He stood with his arms crossed and contemplated me. He seemed sorry for me. He was broad and strong, and from his shoulders and upward he was higher than hawk-featured Abner and all of the other officers about him. After Goliath, he was one of the tallest men I had ever seen.

"You are just a youth," he observed at last, "and he has been a great man of war from his boyhood. Thou are not able to go up against this Philistine to fight with him."

"The bigger they are," I replied, "the harder they fall." That went over rather well. "Thy servant kept his father's sheep," I pressed my advantage, "and there came a lion one day and a bear another and took a lamb out of the flock. Thy servant slew both the lion and the bear—I swear to God I did—and this uncircumcised Philistine shall be as one of them. The selfsame Lord that delivered me out of the paw of the lion, and out of the paw of the bear, will deliver me out of the hand of this Philistine."

"My lord the king, why not?" Abner suggested. "It's certainly worth a try."

Saul told him why not. "The Philistine hath said that if we choose a man able to fight with him and kill him, they will all be our servants. But if he prevails against him and kills our man, then shall we be their servants and serve them."

"My lord the king," importuned practical Abner, drawing closer to Saul's side, "don't be a *naar*. Saul, Saul, do you really believe those Philistines are going to become our slaves if we win? Or that we will be theirs if we lose? That dumb we're not. Neither are they. Let the lad go down if he chooses to. What have we got to lose but his life?"

When Saul yielded finally, his reluctance gave way to a solicitude almost embarrassingly paternal. He decked me out in his personal armor, his helmet of brass and his coat of mail, and girded me with his own sword, and after he had completed preparing me for battle in his splendid panoply, I found I couldn't move. I barely could see. Big I'm not, you know, and the rim of his helmet rested upon the bridge of my nose and hurt. I ungirded myself of his sword and handed it back. I told Saul right out that I did not want his armor or his sword because I had never tested myself with them and had no experience fighting that way. I saw no profit in adding that I had not the least intention of coming near enough to Goliath to touch him with a sword, or allowing him to come near enough to reach me with his. Only a consummate nitwit would have faced the big Philistine hand to hand with a sword, shield, and coat of mail and expect to survive. One blow of that sword by that enormous man would rip from your hands whatever weapon you were wielding; the second would separate you from your soul.

"Let me go as I am," I requested with a perfectly straight face, stripping back down to the lovely new tunic into which I had changed, "for the Lord saveth not with sword and spear. The battle is the Lord's, and I know He will deliver the Philistine into our hands."

The patronizing looks of disbelief passing slyly among my hearers communicated their doubts about my sanity, which was just fine with me. Mention of sword or spear was as far as I wanted to go. I had no desire for Saul or anyone else to plumb my thoughts. Did I have to remind them that the Lord might also save with the sling? Let them believe it was a miracle.

Certainly I was already feeling very much like a king as I made ready to parade from Saul's tent and begin my deliberate and suspenseful walk down into the plain of the valley where Goliath stood waiting, with his massive legs planted apart like a colossus bestriding the earth. After all, hadn't I been anointed king by Samuel two years earlier with all that scented olive oil he had smeared on my face? I recall how credulously I listened as Samuel made known that the Lord had rent the kingdom from Saul and was giving it to a neighbor more after His own heart.

"Is that person me?" It seemed to me not in the slightest an unreasonable surmise.

And Samuel responded: "Who else?"

And nothing more had occurred, not a blessed thing, not then or since. No trumpet sounded. No wise men brought gifts. I heard no hosannas. Bach wrote no cantatas, not even one. My brothers gloated. No wonder I felt so awfully let down there in Bethlehem; it was as though nothing out of the ordinary had taken place. The earth didn't move. There were no hallelujah choruses. All I got out of that whole day was a face full of oil.

Well, being king is not much fun if nobody knows you are one, is it, and I could see it would be useless trying to get my brothers or anyone else to bow down in subservience. How different it was years later when, with Saul dead and the army of Israelites dispersed by the Philistines, I walked triumphantly into Hebron to allow the elders of the city to acclaim me king of Judah. First, though, I dispatched the youngest of my nephews, fleet-footed Asahel, to see how my idea sat with them.

"Ask them," I directed, "if they would like to acclaim me king of Judah now that Saul is no more. Remind them that I have six hundred fighting men, that the army of Israelites is scattered about the hills like sheep that know no shepherd, and that there is now no other fighting force stronger than mine remaining in the country. Remind them I am thin-skinned and very easily insulted."

My idea sat well with the elders of Hebron. "They want very much to acclaim you king of Judah," my nephew Asahel reported back.

I had just turned thirty.

I FELT NO LESS exhilarated on that day of my killing of Goliath when I finally emerged from Saul's tent and started down the hill, a harmless shepherd boy out of uniform, with my staff in my hand and my sling hung inconspicuously toward the rear of my girdle. I paused a moment on the peak of the low ridge to let everyone get a good look. I was far from uninterested in the effect I was creating. My only regret was that I could not see myself as others were seeing me.

I knew, of course, that every eye was upon me. Who among those multitudes of gawking spectators on both sides could have guessed what would follow as I made my way downward along the declining green slope profusely colored with violets, white daisies, and yellow cabbage flowers? No one, not in a billion years. Certainly not Goliath. We know that now. I could tell then, just by watching him. When I came to level ground, I slowed my pace and looked across the stream at him. He was squinting as he regarded me across the narrowing distance, his sword sheathed, waiting like a man very much affected by a sense of his own invincibility. His shield carrier stood deferentially a few paces behind. Goliath studied my approach with a look growing more and more quizzical. Again I wanted to laugh. The skirt of my smashing new tunic was extremely brief, affording free movement to my legs without my girding up my loins. I did not wish to disturb his complacency by coming to him with the hem of my garment tucked up into my goatskin sash. My entire aspect was no more threatening than a snail's. I wanted him to judge me someone paltry—as a messenger, perhaps, bearing words of capitulation, or as a local youth accidentally straying onto the battlefield in search of a lost lamb or kid.

If you want to believe what you've heard, I halted along the way to choose five smooth stones out of the brook. That was just for show. Any slinger worth his salt always carries his stones with him; and as I knelt with my knees in the water, I was unobtrusively removing two from the leather pouch at my waist, concealing them in the palm of my right hand. Two would certainly be enough; if I didn't disable the big warrior with my first shot, I probably wouldn't have time even for a second. As I rose to cross the shallow stream, I transferred my shepherd's staff to my left hand. Goliath did not appear to notice. I had to suppress a smile. With my right hand, I stealthily began unfastening the cords of my sling from my belt and clearing the loops.

Let's call him a giant. *His* teeth, not Bathsheba's, were like a flock of sheep that have been even shorn. With her it was merely flattery. But everything about Goliath was larger than life. I have to chortle even now at the violent transformations he underwent when it finally began to dawn on him why I was there. How his eyes bulged with amazement. How his massive face darkened with outrage and purpled with wrath. How he howled and roared when he finally recovered from his initial moment of shock. You'd think he'd been speared in the liver. For forty days he had asked of the Israelites that they send down a man worthy to engage a Philistine champion of his mettle in single combat. Instead, he'd been given a youthful shepherd who was ruddy and of a fair countenance. He had expected Achilles. He'd been given me. And to top it all off, I was carrying a stick.

Doubts that I could kill him continued to evaporate as he allowed me to draw closer and closer without arming himself, and I observed the sequence of responses with which he observed me. He was befuddled. He was curious. He was aghast. And then—oh, boy, was that an angry giant!

It amuses me still to recall his blackening expression of astounded disbelief when my objective in approaching him began to sink in. He gaped and he glared and he stood rooted to the spot as though paralyzed. His shield carrier hovered behind him in a state of vacillating perplexity. Goliath was not really a giant, I guess, but he was big enough. The sunlight blazed on his armor. His eyes were like coals, his beardless, mottled face was darkly stubbled. I saw his lips move as he began to mutter to himself. Not for a second was I in fear of him. It was that stick I carried that really touched him off. The veins and tendons in his muscled neck swelled vividly when he finally drew a gargantuan breath and opened wide his jaws to speak. His voice was deafening. His roaring words were aimed less at me than at the battalions of Israelites clinging in terror and suspense to the thickets, rocks, and hollows of the sides of the mountains in back of me.

"Am I a dog?" he raged, and drew another large breath to rage some more.

Feigning deafness, I interrupted immediately. "What?" I called in reply.

I slipped the larger of my two stones into the hollow of my sling, which now was free and held furtively against my thigh.

"Am I a dog, I said!" he bellowed with annoyance. "Are you deaf or something? Am I a dog that thou comest to me with staves?" As I moved steadily toward him, he began to curse me by his gods—by Dagon and Moloch, and Baal, and Belial. Oh, what a mouth there was on that giant! "Come to me—come on, come on!" He was moving both arms now, rabidly beckoning me toward him. "And I will give thy flesh unto the fowls of the air and to the beasts of the field."

"What?" Again I pretended to be unable to hear.

He repeated his threat verbatim as, barefoot, I slid closer and closer to him. Now he was addressing himself only to me. This time I chose to answer.

"You'll give *my* flesh unto the fowls of the air and to the beasts of the field?" I replied with an insulted passion of my own. "I'll give you *flesh*. I'll show you who'll give whose flesh. *I'll* give *your* flesh unto the fowls of the air and to the beasts of the field. Thou comest to me with a sword and with a spear and with a shield."

"Where is the shield?" he sneered, and raised his hands to display them empty. "Where is my spear, where is my sword?"

"But I come to thee in the name of the Lord of hosts," I proceeded without answering his questions, "the God of the armies of Israel, whom thou hast defied." My voice was filled with righteousness. Ask me to this day what I thought I was talking about when I said "Lord of hosts" and I still will be unable to tell you. I have many phrases whose meaning is likewise unintelligible to me, but rhetoric is rhetoric. "This day will the Lord deliver thee into my hand," I informed him gamely. "And I will smite thee and take thy head from thee. And I will give the carcasses of the host of the Philistines this day unto the fowls of the air and to the wild beasts of the earth, that all the earth may know there is a God in Israel. And all this assembly shall know that the Lord saveth not with sword and spear, for the battle is the Lord's, and He will give you unto our hands."

Now, quite frankly, this doesn't sound to me like anything I would have said under normal circumstances, although back then the underlying sentiments might have been mine. Those were my salad days, when I was green in judgment, and I believed in a great number of things about which I'm skeptical now. I believed in the future. I still believed in God. I even believed in Saul. I have had three fathers in my life—Jesse, Saul, and God. All three have disappointed me. I have lived without God a long time now, and probably I can learn to die without Him too.

The response of Goliath to my rather stilted announcement was unexpected. Cupping his hand to his ear, he said: "What?" Imagine my surprise to discover that Goliath the Philistine giant truly was a little hard of hearing. That may be why he talked so loud.

I shook my head, refusing to repeat a syllable, and thumbed my nose at him. Next I stuck out my tongue. I was conserving my breath for the sudden sprint I intended to begin in a matter of moments.

This time when Goliath began to curse me by his heathen gods, he even threw Astarte and Chemosh in with the others, but he never got to complete his list. He was still dilating on Baal when I began my charge. Casting away my staff when I was less than fifty paces off, I rushed toward him without warning, running at him in a straight line as fleetly as I could and lifting my sling to whirl it above my head with an accelerating momentum greater than any I had ever been able to muster before in my whole life. The mass of the stone in the hollow of my sling seemed to double in weight by the second. Goliath stood riveted in place like something inanimate, his mouth gaping. I felt wonderful. Who could put it into words? The mounting pull on my muscles of the centrifugal force I was generating was more exquisite in its pleasure than any sensation I had ever experienced or could possibly have dreamed of. An intoxication of overconfidence brought me nearer and nearer, and my reason was in peril of being swept away. Fortunately, I took hold of myself. Thirty paces was about near enough, I decided, and skidded to a stop when I was already closer than that, digging my legs in for my throw. It was with all my strength that I brought my arm about the next two times. I took dead aim at the dark hole of the open mouth between his huge and repulsive teeth. Coming around on my final spin, I let slip the loop from my thumb. I felt my shot unroll with the sling and fly from the pocket without the slightest waver, and I knew in my bones that there really was no way I could possibly miss. I missed. I caught him in the forehead instead, above the left eye. Blood gushed out yards in front of him for the second or two he remained standing. Then he dropped like a boulder. He struck the ground with a crash. His shield carrier fled. Goliath lay where he had fallen, staining the sandy earth brown. There was not even a twitch. My joy was immense.

It was all over but the shouting, and God knows there was plenty of that. Wails of anguish came from the Philistines when they saw their champion so suddenly dead. They scurried about in frenzied circles, preparing to assemble their equipment and flee. At the same time, the men of Judah and Israel arose from the mountains with wild cries and came plunging down past me to assail the retreating Philistines with axes, clubs, and cutting weapons and to pursue them where they fell down by the way to Shaaraim, and even unto Gath, and unto Ekron too.

For my part, I was taking no chances. I watched the fallen giant warily. When a full minute passed without the smallest hint of life from him, I sprang forward and ran the rest of the distance to his still figure, took his sword out of the sheath, and, to put my mind at rest, cut off his head. Now, at least, I could be sure he was slain. Barbaric? Who cares! Remember, those were primitive times. They did much worse to Saul and Jonathan and the other two sons when they found them fallen on Mount Gilboa, didn't they? They fastened Saul's head in their temple of Dagon. And nailed all the rest of the four bodies to the outer wall of their bastion city of Bethshan, until the valiant men of Jabesh-gilead came in the night to take their bodies down and burn them respectfully and bury their bones, to end the sacrilege. Compared to that, I was practically too full of the milk of human kindness. I wanted to bring back Goliath's head as a trophy. The remainder of him, of course, would be left unto the fowls of the air and the beasts of the field. Didn't he say he would have done the same to me?

The danger from Goliath past, I relaxed awhile in total contentment with my foot on his chest. The dirty work lay ahead, removing those greaves of brass from his gigantic legs, his target of brass from his strapping shoulders, his coat of mail weighing five thousand shekels of more brass. How was I going to carry that spear of his with a staff like a weaver's beam? And I still had his head to manage, with yet more brass in the helmet. That head of his would weigh a ton.

I hadn't counted on the overwhelming charm of celebrity. Luckily, I was soon engulfed and aided by those children of Israel streaming back after routing the Philistines from their bases and spoiling their tents. Whooping with cheers and congratulations, they relieved me of these burdens and hoisted me upon their shoulders. With boisterous cries and songs of victory, they bore me back up the hill and set me down in Saul's compound. Somewhat reserved and puzzled, Saul peered at me strangely, his eyes blinking and watery, regarding me once more as though he had never had sight of me before.

Looking sideways at his commander of the host, he asked, "Abner, whose son is this youth?"

"I am the son of thy servant Jesse the Bethlehemite," I spoke up boldly before Abner could answer, and then waited with my heart in my mouth for what I prayed would follow.

I got what I wanted. Saul took me into his army.

Naturally, I was acclaimed all along the way on the journey back to Gibeah. Who wouldn't be, after what I had done? They set me on an ass, elevating me above all the rest, even above Saul, so that all could see me. I was pleased people stared. My cheeks were flushed, my neck was as a tower of ivory, my curls were black as a raven's, my head was of beaten gold. Reports of my spectacular triumph preceded us into the city. Michal painted her face and sat by her window. Imagine how doubly blessed—no, thricely blessed—she considered herself when I traveled past and she saw how goodly I was to look at. I was not unaware of the splendid appearance I made. I was happy as a pig in shit. I remembered my Creator in the days of my youth, and I loved what He created when He created me!

4

THE
DAYS OF
MY YOUTH

That was the best day of my life. Most days now feel like the worst. My palace is drafty, yet permeated by strong, unpleasant odors. If I were Adonijah, I would fumigate the whole fucking harem. It tickles me to consider what Bathsheba has thus far overlooked: that she will be part of the harem he succeeds to. My mind is somewhat troubled about Abishag. I don't think I want her in anyone's arms but mine—yet. That's how new love is, as terrible as an army of banners.

No such nagging concerns about women and harems clouded my mind on the day I killed Goliath. There was no envy or suspicion yet of which I was the object, no enmity, or fear, no shadow of danger stretching toward me like the spearhead of some unavoidable angel of fate, no intimations of a forlorn destiny ahead. Who could have thought back then that a king like me might someday find himself embarrassed by hemorrhoids and an enlarged prostate, or that one favored with so hale and auspicious a beginning would eventually lapse almost daily into moldering spells of solitary depression and anxiety? Who needs it? Who can stand it? My teeth chatter a hundred times a minute when the chills take possession of me. Desire has failed. I get up with the fucking cricket. I can't keep awake and I can't fall asleep. In the morning I wish it were evening, in the evening I wish it were dawn. And I have the discouraging impression now that it has been this way for me always. How a person feels at the end of his life will tell you what he feels to have been the quality of it all. Who would have believed that a time might come when a man like me would regard the day of his death as better than the day of his birth?

Nothing fails like success.

Believe me, don't I know? How dispiriting I find it, even after all my personal triumphs, that we must grow up and grow sad, that we must age, weaken, and in time go down to our long home in the ground, and that even golden lads and girls all must, as chimney sweepers, come to dust. I've missed Saul. I've missed even my old and innocuous father. I have dreams about both of them, in which they are interchangeable figures and occupy the same roles. I want their love. And both are gone. And ironically, I'm drawn to repeat my well-known apothegm of futility: that, just as the person who wants praise will never be satisfied with praise, the person who wants love cannot be satisfied with love. No want is ever fulfilled. And I therefore still don't know whether it is better to fear God and keep His commandments or to curse God and die. Fortunately, I've been able to get by very neatly without doing either.

Back then I had no Nathan castigating me with allegations of fornication and murder. It was a grave indiscretion for me to employ Joab to have Uriah killed; Joab knows of my crime, and I know that he knows. We each know a bit too much about the other. I had no raped daughter then and no butchered sons, no stubborn Abner impeding for seven years my fated reign over a Judah joined with Israel in a united Palestine. Daily I wished that pockmarked son of a bitch dead. When I needed him alive, Joab killed him. Under the fifth rib, he smote him.

Joab sure does love that fifth rib, doesn't he?

Once, in a mood of whimsy, I thought of suggesting to Joab that he stick it to my first wife Michal under the fifth rib. How soothing to my frazzled nerves was the prospect of being rid forever of that venomous witch. How I reproached myself for ever having wanted her back after Saul had given her away to another husband. There are certain men of mild disposition who seem evolved by nature for no other purpose than to be browbeaten by domineering viragoes. I do not think I am one of them. For someone of my estate to be subjected to a henpecking shrew was a gross anomaly. The jealousy and acrimony with which she assailed me regularly after I had demanded her back was intolerable. It is better to dwell in a corner of the housetop than with a brawling woman in a wide house, so much better to live in a fucking wilderness like Ziph, Maon, or Engedi than with a contentious and angry wife. Even for a king this is true. All the more true for a king. A virtuous woman like Abigail is a crown to her husband, but one like Michal that makes him ashamed is as rottenness in his bones. Do you wonder I was so happy when they told me she was dying? She was even in pain.

98

"God is holy! God is good!" I cried, and sacrificed a lamb that same day.

One reason I didn't suggest to Joab that he stick it to Michal under the fifth rib was that I had no doubt he would do it.

No premonitions of such vulgar wrangling to come diminished my spirits on that day of my killing of Goliath. I had no shrews complicating my life, I had no wives at all. No dead babies. My throbbing memory pains me still for the loss of that little child I did not know, and for the grisly, cold-blooded slaying of that older one I loved too much. Poor boy. While the child was ill, I lay with my face on the ground and prayed that God might be gracious and that the moaning infant might live. His parched skin was on fire. I might just as well have been talking to myself. And I found out again what I had known before: there is never, *never* any mercy to be expected from heaven. I have still not forgiven God for getting back at me that way, and I know I never shall, no matter how much He begs me, not if He begs me for a million years, even if it does turn out He was never really there in the beginning. Look how He always does what He wants, not what you want. Look how He lifts the blame from me and kills the guiltless child. Now *there's* an original sin for you, isn't there? Look how He gives me now this angelic, amorous virgin, with eyes as dark as grapes and nut-brown dusky skin, whose heart-shaped face I want to cup with tender warmth in my shivering palms, when I am already much too old to enjoy her fully and fear I lack the power ever to enter a virgin again. And how He has me hungering anew in gnawing frustration for my wife Bathsheba, who tells me she is sick of love and rejects me always in the most demeaning way imaginable: she is oblivious to my need for her. She would not believe how wounding that is. She would not care.

I don't believe I disgust her, for she will usually taste and often finish the food I leave in my bowl, stuffing herself with her fingers while complaining of nightly indigestion and increasing overweight.

"What is that red stuff you're putting on his bread and beans and shredded lettuce?" she inquires of Abishag with a dim stirring of interest in both the girl and the meal she is diligently preparing for me.

"Red chili peppers," says Abishag.

"Why don't you ever call me Your Highness?"

"He tells me you're not a queen."

"What is that green stuff you're putting in his chopped lamb?"

"Green chili peppers."

"What is it you're making?"

"Tacos, with green chili lamb stew and refried beans and sour cream."

"Tacos?"

"Tacos."

"Can I eat some? It looks delicious. I'm hungry. Why do you do so much work for him? That's stupid, to work so hard when you don't have to." Bathsheba makes a face at the first forkful she tastes and puts her bowl on the floor. Abishag bends gracefully at the knees to lift it and carry it away. She moves like a ballerina—you would think she had gone to modeling school. "You'll ruin your looks if you keep doing so much for him," adds Bathsheba. "You'll spoil your skin. Your hands will crack. You should use emollients all over your body when it's hot and dry like this. I do. Look at me." Bathsheba opens her robe without inhibition to expose her oiled limbs and flanks. She is wearing white bloomers, and I feel my privy part give a small jiggle. Bathsheba my blonde wife still uses kohl and antimony to give dark prominence to her small, shrewd eyes. Indolently, she picks at her teeth with the quill of a dove's feather. With her other hand she scratches hard, but absently, at the side of her broad hip and buttock and then at the inside of her thigh, as though troubled by fleabites again. Her legs and waist have remained thin. I am familiar with her uncouth traits from our days of lechery together. I want her again. She arouses desire in me in a way Abishag has not been able to. I gaze at the meaty, obese swell of middle-aged flesh of my wife's thighs and belly, at her rotund pelvis, and feel I could fuck her again if only she would come to my bed and open herself to me. A lot of good that feeling does me. Can I, the king, say to my unfeeling and indifferent wife that if she allows me to do it to her again I will give to her son Solomon the Israel empire I have created and allow her indeed to become the queen mother she wants to be? Why not, the Preacher might saith, since I easily could break that promise afterward? But not for her or anyone else in the universe would I pay so shameful a price as to confess to so desperate a longing for another piece of ass from her.

In the old days, which were my younger days, I could sweep her off her feet and onto her back every time I tried, even when her flowers were upon her, with a dizzying flow of honeyed words that left her dazed and flattered and brought a glistening rush of blood to her face. Oh, the dauntless skill with which I could always conquer her, gushing fluently:

"Open to me, my sweetheart, my love, my dove, my undefiled. Kiss me with the kisses of thy mouth. Thy love is better than wine, I will remember thy love more than wine, O, thou fairest among women. Thy banner over me is love. I have compared thee to a company of horses in Pharaoh's chariots."

You think I always knew what I was talking about? It made no difference. Down on her back she would go every time in a flow of sighs, spreading wide her legs and lifting her knees, opening her arms in her enraptured swoon as though to hug me inside herself.

"Oh, David, David," I would hear her moan. "Where do you get such wonderful words?"

"Out of the blue."

"Out of the blue?"

"They come to me right out of the blue."

"Oh, that's so lovely also."

Nowadays I lie here shivering in bleak and friendless longing, and all she does when bored, my self-absorbed wife, is gaze at Abishag with heavy, painted lids and ply the unspoiled girl with worldly questions and homely bits of female wisdom.

"Don't be so good a cook," Bathsheba advises my servant girl. "Why should you work so hard when you don't have to? Don't comb his hair so carefully or keep him so clean. Hurt him once in a while, let him get dirty. Don't make such good meals, don't be so good around the house. Who needs it? He never finishes what you give him anyway. Let his lamp go out once in a while. Only learn to do well the things you enjoy doing. Do you want to lose your looks?"

Abishag answers, "I enjoy cooking and cleaning for him. I like to see him with his hair combed. I have always enjoyed doing housework."

"Such a pity. Such a waste." Bathsheba frowns in commiseration and pauses a moment, respectfully. "A lot of men go for small dark women like you. You look a little bit Korean. I sometimes had trouble because I was so tall and had this pale skin I still can't stand. And I have these weird blue eyes. You wouldn't believe it,

101

but a lot of people never could understand what he saw in me. A lot of people never could appreciate why he wanted to make me queen. Right?"

"I never wanted to make you queen."

You think she always waits for an answer when she asks a question, or listens when I give her one? She is already addressing Abishag. "It's a shame you're cooped up inside this stinking palace when you're still so young and pretty. Have you ever smelled so many odors? I'm sure none come from me. You're wearing those same robes of divers colors—that's the first thing I look for when I come here every day, you know. I'll let you in on something. As long as you're a virgin, you can still get out. You're not his wife and you're not really his concubine. Make him let you out. Nag him, bother him, aggravate him. Spill hot tea on him. A girl so nice, with such cute tits and such a nice black pubic patch, you should be outside enjoying yourself and learning tricks from other men and from Canaanite whores. Canaanite women know how to get pleasure as well as give it. It's a pity you had to come in here as a servant. Why are you even still a virgin, a sweet girl like you? When I was your age, my closest friends were harlots. That's how I got so smart. The first time I married, Uriah didn't know what hit him. Neither did this one when we first started doing it, did you? And he'd already been married seven times. He never even had his cock sucked until he met me, can you imagine? Once I moved in, I never had to do another stitch of housework. My hands never touched hot water again. Abigail was the dumb one who just kept working. She aged overnight, practically, and her hair turned ugly gray."

"Her hair was pewter and it was beautiful."

"Then how come you kept sleeping with me? He'd go to her to eat and to pour out his troubles. Right off the bat I got an alabaster bathtub, ivory ointment boxes, and one of the largest apartments in the palace, didn't I? I had western exposure from the beginning and got a beautiful breeze from the sea every evening."

It was Bathsheba, of course, from whom I derived my universal axiom that a bad reputation never hurt anybody.

"Leave her alone," I butt in now to the unprincipled mother of my dead baby and my son Solomon. "She does beautifully all she will ever be expected to do. She can have all the maids and kitchen help she wants. What are you bothering her for?"

"You should have waited," Bathsheba comments to Abishag, "and come in here as a queen. You should at least make him marry you before you bathe him again or cook him another meal. Then you would be a queen too, and never have to work again. Let him shiver, let him go hungry and get bedsores if he doesn't want to marry you or let you go."

"We don't have queens," I remind her. "Who says you're a queen?"

"I'm the wife of a king," she tells me. "What do you think that makes me?"

"The wife of a king," I instruct her, "and that's all. Where do you think you are, England? You're starting to sound like Michal."

"That's just what I did," Bathsheba states placidly to Abishag, dismissing my firm objections of a few seconds earlier. "I came in as a queen. You should have done the same. And soon I'm going to be the mother of a king."

The audacity of this enlivens me with a rush of adrenaline I do not frequently experience anymore. "Yeah?" I say. "And just how do you figure that's going to come about?"

"Solomon," she answers, resting her gaze on me.

"Solomon?" The ridicule in my voice is practically a guffaw.

"No?"

"God forbid."

"Why not?"

"You're trying to make me laugh."

"Isn't it better for the future of the country?"

"Over my dead body."

"That," says Bathsheba, "is the sequence in which it usually takes place, isn't it? Except with Adonijah. Your pride and your joy. Adonijah doesn't like to wait until you die, does he? Adonijah thinks he doesn't have to wait."

"What's this about Adonijah?" I inquire with concern. "What are you talking about?"

Bathsheba's breasts shift sensually inside her golden robe with the exaggerated sigh of exasperation she heaves. Her breasts have gotten fuller with age, more shapely and pendulous. My fingers itch to squeeze them. "Don't you know?" she asks, with affected disdain. "Must I be the one to tell you everything? And you say I'm not a queen? Your son Adonijah exalts himself all over the city by saying he will be king. Nobody's told you that? And they say you do nothing to displease him by asking him why he has done so. Have you done anything to displease him by asking him why he has done so?"

"All Adonijah wants is to give an outdoor feast to celebrate the fact that he's next in line, and that he's already willing to pitch in by representing me." I give this explanation rather feebly, hoping to obscure the disturbing effects the points she is scoring are having upon me.

"And isn't that just how Absalom began his rebellion, by representing you?" Bathsheba hits home again with a tenacity and quickness of mind she has demonstrated in the past when pursuing her own interests. "Oh, David, David, don't be a sap. Can't you ever learn? Adonijah will exalt himself once again at his fancy luncheon by saying he will be king and behaving as though he already is. Would Solomon do that? Your subjects will become his subjects. Have you done anything to displease Adonijah," persists Bathsheba, "by asking him why he is doing so?"

"Why should I do anything to displease Adonijah?" is my reply. "Adonijah will be king and Solomon won't. Adonijah is the oldest."

"That doesn't have to count." The alacrity with which she is counterpunching infuses me with the vexing notion that she has been coached. "You weren't the oldest, were you?"

"You think I got where I am as a gift from my father?"

"You think Jacob was the oldest?" she answers with a question, aggressively. "Was Joseph? Was his son Ephraim? But Ephraim got the blessing from Jacob, didn't he? Even though Joseph wanted it to go to Manasseh. That big-shot ancestor of yours, Judah, wasn't the oldest either, was he, and neither was his twin son, Pharez, about whom you also like to boast so much. That's some scandal with Judah you've got back there in your family closet, haven't you? Never mind me and my wild parties with my Canaanites before I was married. Judah doing it with his own daughter-in-law? Oh, boy! A man must not lie with the wife of his son, didn't he know that?"

"She was a widow," I cry out in protest. "And she dressed up as a harlot to trick him. Listen, how come you all of a sudden know so much? You never read a good book in your whole life."

"I've been brushing up. I've been reading my Bible. I've got nothing else to do."

"Horseshit." I know my dearest sweetheart too well to fall for that one. "That's a barefaced lie. You've been listening to Nathan, haven't you? He's the one who's been sending you in here with all those things to say, isn't he?"

Bathsheba looks all the more winning when her face colors a bit. "So where's the lie?" she replies at last. "Listening to Nathan is a lot harder than reading the Bible, isn't it?"

"You said it," I agree, and eye her appreciatively. "Remarks like that remind me of why I still do love you, my darling. Come to me."

Bathsheba gives a peremptory shake of her head. "I am sick of love."

"Then tell your son Solomon to go pee up a rope."

"Are you going to punish the kingdom just because I refuse to do dirty things with you at my age?"

"What's dirty about them? You didn't used to think they were dirty."

"I always thought they were dirty. That's why we enjoyed doing them, you simpleton. Men are so naïve, always."

"And what's all this about punishing the kingdom?" I demand belatedly. "Adonijah is a very goodly man and popular with the people."

"Solomon is wise."

"As my foot."

"The apple doesn't fall far from the tree."

"Don't butter me up. Let him learn from Adonijah, if you think he's so wise, instead of lurking around my hallways all the time with his stylus and his tablet, trying to get in to see me. Why does he have to write everything down? Can't he remember? People believe that Adonijah will be king because he goes about behaving as though he already is."

"How can Solomon exalt himself by saying he will be king?" Bathsheba argues. "Isn't Adonijah the older?"

"You see?" I answer on a soft note of triumph. "Primogeniture does make a difference, doesn't it? Let Solomon try something else, if you're so determined. Why doesn't he start a rebellion? Solomon's so stingy he's probably got enough saved up by now to finance a popular rebellion."

Bathsheba hangs her head moodily. "Solomon isn't popular."

"So there you are."

"And he loves you too much," she says with a sudden flash of invention, "ever to oppose you in anything."

"Was I born yesterday?"

"It's true. Solomon lives only to find out what you wish and make sure it's done."

"In that case, he would never let me set eyes on him again."

"Have dinner with him tonight, my dearest David. Hear it from his own lips."

"Not," I reply genially with a redundancy more in Nathan's character than mine, "for all the tea in China, the perfumes in Arabia, the camphire in Engedi, and the coffee in Brazil. I never want to eat with that penny-pinching imbecile again."

"He'll pay for the food."

"That will be the day."

"I'll make him promise. Solomon does whatever his mother tells him to."

"I can't stand him."

"He's our flesh and blood."

"Don't rub it in."

Solomon keeps records scrupulously. He rarely smiles and never laughs. He has the pinched, drab soul of a landlord with diversified stingy investments who interprets every piddling reverse as a catastrophe uniquely his own. "A pill," was the way my dashing Absalom described him. "The pits. He never laughs. He curses deaf people and places obstacles in the path of the blind. Even then he doesn't laugh. He just looks on. Whatever he gives, he always takes back. Yesterday, I stopped him in the street and asked him to share some raisins with me. By the time I arrived home, he was already waiting at my door with a cup to borrow some lentils." If we had a word for prick then, we would have called him one.

"Solomon," I used to counsel him when I still assumed—preposterously, as it turned out—that every living being has some potential for salutary intellectual change, "there is really no better thing a man hath to do under the sun than to eat and to drink and to be merry, for who can tell when the silver cord shall be loosed and the golden bowl be broken and our dust be returned to the earth as it was?"

The prick wrote it down studiously, pausing with the tip of his tongue protruding from the corner of his mouth before requesting me to please repeat the one about the silver cord. And soon he was noising these words of mine about the city as his own. Solomon writes down on his clay ledger everything I say, as though the ramifications of knowledge were coins to be gained and husbanded avariciously, instead of liberating influences to expand and gladden the psyche.

"Shlomo," I address him familiarly, in a heavyhearted attempt to feed him something that will sink in. "Life is short. The sooner man begins to spend his wealth, the better he uses it. You should learn to spend."

There followed one of the few times in both our lives that I was privileged to see his face brighten. "Last week, my lord, just last week I spent a good deal to buy silver amulets and marble idols from Moab that are already worth more than three times what I paid for them."

"That was saving, Shlomo," I explain, as though talking to a child with a learning disability. "You don't seem able to enjoy the difference between spending and saving."

"I enjoyed it, I enjoyed it a lot," says Solomon soberly. "I Jewed them down."

"You did what?"

"I Jewed them down."

"Solomon." I am forced to break off for a second. "Shlomo, your mother tells me you are very wise. Do you believe that the apple doesn't fall far from the tree?"

"I don't know what that means."

"Write it down anyway, just keep writing everything down. Put it in your book of proverbs. Every wise man should have a book of proverbs."

The prick keeps writing.

Just about all he does know is how little I think of him. He is abashed in the royal presence; but he perseveres in seeking it. He will tense and hang back for safety as though there were a viper at his feet each time he witnesses some glitter of private merriment illuminating my countenance. Sometimes, maliciously, I may smile to myself even when I have nothing more to smile about than the predictable delight of watching his face blanch. He inevitably fears the worst, guessing with good reason that I deplore him for his wooden dullness and uncharitable stupidity. He is one of these dry-natured Jewish men who never want to go out with Jewish girls, or with short ones. He is somewhat notorious already for his predilec-

JOSEPH HELLER

tion for the strange women of Gilead, Ammon, Moab, and Edom, an attraction which in itself would not be so exceptional. It is said, however, that he is equally drawn to their strange gods. I know that not even he can be that stupid, but there are whispers of altars to Ashtoreth and Milcom built by him while he was away on his secretive debauches, and he invariably returns from these desert sprees with more amulets, idols, and models of occult towers to augment his treasured collection. He has told us he would like many wives. He has a bent for accumulation. How many? He isn't sure. Maybe a thousand, he says, without cracking a smile.

"A thousand?" I ask with surprise. He nods. "Why so many?"

He doesn't know, but he really means it. Not in my day has Solomon been noted for intelligence, humor, or good fellowship.

Adonijah, his older half brother, is a vain and convivial popinjay with the complacency of a man who feels he has already come into his estate, and he must surely believe I am brimming inside with uncritical approval every time he observes some pleased expression light briefly on my features. Let him recall, for contrast, the doting love with which I used to gaze on Absalom for a timeless example of undying fatherly devotion. My time of attachment to my children is past; it terminated, I believe, with the death of Absalom in the wood of Ephraim and the arrival of the two runners with reports of the battle. The first to reach me brought tidings of victory. The next brought news of inconsolable loss. I went up to the chamber over the gate and wept. As with the death of my baby, I felt in my heart that my punishment was greater than I could bear.

Since then I've not felt much for anyone but myself, not until Abishag the Shunammite was ushered into my rooms and began endearing herself to me, and not until Bathsheba began coming to my quarters each day to wheedle in her devious ways, and by doing so reawaken my distant memories of the exquisite lust and lewdness we once shared. I want her ass in my hands again. I swear by everything important left to me—which isn't much, I know—that I could swive her mightily at least one more time, from stem to stern and keel to topmast, if she'd just lie down beside me and extend the physical cooperation I'd need. She might have to help me a lot.

She does not mean less to me now because she is heavier. She has a weakness for honeyed grains and dried fish. She does not know how the sight of her flesh now inflames me with a wistful desire to

108

lay myself upon her again. She has stopped wearing bloomers every day, now that she no longer cares to be seductive, and there is more of her bare body to see in the folds and slits of her smocks and negligees. I stare shamelessly, up her carelessly parted thighs and down her unbound bosom, at the clear blue veins beneath the milky, translucent skin of the front of her hips to the livid little venous knots in her calves and ankles. I love those extra sags of age-ripened flesh, I respond to those purple varicose defects, to the chronic edemas I identify in her feet. She has always been human, animal, and real. What I have always relished most about her, I believe, were her blatant and spontaneous indelicacies. She never claimed refinement. All these signs of degenerating, natural, wholesome, breathing life are startlingly appropriate, reminding me bluntly of impermanence; they draw me to my beloved with the old and nearly overwhelming hunger to fling and force my disheveled masculine body atop her disheveled female one as I used to do, and say to her yet again, "I want you, my darling. Open to me, my sister, my love, my dove, my undefiled."

I am injured when she murmurs mechanically in reply that she is sick of love. I am so incensed I could roar, so humbled I could cry.

It was Bathsheba who exemplified to me for all time the vast and telling difference between spilling seed and good fucking. It was she who put that into words for me in a jesting retort to my playful baiting. It was Bathsheba also who told me I have—or had—a big cock. Of course, only Bathsheba among all my women had exposed herself to an adequate sample for valid comparisons.

On the other hand, it was I, without the knowledge that I was doing so, who illuminated for her the inexpressible difference between good fucking and making love. Bathsheba gave me credit for that in words I never wish to forget.

"This isn't fucking" was the way she propounded her philosophical article of faith, in a hushed and startled exclamation, as her rattled pale blue eyes rolled steadily back into focus. Her damp, reddened face stared up at me adoringly. "This is making love."

Ever the innocent in such matters esoteric, I inquired, "What's the difference? How can you tell?"

She nodded wisely. "That knowledge," she informed me, tapping the bone between her breasts and regarding me still with that same slaked expression of overindulgence, "comes from the source." The differing pallors of her milky skin undulated and dissolved in the flickering lamplight from my cedar walls. "It comes right from the heart."

I was all at once filled with an uncontainable joy more gratifying than any I had experienced in my whole life. My hair was drenched with perspiration. I lay my tousled head upon her chest and I thrust my mouth against her breastbone as though to caress with my tongue and lips that same precious heart whose sturdy beat I could feel and hear only an inch beneath, like a sanctified and reassuring roar.

But that was after, so long after, the day of my killing of Goliath. My ordeals with Saul were over and nothing presaged the misfortunes in store. There was no Absalom driving me from the city. Who would have thought such a thing could happen? That a son would rebel against a father with weapons and troops? That the people would flock to him in such large numbers and race toward my city as though borne on the wings of the wind? Someone must have been telling lies about me. Forced labor and high taxation might have had something to do with it. And if that were not heartbreaking enough, then came that ugly Shimei to harangue me obscenely as I fled—Shimei, that repulsive gnome with bent legs and arms and toothless raw-red gums. Vile distant kinsman in the house of Saul, he came bounding out of his hut in Bahurim with sadistic glee as we trudged past in retreat from Jerusalem, to defame me with his gloating taunts and malignant insults.

"Thou bloody man, come out, come out," he howled.

Oh, the impious things that cackling animal said to me. He drew near enough to fling stones at me, even dust. On me, David, our first great king—was there ever a second? At one point, my nephew, faithful Abishai, gripped his sword and asked permission to step off the road to decapitate him. I would not allow that. I had enemies enough. I wanted no more gratuitous acts of violence to enlarge the numbers already convinced I had been treacherous to Saul or wishing me deposed for other reasons. It's a very tangled web we weave when first we practice to deceive.

I spared Shimei that day as I proceeded miserably with my entourage of refugees downward in defeat toward the plain of the wilderness that lies between the mountainous terrain of Jerusalem and the skimpy river Jordan. When I was safely across the river with all of the loyal troops accompanying me, I knew that the outcome of the whole turbulent business was going to be ours. And as soon as that certainty settled within me, I began to sorrow over the ruin in store for my poor son Absalom. His goose was cooked. Poor boy, I mourned. Poor, poor impetuous boy.

My heart sank further when later I found myself brooding on both the stark temerity of Shimei's attack and the substance of his barbarous vilifications. A bloody man, he'd called me. Me? The poet who had lauded Saul so generously in my famous elegy? And mentioned none of his faults? Against Saul and his three legitimate sons I had never raised a weapon. Is it my fault they were all killed at Gilboa and there was no one eligible left alive with a bona fide relationship to the royal family but me, the son-in-law? Who told him to fight when he had no chance of winning?

I was in Ziklag when that happened, serving Achish of Gath in his southern territory with the small private army with which I had fled from Saul to the protection of the Philistines. I sent booty to Achish regularly and spoke of raids upon Hebrews. With commendably sagacious foresight, I sneaked spoils as well to the elders of key Judean cities whose good will I was cultivating for the future—and told them of bountiful forays against Bedouin tribes and desert caravans of wealth. Where did it all really come from? Who remembers! But even while outlawed in the barren sands of Philistia, I made sure that no grass grew under my feet.

And when Saul died, I was ready.

5

ARMS
AND THE
MAN

Everybody's death, I have written, simplifies life for someone, and I will not pretend that the death of Saul and his three legitimate sons did not simplify mine. But don't get the idea I was glad. Of course I grieved. And then I wrote my famous elegy.

Now, frankly, we artists do not normally write well when we are distraught, if we can bestir ourselves to write at all. But my famous elegy is a glorious exception. Though composed rapidly, it's a better elegy than Milton's to Edward King or Shelley's on the death of John Keats, which is pure *dreck*—revolting, sentimental *dreck*. "Oh, weep for Adonais, he is dead." What kind of shit is that? *Adonais* instead of Adonis? Shelley needed that extra syllable? I worked with simple English names like Saul and Jonathan and never had any trouble. And everyone in the world knows the words to mine. But do me a favor and don't take them all as gospel. Forget the ones about Jonathan that gave rise to all those denigrating insinuations about homosexuality that plague me even into the present and will probably dog me to my grave. I wish I could forget them. It is unjust and outrageous that impressionable young people like Abishag the Shunammite might be led to believe I really was gay. Anyone with the slightest knowledge of my private life would know that Jonathan's "love" definitely was *not* more wonderful to me than the love of women! Count my wives. Consider my carnal involvement with Bathsheba. I loved Jonathan as a brother, that's all I meant. But no, people would rather snicker and wallow in smut at someone else's expense, wouldn't they? And how come, if there's even one iota of truth underlying those base rumors, you find me mixed up only with women for the rest of my life and never again linked in that disgusting fashion with any other fellow?

Let me tell you something straight from the shoulder: good

115

name in man or woman is the immediate jewel of their soul. A good name is better than precious ointment. Who steals my purse steals trash, but he that filches from me my good name robs me of that which not enriches him, and makes me poor indeed, and I wish I could set the record straight on this matter of Jonathan and me once and for all. Certainly we were close—do I deny that?—and sure I was flattered when he embraced me so warmly with his avowals of undying friendship right after I killed Goliath and settled in Gibeah. Who wouldn't be? Jonathan was older, legendary, cosmopolitan, and not bad-looking. He was a popular man-about-town in Gibeah. He was the hero of the battle of Michmash, for which he was looked up to by everyone but Saul, who was to remain, until the day they both died, uncontrollably jealous of the initiative shown by his son there. Jonathan told me the story. With me Jonathan held nothing back. He did tend to be effusive on occasion and often expressed himself in a florid way I found disconcerting and even incomprehensible—frankly, I hadn't the slightest idea what he meant when he told me that his soul was knit with my soul, and I still don't. But I can tell you this: we were never fags. Not even once. You want to know who was a fag? King James the First of England was a fag, that's who was a fag. His court was full of fags. And that's why his scholars relied more on Greek sources than Hebrew for their Authorized Version of the Bible. What would you expect them to come up with? They weren't much good with Hebrew, and they weren't much better with English, either. Go figure out what they're saying half the time. I'll tell you honestly that I did not know what was in Jonathan's mind when he told me he loved me as his own soul and then stripped off the robe that was on him and other garments and gave them to me, along with his sword and his bow and his girdle. But I do know what was in mine. I was glad to get them.

Sure, we may have hugged and kissed a little once or twice, and we did cry together; but that was mainly when I was in trouble and we were parting, as friends—just friends—for what we believed would be forever. He had sounded out Saul for me and brought back word that his father was resolved to kill me, had fiercely berated him for stupidity in failing to recognize that he could never establish his own kingdom as long as the son of Jesse, meaning me, lived. And then Saul had hurled a javelin at him!

What is it with these fathers who want to destroy their children?

Whence comes this royal and noble willingness to spill the blood of their own offspring? Saul and Jonathan. Saturn and Chronus, then Chronus and Zeus. Abraham and Isaac, Laius and Oedipus, Agamemnon and Iphigenia, Jephthah and his daughter—the list is long. I never hated Absalom. I know if I were God and possessed His powers, I would sooner obliterate the world I had created than allow any child of mine to be killed in it, for any reason whatsoever. I would have given my own life to save my baby's, and even to spare Absalom's. But that may be because I am Jewish, and God is not.

Jonathan alerted me to my peril when we met secretly in a field outside the city the next morning. My return to Gibeah had been in vain. Crazy Saul. He was mad as a hatter but close to the truth in his irrational belief that I was fated to succeed him and that two of his children were closer to me than they were to him. I saw Jonathan but one more time after I fled for good, when he sought me out in the wilderness of Ziph to cede to me his hereditary right to be king. Crazy Saul guessed right on that one too: Jonathan was not going to establish his kingdom as long as I, the son of Jesse, lived.

It was beginning to look as though more and more people were discovering that Saul had feet of clay. He was as unstable as water, and when Samuel departed and took God with him, he left Israel's first king with no high source of guidance, without traditions for governing or even much of a religion. The truth is that we Jews did not have much of a religion at that time, and we don't have one now. We've got altars and forbidden idols, and we sacrifice lambs, and that's just about it. In that kind of moral void, Saul, selected more for his height than his intelligence, was alone and despairing and had no vision for discerning what was right, or even what was good. He talked to God. He got no answer. Now *there's* a hollow state to be in, isn't it—to believe in God and get no sign that He's there. No wonder he went crazy.

How revealing the difference between Saul's feelings toward his children and my feelings toward mine, even toward Absalom when I was dragging myself away from Jerusalem with my vanished pomp and aching heart. Panting messengers arriving from the city brought compelling exhortations that I lodge not the night in the plains of the wilderness but speedily pass over the waters of Jordan, lest I and all the people with me be overtaken and swallowed up. We plodded onward until we reached the bank of the narrow river and there was not a one of us that was not gone over Jordan. We arose the next morning with the voice of the first bird. And only then was the ghastly truth at the core of my plight driven home to me: Absalom meant to kill me.

How ironic the difference between me and my beloved son Absalom, between his soliciting the soundest means for overtaking me and having my life, while I was cudgeling my brains for a way to spare his. "Deal gently for my sake with the young man Absalom," were my mawkish words to my commanders as their men trooped past me toward the positions they would take up in the field outside the wood of Ephraim for the battle in which he would die. "Beware that none touch the young man Absalom," I urged like a fool. No, not like a fool, but like a fond, doting father who will overlook and excuse everything in the child he loves best, and who breaks his heart. And in that singular disparity in our desires abides his lasting victory over me: I loved him and he did not love me.

If only the young man Absalom had waited. What was his hurry, except a volcanic desire to depose me that overmastered his wish to inherit and govern? How proud of him I would be now, how gratified by reports that it was he, not that vain and simple-minded fop Adonijah, who was riding about the city grandly in his chariot with fifty runners going before him. Or it was he who was bruiting it about, with his princely dark head thrown back in impudent laughter, that he was going to be king. If Absalom were alive, I would not be saddled now with this petty choice I must make between vacuous Adonijah, who puts too much faith in his affable nature and his many friends, and industrious, saturnine Solomon, who glumly detects that he has not too much of either.

With less and less discretion, Adonijah blithely gads about exalting himself, and assumes, because I have not spoken to curb him, that he is not displeasing me. He has taken of late to ogling my precious servant girl Abishag with the rude and self-esteeming eye of one of those despicable roués whom no person of any discrimination can stand. He is an even bigger dolt than I rate him if he supposes I will permit that, or that his stepmother Bathsheba will allow me to.

Much of the derogatory information I receive about him is given me by Bathsheba. I confess to a weakness: I am invariably pleased by her distress, just as I invariably used to be sexually stimulated by our quarrels. I relish the sight of her tiny bright eyes flashing angrily and her blood rising with emotion to color her cheeks with splashes of carmine.

"Adonijah," she complains with agitated movements, "is still going about saying that he will be king. He is also saying that he plans to make important announcements from himself and from you at that big outdoor luncheon feast of his. Solomon would never be so tactless, never so heartless, not my Solomon. Hasn't anyone else told you what I'm saying? It's lucky you have someone like me to look out for your own good."

She takes long steps rapidly, first in one direction and then in the opposite, passing very close to my bed. If I possessed but a fraction of the dexterity and strength of former days, I could seize her suddenly by the crotch and hold her firmly enough to draw her to me. God knows I want to. Today she is clad in a loose pearly robe with a very low neck and a flaring long slit up one side past the plump contour of her hip almost into her narrowing waist. When she halts and whirls in her violent hurry or flings herself into her chair and draws her legs in to start up again, I get frequent, head-on views of her ash-blonde snatch and much of the curving flesh of the exposed half of her backside. The hair of my tall blonde wife is a luminescent yellow today, and her toes are clean. She is wearing a sweet pomade that exudes an essence of lavender fixed in a vaguely acrid underbase.

"You don't seem to be wearing your underwear anymore," I notice.

"Now that I'm sick of love," she mutters abstractedly, "I don't always have to look sexy." We all know underwear never caught on. And Bathsheba had tasted once again the disappointment of creative failure. "You promised," she says, scolding me sharply, "that you were going to stop him."

"*You* said I was going to stop him," I correct her with good humor, making no effort to conceal my mirth when our gazes for a moment lock.

"Why should he be making proclamations that he will be king?"

"Proclamations?" I question her closely.

She gives ground a little. "Well, they're almost proclamations, the way he goes riding around his chariot telling everyone he will be king."

"Adonijah probably will be king. Why shouldn't he make proclamations?"

"You want him to make proclamations?"

"He shouldn't be making proclamations?"

"That he's going to be king?"

"When I die, he will be."

"Do you want him to be king now? And why does it have to be him?"

"He's the oldest, that's why."

"Again the oldest?" Bathsheba stares at me with disgust. "Show me where it's written. We're Jews, not Mesopotamians. Wasn't Reuben Jacob's oldest son? Look how he was dumped."

"You've been meeting with Nathan again, haven't you?" I charge. "Reuben was as unstable as water."

"By you," Bathsheba scoffs, "everybody is as unstable as water. Adonijah is stable? Wasn't Reuben passed over because he slept with one of his father's women? Haven't you noticed the way Adonijah has been staring at Abishag? And winking? Believe me, he doesn't want to wait until you die before he goes in unto her. She knows what I'm talking about." Bathsheba looks toward the modest servant girl, who is seated with her cosmetic pots before a mirror of polished metal, creaming the surfaces of bone circling her eyes and applying a violet dye to her upper lids. "Don't you, child?" Abishag nods with a smile, blushing slightly. "What has he done to you, what has he said?"

"He looks at me straight and giggles a lot," says Abishag. "He winks his eye."

"Has he told you he will be king?"

"He tells me he will be king," answers Abishag, "and asks me to be nice to him now. Will Adonijah be king, my lord?"

"You see?" cries Bathsheba. "Would my Solomon do something like that?"

"Send in Solomon," I decide.

Bathsheba heaves a sigh. "You'll never regret a minute you spend with my Solomon," she exclaims. "He's such a joy, my Solomon. A jewel. He'll make you proud."

"Solomon," I begin very tolerantly with the best intentions, endeavoring one more time to plumb the depths of this our son if ever I should be so blessed as to find any. After all, is Adonijah such an Einstein? "You know—even *you* know—" I falter and have to

120

break off, wincing beneath the discomforting weight of his trans-fixed attention. As usual, he sits listening stolidly to me, his stylus and clay tablet at the ready, his somber head inclined toward me with a deference that is almost offensive, as though all my words ought immediately to be recorded on stone. "Solomon," I resume even more patiently in a softer tone, after wetting my tongue with some water from a cruse, "even you know about Shimei the son of Gera—remember?—who cursed me grievously that day as I fled from Jerusalem to Mahanaim. But he came down to meet me in penitence when I returned to Jordan. And I swore to him by the Lord that I would not put him to death with the sword. Now mark me well." Solomon nods once gravely to show he is marking me well and bends still closer with his rigid expression. I wish it were possible for me to recoil from him farther. His breath is repulsive, much too sweet, and I judge he is using some kind of obnoxious male cologne on his face and beneath his arms. "But I did not swear that *you* wouldn't put him to death, did I?" I conclude with sly emphasis, smacking my tongue, and I cannot restrain myself from chortling at my own cleverness. "You get my meaning, don't you?"

Solomon replies with an elephantine nod. "I get your meaning."

"What is my meaning?"

"You swore that you would not put him to death," he recites in a monotone, reading from his tablet. "But you did not swear that I would not put him to death."

He says this without a glimmer of levity brightening his lugubrious mien, and I begin to fear he does not get my meaning.

"Solomon—Abishag, my darling, let me have a little bit of that stuff you prepare that helps settle my stomach."

"Bicarbonate of soda?"

"No, the stronger stuff today. That mixture of aloes, gentian, zedoary, cinchona, calumba, galangal, rhubarb, angelica, myrrh, chamomile, saffron, and peppermint oil."

"Fernet-Branca?"

"Yes, my pet. Solomon, come a bit closer, closer—no, that's close enough." I can't stand cologne on men or sweeteners on their breath; they reek to me of guilty knowledge of the pile of shit they're leaving behind and are sneakily attempting to disown. "Solomon, my dearest son," I say to him in a voice lowered to a level of seriousness almost sacrosanct, "let me give you now a precious secret about kingship, about how to rule well and be honored by your subjects, even by your enemies. You would like to be a king someday, wouldn't you? Would you like to be a king?"

"I would like to be a king."

"Why would you like to be a king?"

"Peacocks and apes."

"Peacocks and apes? Shlomo, Shlomo, you said peacocks and apes?"

"I like peacocks and apes."

"You like peacocks and apes?"

"I like sapphires too, and a throne of ivory overlaid with the best gold, with carved lions standing by the stays and twelve more lions standing there on one side and there on the other upon the six steps, and houses of cedar carved with knops and open flowers."

"Knops and open flowers?"

"Knops and open flowers."

"That's why you want to be king?"

"Mother wants me to be king."

"What are knops?"

"I don't know. She thinks I'd be happy as king."

"I'm not happy as king," I tell him.

"Maybe if you had some peacocks and apes."

"How many?"

"Lots."

"Solomon, you don't smile when you say that. You never smile. I don't think I've ever seen you smile."

"Maybe I've never had anything to smile about. Maybe if I had some peacocks and apes."

"Solomon, my boy," I say, "let me give you some wisdom. Wisdom is better than rubies, you know, and maybe even better than peacocks and apes."

"Let me write that down," interrupts Solomon politely. "It sounds wise."

"Yes, very wise," I answer, frowning.

"How does it go?"

"Wisdom is better than rubies," I repeat, "and maybe even better than peacocks and apes."

"Wisdom is better than rubies." He cannot write without moving his lips. "And maybe even better than peacocks and apes? Is that wise?"

"Very wise, Solomon. Please hearken to me closely now." My throat is dry again. "If ever you do become a king, and if you want to be honored as a king and deemed worthy as a king, and if ever you find yourself drinking date wine or pomegranate wine from one of the royal goblets in the company of others whose good opinion you wish to retain, always make certain that you drink with your nose inside the brim of the royal goblet."

"Inside the brim?"

"Inside the brim."

"With my nose inside the brim of the royal goblet," Solomon repeats to himself, writing, and waits without the slightest trace of curiosity when he has finished.

"Aren't you going to ask me why?" I prod.

"Why?" he responds obediently. This is about as much mental agility as I've ever been able to whip up in him.

"Because otherwise," I inform him, feeling let down, "the wine will spill down the front of your neck, you goddamned fool! Abishag! Abishag! Show him the door. The fucking door! Show Shlomo the fucking door!"

"I've seen the door."

"Get out, get out, you idiot, you dummy, get out, get out! Abishag, give me some more of that shit for my stomach. Oh, if only my words were written down in a book. Who would believe them?"

Abishag would believe them. Abishag will believe anything from me.

But Bathsheba would not, and tries to convince me that Solomon is the wisest man in the kingdom. "Next to you, of course," she throws in with ritual politeness. "He writes down everything you say."

"And doesn't understand a fucking word of it. And then goes about giving it out as his own. I know what he does. I've got spies."

"Have dinner with him tonight," she dictates to me. She has switched to a robe of aquamarine with a flouncing train that parts at the front and twirls about her ankles as she paces and swerves, and she has put on a pair of those skimpy bloomers she invented that she calls panties. Kneeling at my couch, she takes my hand. The warmth from her palms is agreeable. It is so seldom nowadays that she touches me. "Get to know him better. That would be nice, wouldn't it? Just the two of you, right here. What's wrong?" She feels my shudder and lets go of my hand as though it were something reptilian. "And maybe me too. And maybe Nathan. And Benaiah also."

"No, no, no, no, not in a million years," I tell her. "Not in a billion. I'm not eating a meal with Solomon again in my whole life, and certainly not on one of its last days. He watches every mouthful I eat, and then makes sure to eat exactly as much. If he gives a person the right time, he always asks for it back. He never makes jokes. Do you ever see him laugh?"

"What's there to laugh about?" she answers with a shrug. "His dear father is full of days and soon will be dead."

I turn myself over on my side to confront her. "He still goes around cursing deaf people, doesn't he?"

"That's proof of his sweetness," my wife replies. "Deaf people are unable to hear him and have no idea what he's saying."

"And puts stumbling blocks before the blind, doesn't he?"

"Who else will fall over them?"

"When he takes a man's cloak as a pledge in the morning, he still won't give it back to him at sundown, will he? So the poor beggar will have something warm to sleep in at night."

"How else can he be sure he'll be able to collect?"

"Sure, *collect*. I'll give him *collect*. That's the whole point of the commandment, damn it, that the man won't be forced into paying before he can afford to. The quality of mercy is not strained. You don't know that? It droppeth as the gentle rain from heaven upon the place beneath. Don't you understand Exodus and Deuteronomy?"

"I don't read that stuff anymore."

"No, you'd rather get a brief synopsis from Nathan, wouldn't you?"

"A synopsis from Nathan?"

"Solomon—that cheap prick won't even build a parapet around his roof to protect himself from blood guilt if people fall off. You watch. Deuteronomy will get him if Leviticus doesn't."

"He's wise."

"Solomon?"

"He never has people to his house," she explains with an air of vindication. "So why should he throw out money on a parapet he doesn't need? See how wise? He'll be good for the economy of the kingdom."

"He'll be rotten for the kingdom," I reply. "Let him sell some of those filthy amulets he keeps collecting if he needs money for the battlement on the roof of his house. That's where he puts his money, into amulets. He wants apes and peacocks."

"The amulets are a good investment. They have to go up."

"Never mind *investment*. I'll give him *investment*. They get him hot, that's why he collects them. Oh, that's some Solomon you gave me. He goes a-whoring after strange women in Edom, Moab, and Ammon, doesn't he?"

"You didn't?"

"I took them into my harem. He builds altars to strange gods."

"Ours is not so strange?"

"At least He's ours. And I always was faithful to my wives and concubines."

"When you cheated with me?" she contradicts.

"Almost always," I amend myself sheepishly.

"That was adultery, David. And you knew it, even when we were doing it. And you know what Genesis, Exodus, Leviticus, Numbers, Deuteronomy, and Nathan have to say about that."

Abishag the Shunammite is certainly getting an education just listening to us, I muse, although she tries not to stare and pretends not to hear.

"Come, let us reason together," I suggest more quietly, in my most diplomatic manner. "Solomon will bring ruin to us all if he worships strange gods. He'll bankrupt the kingdom with his apes and his ivory and his peacocks. Do you know what he wants for a throne? Here's what he told me he wants for a throne: a great throne of ivory overlaid with best gold, and two carved lions standing by the stays of the throne and twelve more lions—twelve—standing there on one side and on the other upon the six steps."

"That sounds divine," Bathsheba says with a straight face.

Is it any wonder I'm still so crazy about her? "Fourteen lions?" I exclaim. "Or maybe he means twenty-six. He thinks I should have a throne like that too."

"If Solomon has lions," she says, nodding, "you should have lions too. And so should I."

So different is she from constant, unselfish Abigail, for whom my regard was always higher, and my passion so much less. When Abigail died I was lonely, and I have been lonely ever since.

"God isn't going to take to a throne like that," I think out loud, feasting my eyes upon a face and form so beautiful to me still. "Ours doesn't go in that much for ostentation."

"Ours loves Solomon," Bathsheba insists, "and will go along with anything Solomon wants."

"Don't bet on it," I disagree. "I used to think He felt that way about me. Until he killed our baby. Solomon has no chance of being king."

"That's what you told me from the day he was born," Bathsheba points out, unconvinced. "And now he is second only to Adonijah."

"Adonijah is popular," I say to annoy her. "Solomon is not."

Bathsheba takes an unexpected veer toward the philosophical. "The rich have many friends," she remarks. "But the poor is hateth even of his own neighbor."

"What makes you say that?" I demand touchily.

"I heard Solomon say it, and I thought it was very wise. Why do you ask?"

"He got it from me," I tell her coldly, "that's why I ask. You'll find it among my proverbs."

"Solomon has lots of proverbs too," she boasts.

"And the best of them," I tell her, "are mine. The next thing you know, he'll be claiming he wrote my famous elegy."

"What famous elegy?" asks my wife.

For the moment I am struck completely dumb. "*What* famous elegy?" My piercing cry is one of indignation. "What the hell do you mean, what famous elegy? *My* famous elegy, on the death of Saul and Jonathan. What other famous elegy is there?"

"I don't think I ever heard of it."

"You never heard of it?" I am beside myself with disbelief. "They know it in Sidon. They sing it in Ninevah. 'The beauty of Israel is slain upon thy high places.' You never heard that before? 'They were swifter than eagles, they were stronger than lions.' 'How are the mighty fallen!' 'He clothed you in scarlet, and with other delights, and put ornaments of gold upon your apparel.'"

She sits up straighter, her eyes widening. "You wrote that?" she inquires.

"What, then?" I demand. "Who the fuck do you think wrote it?"

"Solomon?"

"Solomon?" I shout. I have a queasy sensation that none of what is taking place now is really happening. "This was ten years before I even moved to Jerusalem!" I roar at her. "They were telling it in Gath, they were publishing it in the streets of Askelon, a dozen years before I even met you. You don't remember it's mine? Solomon? How the fuck could Solomon have written it when he wasn't even born?"

"David, don't be so cross," she reproaches me. "You know how hopeless I've always been about dates." She seats herself beside me on my bed and places her hand on my chest. For a second, it is like old times. My member thickens slightly. My senses are imbued with the sensual odors of myrrh, cassia, and sweet calamus radiating from her tissues and garments as though from an ivory palace. "Don't," she says when I drop my hand upon her knee.

"You didn't used to mind." I am now the one who is imploring.

"Life doesn't stand still," she observes.

"Another proverb from Solomon?"

"It moves along," she continues without having heard me. "David," she appeals, "I feel danger in my bones. Nathan fears that a royal banquet with Adonijah presiding could make prisoners of us all. Even of you."

"That's funny," I reply with deadpan irony. "Abiathar was in here just this morning to tell me he thinks it's a fine idea."

"Abiathar?" she repeats vacantly, as though the name were an alien sound she had never heard before.

"The one who's been around me just about all my life," I remind her tartly, "since my days as a fugitive."

"You know how bad I've always been with names," she says, faking, and heaves a heavy sigh. "So many A's. Who can keep track of them all? Abigail, Ahinoam, Abishai—and now an Abiathar."

"Not now. For fifty years."

"I sometimes think that Benaiah and I are the only B's in the whole country."

"Abiathar is my priest," I remind her slowly of what we both appreciate she knows very well. "He was one of the first to join up with me, right after Saul killed his father."

"Zadok is your priest."

"I have two."

"Well, Nathan is your prophet," she counters.

"Nathan is a windbag, and he never did approve of you, you know."

"And a prophet is higher than a priest," she calmly goes right on as though she did not hear me speak. "Nathan doesn't think you can trust Adonijah. Goodness gracious, another *A*. We even have an Abishag now. And what was the name of that dead wife of yours, the dowdy one who never spoke? Abital, the mother of Shepatiah."

"I thought you were bad with names."

"And *A*'s are bad luck. Asahel, and Ahitophel, Amnon, Absalom, Abner, Amasa—look what happened to them all. Darling," she wheedles, and I reflect as she leans down toward me again that an expression so quintessentially good just has to be composed of nothing but duplicity, "promise me that you will never pick as king anyone whose name begins with the letter *A*. That's all I ask."

Her temerity does take away my breath. "I'll give that request some serious consideration," I tell her, and wonder just how senile she thinks I fucking am.

"Yesterday," Bathsheba starts right in the following morning, "you gave me your word that you would never name Adonijah king."

She is wearing a fiery red robe of chiffon, and her head is adorned with a diadem of pearls and other precious gems. She is still so provocative when she dresses up that I want, as always, to tear off her clothes and strip her naked.

"That's not the way I remember it," I answer, admiring her effrontery.

"Abishag was here and heard what you said."

Abishag is steadfast in discretion as she sits at her stand of cosmetic pots, and I know she will never betray me.

"Don't you know that Abishag will be witness to whatever I want her to be?" I reply to Bathsheba with pride.

"What smells in here?" she inquires so innocently, executing another one of her nimble changes of subject that never fail to bedazzle me. She looks timorous as a rabbit as she wrinkles her nose, exposing her tiny, chipped teeth. "Someone open a window."

I laugh. Abishag displays dimples when she smiles. A coppery rouge she is applying to her face highlights the domes of her rich brown cheeks.

What smells, of course, is me, musty, linty, withering, old-aging me. They have perfumed my bed with aloes, cinnamon, and myrrh, but I still smell me. I stink of mortality and reek of mankind.

Pungent frankincense smolders everywhere in my palace. There are maybe a thousand incense burners. It must cost me a king's ransom each year in aromatic gums and resins. No wonder our balance of trade is poor. There is antiseptic myrrh and honey in the sweet-smelling ointments and medicines with which Abishag dresses my scratches and bedsores. My rashes and pimples she covers with a poultice of figs. The girl is loving and tireless in the care she lavishes upon me and is always entirely at my service. She glides about gracefully on soundless steps, her carriage poised in perfect alignment. There is never a moment of imbalance. Do I imagine Abishag the Shunammite, construct her out of wishes? She is as fragrant as grapes on a mountain of spices and like apples of gold in a picture of silver. She is vibrant with bliss when I pet and stroke her and cup her face in my hand and softly rest her head upon my chest or in the hollow of my shoulder. I regret in such moments of soulful union that the dear girl did not know me at my best, long before the hair on my chest turned white. The glory of young men is their strength, you know, and the beauty of old men is their gray hair. God knows I've got plenty of that kind of beauty now, but Abishag confides that she is drawn to the white hair on my chest. She caresses me there often, fingering the curls. She would not like a hairless man. She would not like a shaggy one, she admits with a pout, a man like Esau with bushy growths on his shoulders and back. It seems I fit the bill, if the child is not lying, and I know she is not.

In Shunem, Abishag informs us with native candor when queried, her father owns good land and her life was opulent. She kept the vineyards of the other children of her mother and neglected her own. The youngest and shyest in her large, flourishing family, she was often jollied by the others and was readily self-persuaded of her own inadequacies. To them it was play. She has always been anxious for praise. That same relentless inclination to please and sacrifice herself for others is manifest now with me. I wish I were sufficiently spry to do things for her. I would like to serve *her* a meal now and then, help *her* on or off with her clothing, carry in for her use a basin of fresh water, or bring to her a basket of summer fruits. They searched and found her for me because she was the most beautiful virgin to be located throughout all the coasts of Israel. I induce her to talk. I love hearing her.

"I remember the song with which they used to tease me and make me so unhappy," she relates in her lowered voice. " 'We have a little sister and she has no breasts.' Once they sang it about me at a wedding. I hid my face in my hands and ran out into the darkness. I wanted to die. I did not return until morning. I did not answer when I heard them searching for me. I wept on the ground, feeling frail as a leaf, and slept amid melons near the roots of trees."

"You have breasts now," I comfort her.

"Are they too small?"

"For what?" My smile is indulgent.

"For you."

"I'm a little past seventy, dearest," I counsel her apologetically. "Adonijah desires you already, and Solomon will want you too. Because you are beautiful, and because you have been with a king."

"Am I more beautiful than Bathsheba?"

"Much more beautiful."

"Than when you saw her the first time?"

"You are a garden enclosed, a spring shut up, a fountain sealed. You are more beautiful to me now than anyone in the world has ever been."

She would trade both my sons for me. I know how to talk to a woman now and they do not. Her darkly nippled breasts are like twin roes that feed among the lilies, her perfect buttocks like matched hinds. I am the first person in her life who delights in conversing with her, who will listen entranced to her replies and to all her casual meditations. Where could she find another like me?

She knows she is free now to say to me without shame anything that comes to her mind, and she knows that to me she can never say anything she will wish to take back. No wonder she thinks she is deeply in love with me and feels secure. When her head does rest in the hollow of my shoulder, I trace with my thumb the contour of her brow or the line of the side of her nose to the yielding rim of her spongy upper lip, which, in the dimming hues of my flickering and guttering lamplight, is the color of plums or pomegranate. I caress her that way addictively, insatiably. What good would the world be to me now without my Abishag? No other man she ever meets will draw as much happiness from her as I do, from simply contemplating her face and touching it, from the plain awareness of her presence. Through Abishag the Shunammite I now know about myself what I learned from Bathsheba and had forgotten, that all my life I have wanted to be in love. I can kiss her ears, her temples, neck, and eyes until the insides of my cheeks grow parched and my words barely audible, and then go on kissing her more and more with lips and tongue grown feeble with dryness. For reasons I cannot know, I frequently shy away from kissing her fully on the mouth.

She is my rose of Sharon, I have told her from my heart with my face in her hair and my breath upon her ear, and she is my lily of the valley. I have made her more contented by doing just that than Bathsheba would be were I to yield to her entreaties and give my kingdom to Solomon. Bathsheba would feel relief but no gratitude, never gratitude; and in less than half a day she would feel herself unjustly disadvantaged again in some other respect and be anguished prey to the need for something else. As with the alabaster bathtub.

No sooner had she moved into my palace than she asked for a bathtub of alabaster and got one. Michal yelled blue murder and got an alabaster bathtub too.

What do women want, I have often wondered aloud in moods of matrimonial exasperation; what in the world do women want? An answer as good as any came from my gracious Abigail one afternoon when I dropped in to rest.

"It takes very little to make us happy," Abigail explained, "and more than is contained in heaven and earth to keep us that way."

"That's a discerning answer, Abigail," I said. "And I shall always be so very, very grateful for your intelligence and your kindness. Would you like a bathtub of alabaster too?"

"No thank you, David. I'm perfectly content with the one I have."

"You never ask for anything, do you?"

"I have everything I need to be happy."

"Are you the woman who's the exception to what you've just described?"

Abigail smiled once more. "Perhaps I'm the exception."

"Isn't there anything you want, my darling? Really, Abigail, I would like to give you something."

Abigail shook her head. "No, David, there isn't. My cup runneth over."

"That's sweet, Abigail, really a very sweet thing to say. I will remember it always."

What Bathsheba wants now for her own quarters are my enormous, lush cushions of ramskin and badger dyed red and dyed blue. Solomon, she reflects, will let her have them when he is king. Solomon, I have fun in reminding her, will not be king.

"Suppose," she conjectures, "Adonijah dies."

"Don't you dare," I admonish her with a penetrating glance, "even give one moment's thought to a possibility like that. Why should Adonijah die?"

"I've always wanted to have skin like yours," she replies, to Abishag. "Mine was never so smooth and silken. Even now I'd give anything to be that dark."

"I would give anything to have skin that fair," answers Abishag with sincerity. "I got dark from the sun." Abishag is black but comely, and most particular to let us know she is black only because the sun has looked upon her. "It never went away."

Save for a Persian rug in my dining room that she knows is expensive and a tapestry wall-hanging of umber and viridian that depicts two pairs of cherubims of ocher with outspread wings touching, everything in my rooms is inferior to Bathsheba's standard, although the posts of my doors are of olive tree. Bathsheba does not like wood from olive trees. My bed, I think, is of applewood. Adonijah and Solomon both already lie upon beds of ivory and stretch themselves upon their couches. Bathsheba would also like a bed of ivory upon which to stretch herself. Did you hear her before, that cunt? With her "What famous elegy?" She knew, of course. That's just her nasty, selfish way of baiting me. With scheming vigilance, she takes note daily that Abishag my Shunammite is still attired in a maiden's robe of many colors. Adonijah notes it too. In just such a lively, carefree gown of divers colors was my virgin daughter Tamar, Absalom's sister, desired, deceived, raped, despised, and ejected.

There is import both moral and political in Abishag's virginity. Until I know her carnally, she is servant rather than concubine, and need not inevitably remain or pass on with my harem as a royal possession to go to my successor. A man going into another's woman is attempting to usurp the prerogatives of that other's office. You know what Absalom did in the sight of the sun with those ten concubines I left behind to keep the palace clean. You think it was because they were so beautiful? A streak of pragmatic election-eering is involved in the sporting eye Adonijah now rolls at Abi-shag. And canny Bathsheba is wary that I might encourage the union.

"You can still get out," she advises Abishag frankly with me looking on, as though I were invisible, deaf, or absent. "Nag him, aggravate him. Hurt him when you comb his hair. Bump into things and knock them over. I know how to drive him crazy. Don't bathe every day. Serve soup to him cold. Lose your temper. Com-plain. He'll give in. Don't make the same mistake I did. It's so much better outside."

"I *told* you to stay outside," I remind Bathsheba. "You wouldn't listen."

"Why don't you listen?" Bathsheba presses Abishag.

Smiling guardedly, my servant girl lowers her face and shakes her head. She glances at me shyly with eyes that are lustrous. I am David the king. Though ancient and decrepit, I am nonetheless her prince. I am her legend. She has no vision, she says, of ever being with anyone else.

"Where there is no vision," Bathsheba observes dully, "the peo-ple perish."

"What's that supposed to mean?" I want to know.

Bathsheba admits she doesn't know. "I was just thinking out loud."

"Is that another gem of wisdom from Solomon?"

"The apple doesn't fall far from the tree."

"That's another one I still don't get."

"Solomon says it all the time."

"That the apple doesn't fall far from the tree? What does it mean?"

"Why don't you ask him?"

"Where is the apple supposed to fall? How far away do you think a pear falls?"

"Solomon will like you," says Bathsheba to Abishag, skirting the need to reply. "He is beginning to think well of you already."

"If I do release her"—Bathsheba is not paying attention to me, and I turn and begin again with Abishag—"if I do release you, my dove, you will not go away from me with a light heart, will you? Yet my heart would fly away with you." What awaits her outside? She would be wife to whatever man her father took the price from, spend a lifetime in pregnancy and household drudgery. In sorrow and pain would she bring forth children, manage a home, and endlessly toil a thousand times harder than she would ever have to do for me. Where is the advantage?

"Husbands die, thank God," Bathsheba answers in her matter-of-fact way. "That's how he got Abigail, and that's how he got me. Or they can easily be provoked to get rid of you by divorce. Begin to aggravate him and see. Nag him and holler on him just to keep in trim. You'll see how easy it is to get what you want."

"I get what I want."

Bathsheba pays no more attention to her words than to mine. "Never forget how to aggravate, aggravate," she goes on, as though Abishag had answered in agreement. "Nag and demand. And always aggravate. Marry an old one—they aggravate more quickly—and spy out the young ones you'd like to cavort with after he dies. That's so much fun." Drink and painted harlotry, she advises the younger woman, have their wages too, and silver, gold, and precious stones are among them. Kneeling at the clay oven with the grace of a lovely figurine, Abishag, meek but resolute, gives a tiny shake to her head and blushes a dark crimson. She keeps the charcoal fire low. She would rather remain with me. She gladdens my heart when she declares that.

"He is my love," she says modestly, with her large eyes cast downward toward the embers, "and he has taken me into his garden."

The girl is heaven-sent; I cannot avoid the feeling that perhaps I am entertaining an angel unawares. Is she too good to be true? Her figure is flawless, her spirit hypnotic. Her face is as brown garnet, her hair like sable at midnight, her stately neck is a column of molded copper, and her legs from the rear are as pillars of marble set upon sockets of fine gold. Her mouth is most sweet. The scent from between her legs is almost always of apples and acacia, of perfumes out of Lebanon. In front, her navel is like a round goblet that wanteth not liquor, and the patch of her thing is perfectly deltoid and as shiny and indelible as black coral.

"So much beauty," warns Bathsheba in a dirge, "so much loveliness you'll be wasting on him. There's nothing to do in here. I thought I would be the queen."

"Sure, the queen," I am quick to gloat. "And I told her no queens. We have no queens."

"And I wouldn't listen," she concedes. Then she comes alive with another good idea for Abishag. "Why don't you marry my Solomon now? He'll give you permission if we nag him enough. Will you let her marry Solomon? Hey, David, give me an answer, don't just lie there like a pancake. Then she and I can rule together and get everything we want. I believe my Solomon could learn to like her very much."

"My other son Adonijah," I interrupt sharply, "already likes her very much."

"And that's another reason you ought to marry my Solomon now," Bathsheba goes on enthusiastically. "Otherwise you might have to sleep with that conceited monkey Adonijah if he's the one that gets to be king. You'll belong to his harem."

"And so," I say with a malicious emphasis, "will you."

Her stricken gasp is music to my ears, her look of stunned revulsion a feast for sore eyes. Is it possible to hear a face fall?

"That's impossible!" she declares, as though able to nullify by her mere opposition all of the natural laws of society and the universe.

"He inherits the harem," I point out smugly.

"He'll want to lie with me?"

"It's out of the question?"

"Deuteronomy won't stop him? Leviticus? A son can lie with the wife of his father?"

"Has Leviticus stopped others?"

"He'll really want to? That's not disgusting?"

"Don't I want to?"

"You're not disgusting?"

"He'd be stupid not to. What better way to solidify his rule than to possess the favorite wife of the former king?"

"Well, my son Solomon," she asserts through drawn lips, "would never allow that. My son Solomon would kill him if he tried."

"Your son Solomon," I warn her, staring fully into her face, "will probably be dead in a matter of seconds if you keep this up, you dear, designing, confused old goose." I have begun like a lion and am concluding like a lamb. "And so will you be if you don't give up your campaign instantly and become more discreet. Didn't I warn you from the day he was born that you would be placing both your lives in jeopardy if you didn't stop talking about him as the future king?"

"Didn't you promise me that he would be king?"

"Why in the world would I promise you that?"

"Because I was giving you great fucking, that's why," she retorts defiantly without an instant's delay. "Wasn't I giving you the best head you ever had?"

"You were giving me the only head I ever had," I answer, feeling very pleased with myself. "How could I tell if it was good or not? But that's hardly going to carry much weight with Adonijah if you don't start doing everything possible to make him like you and get on his good side now."

"I think I would rather die," says Bathsheba with her jaw lifted stubbornly.

"That just might be the alternative," I caution her sternly. "You're playing politics and you don't know how. And I will not be alive to save you when you fail. There is just no way, no way in the world, you can succeed in making Solomon king."

For only one moment does she appear to be sobered. And then the spell is over. "There is always a way," she responds, as though thinking aloud, "where there is a will."

"Another insufferable platitude from Solomon?"

"That one was mine."

"What does it mean?"

"I don't think I know."

"Well, it doesn't make any sense. Now will you please desist from your kingmaking? Dye your hair again, or tweeze some hairs from your mole, or invent more underwear. It's just no contest. Adonijah will be king, and Solomon will not."

But hope, unfortunately, springs eternal in the human breast, and I know that this wife of mine is not the type to comply. I rail introspectively again at the libidinous male vanity that made me want so many wives when younger. Look at the trouble they cause me. And their children too.

Celibacy has few pleasures, I know, but marriage has many pains. And harems are not always what they're cracked up to be. Rarely in the long run are they worth the cost and endless bother.

They congest the palace with people, noise, and odors, and they intensify the problems of garbage removal and sewage disposal, which are already hopelessly insurmountable throughout this raucous, teeming city. So many people these days are pissing against the walls that they practically have to wear boots. It's futile to try to divert any of my sons from their pleasures and personal goals to contend with the commonplace problems of civic administration. A lot they care, these fruits of my unions. And if marriage has many pains, polygamous marriage multiplies those pains to an unforeseeable extent with the commotion generating from squabbling wives and contending offspring. Even God's faithful servant Abraham had his poor hands full, didn't he?

In the beginning there was Abraham, in that first Jewish family, expelling, with Sarah egging him on, the one son Ishmael from the nomadic fold for mocking the second son Isaac at the celebration of his weaning and for any future aggressions against him foreshadowed by that action. Ishmael, the son of that alien bondswoman Hagar, was an archer who would turn out to be a wild man with his hand against every man, and with every man's hand against him. They were better off without him. But then—when Abraham was finally rid of Hagar and Ishmael, guess what he did next. He took another wife! He had six more children! And at his age?

He needed more children? Like a hole in the head. He couldn't live without another wife? A man like him so full of years? I guess he did need another woman. Sex is so powerful in this Mediterranean heat, and I was not the first to turn at times as horny as a goat. Reuben humped Bilhah, and Judah swerved off the road to stick it to the woman in harlot's dress who proved to be his dead son's wife. Lust isn't bad in a warm climate with long dry summers. Return, O my Shunammite, that I might fondle and contemplate thee once more. Bathsheba, my old love, stretch thyself down beside me and place your fat ass in my hands again; open thy legs to me as thou did in the past, that I might indeed know thee at least one more time and taste again, perhaps, that joy that cometh in the morning. Lay your sleeping head, my love, upon my arm, I wish when most sad to croon to her, as though a full lifetime of enchantments still were in store, for we must needs love each other or die.

Saul had no harem—I was the first in Israel to think up that extravagance—but he had troubles enough without one after Samuel dumped him. Saul begged to be pardoned for his transgression and for Samuel to return to him so that he could continue worshipping the Lord. What was so bad about taking some cattle and sparing a king for ransom? The Lord has forgiven worse. But Samuel would not be swayed. As he whirled to depart, Saul laid hold upon the skirt of his mantle to detain him, and it rent. Some days Saul couldn't do anything right; that day was among his worst.

And Samuel said unto Saul stringently, "The Lord hath rent the kingdom of Israel from thee this day and hath given it to a neighbor of thine, that is better than thou."

Now, strictly speaking, this was not true. In fact, it was a bald lie, for it was not until afterward, in Samuel I, Chapter 16, that the Lord, repenting that He had made Saul king over Israel, commanded Samuel to go to Jesse of Bethlehem to find the king He had provided Himself from among Jesse's sons.

The rest, of course, is history, and everything occurring in the universe earlier seems but an overture to my birth and a prelude to the eminence I've enjoyed. Samuel came to Bethlehem with his red heifer on a rope. The elders of the town trembled at his arrival, of course, until he assured them he had come in peace to sacrifice to the Lord. No one but me would have questioned why he had to come to Bethlehem in Judah to sacrifice. They had no altars in Benjamin? He calls for Jesse and his sons and that's pretty much the way I come into the picture, when none of my brothers could qualify with God. The spirit of the Lord came upon me from that day forward, and the spirit of the Lord departed from Saul at that identical time, leaving him mad as a hatter and lonely as a stone. In no time at all he was ready for the nuthouse.

Saul's basic failing, I believe, was a parochial inability to understand that the same theocracy plucking him up from a hillside meadow to be ruler over Israel would be quick to disown him as soon as he began to reign like one. His offenses were inconsequential. At Michmash, earlier, Saul performed the sacrifice before battle when Samuel was late showing up. That wasn't his fault. When his men were famished, they ate meat with the blood. That wasn't his fault either, and he castigated them for having done so. And who but God could blame him for his failure to follow through on his curse and execute Jonathan?

138

GOD KNOWS

For this you fire a king? Not by me you don't, even though I was the beneficiary.

I never had such conflicts with prophets and priests, thanks to Saul, who left a clear path for me by reducing their number and their authority. What did it cost me to throw Zadok and Abiathar a smile and a nod every now and then, to resign myself to the garrulous homilies of Nathan when I had to? We had no temples or synagogues, no rabbis, and we could forget to observe the Passover each year if we had something more entertaining to do. We kindled fires on the Sabbath and could even work if we wanted to. No one reprimanded us for keeping our household idols. We had no daily or weekly prayers to recite, and our God, like the slumbering volcano He once was reputed to be, was dormant for the most part, and tended to say little when He wasn't talking to me. All I had to do was bring a lamb to the altar of the priests every once in a while; they slaughtered it and I was finished. Thank you too, my good fellow, and a very merry Christmas to all of you as well; of course I'll be happy to come again. Neither God nor Saul ever thought of naming another Judge to follow Samuel, and Saul kept near him no prophet or priest. What was the poor creature to do? It isn't easy to be a king if you've got no real feel for the job and no footsteps of a predecessor in which to follow. No wonder he worried. Great wonder, though, that he plunged into the first of his numbing depressions on the very day that the spirit of the Lord departed from him and moved to me, and that I was the one they sent for to snap him out of it. For reasons still mysterious to me, I was already known in Gibeah as someone with a cunning hand on the harp and a person skilled in the arts of war. I had never even been to war. But I could carry a tune and I was damned good with the sling.

As far as anyone knows, Saul had no history of emotional instability prior to the day Samuel anointed me, other than a single episode of religious ecstasy with other prophesying fanatics among whom he chanced to fall and with whom he went dancing about wildly down the mountain, stripped off his clothes, and rolled about naked in the dirt awhile with his mouth frothing. That would have been tip-off enough of trouble to come to anyone less enamored than God with the concept of His own infallibility.

How I loved that man Saul. How I looked up to him, even when he drove me away and hunted me; how I yearned to be sealed into

139

his embrace and taken into his household as a member of his family. That never happened.

He meant more to me than God. I still have dreams about Saul; I have never in my life had a dream about God. My dreams of Saul are of longing, remorse, and reconciliation. When they sent to fetch me to cure him, I walked from Bethlehem to Gibeah as though every step were on hallowed ground. I went barefoot, my mission seemed holy. For much of the way I felt out of breath from awe. He was Saul the famous, I was going to meet him. He was my lord the king. He was the savior of Israel, the military leader who had routed at Jabesh-gilead the besieging Ammonites for his first big victory, and had trounced the Philistines at Michmash for his next. And now he was feeling low.

Irony of irony, said the Preacher, that I, the unwitting cause of his disease, was called upon to supply the remedy.

I wanted to call him father. I did call him father. Each time I addressed him as my lord the king, I was calling him father. Each time he answered, he called me his son. In the years I was near him, I wanted to hug him. In the years I was distant, I wanted to be back. He was impassive in affection and kept me at bay. He said he would make me his armor bearer and forgot to. He said he would always remember me and didn't. He said I would be to him always as one of his own sons. Had I known at that time how he felt about his children, this would have been cause for concern.

When I arrived with my harp at the mud-brick house in Gibeah, they invited me to bathe my feet. Of course I jumped at the chance. I soaked my tired feet in cool water in a clay basin awhile and dried them thoroughly with the woolen towels offered me. I followed timidly to the doorway to which I was led. I stepped through the entrance alone into the low-roofed chamber in which Saul had been brooding so terribly in silence and in solitude.

My heart sank the minute I saw him. My lord the king was clearly in a very bad way. A tall and barrel-chested man of almost unbelievably massive muscular development, he was slumped forward like something inanimate in a half-reclining position on a small wooden bench at the rear of the room. His shoulders sagged and his head was hanging. His hair was tangled, his beard matted. His sun-browned forearms, heavily veined, lay limp on his thighs. At first he did not stir and he struck me tragically as a mighty machine fallen into disuse. There was a minute in which I was frightened. He sat with an expression of resigned and incurable agony, diffusing a silent gloom that seemed to me almost as painful to witness as to suffer. The room was dim, the atmosphere thick, but the entire experience was nothing at all as you may have been led to imagine it was by Robert Browning—no, not the least bit like Robert Browning. Why listen to him? I was there, Browning wasn't; he was in Italy sending home thoughts from abroad. At no time did Saul climb laboriously to his feet like a man weighted with an unutterable misery and unfold his tortured physique with upraised arms extended sideways to station himself in the figure of a cross. Crucifixion was a Roman invention, not a Hebrew, and this was a thousand years before the Romans even existed. Our preference in executing people was to burn them with fire and stone them with stones, and we did very little of either. It was so much easier to tolerate our sinners and live with the headaches they gave us than to judge them and kill them. Why make a fuss? More often than not, we would leave them to heaven or simply have somebody fall with their swords on our enemies. And here's something else: not a one of us then would have cared a pinch of snuff about any second coming of a Messiah, let alone a first, or even said a single word about either. Who needed a Messiah? We had no heaven, we had no hell, we had no eternity, we had no afterlife. We had no need for a Messiah then, and we have none now, and the last thing any sensible human being should want, to my way of thinking, is immortality. As it is, life lasts too long for most of us.

I'm not even sure we really had that much need for a God as much as we did seem to have a need to believe in Him. I do know that just about every good idea emerging in my chats with Him originated with me. The plan of stealing through the mulberry trees to encircle the Philistines at night at the second battle of Rephaim was His. But I'm not sure it made that much difference, or that I wouldn't have thought of it myself. I do know that Joab's idea of attacking them frontally at dawn did not sit well with me.

Saul, by the wretched, inert look of him, probably held a different attitude from mine about the need for a God. Although a foot basin had been prepared for him and placed nearby, his toes and ankles were caked with the dust of the earth. Shapeless slippers of sheepskin lay overturned on their sides near the wall against which his javelin and his spear leaned with their points upward. A mat of roped wool was unrolled on the floor, with a bolster of coarse goatskin at the head. Even though he was king, Saul spurned a bed and slept on the ground.

I had no doubt he knew I was there from the instant I entered. It took awhile, though, before he stirred and turned slowly to contemplate me. He lifted his hand above his eyes as though to shade them from the glare from the doorway behind me. I stared back at him intently. He looked like a man who wanted to weep. He had that desolate, ruined look of someone in love. I know that lifeless, empty anguish of love from my first years with Bathsheba when things were going so frenetically well, and know it also from those endless fits of longing afterward when they began so uncontrollably to change. In good times and in bad, those incomparable requirements of the aching heart seldom lessened much.

"Who are you?" Saul asked at last, pathetically, almost whispering from a throat that sounded inordinately dry. "I have trouble remembering things."

I was choked for a moment by a sudden flood of compassion that filled me with both tears and nausea. "I am David, the son of your subject Jesse the Bethlehemite."

"I have trouble remembering," he repeated.

"I am going to play for you," I told him.

"Are you going to play for me?" he inquired distantly, and paused for some answer from me with his mouth hanging open, like a man with a stroke.

"I am going to play and sing for you."

"They tell me," he mused inquiringly, "that music hath charms to soothe the savage breast."

"I've often heard that too," I answered meekly in my youthful tenor as pure as a choirboy's.

But frankly, I didn't put much stock in that adage. My nephew Joab has always owned as savage a breast as existed anywhere in the world, and the effect upon him of my music has always been to exacerbate rather than tranquilize his turbulent nature. Even as children of the same age growing up together in Bethlehem, my playing and singing had always put a gulf of antagonistic incompatibility between us. He would jog and lift weights; and I would compose an ode to a daffodil.

With an apathetic nod, Saul signaled for me to enter farther and find what I thought was a suitable place, and then he looked away with downcast eyes and waited. I had come to Gibeah with my eight-stringed lyre in order to demonstrate my considerable technical skill to fullest advantage. Now I clasped the instrument tightly to my chest in an effort to conceal the trembling of my hands. My mouth felt paralyzed. Saul appeared no longer interested. Tensely, I made myself ready on a low stool, with one bare knee bent to the ground. I licked my lips and upper palate with a tongue that felt stiff, and I tried to begin. My first note smothered in my gullet with a little muffled sound, almost a croak. I was grateful Saul didn't seem to be paying attention. My voice quavered off key on the two notes following, and I began to lose heart. But then I saw him quiver and start with surprise at the first full touch of my fingers to the strings, as though the tremulous chords lingering in the air were setting in motion somewhere inside him sympathetic vibrations of response that resonated through his entire being. My confidence was restored without my even realizing it was back. I felt in firm control and knew with certainty that I was sounding better and better as I went on, singing like an angel in a voice that was too young for a man's and too sweet for a girl's.

I began with a simple and brief Russian lullaby of my mother's with which she used to croon me to sleep when I was a child and afraid of the dark and which in later years she would hum to herself about the house when content. Saul heard me attentively and was pleased, I thought, and I proceeded boldly to some lengthier and more complex inventions of my own. Of arms and the man I sang, of the wrath of Achilles, and of man's first disobedience to God, in that order, little supposing in my arcadian naïveté that I was embroidering on topics which would either excite his prejudices and anger him, or move him to nostalgia and compunction. Lucky for me it was the latter. In my fortuitous choice of subject matter I might well have been unknowingly guided by a higher power, and then again I might not have been. I heard Saul sigh. I saw his limbs relax and gently regain their flexibility. I watched the dark, rigid lines of his face disappear, saw his expression loosen itself from the grip of fatalistic despair and soften into an attitude of pensive reverie. His head began to dip ever so slightly in tempo with the melodic flow of my music.

I was pleased by these visible proofs of my success. What a splendid and inspiring picture I must have made! I was so white and ruddy. And it was obvious I was working miracles. While the last notes of my epic on man's first disobedience to God still floated in the air, Saul roused himself and straightened with something of a smile. He flexed his shoulders as though rediscovering his ability to move them and then stretched out his arms. He opened wide his jaws and yawned serenely. I concluded my performance with my early ode to a daffodil.

Of course I was eager to do more. For a change of pace, I had in mind for an encore, had he insisted upon one, a lively and mildly risqué ditty of my own about a passionate shepherd to his mistress. But Saul stood up from his bench like a man exhausted who knows what he is about and informed me with a gesture that he had heard enough and was satisfied. He shambled slowly across the room and lowered himself to his sleeping mat with a moan of content, sitting in utter silence for several moments with his arms crossed upon his knees. I feared again that he had forgotten me. I did not want to move. The sound of his breathing was loud and regular. After another minute had passed, he lifted a hand and motioned me to come to him. I approached diffidently and knelt to the level of his eyes when I was before him. He took my head delicately in both his enormous hands and looked deeply into my face with a kind of reverent and solemn gratitude. My heart beat rapidly.

"I will never forget you," he told me in a low voice. "I shall want you always with me. You shall be to me as one of my children. As of morning tomorrow, I will want you to serve me as my armor bearer."

I spent the night in my cloak on a smooth dry patch of earth I located near the front corner of his house. I could not sleep much. My mind was a carnival of glittering hopes and dizzying expectations. In the morning they sent me away. When Saul and I again faced each other two years afterward on the day of my killing of Goliath, it was as though he had never set eyes on me before.

6

IN THE
SERVICE OF
SAUL

In the service of Saul I soon found it almost impossible to do anything right. The more I succeeded, the more I failed. I survived and excelled and began to get a name for myself for smiting Philistines. You think Saul was proud? Jonathan was. Even Abner approved of my cunning, prudence, valor, and growing military reputation. But there was just no pleasing Saul with anything after the first time he beheld for himself the women coming out of the cities of Israel with tabrets, with joy, and with instruments of music to greet me and to answer one another melodiously, singing:

הִכָּה שָׁאוּל בַּאֲלָפָו
וְדָוִד בְּרִבְבֹתָיו׃

Or, in translation:

> *"Saul hath slain his thousands*
> *and David his ten thousands."*

What could I do if I was turning out to be ten times the warrior Saul was?

Nevertheless, it perplexed me tremendously to see him grow so very wroth. If looks could kill, I would have been finished, and he eyed me narrowly from that day and forward, even after I was his son-in-law and was expected to eat most evenings at the royal table in his house in Gibeah. Who could eat with so much aggravation?

I can clearly recall the hour that my fortunes with Saul took their disquieting turn for the worse. We were buoyantly trooping along homeward, in jaunty return from another victory over the Philistines in which I had again acquitted myself with distinction.

Then the women came out with their tabrets and other instruments of playing to sing of Saul's thousands and my ten thousands. Their refrain was music to my ears, and I grinned, of course, honestly anticipating that Saul would rejoice with some display of paternal pride in the acclaim I was receiving. I could not have been more mistaken. It was with a startled and lowering face that Saul heard them. I saw him look daggers at me as he quickened our marching cadence to hurry away from the throngs lauding me. After the women had been left behind, Saul drew Abner with him in my direction as though to make inescapably certain I would overhear his words and observe his reprimanding demeanor.

"They have ascribed unto David ten thousands," he said loudly. "Did you hear them?"

"I heard them."

"Ten thousands? You heard?"

"I heard, I heard," answered Abner uncomfortably.

"And to me they have ascribed but thousands. You heard that too?"

"I heard them, I heard them."

"He was nowhere near ten thousand."

"You know how women are."

"But I achieved my thousands, didn't I?"

"Easily."

"They were singing just for him—you heard them, didn't you?—and dancing for him too. They were paying practically no attention to me. You saw? You heard?"

"I heard, I heard," said Abner. "What do you want from me? I've heard them before."

"You heard them before?" demanded Saul. "When?"

"Lots of times."

"Why didn't you tell me?"

"Why should I aggravate you?"

Saul was glaring at me murderously when he growled, "What can he have more to satisfy him than the kingdom?"

To tell you the truth, something akin to that very thought had been rattling around in my own mind since the time I joined Saul and began doing so well, but always, I swear, with the airiness of an adolescent fancy rather than the constancy of a vaulting ambition that might someday overleap itself. I made no play for the throne of Saul until after he was dead. Ask anyone. Ask Achish, king of Gath.

To understand my bafflement, keep in mind that I was but a child at the time, as green about the ears as a youth from the country could be, with little knowledge of the corroding perversities and ambivalences with which the human heart is capable of polluting itself. Who could conceive back then of the enormity of Saul's brooding hatred for me or comprehend the threatening paradox that the more I accomplished to gratify him, the greater would grow the jealousy and wrath he felt toward me? I know I was hurt when I saw him so angry with me that first time, and I was flustered in a queer and guilt-ridden way each time I found him so thereafter.

The evil spirit came upon Saul for the second time in his life the very next day. Word spread fast through Gibeah that he was again in a state of mysterious melancholia. I took my harp from its kidskin cover at the first report and waited. Saul could not stir from his chamber, rumor had it. He would not taste food or wash his hands or the dust of the earth from his feet. He had no desire for sex. He refused to comb his hair or clean his fingernails. When they lit the olive oil in his lamps, he blew out the flames, muttering uncivilly that he preferred to curse the darkness. They thought of me quickly. No more time-wasting attempts to stay him with flagons or comfort him with apples. Music, they wanted. I jumped at the invitation to play and sing for him, at the opportunity to return to his favor by expunging from his brain the sinister phantoms by which he was tortured. I felt blessed by Abner's supplications, singled out by heaven as someone meant for unique things, touched with sublime grace by the magical quality of my music to heal. And once again, I was Johnny-on-the-spot.

I began my serenade to Saul most delicately with my pure and innocent singing voice and my eight-stringed lyre. I was as divine as a castrato. Nothing but the best for my king. I knew by the lucid timbre of the first note from my lips that I had never been better. Again I was privileged to observe the gently restorative effects of my genius as my plaintive melody pervaded his overburdened consciousness. Before my eyes he began to recover, emerging astonishingly from the state of catatonic depression into which he had plummeted overnight and in which I had found him when I entered. He stirred, he moved, he rediscovered himself, he came back among the living. And I had conducted him there. It was marvelous to behold. As I glided without hesitation into my rather stirring "Ode to Joy," Saul stiffly moved his head from side to side, as though searching for my tempo and testing his authority over his neural impulses. He arched his back, then reached his arms out to the side with the elbows bent and rotated the knobs of his shoulders in their girdles of muscle. At last he raised his clouded face to study me. He wore the doleful look of a man who had been given shattering news some time before and who only now felt able to begin pulling himself together. I was glad when I saw him regarding me with what I would call a look of deep gratitude and undying devotion. There was no doubt he knew I had saved him. He smiled slightly, apologetically, a spark of understanding igniting in his bleary, swollen eyes as he made me out and recognized me. I felt redeemed—now he would be more indebted to me than ever before. I gazed at him in happiness. The next thing I knew, the crazy son of a bitch was lunging to his feet for his javelin and casting it at my head with all his might! I was horrified. The javelin landed with a loud thwack in a beam of wood beside me, the quivering shaft humming only inches from my ear. Who would believe it? The bastard was really trying to kill me! For moments I sat there unable to move, my mouth agape, until he dived for a second javelin to fire at me and missed again. Then I bolted to my feet in terror and avoided the hell out of his presence as fast as my legs would carry me.

Abner was unperturbed when I related to him what had occurred. "You have got to learn to take the bad with the good," he advised me philosophically, scratching his pitted face with one hand and pausing to suck on a pomegranate he held in the other. "He missed you, didn't he?"

"Twice."

"So what are you complaining about? It's not as though he hit you, is it?"

"Can you at least get my harp back? It's the best one I've got."

"The thing to do," said Abner, returning with my lyre, "is to stay out of his presence until he has a change of heart."

Saul made that easy by removing me from him. I expected death or demotion. Instead, he appointed me a captain over a thousand. Then he dispatched me on combat missions in remote places with bands of a dozen or two dozen men against invading mobs of

Philistines moving into the valleys or pillaging or occupying our villages in northern Israel or southern Judah. Dutifully, I went out whithersoever Saul sent me and behaved myself wisely in all my ways, endeavoring to gladden him by doing so. Fat chance. All Israel and Judah seemed to grow to love me because I went out and came in before them on my triumphant forays of liberation and safekeeping. But not Saul. The more wisely I behaved, the more afraid and resentful of me he appeared. My desperate, self-defeating efforts to propitiate him were maddening in their futility. I was at a loss. I suffered palpitations, and wrote a splendid psalm about them.

What endures as one of the regrettable facts of my life is that my future father-in-law and I were never again to be at ease with each other after that first episode with the javelins. What had I done to deserve that? You tell me. It seemed to me that we both continued delving for a solution to that riddle and could arrive at only the same one: nothing. Such an answer was equally disturbing to us both. But his attitude of sullen grievance and simmering fury never abated fully. I felt myself in continual peril, and in a continual mood of repentance. How was it possible to atone to this patriarchal figure for what I had not done? At best each of us was embarrassing to the other. It was obvious at other times that he could not bear the sight of me without manifesting visible symptoms of a turbulent and menacing agitation. His antipathy was evident to all about him and a matter of nervous concern to Jonathan and others. I myself could not make head or tail of it. What did he want from me? Who could dream back then that, because of Samuel, he was wrestling every day with an impulse to slay me that was close to ungovernable? The malignant fuck was sending me out on these undermanned expeditions to distant places in the pathetic and distracted hope he could let the hand of the Philistines be upon me instead of his own.

Saul was of the opinion—with good reason, perhaps—that I was loved by God. And he feared, therefore, when in his right mind, to slay me himself. What Saul was attempting with me was what I was much later to perform with more successful results against that unfortunate sucker Uriah the Hittite. I didn't want to slay him myself, yet I had to be free to marry his wife before the indications of her pregnancy grew undeniably evident.

There is no new thing under the sun, is there, certainly no new plots. Show me anything whereof it may be said "See, this is new," and I will show you it hath been. There are only four basic plots in life anyway, and nine in literature, and everything else is but variation, vanity, and vexation of spirit. I sure as hell know I didn't *feel* loved by God in this tempestuous period. Instead, I felt much vexation of spirit, for Saul clearly loathed me incessantly with an animosity that was unappeasable. The error I committed in my trusting naïveté was to assume that he really meant what he said in his logical wish that I triumph over his enemies. But he was enraged and demented each time that I did. You could have knocked me over with a feather again, therefore, when a delegation of his servants arrived to tell me that Saul's daughter loved me and that Saul wanted me to be his son-in-law. Such is the vanity of human wishes that in no time at all I was able to trick myself into believing he now approved of me. All is vanity, you know, *all,* all in the long run is but vanity and vexation of spirit. In almost no time at all, it became to me the most natural thing in the world that the king's daughter should be in love with me.

In retrospect, I see that the more unusual phenomenon was that I took to combat as easily as I did, as though destined for it from birth. I was never warlike as a child. People forget that Goliath was the first man I had ever killed. I had never even been to battle before. Reports that I was a man of war and a valiant man are but the lacework of hero worship; otherwise I would already have been on the scene in the trenches of Shochoh, wouldn't I? Saviors who capture the imagination traditionally arrive unheralded from obscure or pedestrian origins. That was true of me. Where would the climax be if I were merely one famed fighter who'd triumphed over another? Achilles' defeat of Hector is the weakest part of the *Iliad* —he was the odds-on favorite going in. Homer was really not much good at building a story, was he, but then, of course, Homer was stuck with the truth.

Growing up in Bethlehem, I didn't care much for games of war or group activities of any kind. I was never the equal in enthusiasm of my nephews Joab, Abishai, and Asahel for the manly martial arts they indulged in for fun. Because I was the last born in a large family and they were the earliest offspring of my oldest sister, Zeruiah, we were near to each other in age. I was always more deft with the less highly regarded sling and preferred casting stones by myself—a solitary, romantic figure, I thought, meditating on my poetry and musical compositions as I did so, and simultaneously safeguarding my sheep. Joab and the others would spend carefree, exhausting hours lifting weights and doing push-ups and wind sprints, and smashing things with their makeshift hammers and axes in games of war against imaginary hordes of Philistines. I slung stones in far-off pastures; I composed my celebrated "Air for the G String" one overcast, windy day while gazing as though blind at the graying, unshorn rumps of my small herd of sheep.

My fame as a gifted young composer and as a prodigy with a cunning hand on the harp was, however, well deserved and widely known about the countryside while I was still in my teens. I don't think Joab valued that at all. Joab always was churlish on the subject of my songwriting. To Joab, all male singers are suspect, and male dancers too. I'm sure he thought I was queer. To me, on the other hand, the man that hath no music in himself is fit for treasons, stratagems, and spoils, and often I defiantly told that to Joab in just those words, even after I was king. I was also, as I may have hinted, fantastically good-looking as a young man, even pretty in a faintly feminine way. I doubt he liked that either. I never would give him or anyone else satisfaction by pretending to minimize the immense pleasure I took in my handsome bearing and winning smile, and in my self-deprecating ways. Old women clucked over me, young wives and unmarried girls fixed longing stares upon me, and even occasional strange men traveling through would give a start of surprise upon catching sight of me and stare at me hard with inquiring expressions freighted heavily with something more insinuating than normal objective appreciation. I was a comely person and knew I made a good appearance. There was that neck of mine that has been compared to a tower of ivory, and my bushy locks that have been described as black as a raven's— and not just by me. I am not exaggerating when I tell you I often witnessed the most beautiful of my sheep bleat with desire and turn their heads to make wistful cow's eyes at me.

To me, therefore, it shortly began to seem not at all extraordinary that the king's daughter Michal had fallen in love with me. Why shouldn't she? Wasn't my skin whiter than milk and more ruddy than rubies? Who was around that was better? Such is the innate capacity of vain men for self-delusion that I soon reasoned it equally plausible that Saul would so welcome my marriage to his daughter as to make things simple for me in the matter of the means to pay for her. It did not cross my mind that he might spy in the amorous inclination of his daughter an opportunity to set a snare for me by which he thought to make me fall by the hand of the Philistines.

"Is the king displeased?" I inquired when informed that Michal loved me.

"He wants you to be his son-in-law," Abner answered concisely. Only afterward did I discern that the answer he gave was not to my question. Abner never proved easy for me.

"I had the impression he didn't like me," I said diffidently.

"You're first on his list."

"Who am I?" I demurred, with appropriate humility. "And what is my father's family in Israel, that I should be son-in-law to the king? I am lightly esteemed."

"Not by him."

"He really likes me?"

"When you go out and fight with the Philistines," Abner reminded, skillfully begging the question again, "you slay them with a great slaughter, and they flee from you."

"Does the king notice that?"

"Is there salt in the sea?"

"He never says anything in praise of me."

"You know he is shy."

"He gives me the feeling sometimes that he's afraid I am up to something." I squirmed a moment.

"What better way to pacify that fear than to make you a member of his house and keep you close to him?"

"Would that really do it?"

"It was my suggestion."

"Can one say no to a king?" I asked rhetorically.

"Does a bull have tits?"

"Does the wild ass bray when he hath grass?"

"Have we got all day, David?" Abner never did appear much enchanted with me as a person.

"I am a poor man," I cautioned with proper modesty, getting right down to the gist of the matter. "I have no money, I have no land. Even those few poor sheep I used to watch in the wilderness were my father Jesse's, and not my own."

Abner replied with amusement. "Does the king need money? Does Saul suffer in want for land or sheep?"

GOD KNOWS

"Are the sands of the desert made of silver?" I replied brightly.

"Or the weeds of the forest made of gold?" continued Abner, with that deficiency of emotion that rendered him always an enigma to me. "Saul is the king and can always take as much money, land, and sheep as he chooses. No, the king desireth not any such dowry for his daughter. He wants but a token, some tangible earnest of good faith."

"What tangible earnest?" I asked warily.

"A trifle, a pittance for the king's daughter that will not impoverish your father or you or leave you even temporarily strapped. Saul does not want wealth."

"With what will I pay for her, then?" I was now constrained to ask.

"With a pound of flesh," was the answer I got.

"A pound of flesh?" I echoed with surprise.

"Or ten or twelve ounces, whatever they all add up to," Abner remarked in an offhanded way. He watched me levelly with hooded eyes.

I had trouble figuring it out. "What kind of flesh?"

"Philistine flesh."

"I just don't get it," I admitted frankly.

"Foreskins," said Abner with exaggerated patience, as though I had been privy to all conversations and was obtuse in overlooking a fundamental point. "The king wants foreskins. Bring him but a hundred foreskins of the Philistines, to be avenged of his enemies, and you shall be his son-in-law. That's all that he wants. A hundred foreskins."

Foreskins? I nearly jumped for joy when I understood. A hundred Philistine foreskins? I could bring him a thousand!

"I will give him two hundred!" I cried exultantly, in a mixture of boastful liberality and conservative good sense. "When does he want them?"

"The sooner the better, I should think," Abner decided, "from everyone's point of view. While she still has her looks and is young enough to bear children. Saul wants grandsons."

"I'll start at once."

"How long will it take? You can have what men you need."

You would have been charmed by the proficiency with which I began calculating aloud. Abner appeared spellbound. It would require, I projected fluently, a minimum of four able-bodied young

155

Israelites to take hold of a live Philistine and wrest him motionless to the earth in a supine position, a fifth to lay hands on his privy parts and elevate his member with a firmness sufficient to overcome any spontaneous urges to flinch from the surgical procedure intended, and a sixth with a sure hand on the blade to trim the Philistine foreskin expertly from the glans of the penis. I have a mania for neatness in some matters that is almost anal. The last two men could contribute with their weight to the total force necessary to hold the unconsenting subject pinned in place on the ground. I was not counting on voluntary compliance. Allowing about an hour, on average, to locate and seize each Philistine for circumcision, and working with four squads of six men taking their daylight nourishment on the prowl rather than breaking for lunch, I estimated hopefully that we could gather daily—

Abner abruptly shook free from the trance in which he had been listening to me. "David, David," he interrupted. He rolled his eyes skyward and weakly raised a hand, requesting forbearance. "I think you may be missing the underlying goal of this exploit. We want you to *kill* the Philistines, not convert them. We don't care if you bring back the whole prick."

Again I found myself overjoyed, and nearly whooped out my feelings in a squeal of rapturous hallelujahs. I was able to perceive that killing the Philistines and bringing back the whole prick would facilitate my task considerably.

But who would believe it? Who would figure for even one second that someone as artless as Saul could construct so diabolic a snare to secure by the hand of the Philistines the downfall of the man who had begun to assume in his disordered brain the sacred aura of the being picked by God to replace him? Not I for one, not by a long shot, not until the nefarious details of the Machiavellian scheme were unfolded to me by Jonathan long afterward and then confirmed by my wife Michal the night she entreated me in near hysterics to get my ass out the window fast if I was interested in saving it.

And not my bluff nephew Joab, for another, who leaped at the chance when I invited him to assist me as my captain of twenty-four. Even back then, hale Joab desired nothing better than to charge into strife against any adversary, and he hardly ever troubled himself with reasons why. It was blunt Joab who one spring, at that time when kings again went forth to battle, asked my approval to march with six hundred men and Abishai up through Turkey into the Crimea to conquer and occupy Russia and Asia first and then all of the rest of Europe as far northward as Scandinavia and as far to the west as Iberia and the British Isles, even unto the Irish Republic.

"We go to war in the spring, after our harvests are in," was the first of the objections I raised with Joab. "They go to war in autumn, after *their* harvests are in. How could we get together?"

"We can leave in the spring when our harvests are in and fall upon them in the summer before their harvests are in," Joab answered plainly.

"What would you eat if you fall upon them in the summer and don't have the grain of their threshing floors to live on?"

"We could bring along dried figs," he replied. "In Scandinavia we could live on herring."

Perhaps I should have given more consideration to his grand proposal, instead of renewing my campaign against the Ammonites in Jordan and the Syrians to the north. What a name I would have for myself now! Who needed so much sand and rock? I didn't have enough?

It's no puzzle to me any longer that Saul looked so disappointed at the completion of my labor, when I reappeared before him in Gibeah in excellent health and presented the contents of my basket to him in full tale. I was worried initially that he was discontented with the quality of the foreskins or of the Philistine pricks, but I had alerted Joab to leave behind any that were the least bit deficient in size or symmetry, and I had witnessed him sorting through our daily catch diligently. Not until we were half a day's march out of Gibeah had I leaked a word to Joab or anyone else about the peculiar objectives of the quest upon which we were embarked. My information was electrifying.

"Foreskins?" The question sounded from my swift and courageous young nephew Asahel, who even then was like one of the gazelles that are in the open field. "David, why foreskins?"

"Who knows?" I answered candidly. I paused a moment for dramatic effect, licking my lips the while in appreciation of the impact I knew was to follow, and I was flushed with pride in myself when I continued in a rising voice. "It is the dowry Saul hath requested I bring him that I might be that day the king's son-in-law. I am going to marry his daughter Michal."

JOSEPH HELLER

The loudest exclamation among the cries of surprise that resulted was the one erupting from Joab, who seized my arm in his hand and glared at me in disbelief. "Michal!" he repeated loudly. "Is that what you said? Michal?"

Naturally I was taken aback. "What's wrong?"

"I just don't get it," asserted Joab, thrown into a rage as usual by anything he failed to comprehend. "That's what's wrong. Michal? You're really going to marry the king's daughter Michal?"

"Why shouldn't I marry the king's daughter Michal?"

"I thought Jonathan was the one you loved."

I was jolted. "Are you crazy?" I demanded. "Where the hell did you ever get that idea?"

"From Jonathan," Joab returned at once. "Your soul is knit with his soul, isn't it?"

"Says who?"

"Says him," Joab shot back. "He gave you his girdle, didn't he, and his sword and his bow, and his robe and other garments. He tells everyone in Gibeah he loves you as his own soul."

"His soul is knit with my soul, not mine with his," I argued.

"There's a difference?"

"A big difference," I replied with dignity. "Now let's get going, if you don't mind."

But Joab persisted, pulling me aside to counsel me in friendlier terms. "Michal can be rough, David," he said with worry. "Are you sure you know what you're doing?"

"They tell me she loves me."

"You still might be better off marrying Jonathan."

"Let's go get those foreskins," I ordered brusquely.

This time it was Asahel who appeared determined to thwart me. "Foreskins are dangerous, David," softly warned brave Asahel, who would die not from Philistines but on the hinder end of Abner's spear when he would not turn aside from pursuing him in his unremitting chase after a battle in our long civil war. "They take lots of hard work. Whose idea was that anyway? Abner's? Circumcising Philistines is bad news, David, very bad news."

"Well, here comes the good news," I fairly burst out in reply. "They want us to kill the Philistines, not convert them. They say we can bring back the whole prick!"

My announcement went over well, and "bringing back the whole prick" shortly became a folk saying utilized in conversation as widely as the proverb about Saul and the prophets after he fell into that spell with them the first time, and then the second. When I gave the command to regroup, my little band of stouthearted men let out a wild, frolicsome cheer, and away we traipsed with the gaiety of schoolboys unleashed early from class, augmenting our morale with the lusty chorusing of a jolly bit of opportune doggerel I was successful in extemporizing for the occasion, to wit:

> *"Hi-ho, hi-ho.*
> *It's down to Gath we go.*
> *Who'll give two pins*
> *To get foreskins?*
> *Hi-ho, hi-ho."*

My racy pun was received with hilarity, I am satisfied to recall.

I knew exactly where to take my men to find Philistines alone or in groups of two or three. Downward I led them toward Gath, through the rugged mountains of my native Judah into the low hills descending gradually to the marshy plains of the Philistines as one approached the sea.

The first hundred was short work for a man famed in song for having slain tens of thousands of Philistines. The second was child's play as well. Saul should have been much better prepared psychologically for the likelihood of my success. The trip back was a triumph marred only by some curious disturbances that were wholly unexpected. This time when the women came out of the cities with their psalteries and cymbals and tabrets, they sang:

> *"Saul has taken his thousand foreskins.*
> *and David has taken his ten thousands."*

Who else had ever been as heroic in so novel an achievement, or lauded so robustly in song by women? How thrilled I was to be present to hear them. How relieved I felt that Saul was not. As we were almost through that first village, though, all at once, with no warning whatsoever of what was to come, a piercing shriek rent the air and a buxom woman of ripe years fell into the loudest and most terrible fit of weeping I had ever heard. Pointing into the basket displayed on our cart, almost close enough to touch, she howled:

"Urgat is dead! Urgat the Philistine is dead! *Vey's mir.* Urgat is dead!"

The uproar that ensued was indescribable. Other women hurried to her side to hold and console her. Two or three of them began wailing mournfully as well. But others in the crowd were reacting differently, with faces scowling in callous disapproval. Men's brows darkened, eyes shrank into snake-like slits with looks of violated honor, minds moved sullenly through deduction to arrive at irate conclusions.

"Stone her! Stone her!" the cry went up in a minute.

"Spare her! Spare her!" others rallied in her defense. "Isn't she suffering enough?"

"Urgat the Philistine is dead!"

"What's going on?" I inquired of the only person in sight who seemed in his right mind, a shrunken, white-bearded old man with twinkling light eyes who was taking the whole scene in calmly.

"May her thigh rot and her belly swell with salt water," he remarked to me philosophically, in a most benign manner.

"Pardon?"

He spoke a little louder, smiling, "May her thigh rot and her belly swell with salt water."

We were glad to get out of there. But in the next village, which was but a mile or two distant, the identical thing occurred, except that in this second place there were scores of women who were grief-stricken. Again we were all of us refreshed by the general welcome we received as we neared. Again the women in their bright-colored holiday dresses, again the singing and dancing, again the refrain:

> "Saul has taken his thousand foreskins
> and David has taken his ten thousands."

Here as we walked along we were gorged with presents of dates and figs and sesame cakes of almonds and honey. And then all of a sudden that same fucking shriek. Again there was that shock of recognition, again the mood of celebration was shattered by a heart-stopping cry, again the deafening sobs of heartbreak and loss, again those undulating, inconsolable lamentations for the departed Philistine and his defunct and irreplaceable phallus. Urgat was dead—Urgat the Philistine was gone. But here the bereaved women appeared in a violent majority and soon were assailing us with feet and fists over the death of their favorite Philistine. One of them rushed at my face with her fingernails and raked my cheek and my neck into long bloody scratches. The bewildering uproar was out of control. I tell you truthfully it was no easy matter to fend off these countrywomen of ours without smiting them hip and thigh.

"What the hell is happening here?" cried out my nephew Abishai, who normally was as unexcitable as it is possible for a living thing to be.

"Mix them all up!" I bellowed an order to Joab, indicating with alarm our heap of penises in the basket. "Cover the pile!"

"Mix up the fucking pile!" Joab relayed my instructions in a voice even more booming. "Cover the cart! The cart, cover the cart! Which one of you mothers killed Urgat?"

It was a miracle indeed that we escaped with our lives.

"May your thighs rot and all your bellies swell with salt water!" was the imprecation I yelled back at all of the women in that entire village.

The cart covered, and the territories of Philistia left farther and farther to the rear, it was roses, roses, all the way, one victory carnival after another, until we arrived back in Gibeah and I had counted out to the foreskin the two hundred trophies I had brought Saul, who scrutinized me darkly the whole time with a venomous malice, as though, in honoring his request, I had arrogantly confirmed his blackest intuitions and fantasies. True to his word, he would give me his daughter Michal to wife. He knew, he said, that the Lord was with me, but the way in which he uttered this opinion sent a shiver down my back.

He did not dance at my wedding. Neither did Michal. I hardly stopped. Oh, what a good time I had! Egged on by her brothers and her more convivial cousins and uncles and aunts, I danced harder and harder with all my might, kicking up my heels and my knees higher and higher until the skirt of my tunic was awhirl about my waist and I knew at last that my tossing genitals were in open view and could be observed by all present except the blind and the dying. The ovation I received was thunderous. We drank like Ephraimites and perspired like pigs. One goblet of wine after another Jonathan and his brothers poured into me. Every once in a while, I noticed that Michal and Saul were not having much fun.

With rigid and censorious countenances, both kept stubbornly in the background and held themselves aloof from the festivities, the unhappy pair looking, I thought, as though the father had eaten a sour grape and the daughter's teeth had been set on edge. The chilling presentiment struck me as I went reeling happily past and caught her tight, reproachful eyes fixed upon me that it was always going to be impossible for me to please her for long. And the thought crossed my mind that my nephew Joab had perhaps been right and that maybe I would have been better off marrying Jonathan instead. So riotous a good time did I have at my wedding party that six times—six—I was compelled to desist from my carousing to stagger outside the main door of Saul's house in Gibeah to piss against his front wall. They told me later that six was a record for a young man.

The party ending, the musicians and singers departing, unruly revelers carried us homeward through the streets by torchlight in separate mauve blankets of wool, raucously bellowing obscene songs of the multitudinous nuptial couplings to follow. I joined in giddily in a voice as drunken as the rest. It suddenly occurred to me that I had not heard a peep out of Michal the whole evening. Saul had handed her over to me as wife. I had set her to one side to acknowledge with bows the cheers of her relatives. No one from my family had been invited. Comfortably recumbent on my back, I could not see over the border of my blanket and was lazily reluctant to try.

"Michal?" I inquired. "Are you there?"

"Call me princess," I heard her respond.

Hoots of merriment from the young men bearing us broke out at these words, and I felt emboldened, after an instant's uneasiness, to laugh along with them. At the entrance to the dwelling Saul had allotted us, they stood me up and lifted her into my arms. I carried her across the threshold and pulled the door shut behind me. I knew I was in for trouble when I set her down on her feet and beheld the austere look with which she was regarding me. Her eyes, naturally small to begin with, were screwed into glinting, beady pinpoints. Any possibilities that I might be mistaken about her humor were dispelled by her first words.

"Go take a bath," she directed, with a mouth drawn into a taut, bloodless line. "Wash under your arms. Make sure you comb your hair after you've dried it, the back of your head too. Rinse your teeth with a mouthwash. Use a perfume on your face."

She was no more agreeable when I returned to her, all spick-and-span, after complying meticulously with her instructions. She confronted me with her arms folded, as obdurate as a wall, and said nothing. I was as meek as Moses, who at times, as you know, was the meekest man on earth, and importuned her in an abject whimper when I could endure her silence no longer.

"Is anything wrong?" I made myself ask.

"What could be wrong?" she answered with a shrug, eyeing me coldly.

"You don't seem to be saying much to me."

"What's there to say?" A martyred look accompanied this reply, belying her air of passionless indifference.

"You seem to be angry about something."

"Angry?" She spoke with sarcasm, dilating her eyes in mock surprise. "Why should I be angry? What's there to be angry about? Do *I* have anything to be angry about?"

I felt the ground growing shakier beneath me. "Isn't there anything you want to talk to me about?"

"What's there to talk about?"

"Michal," I cajoled.

"I'm a princess," she reminded.

"Must I always call you princess?"

"If you hope for a civil response."

"If there's anything I've done wrong," I begged her almost apologetically, "I'd like you to tell me about it."

"What's there to tell?" she answered with another exaggerated shrug of unconcern. And then, after a menacing silence of about ten seconds during which she seemed to be marking off the time, she proceeded to say a great deal. "That you shamed me and disgraced me in front of my father and my brothers? On my wedding night yet? You did it, David, you did it to me, by drinking and dancing and singing, by having a good time like an ordinary drunken lout. That was gross, David, really gross."

I tried reasoning with her. "Michal, your brothers were the ones who were telling me to dance and sing and drink. They were doing the same thing."

"My brothers," she let me know, "are the sons of a king who can do whatever they want and never be gross. You are gross for suggesting they're gross. I guess I'm only getting what I deserve." Her voice dipped an octave and she seemed to be blinking back tears. "I never should have married a commoner."

I continued trying to reason with her in a manner most conciliatory. "Michal, my dear—"

"Princess Michal," she broke in.

"Anybody you married *had* to be commoner. Saul is our first king and we have no aristocracy. You aren't being entirely fair."

"Where does it say I have to be fair?" she retorted. "Show me where it's written that I have to be fair. And how dare you, from Judah, accuse me, a princess, of being unfair? You didn't find me in the gutter, you know, I found you in the gutter, that's where I found you."

"Michal," I corrected her firmly, "I was at the head of a parade when you saw me in the gutter. I was a hero and everyone was cheering me. That was right after I slew Goliath."

"Who?" she asked.

"Goliath, the giant, the Philistine champion everyone was afraid of, even your father. You painted your face and sat by the window to see me, didn't you? Of course I was in the gutter. Did you expect them to hold the parade on the sidewalk?"

"We have no sidewalks in Gibeah."

"So? Anyone you found would have to have been in the gutter."

"But I took you out," she asserted, and adamantly crossed her arms.

"Saul took me out, by letting me go no more home to my father and then making me captain of a thousand. He sent word that you loved me, and that's why we married." I looked at her longingly and asked, "Michal, aren't you in love with me, at least a little?"

"Yes, David, I am in love with you," she admitted, relenting slightly. "But only in my own fashion, as a member of the royal family who expects always to be obeyed."

"Your Highness."

"That's better. Promise you will always remember that you are married to a princess."

"I very much doubt you will let me forget it," I replied.

"I will want you to bathe every night and to brush your teeth after every meal. Always use deodorants. You must wash your hands with strong soap after defecating and urinating, especially before you start preparing my food. Always make sure that your hair is combed, especially in the back. I can't stand a man with flat hair in the back; it always looks as though he's been lying down and is lazy. Don't pick your nose in front of me. That's gross."

"I'm not picking my nose. I never pick my nose."

"Don't contradict me. That's gross too. Never fart."

"Never?"

"That's what I said. You must change your clothes when you come home each afternoon. Can a man be at ease in the evening with the raiment he wore in the day?"

"I do all right."

"I will want you to sleep in pajamas. File your nails and keep them clean. I like well-groomed men with an air of authority who dress impeccably and always smell of soap and deodorants."

"I will do my best."

"I want to be mother to a great race of kings."

"I'll do my best with that too."

Mollified at last, she relaxed her arms, and we moved side by side to the mat of straw unrolled on the floor. Our bed had not been delivered yet. Michal was a virgin when she allowed me to hold her and sank down beneath me. She was no longer a virgin when she rose to her feet less than ten seconds later.

"Well, thank God that's over with," said the first of my brides on our wedding night. "I certainly hope we have a son so I'll never have to go through *that* again!"

It took but an instant for her words to sink in with all their implications and for me to comprehend the seriousness of my plight. Michal, my bride, was not just the daughter of a king but a bona-fide Jewish American Princess! I had married a JAP! I am the first in the Old Testament to be stuck with one.

MICHAL DID NOT conceive a son on our wedding night and looked as crabby as Saul in disillusionment with me when the custom of women was upon her and it was unmistakably clear I had fallen short of her expectations in that solitary connubial encounter. As soon as her flowers were no longer upon her and she had completed cleansing herself from her menstrual impurity, she summoned me back to her side with a grimace of painful submission to a duty that was repugnant, and permitted me to get into her pants for the second time. In the interim, she had caused me to sleep by myself on a narrow couch in the chamber adjacent to hers. By that time, all our furniture had arrived. Saul had provided us with a fine two-story house in a good neighborhood of Gibeah, and both our private rooms were on the upper floor, separated from each other by a door of limed wattle. Again there was but one quick coupling, followed by another month of inviolable abstinence and deprivation in which I was banished each evening to my lonely couch in the other room. Something told me the results would be no more fruitful than before, yet I held my tongue until the new moon waxed full once more and the custom of women was upon her again. Never was there a woman, I'll bet, who suffered the multifarious pangs of her period with more ill grace. I failed miserably in my efforts to convince her that, statistically at the least, she was reducing enormously the chances for impregnation by this puritanical rhythm system of sexual congress she was imposing so inflexibly. She thought my efforts at persuasion were bestial, self-serving, and gross.

"You must not think I am frigid," she edified me. "It's just that I don't ever like being unclean, not even for a minute. You must have noticed that I bathe every day."

By that time, so did I.

And even in those first disenchanting months of our marriage, I quickly discovered that I had much bigger problems to contend with than bathing regularly or a nagging and fastidious wife. Specifically, there was my father-in-law, Saul, who was yet the more afraid of me than formerly and had become my enemy continually. Saul was not so determined as his daughter that she be mother to a great race of kings. He was more obsessed with seeing me dead, consumed as he was by the dilemma my sanctified existence personified for him: he could not bear having me alive, he did not dare harm me. His teeming paranoid mind found testimony everywhere that the Lord was with me and that he would have to arrange for my slaughter himself if he wanted me out of the way. Certainly against the Philistines I seemed to have a charmed life. God was not going to let him off the hook.

It had to happen, I suppose, that he would finally round the bend, and the day inevitably arrived when he lost self-control and spoke to Jonathan and all his servants that they should kill me. Now how do you like that for a development? That was some fortunate marriage I had made, wasn't it? Jonathan, who delighted in me much—why shouldn't he delight in me much?—was the first to tip me off, exhorting me to take heed of myself until the morning and abide in a secret place and hide myself. Did Saul care at all that his daughter would be a widow? All night long I lay huddled in my cloak, sleepless and trembling, and dreamed of someone as caring and as tender to me as Abishag the Shunammite turned out to be too late in my life. I thanked God fervently when I learned at dawn the next day that Jonathan had been triumphant in remonstrating with his father and inducing him to rescind his drastic orders against me.

"Let not the king sin against his servant, against David," Jonathan reported to me he had said, "because he hath not sinned against thee, and because his words toward thee have been very good. He slew the Philistine and did put his life in thy hand. Thou sawest it and didst rejoice at first."

"The Lord loves him, Jonathan." Saul was perturbed.

"So much the better, my father. Wherefore wilt thou sin against innocent blood, to slay David without a cause?"

Saul hearkened unto the voice of Jonathan and spoke with a radiant face, as though the scales were dropping from his eyes and he was all at once illuminated from within by the most enlightening of insights. "As the Lord liveth," Saul burst out, "he shall not be slain. I swear from the heart. Bring him to me this same evening and it shall be with him as in times past. There shall not be bad blood between us again."

Jonathan acquainted me with all these things and brought me into Saul's presence that day, and it was better than it had been in times past. Saul sat me at his right hand, honoring me. He looked with favor on me throughout my dinner, helped me to food, addressed me constantly, paid me compliments, catering to me throughout as though I were his most beloved son and he was making amends. Never in my life had I felt so complete as I did that evening. Never had I felt so serenely at one with my king and master and with the fulfilled miracle of my existence.

There could be no doubt in my mind that our reconciliation was whole when, afterward, he took me alone to accompany him on a walk through a field of reaped wheat on a descending incline just outside the gate of the city. In a rich atmosphere of mutual good feeling, we walked beside each other in silence along a path of turned soil between rows of broken stalks whose sheaves had already been bound and borne away for threshing and winnowing. A prize of some kind should be given to the person who first figured out what could be done with grain. The aromas of the earth were as good wine. There was something mystical in that starry night, the gigantic orange harvest moon so low and pregnant, the lush black, depthless sky brilliant and shimmering with hard flickers of white and gold as numerous as the sands of the sea. The heavens were so close a part of the density of our air that I felt I was sucking immortality into my lungs with every breath. An exquisite surprise came when Saul lifted his huge, gnarled hand to lower it ever so lightly upon the back of my head. And I felt for the second time in my life that I had been touched magically by someone godlike, fatherly, and immortal and brought somehow to a life that was now new and preciously enhanced. Beginnings of that kind are incredibly sublime: falling in love with Bathsheba was incredibly sublime. Just once before had I experienced that same profoundly satisfying feeling of being born afresh, when they brought me from Bethlehem to play for Saul and he took my face in his hands afterward to gaze into my eyes with such transfixing intensity and make me those deep-sworn promises that were forgotten by him and everyone else in the morning. I had never suffered such dismal disappointment.

"David, my son, I have a thing I must reveal to you," he began hoarsely as we walked in starlight that balmy evening. "Uneasy lies the head that wears a crown. Believe me, I know."

Continuing in a low voice embarrassingly frank in its bare contrition, he imparted to me a good deal about his history. Much of it was untrue. When I reflect on the candor with which we addressed each other in that conversation, I am astonished to recall that it was our longest and our last.

Saul had never aspired to be a leader of any kind. For most of his young life he had thought of himself as ungainly and clumsy, because of a great height that stood him head and shoulders above others about him.

"Maybe that's the only reason I was picked," he conjectured dolefully, as though ruminating over a familiar mystery. "From my shoulders and upward I was aways higher than any of the other people. They used to ask me how the air was up there. To tell you the truth, I never gave much thought to God, and I was as unprepared as anyone to hear from Samuel that I was the one whom the Lord had chosen to be captain over His inheritance."

"You believe Samuel?" I inquired.

"What choice do I have? He thinks about the Lord, I don't. I believed him then. I believe him now."

And to tell me another truth, Saul confided that he had not been all that happy with his selection then and was not too pleased with his situation now.

"I don't always know what to do."

His sole ambition the day Samuel plucked him out of obscurity was to find those lost asses of his father, which had been gone for three days. And Saul, unlike his daughter Michal, made no bones about the fact that he was from one of the least of all the families of the tribe of Benjamin. I effectively used this knowledge in marital disputes with Michal long after he was dead and I had succeeded in replacing him. When she sought to demean me by calling me a shepherd, I retaliated that her father had been an assherd, and from one of the least of all the families of the tribe of Benjamin to boot. Invariably, these arguments came down to the same basic disagreement, whether it was superior to be the daughter of a king or to be the king himself. I always won: I always proved my point by having her dragged from my room back to her place in the harem.

"Power corrupts, I've noticed," he observed, and averted his eyes as though in shamefaced confession. "And absolute power corrupts absolutely. I can have done whatever I want to. No one now interferes. Not even Samuel. Jonathan will try to talk to me sometimes, but even he will submit to my commands. Would you believe this, David—I've never told this to a soul—would you believe that the thought once crossed my mind, just for a second, you must know, to have you killed? Can you believe that?"

"No."

"We must never breathe a word about that to anybody."

"Why were you going to have me killed?"

"To teach you a lesson, I think."

"What lesson?"

"I sometimes have trouble figuring things like that out. The trouble with me," Saul resumed after a pause, "is that I almost never have more than one idea in my head at a time. Once I can think of something to do, I do it. People give me too much credit

169

for the way I responded to the news of the siege at Jabesh-gilead. It was all that came to mind. There was this yoke of oxen right before me—I had just come after the herd out of the field—and all I could think of was to hew them in pieces and send them throughout all the coasts of Israel as a warning to the people of what would be done to the oxen of those who did not send people to aid me. My only hesitations were over who to send pieces to and how to hack up the oxen to make sure there'd be enough. I didn't want to use more than two."

"What would you have done if the threat failed and the people had not responded?" I had long wondered about that.

"I'm not much good at looking ahead," admitted Saul.

Saul's first action as king, overcoming the Ammonites to lift the siege of Jabesh-gilead, was his best, and nothing in his life after that became him so much as the leaving it; he fell upon his own sword at the battle of Gilboa, by one account, when he found himself too sorely wounded of the archers to flee, and his armor bearer, sore afraid, declined his request to thrust him through and finish him off before the Philistines found him alive and abused him. The armor bearer, seeing Saul dead, fell likewise upon his sword and died with him. Something like that happened to Brutus at Philippi, didn't it, and to Marc Antony after Actium, according to that *gonoph* William Shakespeare, who pilfered from Plutarch too, as well as from Saul and me. A bard of Avon they called him yet. Some bard. *Him* I have to be measured against? In my day, a bard like him would be rolling out pancake dough in the street of bakers in Jerusalem or shrinking cloth in the fullers' field. O that mine adversary had written a book, instead of that mulligan stew of jumbled five-act plays with stupid plots cluttered with warm bodies and filled with sound and fury and signifying nothing. You watch. You watch. To him they'll give a Nobel prize for literature yet someday. And I still won't have a book of the Bible named after me, unless I rewrite the whole thing myself, and who has so much time? While nobodies like Obadiah, Nehemiah, Zephaniah, Habakkuk, and Zechariah do. Believe me, it's not *what* you know, but who you know. But fame is the spur that the clear spirit doth raise, and I don't give up hoping. At any rate, Saul did die gallantly—stupidly but gallantly—and I pay lofty and eloquent tribute to him in my famous elegy. I did better by him than he ever did by me. I immortalize him. Why criticize? The good that men do lives after them, while the evil is oft interred with their bones. So let it be with Saul, I decided, and made no mention at all of his killing of the priests, that bloody nut, and his occasional spells of looniness with the prophets.

Saul looked at me askance a moment on that enchanted night when I made bold to allude most gingerly to his weird episode with the prophets, about which all of us had heard.

"I still don't know what came over me." He shook his head disconsolately, affirming with embarrassment that reports of the epileptic religious seizure into which he had fallen were not unfounded. "Nothing like that had ever happened to me before."

It did happen to him once more since, when he was engrossed in wild-eyed pursuit of me and just about had me captured in Naioth in Ramah, where I had fled with Samuel after escaping out my window in the nick of time with the skin of my teeth. What followed seemed a miracle. Just when we had abandoned all hope of evading him, Saul was possessed once again by an irresistible need to prophesy. And he stripped off his clothes and lay down naked in a swoon all that day and all that night. Crazy? You tell me. Regaining his senses in the morning, he was a man of weakened resolution, and he turned tail and retreated to his house in Gibeah to ponder the mystery of the fit of religious ecstasy by which he had been so helplessly overwhelmed. Freud and his followers could explain that naked swoon—and would probably be wrong.

As Samuel had foretold in that first encounter with Saul, which was so fraught with consequences for the future, Saul did meet a company of prophets coming down from the high place of a hill of God with a psaltery, and a tabret, and a pipe, and a harp. And as Samuel had instructed, Saul did go up to prophesy with them, to allow the spirit of the Lord to come upon him and to be turned into another man.

"I can't really explain what happened to me after that."

The next thing he knew, he was lying on the ground at the bottom of the hill, surrounded by the small crowd of gaping onlookers who had been attracted by the unusual spectacle. He was mortified and disoriented.

"My memory of the whole event is still the most terrifying of my life."

Only from the derisive comments of the people gaping at him was he able to reconstruct what had happened—that he had done the dervish in company with these fanatical enthusiasts, howled out the mantras, harmonized the Hare Krishnas, stripped off his clothing, and gone tumbling down the hill with the others to lie thrashing about in the dust in a foaming, spastic, orgiastic frenzy.

"My chin was still wet from drooling. I did not know how to go about finding my cloak to cover my nakedness. I have never been so ashamed in my life."

Of course he was recognized as the son of Kish by disbelieving neighbors astonished to see him in such a state. He was further disconcerted by the murmurs of ridicule resonating among them with the facile repetitiveness that transmutes conversational statements into tiresome proverbs.

"Is Saul also among the prophets?" he heard more times than he could count.

"What then? It's not Saul among the prophets?"

"Can Saul be among the prophets?"

"Saul can't be among the prophets?"

"How can Saul be among the prophets?"

"Go give a look."

"With my own eyes I saw Saul among the prophets."

Is it any wonder there were many opposed to accepting Saul the son of Kish as king?

"I would have had trouble enough without that. After all, I was only the son of Kish, a Benjamite, of the smallest of the tribes of Israel, and my family the least of all the families of the tribe of Benjamin. What did I know about management, religion, or warfare?"

Filthy children of Belial, Samuel called the people who rejected Saul because they did not see how such a man could save them. These despised Saul and brought him no presents, and Saul went home to Gibeah and held his peace until the Ammonites came up and encamped against Jabesh-gilead.

"That was my chance," observed Saul.

"As Goliath was mine," I could not help reminding.

Saul went on without bestowing upon me the moment of acknowledgment I had fished for.

When Nahash the Ammonite came up out of the desert and encamped against the city, all the men of Jabesh were ready to surrender and serve, and they sued for peace. As a condition of peace, Nahash wanted to thrust out the right eye of all of them. This seemed not unreasonable to me.

"I saw it as a sign of weakness too," Saul agreed. "So I took that yoke of oxen, and hewed them in pieces, and sent them throughout all the coasts of Israel by the hands of messengers, saying that whoever cameth not forth after me and after Samuel, so would it be done unto *his* oxen."

The act to me seemed less effective as threat than as drama; yet the fear of the Lord fell on the people, and they came out with one consent. Dividing his men in three companies, Saul moved into the midst of the host in the morning watch and slew the Ammonites until the heat of the day. Those that remained were so scattered that no two of them were left together. It was a famous victory.

"When I was growing up in Bethlehem," I disclosed shyly, "we often used to play at war, and one of our favorite games was to play at war as Saul against Nahash at Jabesh-gilead. We loved the part of hewing the oxen into pieces."

"And which role did you play?" Saul asked quickly, fixing a searching gaze upon me.

I felt a fleeting chill. "None of us ever took the role of an enemy."

"Did you ever wish to play the part of one of the oxen?" It seemed bizarre that he was not joking.

"All of us wished to take the part of the king."

"Do you still wish to take the part of the king?"

The jarring presence of something dangerous in the atmosphere was now unmistakable. "All of us wished to play the part of the hero, my lord," I replied as tactfully as I knew how. "Of our hero Saul, the great man who was made king before the Lord in Gilgal by all the people, because he gathered an army as he did and saved Jabesh, and all of the men of Israel could rejoice greatly in him."

My flattery was disarming, and I watched his face soften and his symptoms of apprehension recede. Everything for him after that, he recounted, was downhill. His impressive victory over the Philistines at Michmash was blighted by his quarrel with Samuel over the performance of the sacrifice and by the implacable resistance after the battle of the people serving him, who would not let one hair of Jonathan's head fall to the ground when Saul sought to make him die. His success against the Amelekites led to his second quarrel with Samuel and the final breach in their relationship.

JOSEPH HELLER

"What was I supposed to do when Samuel failed to arrive before the battle of Michmash to sacrifice the sacrifice?" Saul wondered out loud, haunted anew by a quandary which eternally confounded him. "Was it my fault or his? He was late in coming and my men were beginning to tremble as they saw the number of Philistines increase. We could have swept them away easily if we had struck right away. No Samuel. I had come with an army eager to fight, but steadily they beheld the Philistines gathering themselves together in greater and greater numbers, with chariots and with horsemen and with people that began to look like the sand which is on the seashore in multitude. Still no Samuel. When the men of Israel saw the strait they were in, they were distressed, and they did scatter from me and hide themselves in caves, and in thickets, and in rocks, and in high places, and in pits. And some of my Hebrews even went back over Jordan to the land of Gad and Gilead. We weren't supposed to fight until we had first made supplication to the Lord with a sacrifice. We couldn't sacrifice without Samuel. No Samuel. When the seven days appointed passed and there was still no Samuel, I finally offered the burnt offering myself. No sooner had I made an end than, behold, Samuel was already there. He told me I had done foolishly and that my kingdom would not now continue, that the Lord hath sought Him a man after His own heart and had commanded him to be captain over the people instead of me. 'So fast?' I cried. 'The burnt offering isn't even cold yet!' 'He built the world in seven days,' Samuel answered."

"Six," I could not help interjecting.

"Exactly." Saul gave a single nod of his head. "Samuel isn't perfect, you see. And I think he was at least as much to blame as I was. Can one reason with God? I was expected to win, wasn't I? Well, I did win, without Samuel, and maybe even without God. And then after the big victory, there was all that trouble with my son Jonathan. I hope you never have from your children the troubles I get from mine. I guess you know what Jonathan did to me there."

"Did to you?" I exclaimed, gawking.

"You've never heard?"

"Tasting the honey?"

"After I put a ban upon eating until evening? And a curse before God on any man who violated it?"

174

"You think God expected you to kill your son for tasting a bit of honey?"

"You think he didn't? When I built an altar unto the Lord that day and asked counsel whether to go down after the Philistines, I got no answer, no answer at all. That's how I first knew somebody had done something wrong."

"Did Jonathan know of your ban?"

"Sure he knew," Saul answered promptly, lying. "It was no secret. What was I to do when I found him out?"

"Ask God?" I guessed.

"Ask God," he repeated, and looked at me pityingly. "What good is God? God wouldn't tell me. God hasn't answered me since."

"You blame Jonathan for that?"

"I haven't killed him, have I?"

And then Samuel came no more to see him after repudiating Saul's actions following his triumph over the Amelekites. Taking King Agag for ransom and the best of the cattle for booty, instead of putting all to the sword as instructed, was only the second or third of Saul's lapses, and his only act of noncompliance; yet it was enough for Samuel to depart from him forever, taking God with him.

"He told me it was the last straw," Saul continued moodily. "He hewed Agag to pieces and went to his home in Ramah. He told me the Lord had rent the kingdom from me."

"For just one act of disobedience?" I wondered aloud in sympathy.

"Not even Adam was given a second chance."

"Adam talked with God directly. You have only Samuel's word."

"Samuel told me to be king."

"That part I would believe."

Saul cogitated a minute in silence and then turned his face to look at mine. "Is there word from the Lord, David?"

"I don't know what you mean." My manner was wary, his was crafty.

"Has God ever spoken to you?"

"If He has, I didn't notice." At that time, my answer was true.

"What happens when you sacrifice?" asked Saul.

"I don't sacrifice."

175

"Do you know what happens when I sacrifice? Nothing. The meat doesn't burn, the fat hardly melts."

"Maybe you need a hotter fire," I suggested, "or better meat."

He paid no attention to my guesses. "I get no omens, I get no advice. God just doesn't answer me anymore."

"Maybe God is dead."

"How can God be dead?"

"God can't be dead?"

"If God was dead, could I feel this bad?"

"Go to Samuel," I urged. "Go to the priests."

"I don't trust the priests, they side with Samuel."

And Samuel had rejected him in the presence of the elders. Samuel came no more to see Saul, as it turned out, until the night before Saul's death. And then it was Samuel's spirit, summoned by the witch of Endor.

"I think he wanted me to be king," Saul theorized, "but he wanted to be the one who ruled. When he left that day, he told me that the Lord had already given the kingdom to a neighbor of mine that was better than me." Saul glanced at me intently again, his brow beetling. "David, were you the neighbor he meant?"

My answer was fearful. "I have no way of knowing, my lord. I was not there—"

"David, David," Saul interrupted impatiently, "I am drained of choler. I have no anger left. I love you as I do my own sons. Did Samuel make you a king?"

"Only God can make a king," I replied.

"If God is dead?"

Now he had me. "There's only Samuel."

"We know he traveled to Bethlehem," said Saul. "He came with a red heifer on a rope that he said was to sacrifice. We know he stopped in your father's house and went no farther, and we know they sent to fetch you where you were keeping the sheep. He went back with the heifer. David, David, did Samuel make you king?"

There was no room left to temporize. "He put oil on my face," I replied, "and told me the Lord had provided for me to be king. But in Bethlehem things like that are always happening. Some people say it has something to do with the drinking water."

"Have you been intriguing with him?" said Saul. "What has he told you since?"

"Oh, no, my Lord, I have not seen or heard from him since," I avowed honestly. "He did not tell me when or how it would come about that I would be king. I have done no plotting. I have sought only to serve thee since the day of my killing of Goliath."

"Goliath?" Saul looked at me inquisitively.

"The Philistine giant," I reminded him. It was beginning to irk me that nobody but me seemed to be talking anymore about my killing the terrifying warrior that day with just my sling.

"What Philistine giant?" asked Saul.

"The one that I slew with my sling that day in the valley of Elah. You took me into your service then, and I have put my life in thy hand to slay the Philistine and preserve thee ever since. Don't you remember?"

"For my own life I care not," Saul said without answering me. "After all, David, we owe God a death, and he who dies this year is quit for the next. But for you to follow me as king would require that Jonathan and my other sons go down to the grave with me too. My line and my name would be cut off among my brethren."

"My lord, I pray thee, let there be no strife ever between thee and me," I implored him. "Do you believe I could ever wish evil to thy son Jonathan, whose soul is knit with my soul, and who goes about saying that he loves me as his own soul?"

"Yes, I've heard him." Saul studied me, squinting a bit, and demanded, "What does he mean by that?"

"That we're good friends," I hastened to say.

"Just that?"

"Only that."

"Then why doesn't he put it that way?" Saul mumbled.

"He tends to be poetic sometimes, my lord," I explained.

"So do you," Saul said. "I hate poetry. But I like your music."

"I like to sing for you," I confessed with feeling. "And I swear I will never lift a weapon against you or any of your house. And that I will serve Jonathan after you." I meant it too.

Saul sighed. "Let there be peace then forever between thee and me," he offered. It was then that he embraced me, clasping me warmly to his great chest with a tender and suffusing affection. "You have my sacred word, I will never doubt thee again or seek to do thee harm. David, will you come play for me again soon, perhaps the next time I'm feeling blue?"

"But give me the chance!" I promised gladly. "I long for nothing more."

I could not have guessed that he would oblige me so quickly.

The very next day it was that the evil spirit from the Lord was upon Saul again as he sat in his house, and I was sent for still one more time to soothe and lighten with song and harp his grievously troubled heart. I came with an armful of music, intending to entertain him—for hours, if necessary—first with my "Ave Maria" and Moonlight Sonata and next with the première of my Goldberg Variations, a work I had recently composed for a neighbor of mine in Gibeah with insomnia on the gamble that the charming air on which the whole is based would lull him toward sleep more easily. This time Saul was awaiting me eagerly, cross-legged on a bench with a javelin already in his lap. That should, I suppose, have alerted me. I was too enthusiastic to care. He looked just awful again, I was glad to see. The worse his condition, the greater his need for me and the richer the opportunity to ingratiate myself with him and to convince him still further of my patriotic devotion. I was glad I had worn my burgundy tunic and taken the trouble to groom myself. I had oiled my arms and face and pomaded my curls. With the second joints of my fingers I had rubbed my cheeks with vigor to enrich their natural color. I should have stood in bed.

All of my preparations were wasted. No sooner did I lift my head to pose like an angel and part my lips for my first dulcet note than he rose from his bench and let fly at me with the javelin, seeking again to smite me even to the wall with it. Holy shit, I thought with terror. Again I was stupefied. Again he missed me by inches, the weapon embedding itself in the wood behind me with a loud report. This time, though, I made up my mind at once. Fuck *him*, I decided, and leaped to my feet. Enough is enough! Music he wants? *Balls* he'll get! I ducked my head and bounded away.

7

FLIGHT
INTO
GATH

At Nob I told some lies and eighty-five priests were slain. Not only that, but all of the men, women, and children in their households, and all of the livestock in that sacred city, were put to death as well. Who is to blame? Saul, Doeg the Edomite, or old Ahimelech, the gullible reigning priest I hoodwinked into supplying me? Saul, who originated the orders for the massacre, was already infamous as a rampaging, bloodthirsty lunatic. Doeg the Edomite, chiefest herdsman of Saul, did the butchering, after every one of the servants of the king, even Abner, refused to put forth his hand to fall upon the priests of the Lord. Ahimelech, officiating that day at the horns of the altar, was methodical and credulous in the performance of his functions and had no obligation to suppose he was being cozened into providing succor to a fugitive from the king's wrath. Doeg the Edomite was most to blame, by my way of thinking; he was doing his duty in the hope of advancement, and he that maketh haste to be rich cannot be innocent. Haven't I found out that much by now from a lifetime of observing others?

Me? Where do I come in for any of the guilt? How can anyone reasonable assert that the responsibility should be mine? I was running for my life and had never, not once, done anything wrong. And even Ahimelech's son Abiathar, sole survivor from Nob after Saul smote with the edge of the sword both men and women, children and sucklings, and oxen, and asses, and sheep, even Abiathar laid none of the fault at my door and fled after me for protection when I had gathered some men about me and come farther up into Judah from the quarters I had established in the cave of Adullam. Inadvertently, I had occasioned the death of all the persons in his father's house; yet Abiathar sought refuge with me. He brought news of the slaughter with him. I took him in and vowed to safeguard .him. And Abiathar has abided with me as

181

priest ever since, even though Bathsheba pretends not to remember who he is each time the matter of his support for Adonijah comes up, or derogates him as one who has lost his wits and is not to be taken seriously.

"You should help a father in his age," I tried moralizing with Bathsheba one time. "If his understanding fail, have patience with him."

"You've got one foot in the grave," was her unmoved retort. "It's all I can do to keep patience with you."

Of Ahimelech that day, all I asked was a sword and some victuals. I wanted bread and saw five newly baked loaves.

He was rightfully afraid at seeing me in Nob. "Why art thou alone?" he wished to know.

I falsely replied that the king had commanded me out on a business with orders to let no man know where or why I was going, and that I was to rendezvous in stealth with the others assigned to my party at such and such a place already appointed; we wanted no questions raised about my coming and my going. This conversation with Ahimelech was conducted in the open, and I grew greatly concerned for myself when I recognized Doeg the Edomite skulking about in the small crowd attracted by my arrival. I knew he would acquaint Saul with the direction I had traveled when he arrived back in Gibeah and learned I was sought for execution, but I did not envision the awful consequences his report would produce. Nor can I convince myself that I would have acted any differently if I *had* given thought to what could result, or even that I should have. I was a young man in panic. I had committed no sin. I was above reproach and felt I had as much right to live as everyone else.

In earshot of all, I requested of Ahimelech the sword or the spear I said I needed to conduct my action, stating that the king's business required haste and that Saul had commissioned me to requisition a weapon from him. I also asked for the five loaves of bread I counted under his hand, still steaming and aromatic from the fire in the altar, and as many more loaves as he could spare. Even before I finished, he was shaking his head.

"There is no bread here to give you," he told me apologetically, "but the shewbread."

"What's shewbread?" I asked.

"This is no common bread under my hand," Ahimelech the

priest explained, "but there is hallowed bread I can give thee, if the young men with thee have kept themselves from women for at least these three days past and are not unclean."

"For more than three days," I assured him with celerity, anxious to be gone before the curiosity of Doeg the Edomite was fanned into expressing some kind of doubt. "We are as clean as can be."

Only in this last statement was there anything like truth, for I had not lain with another woman since parting from Michal at my window three weeks earlier, nor had I lain with her more than once in the weeks preceding that. Our farewells had been rushed, leaving little time for horseplay. Bounding from Saul's room after his newest effort to smite me, I had bolted first into Abner, who listened without arching an eyebrow to what for me was an account of a most extraordinary and hair-raising event. Abner bit into a pomegranate he was eating and continued grinding away noisily on the seeds as I spoke.

"I myself would not make too much of it," he decided a few seconds after I had finished. "Accidents will happen."

"Accidents?" Could I believe my ears?

"Is it not an accident that your anointed king wishes to kill you every now and then?" Abner argued in his friendly and sophistic way. "Or do you feel he has good cause?"

"He has no cause," I declared emphatically.

"And he still hasn't hurt you, has he? Be reasonable, David," Abner added, as though urging me to grow up. "Life is to be lived. If it makes him feel better to throw a javelin at you, let him throw the javelin. Saul is our king. He seems to perk up afterward. He lets off steam."

"You call that fair?"

"Is the moon made of cheese?"

Had I taste for such drollery at a time like that?

It was good Joab murdered Abner for me, although I did not think so at the time and had to simulate much public grief at his burial. It was good in the long run that he killed Absalom for me too, I guess, although I will never get over my love for that handsome second son of mine. He murdered my other nephew, Amasa, too, the son of my second sister, after we had put down Absalom's rebellion, but Amasa hardly mattered, except to remind me again that Joab could be ruthless and disobedient in his jealousy of sharing power. I prepared Benaiah for Joab's potential for enmity when

I placed him rather than Joab in charge of the palace guard of Cherethite and Pelethite mercenaries I had created for my personal safety, to be responsible only to me. What a blow that was to Joab. He was an idiot to suppose I would have put myself entirely at his mercy.

Michal saved me that day Saul tried to smite me in his room. From Abner I headed home as fast as my legs would carry me and was a bundle of nerves by nightfall when Michal arrived. Like an animal encaged, I paced without letup from one section of our house to the other, vacillating between spasms of furious outrage and spells of tearful self-pity. I wanted to howl and I wanted to whimper. Part of the turmoil I suffered sprang from my need to find some way of protesting to Michal about her father without provoking from her another angry outburst against me. My misgivings were unnecessary, for she was in a very bad state herself when she finally came bursting in.

"You'll never believe it!" we shouted at each other at exactly the same moment, and for the next half minute or so communicated with each other in a flurry of alarms.

"It's terrible, terrible!" I cried indignantly. "I'm not going to stand for it. You're not going to believe me."

"It's awful, awful," she was telling me even as I was protesting to her. "The news I've got for you is awful. I can't believe such awful news."

"He threw a javelin at me again."

"Murderers are coming."

"I knew you wouldn't believe me," I accused.

"Never mind what I believe," she retorted. "What I'm telling you is worse."

"You never believe me when it comes to your father. He threw a javelin. What could be worse?"

"Murderers outside, that could be worse," answered Michal.

"Murderers? What are you talking about?"

"They're on the way."

"Yeah-yeah."

"You don't believe me? Assassins, David," she emphasized in my face. "Don't you understand? They're coming to kill you. *Oy*, they're already here, in the street outside, to watch the house through the night and slay you when you leave in the morning."

"I know you're joking."

"Go look."

"Holy shit!"

Furtive hooded men with cloaks and daggers were already positioning themselves in doorways and alleys in the street in front of my house and at both ends, shutting off flight and closing me in. Their dark robes were of solid colors and the blades and handles of their swords and daggers could be seen jutting from beneath. Some were waiting with their hands already on the hilt.

Michal was breathing deeply. "What can we do?"

"I think I know exactly what to do," I replied with authority. "They would not dare detain or harm you, the daughter of the king. You go out now, go to the house of your father the king as quickly as you can, and report to your father the thing that is happening here."

"David, guess who sent them."

I was now able to discern, in shadowy profile in a recess between two houses, the vulpine silhouette of Abner and one of his pomegranates. Abner always did have a very big nose. Prompted by Michal, I was able to put two and two together and see that she was right.

"Michal, what *can* we do?" I whispered. "What does it all mean?"

"It means that if thou save not thy life tonight," was the sage counsel she gave me, "tomorrow thou shalt be slain."

It was Michal who concocted most of the elements in the scheme that allowed me to save my skin and who took upon herself most of the burden of implementing them: we laid an image in the bed with a pillow of goat's hair for a bolster and covered it with a blanket, to represent me sleeping; she let me down by a rope through a rear window; in the morning, she would give it out that I was sick when the messengers from Saul came inquiring about my failure to appear from my house as usual. By that time I would be far off, and the lie and the ruse would give me hours more. It was Michal too who, sooner or later, would have to face the music when the deception inevitably was exposed, and justify herself against the ire of her father with the precarious excuse that I had threatened I would kill her. To the questions of why, if she had indeed been in such fear of me, she had not raised a hue and cry the instant I was departed, or had not thrown herself under the protection of the messengers from her father instead of delaying them with fabrications, she could give whatever lame explanation came to mind. Or she could weep or faint. Or both. We put together a shepherd's ration of bread, cheese, dates, olives, and raisins, along with a water bag and another bag of curdled goat's milk. And some fig cakes and pistachio nuts. She took hold of the rope.

"I love you," she said in a clipped voice. "I hope you know that."

I could see that she did, but in the only way she knew how, with acrimony, injury, envy, and disdain, and with consummate selfishness and egocentricity. We kissed goodbye on the sill of the window.

"Do you have your mouthwash?"

I lied and said yes. And out the window I went, like some hairy-legged clown in a dirty burlesque. When next we met, I had been king in Hebron for over seven years and she had been given by her father to another man as wife. And neither one of us was that much fond of the other.

It's a wonder to me still that I landed on my feet and escaped in one piece. I headed directly for Ramah to the abode of Samuel, seeking shelter, solace, and wisdom from the one man left in the kingdom who I thought might still have influence over Saul and the strength of character to exercise it in my behalf. It was a waste of energy. What I found instead was a man with frantic woes commensurate with my own who was vexed with me for having added to his.

"What do you want?" was the irascible way he greeted me. "Why did you have to come here? What are you doing to me?"

With his shaggy hands he was rapidly throwing things into his knapsack, and he seemed to be grumbling in his beard while I did my best to explain. Samuel was just about the crankiest individual I had ever met, and I have not come upon any since to rival him. He was even hairier than I remembered him: his endless black beard, profusely lined now with wiry strands of dingy gray, was, it embarrasses me to reveal, a bit unkempt.

"From me you want wisdom?" he demanded curtly. "From me you want influence and shelter? Solace I should give you? How should I be the one to tell you what to do?"

"You're a prophet, aren't you?" I shot back.

"When was the last time you heard of me doing any of that?"

"You're also a Judge."

"When was the last time you heard me judge anything? Listen, even when I was speaking directly for the Lord I wasn't always sure I was telling the truth."

"You can still give me advice, can't you?"

"You want advice?" spoke Samuel. "I'll give you a beautiful piece. Go far, far away."

"From where? From whom?"

"From me, you damned fool," Samuel sputtered. "Haven't I got troubles enough? Now he'll think I've been helping you. You had to come here?"

"You had to start the whole thing?"

"Me? What did I start? I started nothing."

"Did I ask you to anoint me? You came and said I'd be king, didn't you?"

"You want to be king?" Samuel retorted with a snarl. "Go be king somewhere else, and leave me alone. I've got to run now—thanks to you."

"To where?"

"Naioth. You think I'm staying here, now that you showed up?" Samuel was squeezing his hands and chanting distractedly. "Look at me, look at me," he grieved. "A Judge, a prophet, yet. I used to be the most powerful man in the country until God told me to turn away from Saul and go to you. Why did I have to listen to Him?"

"Why did you have to make Saul king?"

"*I* made Saul king?" Samuel shook his head vehemently. "Oh, no, sir, mister. Not me. God made Saul king. I just delivered the message. None of it was my idea. It was the people who wanted a king, not me. They weren't satisfied with just me, with just a Judge. They want a king, make them a king, said God. He told me pick Saul, I picked Saul. Who would have guessed that He'd pick such a *meshugana?*"

"Are you sure He told you later to pick me?"

"What then? I'd choose you myself?"

"You made no mistake?"

"God makes mistakes, not Judges. You want the truth? If it was up to me, I would have chosen your brother Eliab, or Abinadab, or even Shammah—they're bigger than you. And they were born first. But the Lord told me to look not on the outward appearance or the countenance. The Lord looketh on the heart, He told me. Sure—

the heart, He told me. And He saw something special in yours. What it is I cannot guess. Do me a favor and give me a clue."

"A lot of good He's done me," I sulked. "I can't even go back to Bethlehem—that's the first place Saul will look."

"*Here* is the first place he'll look when he learns you didn't go back into Judah," Samuel reproved me bitterly. The only prophecy Samuel would make was that Saul would go wild when he heard I'd come to Ramah to him. "That's why I'm going to Naioth, fast."

"Naioth?" I complained some more. "There's nothing to do in Naioth. Now I have to run to Naioth with you."

"With me?" Samuel's words were a cry of alarm. "Oh, no, mister, not with me. Run somewhere else and leave me alone. I know trouble when I see it. Goodbye, goodbye, parting is such sweet sorrow, but not from you."

I let him know I was sticking to him like glue. Where else could I go? How we squabbled from the beginning! He insisted on taking his cow.

"She brings me good luck," he explained.

"She'll slow us down," I objected.

"Who tells you to wait?" he wanted to know.

"And why go to Naioth?"

"Who asks you to come?"

If consolation was my goal, I was not going to obtain it from him.

Samuel was accurate in his prediction about Saul, who lost no time sending messengers to Naioth to take me once it was told him where his bird had flown. His men never got there; strangely, they fell to prophesying along the way. When that same thing came to pass with a second contingent, Saul set out to take me himself. Then the unforeseen occurred again. You wouldn't believe what happened. I had given up. Samuel and his cow would go no farther. Just as I was practically in his grasp, Saul was irresistibly possessed for the second time in his life with the need to prophesy.

It began at a great well in Sechu, where he learned by inquiring that we were still in Naioth. And as he went thither to Naioth, behold, as had befallen the men he had sent earlier to seize me, the spirit of God was upon him also, just like that, and he began to prophesy. And he went on and on and prophesied all the way into Naioth until he came to Samuel, and guess what he did then? He stripped off his clothes also, and prophesied before Samuel in like manner, and lay down naked all the rest of that day and, as it turned out, all that night. Wherefore, it could again be seen and said that Saul also was among the prophets. This time, though, I saw it with my own eyes.

"It's a miracle," I said in a hushed voice when Samuel and I were again by ourselves.

"Don't bet on it." We spoke on the ground by torchlight. He was sweating from exhaustion. "At least now I have a little room to breathe."

"How long will it last?"

"He'll lie until morning, probably," Samuel answered. "Then maybe, if we're lucky, he'll go back home to pull himself together, until something else comes up to make him crazy again. What more can I tell you? Saul is miserable, murderous, and unstable. Saul is the unhappiest person I know—except, maybe, for me."

"Samuel," I proposed, with the germ of an idea stirring, "you can help him, you can help all of us. Let Saul be king again."

"Let Saul be king again?" Samuel echoed with disdain. "How can Saul be king again? You're the king."

"Does Saul know that?"

"Why do you think he wants to kill you? Why do you question me?"

"Why do I question you?" I repeated, amazed. The scruffy old goat was totally without imagination. "Because I'm living in a fucking ditch, that's why. I have no home in Gibeah anymore, I can't be with my wife, and every Monday and Thursday I find myself dodging javelins from Saul. You call this being king? What the hell good is it?"

"You'll be king, you'll be king," Samuel muttered without conviction. "Why worry, what's your hurry? Bide your time. Rome wasn't built in a day."

"From a Judge like you I don't need banalities like that," I let him know. "Saul is mad."

"You're telling me? Whom the gods would destroy they first make mad."

"A lot of good that does me. I'm tired of waiting. I live like a bum."

"What's the big rush? It's the mills of the gods."

"What about them?"

"The mills of the gods grind slowly," he told me, "yet they grind exceedingly fine."

"And what am I supposed to do while they're grinding?"

Now it was Samuel's turn to blow up. "What do I care what you do?" he shouted. "Bang your head against the wall. Go shit in the ocean. You can grow like an onion with your head in the ground and your feet in the air, for all I care."

We each spent a minute calming down. With long-nailed yellow fingers, Samuel peevishly picked bits of food, foliage, and other refuse from the dangling knots of hair falling down on his shoulders and his chest. I gave him a drink from my bag of water and he thanked me grumpily. I gave him pistachio nuts.

"Samuel, Samuel," I implored diplomatically. "Let us try to reason together."

"I used to be the most powerful man in the country," he reminisced again. "I should have stuck with Saul, no matter what I thought God said He wanted."

"Then let Saul be king again," I advised, "at least until the mills of the gods finish grinding. Go tell him. How can it hurt us?"

"It isn't true," Samuel answered.

"Does he have to know? Let him think he's king. Ask God if it's all right."

Unintentionally, I had touched another nerve; Samuel looked hurt for a second but answered gently. "Don't you think I've done that? You think I'm dumb or something? Of course I asked God."

"Did God say yes?"

"He didn't say no," Samuel retorted, and then went on more candidly. "He didn't say anything. God answereth me no more," he confessed, in a voice weak with humiliation.

"Not you either?" I exclaimed. "Saul told me the same thing about himself. What the devil is wrong with God these days?"

Samuel shrugged. "Do I know?"

"Maybe," I hypothesized, venturing forth again into the same uncharted intellectual territory which I had once started incautiously to explore with Saul, "God is dead."

Samuel's reply was terse. "God can be dead?"

"God can't be dead?"

"If He's God, He can't be dead, stupid," Samuel instructed me. "If He's dead, He can't be God. It's someone else. Enough of your foolishness."

"Then let's ask Him again," I proposed eagerly. "They say He likes me. Come on, Samuel. Try another sacrifice."

"Why waste a cow?"

"Then do it without the sacrifice," I persisted. "It doesn't hurt to ask, does it? See if Saul can be king."

"King-schming," Samuel intoned.

I found his message incomprehensible. "I don't think I understand that."

"It's a saying."

"An old saying?"

My question irritated him. "How old can it be, you dummy? Isn't Saul our first king? Listen, you think I didn't ask enough times already? I asked and I asked. You think we have no feeling for Saul, God and me? No love? We pity him, repent for him, feel mercy toward him. God even chastised me once for mourning for Saul too long. That was just before He ordered me to fill my horn with oil and go find you. What a sad day that was. You've no idea how I hate the sight of you. I was much better off with Saul. All Saul did was disobey me once. I'm sorry I lost my temper and said those mean things to him."

"Then go back to him and apologize," I advised, nobly allowing his gratuitously insulting comments to pass without objection. "Tell him you made a mistake."

Samuel drew himself up frigidly. "I should tell him I made a mistake?"

"Then tell him God did."

"That's more like it," Samuel agreed. "Saul would believe that. But the Lord is not a man that He should ever repent."

"But you can do it all on your own," I coaxed. "Tell Saul you decided to give him another chance. You told me he's miserable. Let him feel good again for a while."

Samuel spoke with wicked relish. "Let him twist slowly," he said, his eyes smoldering, "slowly in the wind."

For the moment I was speechless. "I thought you loved Saul," I finally exclaimed. "You said that you and God had pity and compassion for him and that you wanted to be merciful toward him."

"That's the way we show it."

Samuel went back to Ramah, where it was his good fortune to die before Saul got around to killing him too after slaughtering the priests at Nob and discovering through trial and error that people in high position get away with murder.

LIKE A DOG returning to its vomit, or a fool repeating his folly, I found myself journeying back to Gibeah, even though alerted by common sense that a lion could be awaiting me there in the streets. I walked on high winding paths deserted after dark, skirting the main ways through the villages in between, lest there be a lion in the streets of one of those too. I moped all the way. I came back toward Saul as though hypnotized, drawn by my wistful need to re-establish myself in the good graces of the man on earth who had made a deeper impression on me than any other—even though I now understood him to be mad and homicidal and even, perhaps, stupid and boring. I felt he was my father, my patron still, and I wanted to be near him no matter what. Believe it or not, I even wanted to be back with Michal. He was the only being I had ever succeeded in loving as a parent; his, for better or for worse, was the only house in which I had ever felt myself at home. Had Saul been just a bit more fatherly to me, I would have worshipped him as a god. Had God ever been the least bit paternal, I might have loved Him like a father. Even when God has been good to me it has not been with much kindness.

At the same time, I will admit that the notion of my succeeding Saul as king had never been entirely obnoxious to me or out of my daydreams for long.

My head told me that this final endeavor to reinstate myself with Saul would prove hopeless. My heart told me I was exiled forever from the only nest in which I could ever dwell without feeling myself estranged and adrift, disconnected from my own past, and with no strong sense of attachment to my future. I was nevertheless compelled to try, despite my foreknowledge of futility, which weighed in my breast like an anvil. I was much less stiff-necked with Saul than I have been with God. I knew he was crazy; yet I wanted to win his devotion and forgiveness. I would want to try again even now if he were still alive. I can't bear feeling alone. I never could.

Entering Gibeah after sundown, I conferred with Jonathan in secrecy, wretchedly craving to glean from him, the king's oldest son, even the dimmest ray of hope. What I obtained instead was a befuddling surprise.

"Jonathan, please help me," I begged at the beginning, trusting no one fully, not even him. We conversed in a wooded corner of that same oblong field of moldering stalks of scythed wheat in which Saul and I had talked so familiarly on that magical moonlit night. Again the balmy air blowing in from the distant sea was caressing in texture and laden with the intoxicating fragrances of plums and melons and of blue grapes in the winepresses. "You can talk to him again for me. Observe him closely at dinner tomorrow night. Find out if he has forgiven me or if he still means to kill me. Then come and tell me."

"You can observe him yourself," was the answer with which Jonathan caught me unprepared. "You're expected at dinner tomorrow."

"That's insane!" I cried, suspecting a trick.

It was that time of month again when the moon was new, and I learned from Jonathan that I was expected to sit with the king at meat in the evening as in normal times, positively without fail. What kind of nonsense was that, I wanted to know. I was highly indignant. Wasn't I a fugitive? It was as though nothing at all untoward had occurred, as though Saul had not tried to smite me even to the wall with his javelin, sent minions to my house to slay me, ordered messengers to Naioth to seize me, and even come after me himself for the pleasure of apprehending me and ordering my death on the spot. What the hell was going on? Was all of that forgotten, did it count for nothing? Apparently yes, for a place would be set for me at the king's table the night following, and my failure to appear would be judged insubordinate. I felt myself enmeshed in absurdity. How did they even know I was there? With a logic that appeared irrefutable to him, Jonathan proposed that inasmuch as the king was not then pursuing me, I had no good reason to avoid him and was without legitimate cause for flight or truancy.

I wasn't buying it. "They commissioned you to bring me?"

"There was no talk of that," answered Jonathan. "But as long as you're here, you can come tomorrow. You will come with me."

They all must be crazy. "Why shouldest thou bring me to thy father?" I pleaded with Jonathan. "I know he still means to slay me."

"I can't believe that."

"Then you find out for me. What have I done? You ask him. What is mine iniquity, and what is my sin that he seeketh my life?"

Jonathan was disposed toward a rosier view. "Behold, my father will do nothing either great or small, but that he will show it to me. Why should he hide this thing from me?"

"Jonathan, your father isn't that wild about you, remember?" I answered. "Thy father certainly knoweth by now that I have found grace in thy eyes. You go about telling that to everybody. Perhaps he does not want you to grieve, or is afraid you might talk secretly with me, as we are doing now. What made him think I would even be back here after all that has taken place? He sent murderers to my house to kill me."

"I can't believe that."

"Ask your sister."

"Michal exaggerates. The moon will be new."

"Does he think I'd come back to have dinner with him just because the moon is new?"

"You know how crazy he is," Jonathan tried to explain. "He forgives and forgets."

"And then he forgets he's forgiven," I replied. "As the Lord liveth, Jonathan, and as thy soul liveth, there is but a step between me and death. I feel it in my bones."

Jonathan looked horrified and said unto me, "God forbid—thou shalt not die. Whatsoever thy soul desireth, I will even do it for thee."

"Then let me go," I suggested, "that I may hide myself in the field at least unto the third evening and the morning after. You watch and see if thy father at all misses me. If he does, then say that I asked leave of thee to run to my city of Bethlehem for the yearly sacrifice there for all my family. If he says that it is well and that I shall have peace, I will return to him that same day. But if he be very wroth, then we can be sure that evil is determined by him. Who shall tell me if thy father answer thee roughly?"

"Would not I tell thee?" earnestly responded Jonathan, who'd been bobbing his head with assent all the while I'd been talking. "Do not I love thee as I do my own soul?" I had no doubt Jonathan did love me as he did his own soul, although I wasn't sure what that meant. And I did believe he would do everything feasible to insure my safety. "Tomorrow is a new moon," he began rapidly, outlining a plan of his own, "and thou shalt be missed, we know, because thy seat will be empty. Don't come to my house. Don't even come into the city."

"A lion is in the streets?"

"For you, it may indeed turn out that a lion is in the streets. Abide thou three days in the field in one place or the other. Then thou shalt go down quickly every morning and come to the place where thou didst hide thyself when the business was in hand, and shalt remain by the stone Ezel until the morning I shalt have word for thee and appear."

"Ezel?"

"Yes. Ezel is the one to the south of stone Rogellen. And I will shoot three arrows on the side thereof, as though I shot at a mark. And behold, I will send a lad, saying, 'Go find out the arrows.' Now, if I expressly say unto the lad, 'Behold, the arrows are on this side of thee, take them,' then come thou, for there is peace in thee, and no hurt, as the Lord liveth. But if I say thus unto the young man, 'Behold, the arrows are beyond thee,' go thy way, for the Lord hath sent thee away."

"Say that all again?" I requested, my mind starting to reel.

"Please do it my way," Jonathan asked. He was still struggling for breath and I did not have the heart to oppose him. "Behold, if there be good toward David when I have sounded my father and I then not send unto thee, the Lord do so and much more to Jonathan. But if it please my father to do thee evil, then I will show it thee and send thee away, that thou mayest go in peace."

"I'm not sure I have that one straight either."

"Let's just see what happens with my father at dinner the first night and the second night and the third. I worry so about him when the moon is new."

Jonathan came on the last day at the appointed time. For the third morning in succession, I arose stiffly from another night of fitful sleep, with dead insects drying on my mouth and the rustle of a small animal scratching on fallen leaves nearby. I concealed myself as bidden near the stone Ezel, after I had relieved myself in a patch of stubby brown weeds deep inside the stand of green laurel in which I had cleared my lonely nocturnal burrow. A little lad was with Jonathan. I held my breath to hear better. And Jonathan said unto his lad, in a voice meant to carry, "Run, find out now the arrows which I shoot." And as I peeked out in suspense, I saw the lad run, and I saw Jonathan shoot an arrow far over his head, and I heard Jonathan cry after the lad, and say, "Is not the arrow beyond thee?" I felt my strength fail with the long trajectory of the arrow. Jonathan was one of the very few among us then who had learned how to use a bow. The look of leaden sorrow on his countenance confirmed my grim conviction that my fate had now been sealed beyond any chance of reprieve. I wanted to cry. Jonathan shot two more. A weird and awkward interval occurred after Jonathan's lad had gathered up the arrows and come back to his master. Jonathan looked about in all directions confusedly. We had both forgotten the remainder of the code. Everything came to a clumsy standstill. Giving up, Jonathan handed all his artillery unto his lad and instructed him, "Go carry them into the city." And Jonathan cried after the lad, "Make speed, haste, stay not."

The lad knew not anything. And as soon as he was gone, I arose out of my place toward the south, feeling terrible, just terrible, and I fell on my face to the ground when I reached Jonathan and bowed three times. I knew it was the end, that all hope of effecting the longed-for reunion with his father was over. Jonathan's eyes too were filling with tears when he helped me up, and I could read in his forlorn and agitated look the unmistakable message of my failure and doom. It was then, and only then, that we fell into each other's arms and hugged, that we kissed one another and wept one with the other, until I exceeded him in weeping, and that was the only time. And that's all that we did. Show me proof there was ever more.

Jonathan was voluble with details as he sounded my death knell. On the first day of the new moon, which was the first day of the month by our calendar then, the king sat upon his seat; as at other times, Abner sat by his side, and my place was empty. Saul's glance fixed itself continually upon my empty place that first evening as though he were staring at some baleful omen, but he raised not a question to anyone about my absence. Instead, he murmured aloud that something surely must have befallen me to account for my empty place; perhaps I was unclean, surely that was it, I was not clean. Perhaps I had even lain with my wife. It was a different story on the following day when he saw my place empty again. This time he inquired point-blank of Jonathan why I had not come to meat neither that day nor the day previous. His anger was kindled against Jonathan when he heard the reply I had devised, that I had sought Jonathan out for leave to go to my family to sacrifice in Bethlehem and that Jonathan had given it. And Saul flew into a fury at the knowledge that Jonathan and I had met and that Jonathan had offered nothing about me until asked. What followed was somewhat chaotic. He commanded Jonathan to fetch me unto him forthwith to be slain, cast a javelin at him when Jonathan spoke up in my defense, and then excoriated him in a rambling, incoherent diatribe denouncing his allegiance, his intelligence, and even, incongruously, his maternal parenthood, whereby Jonathan at last knew that it was determined of his father to slay me.

"There was more, David, much more," Jonathan went on, with his stricken look. "He called me an imbecile too, practically. Then he told me I was the son of a perverse, rebellious woman, and that I had chosen to side with you to my own confusion. Half the time I did not know what he was talking about. He added something else that makes no sense to me at all. David, you're smart, maybe you can figure it out. He told me also—this is not easy to say—that I was a confusion to my mother's nakedness."

"A confusion to your mother's nakedness?"

"Do you know what that means?"

"A confusion to your mother's nakedness?" I repeated a second time, to make sure I had heard him aright.

"That's exactly it," Jonathan affirmed. "He told me I had chosen you to my own confusion and unto the confusion of my mother's nakedness. It kept me awake all night."

"What did he mean by that?"

"I asked you."

"It's Greek to me," I was forced to confess. "Jonathan, there's something more that's troubling you. I can tell it by your eyes."

"He also said," Jonathan revealed with great difficulty, glancing away, "that neither I nor my kingdom would be established as long as the son of Jesse was allowed to remain alive on the ground."

In the silence that followed, our eyes met. "That's me."

"I know."

"Do you believe him?"

He was truthful. "I don't know."

I had no weapon. My death had been sanctioned. He could again be a hero. He wore his short sword in a scabbard and a knife in his girdle. He was older than I and much the larger and stronger, and I knew he could have seized me by the hair in his grip and stabbed or slashed me or run me through, as he desired. And I also knew by the look of him that if I had asked him for his sword and his knife, he would have lain both in my hand without question.

We wept again, bursting into tears at the same instant, parting for what we believed to be forever, although we did meet as friends one more time before his death, when he sought me out in my hiding place in the wilderness of Ziph to confide that he too now was sure I would be king over Israel soon and to pledge that he would sit next to me loyally. We made a covenant on that before the Lord, and Jonathan stole back to his house. In my mind during that conversation, and left unmentioned, was the underlying knowledge that his oath, though earnest, was more sentimental than practical, for Jonathan would certainly have to be dead before my accession to kingship could come about. We shook hands on it anyway. We made covenant after covenant also at the tearful leave-taking in the field earlier, pledging eternal amity between him and me, and between his seed and my seed forever, for all that was worth. I know I did look after his only son, who was lamed on both his feet after a panicking nurse dropped him while trying to flee after hearing the news of the great Philistine victory at Gilboa and of the death of Saul and Jonathan both. And again when we wept, Jonathan and I, I exceeded him. I'll admit I exceeded him. Why wouldn't I exceed him? God only knows what *he* was weeping about. I was crying because I had lost everything and was shit out of luck.

A poor man, you may find it written, is better than a liar. Don't you believe it. I've been both. I've even been both at the same time, and it's much better to lie than to be poor. Ask anyone rich, if you don't believe that. After we separated, Jonathan could, as he did when he arose and departed, go back into the city to his house. But what about me? The foxes have their holes, and the birds of the air have their nests, but this son of man, of Jesse the Bethlehemite, had nowhere to lay his head. I could not go home again. Bethlehem in Judah would be the first place Saul would look; and as sure as the night follows day, he would soon have his messengers out scouring the whole country for word of my whereabouts now that he was more convinced than ever that the Lord loved me and that I would succeed him as king if I were permitted to live. His wrath was cruel and his anger outrageous; but who was able to stand before his envy?

I could not depend much on the kindness of strangers, and certainly not of friends and relations. A rich man beginning to fall is held up by his friends, but a poor man being down is thrust away quickly by everyone, by his friends also. Wealth makes many friends, of course, but the poor is separated from his neighbor, and if all the brethren of the poor do hate him, how much more do his friends go far from him? Besides, what friends could I go to? Joab? Abishai? Who can number the sand of the sea, and the drops of rain, and the days of eternity? All of this, though commonplace now and wryly humorous, I found out directly through rigorous personal experience in the months that followed. Not until I was thrown out of Gath by the Philistines and came to rest at last in my hiding place in the cave of Adullam did I find some surcease from sorrow. From gross and gluttonous Nabal in Carmel I got the slap in the face demonstrating that as the proud hate humility, so do the rich abhor the poor. No wonder I grew wise so soon. I was striding with my band to avenge with blood Nabal's demeaning rebuff when Abigail intercepted us with her string of asses bearing the provisions I politely had solicited, and she made humble apology for the arrogant rudeness of her fat husband. Nabal died with relief when he heard how narrowly he had escaped being slain, and I wound up with his wife and a good-sized share of his transportable belongings.

But in between, I could scarcely draw a peaceful breath or enjoy a good night's sleep. I was anathema to anyone who knew me, an outcast hated by the brutal king, a danger to anyone I approached, an accursed stranger in a strange land who could not without mortal risk to everyone in the vicinity walk up to anyone I beheld with the simple plea "Give me, I pray thee, a little water to drink, for I am thirsty." Anyone aiding me even innocently in my solitary struggle to survive would be putting his own life in peril. Look what happened to Ahimelech and the other priests from Nob, and to their families.

So it was to foil expectations and evade capture that, instead of returning south into Judah, I hastened in the opposite direction to the city of Nob for my sword and my breads, told my lies, and left such barbarous and unimaginable destruction in my wake. Noting Doeg the Edomite in Nob brought home to me the desperate seriousness of my plight: my time of free travel in Israel was going to be short. I pretended not to recognize him, but arose as soon as I had rested and I fled that same day for fear of Saul. Any kind of deal we might have struck in those circumstances would have been of little value, for the heart is deceitful in all things. Don't I know that from my own bouts of self-examination? The unexamined life is not worth living, I know. The examined life is? There's just no escaping our original sins, for without committing a single one of the acts for which Saul held me at fault, I was nonetheless guilty of all. In Saul's fevered imagination I wanted his kingdom and his life. Whereas all I really aimed for most days now was a basin of clean water in which to wash my feet and a hot bowl of lentil soup. Many's the time I would have traded my birthright for a mess of pottage.

The fool walks in darkness, but what choice did I have? I reversed my course and headed south. As much as I could, I traveled by night, knowing it was a far, far better thing I was doing skirting the familiar resting places of my native Judah and fleeing downward into the land of the Philistines than I had ever done before. I snatched sleep in wadis for an hour at a time when the weather was dry. In storms I took refuge in limestone caves, listening to the rain lashing down outside in windswept gusts and cropping away like deadly locusts at the soft sides of the natural portals into which I had crawled. One day after the next, glowworms and gecko lizards were the most agreeable of my companions. There was hail, and fire mingled with the hail. Take it from me, the king's wrath is as the roaring of a lion, and Saul's wrath had transmogrified me into a fugitive and a vagabond and had caused me to stink among the inhabitants. You think I was used to living that way? The whole thing was a desolation and an astonishment to me, as though suddenly the earth was again without form, and void, and darkness was upon the face of the deep. I avoided the company of humans. How I remembered and missed the voice of mirth, the sound of the millstones, the light of the candle. I traveled invisibly through tangled thickets of brier on high ground when I did move by day, and crept along paths at night through villages and small towns only when the streets were empty. I stole food, gathered wine and summer fruits from the cellars and orchards of others. Downward and seaward I proceeded doggedly through stony hills, until Judah had been left behind me and the land of the Philistines lay before me like a sanctuary. I felt I had triumphed, although I had only lasted. I was still far from the coast, but I had made it to Gath.

GOD KNOWS

Twice in my long and rather eventful life, I fled to the city of
King Achish of Gath for protection. The first time, he threw me
out. The next, he welcomed me and my small army of six hundred
with open arms, so to speak, and allocated to me his southern
territory of Ziklag to oversee, police, and plunder. This was the
first time. Believe me, when sorrows come, they come not single
spies, but in battalions. It never rains but it pours.

I was spotted within minutes of walking into the first inn I saw
after passing through the gates of the city. I don't know why I was
identified so quickly—we're not allowed to make pictures of each
other and never did. And it wasn't because I looked Jewish. I've
never looked *that* Jewish, and the patrons in the spacious rooms
already included a colorful sprinkling of other Hebrews from vari-
ous places, as well as some Hittites, Midianites, Canaanites, and
other Semites. I was famous, I guess, and probably had been
pointed out in the past to some of the Philistine fighting men present. I was, I will have to grant, already something of a legend in
my own time.

The last thing I wanted was more trouble, especially in Gath.
What I needed most was a bath and a good meal. The catch of the
day at the Philistine inn was water snake and baby eel. I had a beer
and ordered some baked whitefish with prawns and kasha varnish-
kas, and a pork chop with potato pancakes to start. Before any of it
could come, I began to grow uncomfortably aware of a stir of
recognition developing beneath the normal hubbub of the place. I
could see I was the cynosure of conjecture by different small
groups of Philistine soldiers, who pressed closer together and in
upon me with a hunger for information. Was this not David, they
wished to know, first from each other and then from me. Which
David? David who? The David of whom they did used to sing one
to another of him in dances, saying Saul hath slain his thousands,
and David his ten thousands? Was this not that David? Like a
schmuck, I said yes.

Say what you will about the coarse aesthetic insensibilities of the
Philistines; they are of husky physique, and in no time at all they
had me rolled up in a rug and delivered like a bolt of woolen cloth
to the room in which King Achish of Gath sat in a monstrous oak
chair he called a throne. Even as they were unrolling me from the
filthy rug in which I had been bound, they began to reminisce, and
horrible visions of Samson eyeless in Gaza began dancing in my

brain as I listened. They talked of blinding me and then of cutting off my thumbs and my big toes. I laid up these words in my heart and was sore afraid. I was not in a good bargaining position, and could see that in one way or another I would have to change my behavior. So on the spot I decided to put on an antic disposition and stake everything on the effect. Where do you think Shakespeare really got the idea for *Hamlet?*

I began with a song. "When there are gray skies, I don't mind the gray skies, you make them blue, sonny boy," I sang out without warning in the loudest, most melodramatic voice I could produce, riveting everyone in that great timbered hall with amazement.

Philistine doctrine back then insisted that madness was contagious, and subsequent scientific studies have proved this primitive superstition largely correct.

Following up my initial advantage of surprise, I pulled out all the stops. Plunging toward the flabbergasted monarch, I dropped to one knee, grasped his hand in one of mine, and spread my other over my chest in a manner denoting unbearably deep feeling, and I opened wide my jaws as though to go further with my song. Achish pulled back from me as though I were leprous. He bounded out of his throne with a yelp, and I followed as he retreated backward in horror. Poor Achish. I rolled my eyes about full circle in their sockets and regaled him with my very admirable imitation of a Jewish laughing hyena. In all ways I could think of I feigned myself mad in their hands. I scrabbled at the doors of the gate, making canine epileptic noises, and I let my spittle fall down all over my beard. Achish squealed and whimpered in panic each time I made a motion toward him with my arms outspread, as though I were ambitious to afflict him fatally with something catching. He glared wildly at the men who had brought me to him.

"Lo, you see the man is mad!" he berated them, screaming. "Wherefore then have you brought him to me? I am king of Gath. Have I need of *more* madmen that you have brought this fellow to play the madman in my presence? Shall this fellow come to my house? Better he should bring me boils, palsy. Get him out, put him out quickly lest he cast his plague upon all our houses."

I did better than Hamlet with my madness. I saved my life. All he did was carry on precociously and divert attention from the fact that nothing much believable goes on in the play between the second act and the last.

They drove me from the palace and out the gate of the city, beating and prodding me from a hygienic distance with long staves and with the hinder end of their spears.

"Where shall I go?" I bewailed them. "Saul seeks my life."

"Try Gaza," one of them advised conspiratorially, "or even Askelon. But tell it not in Gaza that we put you out. And publish it not in the streets of Askelon. Maybe they will let you in. In Askelon, madmen do not stand out."

I elected not to go to Gaza or Askelon, but to wend my way back into the remote places of Judah and eventually to make my lair in the cave of Adullam. The choice proved a good one ultimately.

But that night I bedded down alone again, in another forsaken place, after I had walked dispiritedly as far from the city as I could go before I tired. I sat myself down on a fallen tree beside a small pool in a wood near the fork in the road. I hung my harp on a willow and wept when I remembered Gibeah, recalled my auspicious beginning and all of the good things in the offing that now seemed out of reach forever. I had never in my life been in lower mood than I was that evening. I wondered where in the world I could go. Adam out of Eden had a more coherent sense of direction than I did and was much better off.

With fresh water from the pond, I washed the spittle from my beard with my bare hands and wiped my face with the sleeve of my dirty cloak, and that's another thing that pisses me off about that stupid statue of Michelangelo's in Florence that's supposed to be me: he's got me beardless, clean-shaven, without a hair on my face —and not only that, he's got me standing there in public stark naked, with that uncircumcised prick! If that Michelangelo Buonarroti had possessed even the dimmest idea of how we Jews felt about nudity then, he never would have put me up there on that pedestal out in the open with my *schlong* hanging down, and with that homely, funny foreskin no self-respecting Jew would let himself be caught dead with. We're not even allowed to go up by steps to the altar, that our nakedness be not discovered thereon. Besides, I was already much too busy when I was that age; I never had time like his David did to stand around all day for centuries doing nothing, with just a sling on my shoulders and no clothes on, not

JOSEPH HELLER

even a loincloth to hide my nakedness, just waiting for something interesting to show up. It may be a good piece of work, taken all in all, but it just isn't me. And besides, if Bathsheba was telling me the truth, I have, or did have, a much bigger dick than he does, even without the funny foreskin. Foreskins are always so funny-looking I'm surprised anyone keeps them. That's the real reason we circumcise; we like to look nice. There's nothing mysterious about it. The statue of me by Donatello in Florence is even worse —a scandal, a sacrilege—but at least they've got that one off the beaten track in the Bargello, where no one important ever goes.

No, what we have from Michelangelo, I'm afraid, is not David from Bethlehem in Judah but a Florentine fag's idea of what a handsome Israelite youth might look like if he were a naked Greek catamite instead of the hardy, ruddy-faced shepherd boy who walked to Shochoh with a carriage of provisions for his three brothers that day and stayed to beat down the detestable boasting of the Philistine giant Goliath.

And that was another melancholy thought crossing my mind that night outside Gath and plaguing me further with a deep sense of unfairness. This was a hell of an unjust spot for the guy who had killed Goliath to find himself in!

Eventually, I slept, and my lashes were stuck together with tears I shed while I slumbered. When I awoke, my head was filled with dew and my locks with the drops of the earth. At once I felt worse. Watching the morn in russet mantle clad creep o'er the hills, I felt my heart die within me as I realized suddenly that just about no one ever mentioned Goliath anymore, neither Philistine nor Israelite, and I began to wonder if the day of my killing him had ever really taken place.

8

IN THE
CAVE OF
ADULLAM

In the cave of Adullam in the outskirts of Judah above the plain of the Philistines, where I climbed by myself to hide out for a while after coming back up from Gath, my fortunes began to take their turn for the better. It was no fun at the start, and the improvement did not occur overnight. I slept on the ground in a worn cloak amid menacing black things changing shape in the darkness, and pondered the phenomenon that man that is born of a woman is of few days, and full of trouble. I watched fireflies for diversion.

As knowledge of my lurking place leaked out and spread, people, to my surprise, began laboring their way up through the steep and barren rock-strewn hills to enlist in my service. They trudged in alone or in groups of two or three, some days faster than I could keep count, arriving to join up with me in an ever-swelling stream. And such people you wouldn't believe! Riffraff. Scum. Ne'er-do-wells. Thugs and ruffians. Everyone that was in distress, and everyone that was in debt, and everyone that was discontented, all gathered themselves unto me, and I became a captain over them. It began to look as though every deadbeat, misfit, rascal, and freebooter in the land was ambitious to throw in with me. I was soon posting sentinels to beat back all but the most formidable and battle-hardened. Those I let stay were durable, fearless, and experienced, for life as fugitive outlaws in the wildernesses of Judah through which we were soon set to roam is not for the timid or the weak or for people who, like all my sons, were spoiled by easy circumstances.

Joab was one of the first to join up with me. He came for the adventure, bringing two more of my nephews, his brothers Abishai and Asahel, with him. The rest of my family sped to me for their lives. Fearing a bloodbath from Saul, all of my brethren and all of the others in my father's house came down hither to me as fast as they could make it when they heard of the stronghold I was establishing in the holes in the walls of the caves of Adullam. Everything left behind was confiscated. I took them in, of course, even my ratty brothers, who were all, I was gratified to observe with the passage of time, destined to lead obscure lives that brought them to the attention of nobody. There were soon with me about four hundred men. We knew the countryside and were fleet of foot. One of the first things I did was put my mother and father out of the way. I traveled west to Engedi and thence across the Dead Sea to Mizpeh in Moab to see if I could place them there with the king for safety, and he did allow them to come forth and dwell with him. The old family tie through my paternal great-grandmother, Ruth the Moabitess, paid off, and I was able to discharge my filial obligations to my parents with good conscience. My father now was doddering with old age, and Moab was as good a nursing home as any in which to divest myself of him and my mother.

As the numbers of my men increased, we made for ourselves the dens which are still found in the mountains and caves and strongholds. In these early stages, Fineberg's law operated greatly to my advantage in my apprehensions about Saul and my foreboding that sooner or later he would set out with thousands to take me. Fineberg's law held that if he could see me where I was hiding, I could see him coming and therefore have time to take whatever steps I deemed appropriate. I could pack and get out of his way. And if the terrain into which he had confined us was hard, bleak, and forbidding, it was also relatively inaccessible and was impregnable to frontal assault and invulnerable to siege. We could simply circle off to the side away from him and give him the slip each time he advanced with his superior numbers. And that's pretty much the way it worked out each time he did come down into the wilderness of Engedi, into the wilderness of Maon, and into the wilderness of Ziph. I was able to elude him easily and there were those two times I had him lying on the ground asleep before me and could have killed him. I made sure he knew it, too.

"Is this thy voice, my son David?" he asked each time, blinking and squinting as though smarting with pain, and wept when he understood I had spared him.

Engedi was funny because Saul traipsed right into the cave in which we were hiding and did not detect our presence. Something similarly farfetched happened to Odysseus with the Cyclops, didn't it? The one time Saul did have us nearly encompassed in the wilderness of Maon, the Philistines obligingly came to my rescue by putting pressure on him elsewhere and compelled him to withdraw to resist them. That was not, you know, the only time that Philistine and I cooperated to the advantage of both. In fact, my only compunction when I went with King Achish to fight for the Philistines against Saul at Gilboa was that I had no compunction. This caused me often to wonder about myself. My dilemma, in retrospect, in going to fight against Saul and my own people is that I had no dilemma. Who asked them to remain obedient to Saul when they already knew he was such a fucking lunatic? I had no dilemma with Uriah, either. Bathsheba was pregnant, he obstinately declined to sleep with her and unwittingly disguise her infidelity, I sent him back to be killed. I gave him two chances, didn't I? Did I kill Uriah to avoid a scandal or because I already had settled in my soul that I wanted his wife? God knows. For not only is the heart deceitful in all things, it is also desperately wicked. Even mine. This danger in being a king is that after a while you begin to believe you really are one.

Fineberg, you know, is capricious, and Fineberg's law ceased operating to my benefit as the size of my private army grew larger. If the craggy region in which we dwelt provided a natural fortress, it was also sufficiently inhospitable to deny the formidable force that developed around me the comforts and luxuries that might have induced us to remain. It was no kind of life. Thus, the day inevitably dawned when it was expedient to roll up our belongings and penetrate farther into Judah from the boundary of the Philistines. We made the move with considerable vim and some trepidation. Faint heart never fucked a cook. Off we went from Adullam to a new site in the forest of Hareth. And next, after due discussion and deliberation, we took our first dynamic step and embarked upon a bold martial venture against a troop of Philistines who had stormed into the Judean town of Keilah and were pillaging the threshing floors.

It was just before we ventured to Keilah that I talked to God for the first time. And He answered. He helped me decide. Back then, He always answered me, and I had no need for a Samuel or a Nathan. I could speak for myself. I was on even better terms with my God, back then, than they ever were. No wonder I grew proud.

I had to learn later that pride goeth before destruction, and a haughty spirit before a fall.

Abiathar, sole survivor of the horrendous massacre of the priests and their households, fled down to me then, holding the sacred ephod of his dead father, high priest at Nob, in his hand. He brought news of the carnage. It dumbfounds me still that others went on serving Saul after that, and that he was always able to muster his three thousand to chase me. Because he was a king? What is a king? I have been a king for forty years and still don't know why people rejoiced to see me, felt sanctified by a word or look from me, why my soldiers cared enough about my life to risk their own to preserve me. I took Abiathar in because his father had died praising me.

"Who is so faithful as David among all thy servants?" his father had said defiantly, defending me to Saul.

To which Saul decreed, "Thou shalt surely die."

"Abide thou with me, fear not," I hastened to assure the young Abiathar, who looked like a ghost and was quailing with fright. "For he that seeketh thy life seeketh my life. With me thou shalt be shielded. I will be an enemy to your enemies and an adversary to your adversaries."

I have kept that promise and want to make certain that my old friend will be secure after I'm gone. Adonijah is no problem, for Abiathar, naïve and orthodox as always, is helpful toward Adonijah and endorses his idea for a big outdoor luncheon on the hill. Bathsheba and Solomon leave me in doubt.

"Be charitable," I observe to the former, "to those who are old and well stricken with age, like Abiathar. Someday, you know, you too will be old."

"Abiathar?" my blonde Bathsheba replies vaguely, and allows the substance of my thought to go right by her while fingering sensuously one of the gold hoop earrings she is wearing.

Solomon is harder work, because he doesn't simulate.

"Shlomo, please pay very close attention to what I'm about to say to you. I have great concern for my priest Abiathar." I find myself pausing with a frown. My son the prince is conscientiously indenting even these prefatory remarks of mine in his tablet of clay. "When I am dead and buried—"

"May you live forever," he breaks in.

"—it will probably fall to your brother Adonijah to be king."

"He is only my half brother," Solomon is punctilious in reminding me.

"Should anything unforeseen betide Adonijah to prevent his becoming king—"

"Yes?" says Solomon, looking up quickly.

"—I would want you to follow to the letter what I say now about Abiathar."

"What could happen to Adonijah to prevent him from becoming king?"

"We are here now to talk about Abiathar," I reprove him. And then I am distracted again by his busyness with his stylus. "Solomon, give me the answer to something that intrigues me. Why do you still write in clay when almost everybody else now uses papyrus?"

"I think I'm getting smart," he says with a nuance of vanity.

"How are you getting smart?"

"Paper rots in our wet weather and the ink always begins to run."

Maybe he is getting smart. I nod sadly. "I worry so much already about all of my scrolls," I admit. "Sooner or later they will spoil, and no one will ever be able to read a word about me after I'm gone. I wish I had taken my words down in clay."

"I take your words down in clay."

"I mean all of my words, even those I say to other people, especially those I've written. My proverbs and my psalms and my other songs."

"Put your scrolls in a cave at Engedi at the Dead Sea," Solomon tells me with a certitude bordering on presumption.

"What are you talking about?" I bridle.

"If you wish to preserve them. That will do it."

"Yeah-yeah."

"They'll last there."

"Never mind."

"I mean it," Solomon insists.

"Have it your way."

"The air is without moisture at the Dead Sea," Solomon goes on, "and your scrolls will last for years if you store them carefully in one of the caves at Engedi."

"Stop talking like a fool," I chastise him when I've had more than I can take. "How can paper last for years? I was telling you. . . ."

"Abiathar," he reads back, in reminder.

"Has been my friend almost all my life." I am annoyed with myself for having allowed him to waste my time. "Through thick and through thin. I want to be at peace concerning him. No matter what ensues after I have given up the ghost, I wish Abiathar to be held guiltless of all things, by you and all others. Do you understand my meaning?"

Solomon nods gravely, as though impressed deeply by the responsibility with which I have just entrusted him. "I understand your meaning."

"What is my meaning?"

"You do not want me to let his hoar head go down in peace to the grave, right?" He is consulting his writing for verification.

Oy vey, I groan silently, and fortify myself with a deep breath. "No, no, no, no, no!" I fairly scream at him. "Are you moronic or something? Can't you get even one thing right?"

Solomon is unshaken by my outburst. "You do want me to kill him, don't you?"

"No, Shlomo," I correct him with a sigh. "I *don't* want you to kill him. There is a difference. Don't you know what guiltless means?"

"No."

"No?" My train of thought, so to speak, is stopped in its track. "You don't know what guiltless means?"

"No," says Solomon.

"Can you figure it out?"

"Hoar head?" he guesses.

"Oh, shit. No, Solomon. Are you sure you are flesh of my flesh and bone of my bone? It will take much to persuade me."

"I don't know what that means," he answers.

"Does the apple ever fall far from the tree?"

"I don't know what that means either."

"Your mother tells me you say that a lot."

"I heard it from you."

"I never said it until I heard it from you."

"I can look it up."

"Look everything up," I direct him emphatically, "because

you've got everything I've been telling you about Abiathar confused with Joab and Shimei."

"Shimei?" He looks blank.

"You forgot already about Shimei?" I am hurt and indignant. "I never told you about Shimei?" I am appalled that he shakes his head. "You really don't know about Shimei? How can that be? How he cursed me and threw filth at me when I was running away from Jerusalem, and how he groveled in the dirt at my feet when I came back triumphant after putting down the rebellion of Absalom? You never heard about Shimei and the rotten things he did to me? Sure I told you about Shimei. I know I told you about Shimei. What the goddamn hell's the matter with you anyway?"

"Tell me again, please," my son requests, poised to write.

"Look it up in your tablets," I reply curtly.

"I've got too many tablets to look anything up in them."

"Who the hell tells you to make them? Answer me truthfully. You really don't know what guiltless means?"

"How should I know what guiltless means?"

"Without guilt, Solomon. Solomon, can't a bright boy like you grasp something like that?"

"Of course I can, once I have it explained to me." He nods briskly. "Now I understand. You do want me to let his hoar head go down in peace to the grave, don't you? Should I or should I not?"

"You should."

His face shows disappointment. "I'll have to redo this whole tablet."

"Just scratch out the word *not.*"

"That does the trick!" He executes the correction with alacrity. "Now, about hoar head?"

"That's not important now," I tell him. "Just remember Abiathar. That's all you have to work on today. Can you remember a simple thing like his name?"

"Of course I can," says Solomon. "Whose?"

"Abishag!"

She walks in beauty like the night of cloudless climes and starry skies, my exquisite Shunammite, and again shows my son Solomon the door. At my request, she brings in Benaiah, of the broad shoulders, deep chest, and strong arms, to whom I reiterate my deathbed bequest of benevolence for Abiathar. Benaiah has kept himself alive, despite the murderous animosity of Joab, of whose lethal jealousy I shrewdly apprised him when I named him to command my palace guard.

"Perhaps you should instruct Nathan as well," Benaiah suggests.

"Nathan," I remark sourly, "is as wise as Solomon."

Benaiah of the broad shoulders, deep chest, and strong arms misses my sarcasm, and another deplorable saying is coined.

I swear I often feel I was much better off in the days when I was struggling to endure and be king than I've been since I became one. Succeeding is more satisfying than success. Believe it or not, God always seemed to reply whenever I talked to Him. I asked a question, He gave me a civil answer, invariably supplying the one I wanted to receive. Our talks went smoothly. He never thundered at me as He did at Moses. He didn't even ask me to take off my shoes. If I wanted to know, I asked. And the first time I asked was before the expedition to Keilah.

A number of my men were balky at that prospect, contending that our survival in Judah was risky enough without revealing ourselves to both Saul and the Philistines in a fashion so provocative to both. The Philistines were making war against the small walled city, and they were not many; the plan to attack them was mine. But I had to be sure, for a failure at the start would mean my immediate finish. I decided to have a crack at talking directly with God. I'd never put much faith in divination by smoke.

"I think I want to mull it over," I made known to those with whom I was in council, and moved off alone to a tree-shaded clearing in the woods. What could I lose? The worst He could do was not say anything. I came right out with it. "Shall I go and smite these Philistines?" I put it to Him bluntly. I was not certain in which direction to look.

And the Lord came through for me. "Go and smite the Philistines," He said unto me at once. "Arise, go down to save Keilah."

"Behold, we are much afraid here in Judah," I informed Him.

"I will deliver the Philistines into thine hand."

I could hardly believe my ears. In a delicious state of elation, I rushed back to the others and proclaimed: "The Lord hath said He will deliver the Philistines into our hand!"

"You talked to God?" They gaped with awe.

"He guarantees it."

So off I went with my men to Keilah and fought with the Philistines, and hocked and *shlugged* them and aggravated them too, until their heads were aching and their bones were breaking and they could not stand it anymore, and we brought away their cattle, and smote them with a great slaughter, saving the inhabitants of Keilah from further oppression and atrocity. We felt like heroes. My men relaxed and celebrated. City life was intoxicating. They smiled incessantly and wanted to stay.

"It's so much better than in the woods," Joab recommended. I was shaking my head. "What's wrong?"

"Saul. How long do you think it will take him to come down after us once he learns we have camped inside a city with walls and gates?"

Joab disagreed. "We can close the gates and lock him out," he argued. "Why not?"

"Fineberg's law."

"Fineberg?"

"If we can lock him out," I elucidated, "he can lock us in. And the men of Keilah?" I went on. "What do you think they are going to do when they hear that Saul seeketh to come to Keilah, to destroy the city for my sake?"

"The men of Keilah?" Joab did not hesitate a moment. "We risked our lives to deliver these people. The men of Keilah are grateful and will be loyal to us."

"Don't bet on it."

"They will stand by us to the end."

"I think I want to mull that one over," I said, and walked off by myself to be alone in the woods again. I could easily picture Saul concluding with glee that God had delivered me into his hand because I had shut myself inside a town that had gates and bars. "Saul," I said to God, coming straight to the point again. I did not want to take up too much of His time. "Will Saul come down to Keilah after me as Thy servant believes?"

"You bet your ass," said the Lord.

"And will the men of Keilah deliver us into the hand of Saul?"

"It's funny you should ask."

"They will?"

"They will deliver thee up."

"Then we'd better get away, right?"

"You don't have to go to college," said the Lord, "to figure that one out for yourself."

Again I went hurrying back with my revelations. "As God is my witness," I announced with urgency, "we must arise and depart from here quickly, for Saul will call his people together for war and come down to Keilah to besiege us here."

So we arose out of Keilah and went whithersoever we could go, and Saul sought us every day. By this time my men had increased to about six hundred. Saul never had less than three thousand. We abode for a while in strongholds in a mountain in the wilderness of Ziph. We moved as well through the wilderness of Maon and the wilderness of Engedi. All are regions of the wilderness of Judah, and it is sometimes difficult for outsiders to tell the individual wildernesses apart. Ziph is near Ziph, Engedi is near Engedi, and the wilderness of Maon surrounds Carmel, where I found Abigail married to Nabal and took my first real woman as my first true wife right after her unmannered pig of a husband died. I did not wait long to propose after I heard she was widowed. Maybe a minute.

It was in a wood in the wilderness of Ziph that Jonathan sought me out to assure me forthrightly of his faith that his father would not find me because I was favored by God and that he saw too now that I would surely be king over Israel in due time.

"From your mouth," I responded with a piety equaling his own, "to God's ears."

He was talking more from feeling than demonstrable fact, but I was glad to hear him anyway, and was not put off by his choked voice and the density of emotions he was manifesting. Neither one of us could know that this was fated to be our last meeting: he would be killed at Gilboa, with me almost on the opposite side, and never enjoy seeing his prophecy fulfilled.

"And I shall serve thee and be next unto thee," he continued solemnly in a vow that events rendered moot, his eyes staring downward with a kind of demoralized humility. "Fear not the hand of my father, for thou shalt be king, and that also my father knoweth. It's the reason he's so confused and unhappy. He doesn't like me, David. He's never really liked me. He would have had me killed after I did so well at the battle of Michmash. Just because I ate the honey, he said, but I believe it was because he was jealous. The people rose up as one to save me. But then, my father has never really liked any of his children. You were the one he seemed to love briefly as the only person who would never disappoint him and never fail at anything. Maybe that's the reason he fears you now and wants to kill you."

"According to him, I'm supposed to want to kill him."

"He isn't sane, David. At Michmash, he wanted to fight them head-on. He still wants to fight them head-on. I think my father never wants anyone to succeed him, and hopes to take all the rest of us to death along with him. At Michmash, I felt I had to do something to stop him. That's why I stole away at night with my armor bearer to try my luck up that twisting path in the mountains to the Philistine outpost. It was a stony, steep trail," he went on, "and I couldn't mount it quickly. I found myself between a sharp rock on the one side and a sharp rock on the other."

He gambled on making known his presence to the enemy sentries, representing himself as a local Israelite who'd hidden in a cave and who now begged permission to return to his own poor house in the wilderness.

"If they allow us to go up," he had whispered to his armor bearer, "we will go up. I will take my spear and hope that the Lord hath delivered them into our hand. If they don't, they don't. We'll go back to the camp. Nothing ventured, nothing gained."

Contemptuously, derisively, they allowed him to come up, prepared to hector him as he passed through and perhaps pull his beard. "Behold, the Hebrews come forth out of the holes where they had hid themselves," they called to each other. "Come up, come up to us, and we will show you a thing or two."

Better for them they should have bitten off their tongues. About twenty of them in a half acre Jonathan slew before they began to comprehend his ruse. Fleeing survivors, believing him the vanguard of a large encirclement, spread chaos in the main camp with their exaggerated reports. Rumor was rampant and pandemonium reigned. By dawn's early light the watchmen of the Israelites beheld the Philistines beating down one another and the multitude melting away in headlong retreat. Saul took advantage of the opportunity with an order to charge, then loused things up with a senseless pledge to God that appeared to be aimed vindictively at Jonathan.

"Cursed be the man that eateth any food until evening," was the harebrained order of the day Saul decreed, having called the roll by then and learned full well that it could be only Jonathan who had started the ball rolling, and that Jonathan, who had not yet returned, would be uninformed of the ban.

Faint from fasting, the Israelites had to leave off pursuing their enemies before the day was ended. They flew upon the spoils of sheep, oxen, and calves, slew them to the ground, and ate them with the blood. Saul disapproved of that. Jonathan returned with his eyes enlightened by the taste of honey he had taken in the wood. He was critical of Saul's prohibition against eating food when he saw how it had interfered with the much greater slaughter among the Philistines that could easily have ensued. Grimly and methodically, Saul embarked on his merciless course of revenge against him. He cast lots in a process of elimination. The tribe was narrowed down to Benjamin, the family to his own, the culprit then to Jonathan.

"I did but taste a little wild honey with the end of my rod," Jonathan admitted affectingly, "and lo, for this I must die?"

"For this," Saul answered with a shrug, as though washing his hands of responsibility, "thou shalt surely die, Jonathan."

But the people knew that it was Jonathan who had wrought this great salvation in Israel that day, and they would not allow one hair of his head to fall to the ground. They rescued him that he died not, and they kept him safe until the resentment of his father had subsided.

"He was envious of me," Jonathan confided. "He was envious of me for the part I had played. He never really trusted or liked me after that. It was his way of getting rid of me. We could see his temper blazing in his eyes. When I understood he really meant to kill me, I realized something. My father the king was mad. And then I realized something worse. The Lord my God was also mad. And when I realized that, I began to weep. My heart was broken, and I did not care."

I gave thanks to God that Jonathan did not weep then. Jonathan did love me, I know now, and I did not love him. And I know that doesn't feel good.

I know because I love Bathsheba and she does not love me. I loved my son Absalom, and he would have killed me if he could, and would have been able to had he set right out to overtake me instead of procrastinating complacently after listening to the counsel of the secret agent I left behind to flatter and mislead him. Yet I

GOD KNOWS

could not kill Saul when I had the chance. It takes all kinds to
make a world, doesn't it? Looking back, I find myself contrite that
I was not more openhearted in my remarks to Jonathan at what
proved to be our final meeting. I was rather cold, imperious. How
could I know he was going to die? Of all sad words of tongue or
pen, the saddest are these: it might have been.

I had those two good chances for killing Saul. My first in the
cave of Engedi, amid the sheepcotes upon the rocks of the wild
goats, when Saul came in to relieve himself where we were hiding
and stretched out on the ground to cover his feet. I could have
killed him just for shitting there. Instead, my heart was wrung by a
nauseating mixture of pity and dread when I found the opportunity
to obtain his death so close at hand, and I let him go.

"The Lord delivered him right into your hand," charged Abishai
after Saul had gone. "Why would you not let me smite him with
my spear even to the earth at once? I would not have had to smite
him a second time."

I responded simply. "I thought he reminded me of my father as
he slept."

"Grandpa Jesse doesn't look like Saul at all," Abishai argued
sullenly.

I decided to let the matter drop. It was always casting pearls
before swine to try to reason from sentiment with the three hard
sons of my sister Zeruiah, or with any of the rough six hundred
who were with me then. Uriah the Hittite, then unwed, was among
those six hundred that far back, and was even one of my thirty
mighty men. When all my civil strife was over and won, I rewarded him liberally with an extended estate in the south to culti-
vate for his pleasure and to safeguard as an outpost. Who asked
him to choose a libidinous wife with the hots for Jerusalem? Is it
my fault she took a shine to me after he succumbed to her insis-
tence and agreed to move here? I should have warned him; I could
have told him by then that it is better to dwell with a lion or a
dragon than to keep house with a wicked woman, for I had already
reclaimed my wife Michal from Phalti and she was living with me
in my palace and buzzing all about me like a hornet. As the climb-
ing up a sandy way is to the feet of the aged, so is a wife full of
words to a quiet man. What was a horny young king like me to do
when a radiant treat like Bathsheba laid it all out for me to see that
eveningtide from the roof of my royal residence? I did what any

normal, virile tyrant would do. I saw her, I sent for her, I lay with her, and as simple as that was the imperceptible drift into the turbulent and depressing second half of my life, with its succession of tragedies for which virtually nothing I had undergone had prepared me. By the time I was sixty, I had lost my capacity for experiencing joy, and the years had drawn nigh when I could say I had no pleasure in them. .

I could say that the Devil made me do it. The Devil always comes in handy that way, doesn't he?

Everything was so much easier back there with Abigail; all slipped conveniently into place with an easiness wondrous to behold as we met and came together in those footloose, carefree years of banditry and extortion in the wilds of southern Judah. The substance of me and my men grew with our reputation. We took wives. I took Abigail as soon as she was available, which was about two weeks after I met her. That worked so well that, with Abigail approving, I took Ahimoam too a little later on. A man cannot have too many wives when he is on the move a great deal and there is so much housework to be done. All of them can pitch in.

How did we live?

We lived off the land. Or rather, we lived off the landowners, which is a different thing entirely. That's how I found Abigail.

"Give us food and clothing," I or one of my men would suggest to inhabitants of the region having the largest flocks of sheep and goats, the lushest vineyards and largest groves of olive, fig, date, and nut trees, the broadest, longest fields of wheat and barley, of melons, lentils, flat beans, garlics, and onions, "and we will make it our business to see that no one steals from you even one sheep."

"Who would steal from us a sheep?" they were naïve enough to ask.

"Who knows?" After a long pause I would go on. "But I, David the son of Jesse the Bethlehemite, will protect you from robbery and arson by thieves and plunderers. I and my men will be a wall unto you both day and night."

"There are no thieves and plunderers in Judah," they did answer at first.

"There are now."

I would give this reply without smiling, looking grimly into the face of each landowner I addressed. It was really no mystery to me that the people of Ziph in my native Judah came up often to

Gibeah to Saul, saying where my hiding places were and volunteering to deliver me into the king's hand if he came down after me. Any sense of hurt I may have expressed was synthetic.

Only from a fat slob like Nabal, the husband of my precious Abigail, did I meet with discourteous refusal and decide upon the very violent consequences that were averted narrowly by the prompt diplomacy of the stunning woman herself. Abigail was a woman of exceptional understanding and of a beautiful countenance. As Nabal's wife, she was a jewel of gold in a swine's snout. Didn't I ask him first in a very nice way? I sent ten young men to him with polite solicitations and with discreet reminders that we had not hurt any of his shearers or his shepherds, nor was there aught missing among them all the while we were in Carmel. His shepherds would vouch for the fact that the whole year through I steadfastly had protected him from us.

But the man was an utter boor, and he coarsely rejected the appeal of my messengers that he share with us a small amount of the prosperity we so earnestly wished to be able to allow him to continue to enjoy. Nabal was known by everyone as churlish and evil in his doings, as a potbellied glutton and drunkard who did not appreciate or deserve so fine a wife as the woman who rode out to greet us the following day when I and four hundred were walking with rapid stride to kill not only him but every living thing in his household.

"Who is this David that I owe him anything?" he rashly ridiculed my men in front of his own, eager to return to his gorging and roistering at the feast of the sheepshearing in which he was just then indulging himself with a complete lack of restraint. He mocked my men in their noses with a snap of his fingers. "Who is this son of Jesse? Is he the king, or even a servant of the king, that I must cater to him? A fig for your David—no, not even a fig, not one fig for your David. Ha, ha!"

God knows I was incensed when my messengers acquainted me with the rude fashion in which my modest proposal had been dismissed. I never could bear having emissaries of mine demeaned. When Hanun the son of Nahash of Ammon defiled the people I had sent in peace to help comfort him on the death of his father, I could not rest until I had exacted my revenge. He shaved off the one half of the beards of my messengers, and cut off their garments in the middle even to their buttocks, before he released them to return to me with their asses hanging out. I made war against all the cities of Ammon after that; from one year to the next, I did not let up until the last fortress was overthrown and all the people of Ammon were put under saws, and under harrows of iron, and under axes of iron, and were made to pass through the brick kiln, and their king's crown, the weight whereof was a talent of gold with the precious stones, was taken from off his head and set upon my own. And even then I did not feel wholly appeased. All of that was very much later, when I was already a mighty king, but it was with no less monumental a rage that I determined to avenge Nabal's insult in the only way I knew how, and began firing orders for my men to make ready for battle.

"Come not at your wives this night," I began with a shout.

"We're going to war?"

"Against Nabal of Carmel."

"No shit?"

"And no shit either. I want no one unclean. Gird ye on every man his sword."

I don't kid around. At daybreak, I girded on my sword and set out toward Carmel leading four hundred of my men, leaving two hundred others behind to abide by our stuff.

Luckily I never got there. Luckily, Abigail, alerted by one of the young men in her husband's employ to the danger provoked so needlessly, had busied herself to help make amends and atone for the sin against me committed by her husband. I never knew a woman more practical. She took two hundred loaves, and two bottles of wine, and five sheep already dressed, and five measures of parched corn, and a hundred clusters of raisins, and two hundred cakes of figs, and laid them all on asses. She told not a word to her husband Nabal about what she was doing and rode out to meet us with five pretty damsels who were her servants.

I'm glad she did, for more reasons than one. In the long run, it probably would have redounded strongly to my disadvantage if I had pursued to completion my resolution not to leave alive any in Nabal's house that pissed against the wall.

We were all of us on foot. Forget about horses—we didn't have any, and no one anywhere then knew how to ride them. Abigail had rouged her cheeks and lips, made up her eyes, and brushed and tied her dark hair. She had attired herself in a robe and mantle of brilliant desert scarlet. I brought my march to a halt when I saw a string of asses bearing provisions come into view against the bright sky and move down by the covert of the hill to meet us. I did not know who she was until after she had arrived and dismounted and announced herself.

We had never seen each other before. She had not dreamt I was good-looking. I did not know she was beautiful. I think you could have heard a pin drop there on the road to Carmel as she hasted the final few yards on her animal, lighted off the ass, fell before me on her face at my feet, and bowed herself to the ground.

She prayed I would hear her words and beseeched me to restrain myself from shedding blood. She begged my pardon repeatedly. She was older than I, dear woman, and clearly more knowing and cosmopolitan and, from her place on her knees, she stared upward at me after the first few moments with an unwavering look of frank admiration. A gleam in her eye made no secret of what she thought of me. We were close enough to touch. For the longest time I could not move my gaze from her face. Then I could not take my eyes off her tits. I felt my member harden and begin to stand out. Abigail noticed it all, she confided a fortnight later when we were lying together as man and wife in one of the several good goatskin tents she had included in the dowry she had brought from the estate of her newly deceased husband. She was too much the lady to give any indication at the time. And besides, she was pleading for her life and, though she could hardly be certain, for the lives of all in the house of Nabal as well. Ten years later, I was struck for the second time in my life with that same dumbfounding thunderbolt of passionate love, when I looked into a bathtub on a roof a half block away and saw Bathsheba, assisted by a servant girl with an azure water pitcher, rinsing her pale and rosy voluptuous body with her head turned brazenly in my direction.

Who ever loved that loved not at first sight? The setting was not as pictorially romantic as it might seem. Her building was low and deteriorated, the space on top littered and cramped. Good housing was already difficult to come by in Jerusalem, and even the roof of my own palace was, as usual, cluttered with figs, dates, and flax set out to dry, along with the family wash strung out on ropes. I had to pick my way along narrow lanes in the relaxing, cooling strolls I took each evening to escape the stenches and stale heat below and the obstreperous, interminable disagreements with Michal and perhaps a few of my other wives. Ahinoam, Maccah, and Haggith were perfect mates—they hardly talked at all, and when they passed away, they attracted barely any notice. Abigail I still miss. I always loved her. Nevertheless, my mouth watered the moment I laid eyes on Bathsheba: she looked to me like peaches and cream, and the mounds of her tiny breasts were tipped with the colors of wild raspberries or fresh currants.

"What woman is that?" I wanted to know.

It was Bathsheba, the daughter of Eliam, the wife of Uriah.

I sent for her anyway and lay with her that same day, for she had finished her bath and was purified from her uncleanliness. Not that the opposite condition would have given either one of us any pause. I could tell within minutes after we began that I had got me a woman with sexual experience considerably more varied than my own. And even while finding her fruits so sweet to my taste, I began to detest the men from whom she had learned, to envy bitterly the very, very many who had enjoyed her and made versatile use of her in the more artless periods of her girlhood when she still looked up to people and it still was possible to impress and surprise her with something different, something new or better. I felt basely overshadowed by them. All I could offer was love. It was with a combination of gladness and dismay that I told myself I had taken a tigress by the tail I would be happy to be rid of and whom I would also feel, hopelessly, I could not live without. I would follow her on bleeding feet. I would follow her as weeping Phalti did my wife Michal when I demanded her back as a preliminary to negotiations.

I was less autocratic with Abigail, and she was more deferential, though I was not yet king. I was bewitched by her eloquence and reserve, by her lustrous grooming and her refinement and dignity.

"Upon me, my lord, upon me let this iniquity be," she humbly began from her place on the ground at my feet. "I pray thee, hear the words of thine handmaid."

It wasn't always clear to me *whose* life she was seeking to save, for she seemed to be condemning Nabal along with all the rest of my enemies. But she gave me her blessing and entreated me to leave the matter of vengeance to heaven sooner than shed blood myself in an enterprise that might bring grief unto me afterward. Abigail always made sense. And she was another in the growing roster of those foreseeing that someday soon the Lord would appoint me ruler over Israel.

"From your mouth," I replied with regal courtesy, dipping my head in assent, "to God's ears. Blessed be the Lord God of Israel," I went on with warmth, "which sent thee this day to meet me. And blessed be thy advice, for in very deed, as the Lord God liveth, if thou hadst not come to meet me, surely there had not been left unto Nabal by the morning light any that pisseth against the wall." I accepted from her the goods she had brought and bestowed upon her the reassurances she had come for. What a nice love story, I thought. I had never met a woman for whom I had a higher regard. "See, I have hearkened to thy voice. Go up in peace to thine house."

It was with a pang that I watched her take leave, an aching sense of unfair deprivation with which I watched her remount and ride away back to her husband with the good news that killed him about ten days later. Joab was studying me sharply. I gave a start of uneasiness.

"What's wrong?" I inquired, fidgeting.

"Why were you lisping?" he demanded angrily.

"Lisping?" I was baffled. "Who was lisping?"

"You were."

"When?"

"Before."

"Lisping?" I repeated in disbelief. "What are you talking about? I wasn't lisping. I never lisp."

"You said pisseth, didn't you?"

"Pisseth?"

"That'th right. You thaid all who pisseth against the wall."

"I thaid pisseth?" I was furious now and answered him with a heat that equaled his own. "I thaid no thuch thing."

"Yeth, you did. Athk anyone."

"Let'th get these provisions moving, Joab, before they thpoil in the sun. I command thee. Pisseth? Indeed!"

He gave ground grudgingly. "I wish she'd brought more."

It ith—it is a source of continual amazement to me that Joab, despite the lifelong antagonism simmering between us, has never once betrayed me, although I was certain he had switched sides the night I abandoned Jerusalem to escape the converging forces of Absalom. Where was he? I felt that night that I had spent half my life running from Saul and the other half fleeing my son and his allies. I still remain unconvinced that Joab was not in league with him at the beginning and broke with him afterward. Against my wishes, he murdered Abner, he murdered Amasa, he executed Absalom as he hung by his head from the boughs of that oak tree by which he had been caught up. For this last, I have never been able to forgive him, although he did me an extraordinary favor by doing so. How could I possibly have spared the life of a beloved child when loyal soldiers had laid down their own lives to prevent him from killing me? Yet how could I have taken it?

But ever since, I have been waiting for Joab to make that one mistake that would give me sufficient public reason to take off his head. I would like to hear a national outcry against him. He may be committing that blunder now when he staunchly befriends my eldest son, Adonijah, and encourages his preparations for that outdoor feast they wish to give. Do they intend to proclaim Adonijah king? There is a significant difference between saying he will be king and declaring he is. Bathsheba snitches to me that Joab has already recommended a caterer for the affair, his wife's brother. And Joab was the one who, with criminal motive or not, induced me to bring back into the city the one thing in the world I wanted most to have near—that same son Absalom.

Go figure out that one. In no time at all, it seemed, Absalom was setting fire to Joab's barley field. I grinned with pride in my audacious son as I listened to doughty Joab complain like a milksop.

"He says he will set fire to all my fields if I do not come and plead with you to let him see you. It's been two years now, David. Why did you allow him to return from exile if you did not wish him to see your face?"

"Why did you urge me to?"

"Don't you want to look at him and talk to him again?"

My heart broke, and I relented and lifted the order of banishment keeping him from my presence, and I did at long last allow Absalom to come into my house. I kissed him when I saw him. I took him in my arms and held him and burst into tears before he even began to justify himself for the slaying of his brother Amnon. I never even forced him to beg my forgiveness. I put him to work as my surrogate, to deal with people with complaints for which I had no patience. Once again he was the apple of my eye.

And in no time at all, it seemed, the apple of my eye was sweeping toward Jerusalem in a whirlwind of fire and in chariots of fiery horses, and I was fleeing my city with my large household as rapidly as I could move. How was he able to mount so large a rebellion so swiftly and fiercely? Why did he want to?

It was not the best of times, I'll admit, but was it the worst? I could not believe he had come so far so fast without the subversive connivance of powerful people very close to me. And I was right. Amasa, my nephew by my other sister, was captain of his host. Ahitophel, the shrewdest and most stoically pragmatic of my advisers, turned traitor too. And I could not drive from my mind that it was Joab, of all people, who had importuned me to terminate the banishment of Absalom and grant him the amnesty allowing his return. As I wended my way downward in a descent that seemed to correspond symbolically to my loss of powers, I saw Joab waiting behind every bush, like a bear.

So surprising it was for this man impervious to all sentimental feelings to read my heart so accurately and take the trouble to intervene that way. It wasn't like him at all. It was, in fact, the only time in our long lives that he made proper obeisance to me as a king, another galling detail that keeps my hunches about him operating even now. I still believe it was the incident of the barley field that divided him from Absalom. Joab does not forgive indignities easily.

He enlisted the aid of the wise woman of Tekoah to play on my emotions in his stratagem for Absalom's return. He dressed her in widow's weeds and sent her in to me with a dolorous cock-and-bull story of family murder and flight paralleling my own distressful tragedy so closely that she was able to turn the charitable verdict I rendered into a moral for resolving my own dilemma. I nearly jumped out of my skin when I heard her say: "Wherefore then doth the king not fetch home again his own banished son? For we must needs die and are as water spilt on the ground, which cannot be gathered up again."

I have never liked parables. "Who put you up to this?" I wanted to know.

Joab was soon on the scene to advocate openly. "Oh, David, David, why be so foolish? Bring him back, bring him back. It's clear you miss him. You're a king. You can do whatever you want."

"He broke a law." I heard quavers in my voice. I could not handle that subject without emotion. "He committed a crime."

Joab was almost patronizing. "There are no laws. This is Joab,

David. No laws are legitimate. And there is no such thing as crime."

"God's laws?"

"God's laws," he echoed cynically.

"Thou shalt not kill?"

"We kill all the time."

"Thou shalt not kill thy brother?"

"He was only a half brother. And where is that written? Cain killed Abel, and didn't God give him a seal of protection? And what difference does it make, if you miss him? Do what you want. David, David, life is short. We shall all return to the dust, even you. Bring him back. Why make yourself suffer? Do I talk to you often about things like this?"

"You can't stand to see me suffer?" I guessed.

"I can stand to see you suffer," he contradicted me calmly. "I just don't like to see a sad king. I never liked Saul. If a king be sad, what little is there left for anyone to hope for? Shall I go to Geshur and bring him?"

"Go." I gave in gladly at the end with a tremendous wave of relief. "Go to Geshur and bring the young man Absalom home again. Let him be as safe as Cain. But let him turn to his own house, and let him not see my face. I can't give him all."

Then it was that Joab fell to the ground—the only time in the forty years I've been king that he did so—and bowed himself and thanked me, saying, "Today thy servant knows I have found grace in thy sight." Who would have supposed that he even thought of himself as my servant?

"Make clear to him also," I added, dropping my voice discreetly as a cue to him, "in a whisper into his ear, so that nobody about will know, that I am sorry. Tell him I apologize. I should have punished Amnon some way after he did what he did, but I still wouldn't know how. Amnon was my child also."

Bet your bottom dollar Joab would have known how. What business was all this of his anyway?

My son Absalom was the talk of the town as soon as he was back, and I waxed with pride in the adulation I knew he was receiving. I longed to see him in the two years I permitted him so near, yet kept him away. I thrived on every piece of information about him. In all Israel there was none to be much praised as Absalom for beauty. From the sole of his foot even to the crown of his head there was no blemish on him. And when he polled his head at every year's end—it was only at year's end that he polled it, for by then the hair was long and heavy on him—he weighed the hair at two hundred shekels, that's more than five pounds of hair. Even with the ointment factored out, that's still a pretty good head of hair. Many's the time I yearned to look upon him and deplored the injunction of separation I had imposed. Absalom prepared him chariots and horses and fifty men to run before him to clear the streets when he rode. No one thought much of Adonijah then, who is but a pallid copy now. Solomon? Ignored. And before you knew it, Absalom was setting Joab's barley field on fire. I must admit I laughed.

"That's Absalom," I commented to Joab, with a happy lift of my arms, and consented to the full reconciliation I craved with the son I now pardoned.

And before you knew it, I was arising with those I could take with me who wanted to come, and fleeing the city lest he find me there and smite Jerusalem with the edge of the sword to capture me. He was humping my concubines. It was with as much incredulity as umbrage that we heard how, in a tent spread for him upon the top of my palace, he went in unto the ten women I had left behind to keep the house.

"On the same day?" I exclaimed with amazement. "All ten?"

"That's what they say."

"But those were my ten worst concubines!"

"That's Absalom," they exclaimed with indulgence.

"It would have taken me a whole year."

It did not seem altogether believable to me that someone so ruthlessly direct as Joab would scheme so ploddingly in his supplication affecting the split between a father and the only one of his children for whom he truly felt love. I have no real evidence that he did. But where was he, I brooded fearfully as I abandoned the city with those who were faithful to me and made my way first to brook Kidron at the edge of Jerusalem. From there I went up barefoot by the ascent of the Mount of Olives to weep with my head covered and to try to take stock of my disastrous predicament. Trumpets proclaiming Absalom king had sounded all over the land, in the south and in the north. My Cherethites and Pelethites were with me. So was Ittai the Gittite, bless his heart, that man without a homeland now, and he brought with him the six hundred mercenaries who had come up with him from Gath after I had subdued and dispersed the Philistines. And Abishai was along with a regiment, muddling with still greater confusion my doleful speculations about Joab. I no sooner had escaped Jerusalem from Absalom than I found myself exposed as I passed Bahurim to the loathsome vituperations of that obscene and obnoxious baboon Shimei, who, red-eyed and red-gummed, subjected me to a tirade of such verbal abuse as I had never been exposed to before. Another bad-tempered Benjamite he was—Sheba, who blew a trumpet to call all Israel to renounce me after I had triumphed over Absalom, was still another intractable Benjamite prick who wanted to make trouble for me. I had to send men all the way north to Abel of Bethmaachah to kill Sheba, and Joab killed Amasa at the start in order to put himself in charge of that assignment himself. I had to restrain my men from killing Shimei.

"Thou bloody man, come out, come out," that Shimei howled and jeered at me with vicious glee. "The Lord hath returned upon thee all the blood of the house of Saul in whose stead thou hast reigned."

What blood? What house of Saul? What was he talking about? And Absalom—he was not bloody? Oh, what a fall was there, that I should have to listen to this from him! He threw stones at me, that Shimei, that revolting jackal. He cast dust on my head. For a famous absolute monarch who, but a week before, was disposed to view himself in the polished mirror of his fancy as uncritically revered, the shocks and insults of which I now unexpectedly found myself the target were almost too grotesque to comprehend.

My nephew Abishai was incensed. "Why should this dead dog curse my lord the king?" he said with livid face. "Let me go across the road, I pray thee, and take off his head."

I put a hand on his arm and said no. "Let him curse," I answered solemnly. "Behold, my son Absalom, which came forth of my bowels, seeketh my life. How much more cause now may this Benjamite have to do it?"

"No cause, no cause," said Abishai.

Where would Shakespeare have been without me? At a brick mold, maybe, or a potter's wheel. Who was it that loved not wisely but too well? Me and Bathsheba, or Othello and that wop? It's not for nothing that I was known as the sweet singer of Israel. I even made up that name.

And of what crimes against the house of Saul was he accusing *me*, David, the boy wonder, who had never raised a hand against my king or any in his family and in whose mouth it had long been said that butter would not melt?

"Fry, lechery, fry," he cackled shrilly like a man possessed.

True, I had killed Uriah, but that was about all. And who the fuck was a repulsive gnome like Shimei to speak for God to me, when I had always been much closer to Him than anyone else in my time? And feel I still am, even though I think He may not be here anymore, and will not lower myself to speak to Him again until He eats crow like a man and apologizes like a decent human being for what He did to my dead baby. Who else but me can ever justify the ways of God to man? The good Lord hasn't got a Chinaman's chance of surviving with His reputation intact if He leaves it to toadies like Nathan, who came sniveling up to me again after Shimei had stopped throwing stones and had been left behind. God talks to Nathan, Nathan says, but He doesn't always talk sense, if you're going to believe what Nathan tells you He talks about.

Nathan had been grumbling in his beard about me from the beginning, holding me responsible for everything bad that was occurring. As though I didn't already have enough troubles on my mind without him. We bickered and snapped at each other constantly, like two old farts near senility. Nathan doesn't like to walk. Now he blamed me for Shimei.

"Maybe the Lord has bidden him to do it," I told him without looking up. "You know, Nathan, there is a time to gather up stones, and a time to cast away stones."

My words did not impress him. "There be three things that go well," he informed me in his sulky way, straying off on a tack of his own.

"What are you bitching about now?"

"Yea, four are comely in going."

"How many guesses do I have?"

"A lion which is strongest among beasts, and turneth not away for any."

"Go on."

"A greyhound."

"That's a good one."

"A he-goat also."

231

JOSEPH HELLER

"That's three."

"And a king against whom there is no rising up." He glanced at me smugly, smacking his lips.

"Nathan, Nathan, what are you trying to tell me?" I asked when he had finished. "The finding out of parables is a wearisome labor of the mind."

"My feet hurt."

"Your feet hurt?"

"Yes."

"Is that all?"

"Can't we stop?"

"We can't stop. Why couldn't you come right out and tell me your feet hurt? Do you always have to be so long-winded?"

"Does the rain have a father?"

"Another abstract question?"

"Or the lion roar when it hath no prey?"

"Nathan, my world is coming down around me in flames. Can't you give me a simple yes or no?"

"From a prophet you want a yes or no?"

"It's not possible?"

"Does the elephant go with the raven?"

"Must you always be such a pain in the ass?"

"There are three things that are never satisfied," Nathan rejoined. "Yea, four things say not, it is enough. Maybe five, even six."

"The sixth would be a prophet like you with a listener like me."

"My arches ache. My toes have blisters."

"Do us both a favor. Go down ahead and ride on one of the asses."

"I'm afraid I'll fall off."

"Get someone to hold you."

Nathan chewed a moment on the inside of his cheek. "And I don't want to be near that slut."

"What slut?"

"Your wife."

"Which wife?"

"You're not going to trap me. You know which wife," he challenged. "You just want me to name her so you can take off my head because I know it's all your fault. You should have listened to me. You should have done exactly what I told you, to the letter."

232

"You didn't tell me to do anything until it was already too late. How could I listen to you?"

"You should have listened anyway," Nathan insisted. "You should have guessed. That sounds mysterious? I'll show you mysterious. There be three things which are too wonderful for me, yea, four which I know not. I'll tell you what I don't know. The way of an eagle in the air; the way of a serpent upon a rock; the way of a ship in the midst of the sea; and the way of a man with a maid. There, I said it, didn't I?"

"What did you say? What are you getting at this time?"

"Why did you have to keep fucking Bathsheba?"

"Did you tell me to stop?"

"Did I know this would happen?"

"You're a prophet, aren't you?"

"Not a fortune-teller. I only know when I'm told. And it's all coming true, isn't it?" he gloated. "Everything I warned you about, the evil rising up against you from your own house, the neighbor with your wives in the sight of the sun. I was right, wasn't I? You wait. You just wait and see what Absalom does with those women you left behind."

"Is this what you meant?" I answered him back. "Why didn't you come right out and tell me you were talking about Absalom?"

"How did I know I was talking about Absalom? You shouldn't have taken Uriah's wife and you shouldn't have slain him with the sword of the children of Ammon, and that's all there is to that."

"Why didn't you tell me that before I did it?"

"How did I know you were going to do it? And there are certain things you're supposed to know for yourself. Did I know you were going to send Uriah back to be killed? I had to be told, didn't I?"

"By who?" I questioned, levying upon him the full weight of my suspicions. "Joab?"

"Joab?" He gaped at me as though I had taken leave of my senses. "Don't be foolish. You know by who. God. Where does Joab come in?"

"Where is Joab?" I regarded him closely.

"Do I know?"

"Is he out there ahead somewhere, waiting to ambush us?"

"God forbid!" Nathan cried out, almost screaming. His face turned ashen. "It's all your fault," he resumed berating me, and paused to sniffle and to choke down a sob. "It will be on your conscience if anything happens to me. I blame only you, only you."

"For three things, Nathan, the earth is disquieted," I told him harshly, running out of patience at last. "And for four which it cannot bear. For a servant when he reigneth, and a fool when he is filled with meat. For an odious woman when she is married, and a handmaid that is heir to her mistress. And worse than all four, put together, is a blubbering nuisance like you filled with whimpers and recriminations at a catastrophic time like this. Do you think I can worry about you? Go get more curses from God. Abishai! *Abishai!*"

I had Abishai transfer him far away from me to the front of our pathetic column, well out of earshot and closer to Bathsheba, whom he'd vilified as a harlot, and with whom he is now in league. Misery makes strange bedfellows. I was sorry at last that Michal was dead. I would have relished placing him between the two of them. I began to torment myself with worries about Joab again. And I began to worry about his brother Abishai as well, suspecting him too of potential treachery.

Crazy as Saul in his deranged fixations about me, I was more and more certain that I detected the hand of Joab in Absalom's successful coup, until we neared the Jordan and I found him awaiting me in staunch support with a large body of mighty men he had mustered to serve me. After that it was only a matter of reaching the river and crossing over to safety. When that was accomplished and we were resting on the other bank, I knew with a sinking heart that Absalom would lose in a battle against me that I couldn't win.

Faithful Joab—how I hated the sight of him, even though he had turned up on my side, *especially* because he had turned up on my side. I was reluctant to believe my eyes. How sad I was for my son. And in those first few hours, I was more vexed to discover my doubts about Joab baseless than thankful for his loyalty and the military advantage he was supplying. I felt absolutely cheated by his failure to justify my worst opinions about him.

Crazy as Saul, I eyed him narrowly as we moved northward to Mahanaim in the land of Gilead to make our base, condemning him for perfidiously biding his time only to turn upon me at some predetermined location more propitious for him. But Joab turned not after Absalom, although he has turned now to the cause of Adonijah, in compliance with what he believes is my wish. It is my wish. But he did not trouble to ask me first. But that is Joab. He is, he has bragged to me, the straw that stirs the drink, and he has always done what he wanted to. He did not trouble to ask if I wanted Absalom executed. "Deal gently for my sake with the young man Absalom" was the charge I had given for all the people to hear. "Beware that none touch the young man Absalom," I had repeated. Joab, ever more practical than I, disregarded my orders and put him to death.

He did me that favor I'll never forget. I have not been able to make whole sense out of him. He knows me too well to be enchanted by the mystiques of royalty and too long to be susceptible to the feelings of hero worship and idolatry I awake in people more distant from me who never make the effort to understand me at all. He does not believe I rule by divine right, and it would make no difference to him if he knew that I did. To him, all I've done is succeed—nothing more.

I am intrigued and annoyed by Joab now because in siding with Adonijah he evokes in me the triumphant notion that he may be losing his touch and might at last overstep himself. Joab is worldly enough to take into account the possibility from which I myself recoil, that in the end I will prove partial to my painted darling, Bathsheba, for reasons having nothing whatsoever to do with God, custom, or country. She gave me head. Whether it was good or not I can't judge; I can only tell you it was good enough for me. She sat on top of me with her knees bent and rode back and forth with her face red as cherries. She hated Absalom when he stood before Solomon, and Amnon too, and I could tell she was glad when each was out of the way. Recollections of past delights mean much to me now. Unsettled scores chafe more each day. I must kill Joab soon for what he did to Absalom, and for what he did to my pride by killing Abner and Amasa, although I probably will have to counterfeit a different reason.

I remember the sight of the runners with their messages from the battlefield. I knew they brought tidings of victory, for there were only two, and they were not part of a rout. Was my son Absalom safe?

"Blessed be the Lord thy God," said the first to reach me, who proved to be Ahimaaz, the goodly son of my other priest, Zadok, falling down to the earth upon his face before me, "which hath delivered up the men that lifted up their hand against my lord the king." I knew that Ahimaaz the son of Zadok would not come running to me with news that was bad.

"Is the young man Absalom safe?" was the first question to come to my lips. He said he did not know.

Why had two runners been sent? I moved him aside, almost roughly, to make room for the other.

"Tidings, my lord the king," said Cushi, the second, "for the Lord avenged thee this day of all them that rose up against thee."

"Is the young man Absalom safe?" I asked again, in a louder voice, feeling my confidence fail.

And the messenger Cushi answered me, "The enemies of my lord the king, and all that rise against thee to do thee hurt, be as that young man is."

He was letting me know in a roundabout way that my son was dead.

"O my son Absalom," I wept with a loud and shattering grief I would not even try to subdue and made no effort to conceal. "O Absalom, my son, my son."

It was Joab who brought me around gruffly. He pulled no punches.

"Thou lovest thy enemies," he told me with hard contempt, in the chamber over the gate in which I had secluded myself. "And thou hatest thy friends, who put out their lives this day to save you from them."

What was I to do?

I put a brave face on the matter and went out to be seen by my servants. And once again, I wished Joab dead.

Crazy as Saul in the unremitting enmity he bore toward me, I have wished Joab dead a thousand times before and since, prayed he'd be taken in one of our plagues or fall dead from a stroke or from a blow at the hand of some enemy in the field. A thousand times I have been disappointed. Dismayed as crazy Saul, I have been brought to the conclusion that I will have to prescribe the deed myself if I surely want it done. The son of a bitch will probably live forever if I don't kill him soon.

That will not be an easy thing to do. No one lusting for blood is ever innocent. Or satisfied. I have not been innocent. Or satisfied. Just as the man who wants silver will not be satisfied with silver, a man who wants the blood of another will not be satisfied with having that blood, nor the woman with jewels be satisfied with jewels, and the man who wants women will not be satisfied with women. Don't try telling me different. Haven't I looked about me in the city and seen how all the labor of man is for the mouth, yet the appetite is not filled? Don't I know myself that no want is ever satisfied? Otto Rank can tell you why. Wishes are granted, goals attained. But wants? Forget them. They live as long as the person they inhabit.

Only with Abigail's crude churl of a husband did my wish for the death of someone come true in a timely fashion. Saul's, you know, took years and years. Nabal was very drunken from the feast he was giving in his house when Abigail returned after meeting with me. Abigail knew her comatose onion, and she waited till morning with the good news that destroyed him: I had spared his life. When he learned he had escaped being killed by my hand, the gross boor leaped to his feet with an exclamation of relief. Then he sank to the earth in a chilly sweat when he realized the close call he'd had and how lucky a man he was. His heart seemed to die within him, and he became as a stone. About ten days later he was no longer alive. Here was a man who died of joy.

"Blessed be the Lord," I observed, and immediately sent and communed with Abigail to take her as wife.

She said yes.

She came with her damsels, and I learned from this poised and accomplished woman of Carmel how to live like a king.

There is a difference between riches and opulence. I learned that when I was king, when I had all that I wanted, and kept wanting more. That was vanity. All that was vanity.

"Oil and perfume make the heart glad," Abigail taught me, seeing me happy and fulfilled in the tent with her.

My palace? Vanity. What's wrong with vanity? It doesn't satisfy.

Who can find a virtuous woman?

Her price is far above rubies. I know that from Abigail. She never let her lamp go out at night. She was good in discretion and beautiful in form. With her five winsome servants, she took care of the folding and raising of the tents wherever we pitched, and the tents she brought on the string of asses with which she had arrived to become my wife were of hand-woven goat's hair. She rose with her maidens while it was yet night to begin giving meat to her household, and in the morning they ground wheat and barley grain into flour on a saddle quern to bake fresh bread. Even while circling about daily to elude the hand of Saul, we ate each evening from a cloth of scarlet or a cloth of blue on a low wood table, and not from a piece of leather on the dirt floor, as I was accustomed to doing. We often had partridge and flagons of wine. There was always time to take our evening meal leisurely. We ate by candlelight. She was clean and particular about her person. She appeared to me always with her lips and cheeks rouged and her eyes colored with malachite, galena, or powdered lapis lazuli, a flowing picture of stately feminine grace each twilight, with a gold net for her hair and her beads of amber and crystal. She slept with a bundle of myrrh between her breasts, and I slept with her. She decked my bed with coverings of tapestry, with carved works, with fine linen out of Egypt, and I was not ashamed that Joab and the other men about me noted with questioning disapproval that I tended to spend all night with her in the garden she made for me in her tent, every night.

"If two lie together," Abigail proved to me, "then they have heat. But how can one be warm alone?"

"How can one be warm alone?" I have tried appealing to Bathsheba lately, designing sneakily to coax her onto my couch.

"You have Abishag for that." She refuses to budge. "That's why they gave her to you."

Bathsheba manages very cozily for warmth with just her burning ambitions for herself and her son.

Abigail was older than I and conceived very late. Well, we had no amniocentesis then, of course; Chileab was born a mongoloid. We tried changing his name to Daniel in Chronicles, but that didn't help. Nothing helped. He remained a mongoloid, and he just sort of died away quietly after that. This remained a perpetual sadness to us. I would have wanted children by Abigail. Even a girl might have been nice. To the end of her days, we would review with affection our years together and marvel at the nature of our coming together so happily through a fortuitous meeting, resulting in a marriage that seems to have been made in heaven. From the start, our conversations were amatory.

"Sweet Abigail, make me immortal with a kiss," I would request.

"Stay with me until the day break, and the shadows flee away," she would respond.

She was afraid of the dark. But her voice was ever soft, an excellent thing in woman.

"I wanted you that first day," I boasted to her so many times in the relaxing talks we shared. "From the moment you bowed and looked up at me, and I had a clear look at your face. You are always so beautiful."

"I wanted you," she never hesitated to admit.

"I thought I could tell. I saw how you kept looking admiringly at the bracelet on my arm."

"I had to look somewhere. I couldn't keep staring up into your eyes."

"I didn't want you to go back."

"I didn't want to."

"But I didn't want to force you."

"No, I would not have wanted to be forced."

"That's not my way."

"But I would want to know you were thinking of doing it."

"When Nabal died, I decided to propose to you the moment I heard about it. I wouldn't say I was glad, but I wouldn't say I was sorry."

"I wanted to hear from you. From the moment he fell sick and was so close to death, that's all I hoped for. If you didn't send for me, I was going to find some excuse for going back to see you again."

"I love you, Abigail. I've loved you from the beginning. I say that to none of my other wives."

"Bathsheba?"

"Except Bathsheba. I do say it to Bathsheba, but it means something else."

"And I love you. But you know that, David. You still suffer so much, my dear, don't you? You never seem able to have much fun."

"I miss the child."

"I do too."

"I'm sorry we couldn't have more. I miss all my dead children. Especially the babies."

"Would you like some barley bread, darling, with lentils, figs, olive oil, and leeks?"

JOSEPH HELLER

"No thank you, Abigail. I just had some."

Whosoever findeth a wife findeth a good thing. And I was so lucky with Abigail that I found fifteen, seven before I triumphed over Abner and his puppet Ishbosheth, and the rest in Jerusalem after I had taken the city from the Jebusites and made it my home and political headquarters. I had the ark of the covenant brought here in a fantastic celebration the likes of which had never been seen before, and made the city a great religious center as well. Solomon the miser tells me seriously that he thinks he might want a thousand wives.

"You need so many?" I ask him, deadpan.

Some of them would have to be for show. None of my other wives came close to Abigail in elegance, taste, and intelligence, although I loved Bathsheba with a heat that was greater. Shall I compare her to a summer's day? Why not? She was so lovely and always more temperate. Ahinoam the Jezreelitess came next in the bridal succession and was with me too when I finally grew weary of running from Saul and crossed over into the service of the Philistines with all of my men and all of our households. Saul had already given my first wife, Michal, to Phalti the son of Laish.

There was never much letup in Saul's obsessive determination to hunt me down, despite the professions of repentance and pardon he called out to me—in front of others yet—so loudly and tearfully after I had him defenseless on the floor of the cave at Engedi and allowed him to depart unharmed. I could have killed him then. I didn't. When I cut that piece from the skirt of his robe, I felt horribly as though I were cutting a strip of flesh from his human person. "My lord the king," I cried after him when there was a good distance between us. "Wherefore hearest thou men's words, saying I seeketh thy hurt?"

"Is this thy voice, my son David?" Saul called back, and lifted up his voice and wept.

"Behold, my father, this day thine eyes can see how the Lord hath delivered thee today in my hand in the cave. I cut off the skirt of thy robe and killed thee not. I have not sinned against thee, yet thou huntest my soul to take it."

And Saul said to me, "Thou art more righteous than I, for thou hast rewarded me with good, whereas I have rewarded thee with evil." He wept some more. It did my heart good to see him so remorseful. It was about time. "When the Lord had delivered me into thine hands, thou killedst me not. And now, behold, I know well that thou shalt surely be king, and that the kingdom of Israel shall be established in thine hand." If I hear that one more time, I thought, I might begin to believe it. "Swear now therefore," Saul continued, wiping his eyes with the back of his hand after another outpouring of tears, "that thou wilt not cut off my seed after me, and that thou wilt not destroy my name out of my father's house."

I swore unto Saul as he asked. It did no good. In almost no time at all he was after me again, for when we encamped in the wilderness of Ziph, the Ziphites came unto Saul in Gibeah to tell him where I hid and offered to help deliver me into his hand. I was disillusioned when I heard that Saul had set out after me again. My spies confirmed he was coming back into Judah, having three thousand chosen men of Israel with him. I moved away to higher ground and witnessed him arriving at the place where we had been. They bedded down there for the night.

"Who will go with me to Saul to the camp to see what is what?" I asked the few nearest me.

I took only Abishai. They had posted no watch. None there were awake. We moved about noiselessly. Things were unnaturally still, as though a deep slumber from the Lord had fallen upon them all. We found Saul lying in a trench, and his spear was stuck in the ground at his bolster. Abner and the other people had pitched nearby and lay sleeping round about him. Saul's expression was haggard, his color sickly, he looked gaunt and soft. There were pockets of lax yellow skin under his jaw, along his neck down to his collarbone. In a month he had aged ten years. He was snoring faintly, his breathing was regular. He moaned in his sleep. Once, he coughed. I had crouched near his face to study him. How could I consent when Abishai asked to kill him? Let him die when he would, I made up my mind, let him go when the Lord came to smite him, when the day did come for him to die, or when he descended into battle and perished. I wanted nothing to do with it.

I took his spear and his cruse of water with me when I left, and this time I made my presence known with a taunting reproach for Abner, admonishing him contemptuously for his failure to post a guard about the king. Against Abner I had been accumulating grievances from the day we met. But first, of course, I prudently put a great space between us and was standing on the top of a hill afar off. Crazy I'm not. Saul had his three thousand. And David never had more than six hundred.

"Answereth thou not, Abner?" I jeered at the top of my voice through hands cupped about my mouth. "Art thou not a valiant man?"

Abner rose with a lurch and whirled to look at me with outrage, answering, "Who art thou that thou criest to the king?"

"Who is like thee in all Israel?" I replied in a voice dripping with scorn. "Ye are worthy to die, for ye have not kept your master, the king thy lord, the Lord's anointed. This thing is not good that thou hast done, for there came one of the people in who could have destroyed him. And now see where the king's spear is, and the cruse of water that was at his bolster. Let one of the young men come over and fetch them back."

By this time Saul had clambered to his feet, looking old. He was tottering as he drew himself fully erect. His face was knotted up against the glare of the sun.

"Is this thy voice?" again I heard him call out in my direction, with deeper feeling this time, as though he had been pining for the sound and sight of only me.

"Who then?" I called back across the chasm between us.

"My son David? It's really thy voice?"

"It is my voice, my lord, O king, my father. They do me wrong who have stirred thee up against me and say I seek to do thee harm. Behold again, I would not stretch forth my hand against thee. Last month it was the skirt of your robe. Today it's your spear and cruse of water. How many more things must I take from you before you believe me? The king of Israel is come out to seek a flea, as when one doth hunt a partridge in the mountains."

Even at that late date, I still clung to the belief that I was an innocent victim of some circumstantial misunderstanding, or the object of invidious slander. I could never believe for long that any-body ever really did want to kill me. Not even in battle. Not even Saul. It was so much easier to deceive myself with that fiction than to accept the fact that this august and imposing figure I still looked up to as king, God, and father truly hated me and was certifiably homicidal.

"Oh, David, David, David," wailed Saul, raising both arms to tear with his fists at his hair. "I have sinned."

"You said it," I concurred.

"Behold, I have played the fool," he cried, "and have erred exceedingly."

"Those are your words, not mine."

"For if a man find his enemy," he reasoned, "will he let him go away?"

"Now you've got it," I assented, rubbing it in. "You're catching on."

"The Lord reward thee well for the good thou hast done unto me this day."

"That's the ticket," I responded encouragingly.

"Blessed be thou, my son David," he went on. His redemption was whole, and it seemed there was now no stopping him. "Thou shalt both do great things and also shalt still prevail."

"From thy mouth," I assented, "unto God's ears."

"Return thou now, my son David," he urged, and went on to make a vow from the bottom of his heart, fervently saying, "for I swear before God that I will no more do thee harm."

Bullshit! I decided from the bottom of mine, and determined on the spot that there was nothing better for me to do than to escape speedily into the land of the Philistines if I did not wish to perish one day by the hand of Saul. A living dog is better than a dead lion, and he who fights and runs away, may live to fight another day.

Negotiations with King Achish were completed swiftly, and I arose and passed over safely into Gath with the six hundred men that were with me, every man with his household, me with my two wives, Ahinoam the Jezreelitess, and Abigail the Carmelitess, Nabal's wife when he lived. Achish gave me the city of Ziklag in the south and all of the territory surrounding it. And this was the end of my troubles with Saul. He sought no more again for me, once it was told him where I had fled.

We dwelt in the country of the Philistines a full year and four months, and then Saul was dead, perishing against the Philistines in the great battle of Gilboa. As though drawn inflexibly toward the goal of his own destruction, he fought them head-on; I would have allowed them entry into the valley of Jezreel and then swept down upon them from the rear and the flanks. I beat them for good at Rephaim by surrounding them at night through the mulberry trees. Saul knew the results beforehand. Samuel had given him the gory details the night before in the hideous revelation he unfolded in the house of the witch of Endor. Ghosts don't lie. It's hard to believe Saul did not cherish that outcome.

He took the initiative in arranging his unholy meeting with Samuel, doing so in dread after all the Philistines had arrived and were ready to fight. When Saul saw the great size of the host of the Philistines against whom he had come to do battle, he was afraid—I don't blame him, because I was with them for a day and a half and was awed by their number—and his heart trembled. Mine knocked about in my chest for a few minutes when the other four kings spotted me with Achish and gave vent to the belief that I was there to turn traitor against them once the fight had begun. All they did, thank God, was send me away.

Saul lost confidence, was stumped. He asked for an omen. The Lord answered him not, neither by dreams, dice, nor prophets. In numb desperation, he sent to inquire and went in disguise for fore-knowledge to the witch of Endor, elevating himself above the ban he had placed upon wizards and all others with access to familiar spirits. Thou shalt not suffer a witch to live, says Exodus, and Saul had endeavored to cut all wizards and witches off from the land. Now he was glad to go underground and felt lucky to find one. He put on other raiment and stole away to the woman by night with two companions he trusted.

"Double, double, toil, and trouble," the witch at Endor greeted him. She became hysterical when she guessed who he was. "Why hast thou deceived me?"

Saul mollified her, promised there would be no penalty if she would just dredge up Samuel for him to talk to. The ghost of the prophet came up at her beckoning, covered with a mantle. When Saul recognized it was indeed Samuel, he stooped with his face to the ground and bowed, making humble and unresisting submission to the figure who loomed before him like a stern and mournful statue.

True to form, Samuel said, "What do you want?"

Saul replied, "The Philistines make war against me, and God is departed and answereth me no more. Please tell me the future."

"You don't want to know."

"Who will triumph in the battle tomorrow?"

"Don't ask."

"What will happen to me?"

"It shouldn't happen to a dog."

And then Samuel gave it to him.

"Tomorrow shalt thou and thy sons be with me. The Lord also shall deliver the host of Israel into the hand of the Philistines."

Saul would die, his sons would die, the Philistines would win, and we would lose. *We?* I wasn't even there. And if I had been, I would have fought for Achish of Gath on the side of the Philistines against my own people. Things worked out perfectly for me. I never would have won the allegiance of Israel if I'd been part of that decisive event in which Saul and all his legitimate heirs died and his army was shattered and dispersed—the people forsook the cities and fled, like harts that find no pasture, and the Philistines came and dwelt in them. Even as it is, I've always had trouble keeping the people of Israel in line.

My men and I responded with fervor when Achish summoned us to make war. We mobilized speedily and came up from Ziklag to Gath to do battle for him and the other Philistine chieftains at Gilboa. We were tough and willing. We were filled with excitement and expectation, we'd been spoiling for a real fight against those who'd been hounding us, and we were impatient for the impending climax that would at last bring one kind of resolution or another to the tension and hostility that had raged so long between Saul and myself and had made exiles and pariahs of me and my men.

We were part of the army of Achish, and we marched under his banner all the way north up to Shunem near Gilboa to the staging area of all the armies of the Philistines. I never saw so many troops. We should have anticipated that I and my band of Hebrews would attract some notice. We certainly did stand out. The princes of the Philistines drew near to look. I was identified, and I began to my horror to hear again those marvelous and euphonic words in the laudatory refrain about me and Saul that by this time I had come to dread.

"Is not this David?" wondered the other princes of the Philistines, huddling closer and ogling me, "of whom they sang one to another in dances, saying Saul slew his thousands, and David his ten thousands?"

If ever I am remembered, it undoubtedly will be for that.

It goes without saying that Achish told the truth.

My men were disgruntled and talked of stoning me when the princes of the Philistines refused to allow us to be near at the time of battle and ordered us back down.

"Let him not go into battle with us," they resolved, "lest in the thick of things he show himself to be an adversary to us."

That was that. My men talked again of stoning me when we returned to Ziklag and discovered that a tribe of Amelekites had smitten the city in our absence and taken as captives all of our wives and daughters and sons, and all of our animals. Abigail was gone and so was Ahinoam. I was brokenhearted. They were ready to kill me. I inquired of God and was advised to go after this troop that had invaded the south and carried away our people.

"Pursue," said God, "for thou shalt surely overtake them and recover all, positively without fail."

We did recover them all safely. Abigail and I embraced with Ahinoam. It felt so good to have them both in my arms again. And three days after we were back in Ziklag, it came to pass that we learned of the annihilation of the Israelite army in the battle of Gilboa and the death of Saul and his three sons. The impact on me of these reports was enormous. According to which account you believe, Saul, sorely wounded by archers and unable to flee farther, either fell upon his sword to take his life or begged a passing Amelekite to slay him in his misery and allow him to escape the agony and ignominy of being found alive by the Philistines. To me it made no difference, for I had his crown and I had the bracelet that was on his arm. I did not know whether the Amelekite who brought them to me was telling the truth or not, and I did not care.

"Go near and fall upon him," I instructed one of my men, who smote him till he died.

I did not want anyone around me to get the idea that one could lift his hand against a king for any reason whatsoever, especially if I was the king. And it was beginning to appear I was going to become one. Who else was now around?

I grieved awhile for Saul and Jonathan, of course. And I composed my very famous elegy, in which I lamented their passing. Also, I bade the Philistines teach the children of Israel the use of the bow. I was truly inspired when I wrote:

The beauty of Israel is slain upon thy high places: how are the mighty fallen!

GOD KNOWS

Tell it not in Gath, publish it not in the streets of Askelon; lest the daughters of the Philistines rejoice, lest the daughters of the uncircumcised triumph.

Ye mountains of Gilboa, let there be no dew, neither let there be rain, upon you, nor fields of offerings: for there the shield of the mighty is vilely cast away, the shield of Saul, as though he had not been anointed with oil.

From the blood of the slain, from the fat of the mighty, the bow of Jonathan turned not back, and the sword of Saul returned not empty.

Saul and Jonathan were lovely and pleasant in their lives, and in their death they were not divided: they were swifter than eagles, they were stronger than lions.

Ye daughters of Israel, weep over Saul, who clothed you in scarlet, with other delights, who put ornaments of gold upon your apparel.

How are the mighty fallen in the midst of the battle! O Jonathan, thou wast slain in thine high places.

I am distressed for thee, my brother Jonathan: very pleasant hast thou been unto me: thy love to me was wonderful, passing the love of women.

You see? I do call him a brother, don't I?

How are the mighty fallen, and the weapons of war perished!

Now what's so bad about any of that, except for that sword of Saul's returning not empty? Where is there anything wrong? What else was I going to say about him? Only a very sordid nature could find in those lines of platonic praise of Jonathan even a hint of any allusion to that reprehensible love that dare not speak its name.

Once again, the creative act had a salutary effect upon me, for I was drained of grief when I finished and of all pity and fear. My beautiful and famous elegy was a catharsis. I must admit I soon grew more absorbed in the writing of it than in the fact of the deaths of Saul and his sons and the total victory of the Philistines. Poetry works like that. My term of mourning ending with the completion of my elegy, I took stock like an able realist, and discovered myself relieved in some ways that Saul was gone. I could now surge ahead to whatever fate the future held for me.

My course seemed clear and unobstructed. There were now no more male children left after Saul but the illegitimate Ishbaal—that Canaanite name alone should tell you how lightly Saul himself regarded this surviving by-blow of some casual roadside rutting in his distant past. I was Saul's son-in-law. Although I no longer had his daughter with me, she was still my wife. No one but a husband has the right to declare a marriage over with a bill of divorce. In addition, my army of six hundred was the only capable military force left for the land of the Hebrews. Who could stop me? I borrowed the sacred ephod from Abiathar for another heart-to-heart discussion with God.

"Shall I go up into any of the cities of Judah?" I asked him. My pulse was quivering. He had not said no to me yet.

And the Lord, God bless Him, answered, "Go up."

So I said, "Whither shall I go up?"

And He said, "Unto Hebron."

So I had His blessing. But just to make sure, I double-checked with another high power.

"Shall I go up into Hebron to be king?" I inquired of the leaders of the Philistines.

And they replied unto me, "By all means."

They thought it was okay. The Philistines found it just dandy, the idea of the land of Judah as a buffer state between Israel and themselves, with someone like me at the head who would remain in liege to them. I did not disclose that I had bigger things in mind. Then came the messengers from the north with a report that stunned me: Ishbaal, surviving son of Saul, had changed his name to Ishbosheth.

"That bastard!" I exploded.

And Abner, who'd escaped from Gilboa alive, was siding with him and putting him forward as king. I could see I was in for a long civil war.

9

SEVEN YEARS I SUFFERED, SEVEN YEARS

It took more than seven years. For seven years I suffered, seven years and six long months. How long, O Lord, how long, I lamented as I saw the weeks grow into months and the months lengthen to years. I gnashed my teeth, I chewed my nails. There were mornings I felt like weeping. Imagine me doing things like that, me, David, the warrior king, the sweet psalmist of Israel.

How long, O Lord, how long I waited. Believe me, that spell of waiting was not an easy time. For seven years I daily wanted Abner dead, seven years and six upsetting months, while I skirmished sporadically with what in Israel still was quaintly known as the house of Saul. Remember, we had no word for family then, and we have none now. Abner made his headquarters far away in Mahanaim in Gilead with that useless figurehead Ishbosheth, born Ishbaal, that lily-livered, illegitimate son of Saul and some unknown Canaanite cooze, who likely was as homely as sin if the offshoot bore any resemblance. Except for busty Rizpah, Saul had the taste of a Philistine when it came to women.

Once I was installed in Hebron as king of Judah, Abner and Ishbosheth were constrained to base themselves someplace remote on the other side of the Jordan, for the Philistines enjoyed unchallenged control of the valley of Jezreel in the middle of Israel. And Mahanaim in Gilead was as good a location as any. Coincidentally, Mahanaim in Gilead was the same haven to which I myself was to retreat a generation afterward, when I fled Jerusalem from the insurgent forces of Absalom hurtling down upon me from the corners of the earth seeking my death. I did not know they were seeking my death until loyal spies brought word of the logical plan of Ahitophel—formerly the sagest of my advisers, consistently so uncanny in judgment that his intelligence was thought to be divine —to set out himself that same night with a fresh mobile force to

251

kill me. I had not a ghost of a chance of surviving had his wisdom prevailed over the slyly flattering counsel of my secret agent, Hushai the Archite. Don't try telling me there is ever anything new under the sun. I was crowned in Hebron, you know, and I announced there first that I reigned in Judah—Hebron, that same city in which my son Absalom chose to uncover his seditious uprising a generation later and sound the first blast of the trumpet to announce that *he* reigned there. What a blow to me that was. Take it from me, the thing that hath been is that which shall be, and that which is done is that which shall be done, and neither shall there be any remembrance of things past that shall not also be a remembrance with those that come after. That which is crooked cannot be made straight, although with that one I believe there are psychotherapists who might disagree.

Life, as Bathsheba said, does not stand still. I took more wives in Hebron while I conducted my struggle for Israel, and I started having children born unto me, almost all of them, fortunately, as with my ancestor Jacob, sons. For wives to begin with, I brought Abigail and Ahinoam when I came to Hebron. By Ahinoam of Jezreel, I had my firstborn Amnon, who grew up a good-looking youth but was indescribably spoiled and vain, so much the affected, self-indulgent scamp that he tricked me shamelessly into helping him set up my daughter, his half sister Tamar, for his nefarious rape. What a sucker he made of me. Why did he eject her afterward from his house with such outspoken revulsion and disapproval? Because she was no longer a virgin? Not even he could explain his abnormal conduct when I had my father-and-son talk with him later. I couldn't even get him to say he was sorry, this firstborn son of mine by Ahinoam of Jezreel. My dutiful, loving Abigail suffered miscarriages until she was finally delivered of Chileab, poor thing, who remained a mongoloid even after we changed his name to Daniel in Chronicles. Chileab went early to his long home, and for him the mourners did not spend much time going about the streets. I had Absalom and Tamar by my next wife, Maccah, the daughter of Talmai, king of Geshur. It was always my instinct to marry well, until I took Bathsheba as wife, and that was my most enriching marriage of all. I did that one for love. She was the penniless one and I was much better off; for a woman, if she maintaineth her husband, is full of anger, impudence, and much reproach, except for Abigail. Bathsheba only asked for everything, and still does. I took Haggith, by whom I had Adonijah; Abital, by whom I had Shepatiah; Eglah, by whom I had Ithream; and Bathsheba, by whom I next had Solomon after our first baby was put to death by God so soon after birth that we had no time to name him. He lies in an unmarked grave. By me she was fertile, if not by Uriah and the countless others who preceded me into her. And after Bathsheba, I took unto me even more wives and concubines and there were yet still more sons born to me, and even some daughters after Tamar, but that's a different story.

My struggles with Abner were generally on a small and indecisive scale. Neither side had sufficient troops to occupy the territory of the other. United, I gauged, we likely would outnumber the Philistines, who maintained themselves politically in separate city states, but we were divided and at war with each other. It was Judah versus Israel, the south against the north, and it was evident to me that sooner or later there would have to be some kind of voluntary surrender and a negotiated peace.

We launched raids into Israel from Judah. At these my nephew Joab was ferociously professional. A tournament at the pool of Gibeon between twelve men of ours and twelve men of theirs erupted into a full-sized melee after every one of the combatants caught his fellow by the head and thrust his sword into the other's side, so that they all fell down dead together. Can you imagine that? I'm sorry I wasn't there to witness that one, or the general action that followed. There was a very sore battle that day, and Abner and the men of Israel were beaten soundly. Lithe Asahel, the youngest of my sister Zeruiah's three sons, was swept from his senses by this success and borne to his death by a delusion of grandeur, the preposterous fancy that he could take on Abner. As light of foot as a wild roe, he pursued after Abner to kill him, and in going he turned not to the right hand nor to the left from following him, nor obeyed the exhortations of Abner that he slacken and desist and chase after someone else. Abner had no choice but to defend himself against his youthful and imprudent assailant. To Joab, after Asahel had been slain, Abner called out sensibly from the top of a hill when the children of Benjamin had regrouped and gathered together after him in one troop: "Turn thee aside. Shall the sword devour forever? Knowest thou not that it will be bitterness in the latter end? How long shall it be then, ere thou bid the people return from following their brethren?"

And Joab, hearing him out, sensibly decided to cease following him that day. He blew a trumpet, and all the people with him stood still and pursued after Israel no more, neither fought they anymore that day. And Joab returned from following Abner to take up his brother Asahel and bury him in the sepulchre of his father, which was in Bethlehem, going all night and coming back to Hebron at break of day. And there was then pause in battle again and a time for all of the principals to take stock of things.

The city of Hebron in Judah is not Versailles, you know, and being king in Hebron is not always a day at the beach. There's usually not much going on socially and little to do, even if you're a king. That's one of the reasons I took so many wives—they helped keep me occupied. And after Abigail, I found myself with a real capacity to enjoy women; she taught me that, too. Bathsheba completed my education. Bathsheba taught me all of the rest and gave me my diploma, and since then I've never been able to enjoy any of the rest of them as much, not even my beloved Abigail. How I miss the way Bathsheba was at the beginning, and the way I used to be with her when we were together. I was in love, and I hadn't been in love that way in all my life until I moved to Jerusalem from Hebron and found her, and had her more than once. I came too quickly the first time. I was just about ready to pop right there on my roof when I first saw her and commanded that she be brought to me. Boredom in Hebron was also a reason I persisted in contending against Abner and the knock-kneed weakling he kept propped up in opposition to me. Ambition, too, kept me going, and war was something else diverting to do that was also invigorating to the spirit. I persevered all the more arduously through the long years of conflict as I observed that my house of David was waxing stronger and stronger and the house of Saul was growing more and more weak.

I intensified the pressure howsoever I could. And at last came the hoped-for breach between my two adversaries, a rift both critical and inevitable. It took place over pussy, of all things; over an ordinary piece of ass, with a good deal of hypersensitive male vanity mixed in. For a people lacking words for genitals, we've certainly had our fill of troubles because of them, haven't we? Ishbosheth was distressed by the mere notion of Abner's sleeping with the hearty woman Rizpah, concubine to Saul while the king was yet alive, and abused him verbally with the charge of having done so. On such piddling occurrences do the histories of great nations frequently revolve. For want of a nail, believe it or not, a shoe may be lost, for want of the shoe a mule may be lost, for want of the mule a battle may be lost, and for want of the battle, who knows? Ishbosheth spoke incautiously. He forgot he was only a cat's-paw and was seduced into rashness by the fantasy that he really was king. And Abner hit the ceiling when subjected to his degrading impertinence.

"Am I a dog's head," he raged, "that thou chargest me today with a fault concerning this woman? Who do you think you are? Have I delivered thee into the hand of David? Could I not, if I wished, translate the kingdom from the house of Saul and set up the throne of David over Israel and over Judah, from Dan even to Beersheba? Overnight? Even if I were guilty of the fault with which thou chargest me, canst thou talk to me that way? Doest thou think, O maggot, thou really are king?"

And Ishbosheth could not answer Abner another word, because he feared him.

By this time too, I'd bet, Abner had seen the handwriting on the wall, and I have a sneaking suspicion that more than injured pride was at the bottom of the overtures he began making to me in secret. He sent messengers suggesting a league. Ishbosheth too began putting out feelers. I did not need a crystal ball to tell me I was now in the driver's seat; I could see I was holding a strong hand, if I might mix up my metaphors, and I played my cards with implacable cunning. I insisted on the return of my wife Michal as a precondition of my dealing with either one of them. There it was, they could take it or leave it. My demand was nonnegotiable.

"Thou shalt not see my face," I sent word to Abner imperially, like the absolute monarch I eventually was to become, "except thou first bring to me Saul's daughter Michal. Deliver me my wife, which I espoused to me for a hundred foreskins of the Philistines." I had no doubt I would get my way.

"Wouldn't you rather have the foreskins?" was the cynical reply sent back by Abner. I occasionally missed Abner after Joab did him in.

I should have said yes.

They sent and took Michal from her other husband, even from Phalti the son of Laish, to return her to me. And Phalti walked along with Michal, weeping behind her all the way to Bahurim, until Abner drove him off, saying unto him, "Go, return home."

Phalti should have been laughing. *I* was the one who should have been crying, for she never gave me a moment's peace or pleasure from the day she stepped back over my threshold. We had not seen each other for more than ten years. Yet the first thing my embittered wife did when she returned to me was to remind me yet again that she *was* a princess. She disliked the exposure from her quarters—she was used to a better view ever since childhood in her home in Gibeah. She found Hebron gross, and she objected to the presence of all of my other wives and their babies in what she said was her palace. She wanted a baby of her own. It was my pleasure to deny her one. It did not take me long to appreciate that I would have been much better off with those Philistine foreskins.

"I don't want those other women in my palace," she scolded sourly.

"It's not a palace," I answered her right back, "and it isn't yours." My earlier feelings of intimidation and inferiority had dwindled away in the interval of our separation. Now I did not give a shit. "It's just a couple of white mud-brick houses with leaking roofs that open into each other and could use a new paint job, inside and out."

"I am a princess," she answered with the customary and peculiar hauteur that was to survive till her death, "and anywhere I live is a palace. Just remember, I found you in the gutter."

"Again in the gutter?"

"I never should have married a commoner."

"Are we back to that?"

"I was brought up in Gibeah," she boasted, "and you are only from Bethlehem in Judah. I am the daughter of a king."

"And I *am* a king!" I thundered.

That never did sink in, no matter how loudly I roared. Do you wonder I was so happy when they told me she was dying? How long, O Lord, how long I had waited to be rid of her, and it took so many years. I did a jig when they brought the news that she was ill. They went through the usual—the bone-marrow and the biopsy. My dreams came true: the biopsy was positive, and we had no chemotherapy. "My cup runneth over!" I cried in my joy. I sang like a lark. She was soon sinking fast. I kicked up my heels. She asked to see me. "Let her wait," I shot back. Only when she was right at death's door did I rush to her bedside, just to watch with a smile and shake my head to any dying requests. Her voice was faint.

"I guess I'm going."

"Good," I said.

"Do you want my blessing?"

"Don't be such a sap."

"I'll bet you're glad."

"You've never made me happier."

"When I was sore with boils?"

"That was nice too."

"You'll dance on my grave," she predicted.

"With all my might."

"After I'm gone, you'll be able to dance with all your might whenever you want to, won't you?"

"I won't even wait, I'll do it right now." To prove it, I began dancing around her bed as hard as I could, winding up with an energetic buck-and-wing and a hey-nonny-nonny and a hot-cha-cha.

"I have a last wish," she said, when I ran out of wind. "Promise you'll grant it."

"Not a chance."

"It isn't much."

"You're out of your mind."

"Even if you lie and don't do it, David. I can go to my grave in peace if only I hear you say that you will."

"You must be kidding."

"You won't say yes?"

"Positively no."

I've only missed her in situations that I knew would inflame her had she lasted as long as I.

Is it any mystery that I valued Abigail still more once Michal had returned to demean and torment me? Or that once established in Jerusalem, I unfailingly preferred the serpentine lecherous writhings of Bathsheba to the grating clangor of Michal's habitual and carping disgruntlement? Take it from me, it is better to dwell in a desert with beetles than in a fine house with a woman who will not be pleased, better to reside with scorpions than with a sullen one whose voice is never still. It is better to marry than to burn, but if your wife go not as thou wouldst have her, it is better to

257

burn: cut her off from thy flesh, and give her a bill of divorce, and let her go, for all wickedness is but little to the wickedness of a woman. The wickedness of a woman changeth her face, and darkeneth her countenance like sackcloth. Her husband shall sit among his neighbors and, when he heareth it, shall sigh bitterly. Let the portion of a sinner fall upon her, for of the woman came the beginning of sin, and through her we all die. From her garments cometh a moth. On the other hand, if you find a woman as virtuous as Abigail, let her be as the loving kind pleasant roe, let her breasts satisfy thee at all times, and be thou ravished always with her love. Unhappily for Abigail, the heart of man being fickle, it was with Bathsheba's love that I was ravished always, and I would be ravished again with Bathsheba's love if only she would give herself to me one more time, settle herself near me on my bed, and assist me in the parting of her thighs. I have tried inducing her. "My sister, my love, my dove, my undefiled," I have flattered. "Let me hear thy voice. Thou hast ravished my heart with one of thine eyes, with one chain of thy neck. Come to me, for sweet is thy voice, and thy countenance is comely. How beautiful are thy feet with shoes."

"That doesn't work anymore," she answered, unmoved.

"How come?"

"You used to be strong enough to make me."

She probably is speaking the truth when she murmurs these days that she is sick of love. Back then, she was wont to emit such delicious and delirious high-pitched cries in her lust, and Michal could hear us both in my harem—I wasn't always quiet as a church mouse either—and Michal would claw at her palms until the blood ran as she waited for me to finish and pass by her doorway on my way out. Often I would dart inside Abigail's rooms to evade her scathing flare-ups. Or I would give her the finger as she raged, and proceed on my way with a smirk.

"How glorious was the king of Israel today," she would snarl, and she would hiss and sputter and stamp her foot.

Oh, the curses I heaped on the head of Hiram king of Tyre for the failure of his architects to provide me a harem with a more serviceable layout. Michal minced no words from the beginning.

"My father," she took pains to remind me on the day we were reunited, "was king over all Israel." I later ordained that day of our reunion a national holiday. I called it Tishah b'Ab. "You are only king of Judah."

There, for the moment, was the only point on which she did have me. But Israel was next on my timetable, and Abner was already out doing whispering work for me with the elders there to bring them over to me. He had communication with them in one place and the next, and recalled to them how in the past, when rankled by Saul and restive with Ishbosheth, they had often sought with each other for me to be king over them. He also spoke all that seemed good about me into the ears of the fighting people and the whole house of Benjamin, the tribe of Saul. It was not that hard to convince them, considering the sad state of the world and their tenuous position in it. What was the alternative?

When the time was ripe, when assents had been given and handshakes exchanged, when the proposal of me as sole universal sovereign seemed as good to the establishment of Israel as it long had seemed to me, Abner came at my invitation to my house in Hebron, and twenty men with him, to finalize the pact. We conferred and shook hands. I made a big feast for him and the twenty men that were with him. With both sides exulting, I sent him away in peace to conclude the arrangements that would at last make it possible for me to rule over all that my heart had desired.

All were exultant but Joab, that perennial fly in my ointment, that albatross about my neck. Joab almost went berserk upon returning to the city with very great spoils after another rapacious swoop into Israel and heard that I had met with Abner, had him wholly in my power in Hebron, and then had permitted him to depart alive. That primitive nature of Joab's never did allow him to appreciate finesse. His anger was terrible.

"What have you done, you dope?" he bellowed at me. Those were still the days when I was king only in Hebron, and neither one of us was much in awe of the other. To him, I was just his Uncle David, and I half surmised that he often made mention of me disparagingly in just that fashion. "Don't you know he came here only to deceive you, to spy on all of us, to know thy going out and thy coming in, and to find out all that you do? How could you be such a *putz?*"

"Joab, Joab," I coaxed, hoping to turn away his wrath with my soft answer. "This is Hebron, not Ai or Jericho. Why would anyone come here to spy? What could a person find out here that isn't already out in the open?"

But Joab was unyielding and merciless. Without speaking anything to me, he sent messengers after Abner to return him to Hebron as though to transmit to him on my behalf some diplomatic afterthoughts. Joab gave him a warm greeting in the gate of the city. He took him aside with the air of a man who wishes to speak in a confidential manner to an esteemed colleague, or breathe into his ear the newest dirty joke making the rounds, while his brother Abishai loitered nearby in an attitude of nonchalance, prepared to leap to Joab's assistance if needed. With Abner thus lulled into a mood of rapt concentration, Joab struck without warning and smote him suddenly there in the side, right out in the open, right under the fifth rib, so that Abner fell down there and died.

It happened so quickly I could hardly believe it. The town was thunderstruck. For seven years and six difficult months I'd wanted Abner dead; and now, when I finally needed him alive, Joab, my nephew Joab, killed him, with Abishai looking on. Oh, those three sons of my sister Zeruiah were too hard for me.

"I did it," Joab repeated obstinately to me, with a face set rigidly, when the roof seemed ready to cave in and I called him on the carpet inside my house to pour out my fury, "to avenge the blood of my brother Asahel."

This time I was the one in a temper. "A lie, a lie, a barefaced and unconscionable lie!" I shouted at him with such volume that I expected the whole country to hear, from Dan all the way even to Beersheba. "That's plain horseshit, Joab. Why in the world did you have to kill him now?" I kept my hand on the hilt of my sword as I took him to task, with the elbow of my other arm at the ready as a buffer protecting my fifth rib.

"And I don't like rivals," Joab continued grimly, without change of expression and without backing away in the least from the first justification he had given. His eyes did not flinch from my gaze. "You would have had to make him your captain over everyone, wouldn't you, even over me."

I begged the question adroitly. "He was delivering unto me all of the armies of Israel that had been loyal unto Saul, and now unto Ishbosheth also."

"And how long, how long," Joab came back at me, "before we began to wonder if he was plotting to depose you with those armies? David, David, I did you a favor. Use your head. I know you, I know your heart. You don't enjoy disagreements. You want praise from everyone, only praise. You will try to get along with anyone if you think it will do you good. I have been with you from the beginning, at Adullam and Keilah and Ziklag. Would you really expect me to consent in our hour of triumph to serve as an underling to the man who hounded us for years? And the one who then killed my brother?"

"That was in war, Joab," I reminded him, "and Abner did not even want to fight with him. But you, Joab, you took Abner aside in peace as a trusting ally and slew him in his innocence with the sharp blade of a knife."

"My sword, David—my short sword, David," Joab corrected. "I kept it hidden inside my cloak while I started to relate to him a dirty joke—"

"You said a dirty joke?"

"Why not?" he admitted with a shrug. "That new one about the traveling knight in armor and the wife of Bath. And when I saw him bob his head and lean closer to hear better, I drew my sword and ran him through."

"Just like that, you ran him through?"

"Just like that."

"You really like killing people. I can see you do."

"It's as easy as pie. Don't you?"

"I don't mind it," I admitted, "when it's necessary. I wouldn't say I enjoyed it. But you really get pleasure out of smiting, don't you? Smiting anyone."

"Just about." He nodded with patent self-satisfaction. "Under the fifth rib I smote him. What a good *zetz* I gave him!"

"You really like that fifth rib, don't you?" I observed.

"It's the best place, David, especially when you're smiting somebody from the side. David, David, tell me the truth, look me in the eye—did you really want Abner alive? Why?"

"What would it hurt to leave him alive?"

"What does it hurt to kill him? You like him so much? He's been such a charming friend to you? Sooner or later you would have felt you had to destroy him. Don't you want to be king?"

"What will I tell to the people?"

"Tell to the people the truth," said Joab virtuously. "That I did it to avenge the blood of my brother Asahel, that was killed by this same Abner at Gibeon."

"That's not the truth," I argued.

"The truth," said Joab, "is whatever people will believe is the truth. Don't you know history?"

"I know history, and I make history, so don't tell me about history. Why should they believe that? Some might believe I was the one who contrived his murder. Oh, Joab, Joab, what have you done to me? There was not much else Abner could do at the battle, was there? Everyone knows that Asahel chased after him without wavering to the left or the right. Didn't Abner keep begging him to stop? How long, how long did he call out to him to turn aside, and to seek after someone else? How many times? Two, three? Was Asahel a match for Abner? Did Asahel listen? What got into him? He brought it all on himself."

"He was still my brother."

"Then why didn't you stop him? Where were you when all this was happening? You were there. You were in command. I know what you were doing. You were probably rooting him on all the time, weren't you? Don't I have witnesses? And you yourself made a truce with Abner afterward, didn't you? Now you murder him—in cold blood you murder him. Oh, Joab, Joab. You call it a family feud? That's horseshit, Joab, plain, unadulterated horseshit, and both of us know it."

I did have witnesses. To this day, every good man present at that battle at the pool in Gibeon will tell his son how Asahel fixed himself upon Abner as a panther upon prey in the disorderly retreat that followed the tournament and how he turned not to the right hand nor to the left from pursuing him. Relentlessly, he narrowed the distance between them with his magically smooth and dazzling speed. A greyhound or a cheetah does not go more fleetly than could Asahel move then. Abner identified him that way. Who else but Asahel could sprint like a hind or be swifter than the eagles of heaven?

"Art thou Asahel?" Abner called back to him, after he had looked behind him and saw he was followed.

And Asahel, flashing a reckless grin, replied, "I am."

"Then turn thee aside to the right hand or the left," Abner beseeched him, "and lay hold of one of the young men and take thee his armor. Believe me, it's for your sake I ask, not mine." But

Asahel would not turn aside from the following of him. And Abner, who, all in all, was both a practical man and a fair one, tried at least one more time to discourage him. "Turn thee aside from following me," he entreated, and gave warning. "I ask you again, in a nice way. Wherefore should I smite thee to the ground? What good would it do? How then should I hold up my face to thy brother Joab? Do us both a big favor. Can't you foresee the tumult in the end if you don't return from chasing me and force me to slay you?" But Asahel would not turn aside. Like a hawk he flew toward him, like an arrow he rushed through the air separating them. Abner endeavored to the last to avoid doing battle with him, even to the turning around of his spear when overtaken to beat back the youth with blows from the butt. Like a strong young lion, Asahel sprang at the veteran older man, and like a skinny, puzzled, astounded, adolescent nincompoop, he found himself mortally impaled when Abner smote at him with the hinder end of his weapon to ward him off. The spear came out behind him under the fifth rib. Poor Asahel was done for. The young man fell down there and died in the same place.

And this was the time picked by Joab to even the score with the killing of Abner, in the gate of the city yet, where everyone could remark and the whole world be told of it. I never did have much luck with my relatives, did I? Remember my father-in-law Saul? My brothers Eliab, Abinadab, and Shammah? And those three sons of my flinty sister Zeruiah—Joab, Abishai, and Asahel—they had always been too hard for me.

I made certain to say so out loud, in exactly those words, in public where everyone could take note and spread the news of my condemnation of the base deed. I put my curse on the house of Joab as I boisterously bewailed the death of Abner, that heroic, gentle Israelite, and denounced the barbarous, treacherous crime. I stormily avowed to eat no meat while it was yet day, or taste bread or aught else till the sun went down. The people took notice of my misery and approved that I fasted. All of the people were pleased with everything I did that day. "Abner died a trusting fool," I wept in the street with heartrending cries and copious tears, "and not as a captive whose hands were bound and whose feet were put into fetters. I had nothing to do with it. My hands, these hands, are clean." I hardly stopped there. I made all of my servants rend their clothes and gird themselves in sackcloth and mourn after Abner with me. "As a man falleth before wicked men, so fellest thou," I said, lifting up my voice in such mighty lamentation that I soon was admiring my own sorrow. How are the mighty fallen, I was tempted to declaim, but I already had used that noble line three times in my famous elegy. "Oh, what a fall was there!" I came out with instead. With my head hanging heavily, I followed the swarthy bastard in his bier and wept at his grave, and all the people pertaining to me wept too. How I eulogized that obdurate, pock-marked, self-serving son of a bitch! "Know ye not that there is a prince and a great man fallen this day in Israel?" I ranted in an-guish at the huge assemblage, as though none but myself had even a glimmer of understanding of the reason for our coming together. "Wasn't this the noblest Israelite of them all?" Onlookers were soon more sorry for me than they were for him.

Now, Abner was not a prince and he was not especially great. And he definitely was not the noblest Israelite of them all. *I* was, even though I was still Judean. Would anyone observing me that day have guessed that these lofty tributes were for the death of a human who, alive, had meant as much to me, precisely, as a stone in my shoe, or a frog in my throat? I used up some of my best phrases on that unfeeling opportunist who'd striven for seven years, seven long years, to bestow monarchical authority upon someone, *anyone,* still left alive from Saul's family, and did so mainly to conserve a share of it for himself. Michal was now the only legitimate issue left in the house of Saul, and Michal belonged to me. Maybe I did know what I was doing when I took her back.

Somehow, as though by a miracle, it all came together. The people took notice of how I carried on at the funeral, and all Israel could see that it was not to my knowing or purpose to slay Abner the son of Ner.

In the end, everything fell neatly into place. In fact, I was better off than I would have been had Joab shown self-restraint, for Ab-ner was now out of the way. And with Abner gone, the days of Ishbosheth were numbered. His hands were feeble when he heard of Abner's death, and all the Israelites yet with him were troubled to see him so sickly and fainthearted. Two of his more enterprising captains chose to act. They entered his house as though fetching wheat and smote him under the fifth rib as he lay in his bed in the heat of day, slaying him and then beheading him, and escaping with his head through the plain all night. They sought favor with

ne by delivering it into my hands. Did I need a head? Like Achish
of Gath had need of a madman. They fawned expectantly, awaiting
my blessing. I rewarded their initiative by having them executed.
Then I cut off their hands and feet and hanged the remains up over
the pool in Hebron as an object lesson. I did not want one soul in
the land to harbor the idea that it was safe to kill even an illegitimate king—or believe for a minute I'd had anything to do with the
slaying of this one.

The liquidation of Ishbosheth just about took care of the con-
tenders for the crown from the house of Saul. But I festered in-
creasingly with mistrust for Joab, and resolved to restrict this brutal man of fiery disposition and independent will who'd just given
evidence that he would not hesitate to do whatever he wanted,
regardless of my wishes. I thought I spied the perfect opportunity
to formalize and make permanent his demotion in status when I
decided to take the city of Jerusalem from the Jebusites and establish my capital in this mountain stronghold near the border between Benjamin and Judah. It made better political sense to move
closer to the neutral center of the united nation of which I was now
the accepted leader than to remain in Judah, far from my latently
antagonistic new subjects, or to headquarter in Gibeah, the city
which was connected so closely to the reign of Saul. He'd been king
for eighteen years, you know. I wished to preclude absolutely the
impression that I was descended in any way from crazy Saul or
indebted to him for a goddamned thing. You can imagine how my
princess Michal reacted to that decision of mine to let slide into an
oblivion of neglect the city in which she'd had her coming-out
party and that otherwise might be immortalized as the site of her
ancestral home. She bawled like a she-ass.

I completed my successful assault against Jerusalem in a single
night with a picked band of mighty men. The walls of the city were
impregnable and we would have failed in an attempt to scale them.
The peaceful Jebusites were confident, and they jeered from inside
that their lame and their blind could safeguard the battlements
against us. And probably they were right. But I had done my
homework meticulously and had ascertained that the subterranean
waterways feeding into the city were shallow and unprotected and
accessible on foot through the caves outside. Taking Jerusalem
began to appear to me no more difficult a feat than eating a piece of
cake.

Before we set out, I gathered my brigade of mighty men before me for the traditional pep talk and read aloud to them from a short scroll the artful and inspiring proclamation I had devised expressly to thwart the aspirations of my nephew Joab. Whoever would be first up the gutter of the large well into the city to smite the Jebusite defenders and open the gates for the rest of us would be, for the rest of his life, chief and captain for me over all the rest—a post which Joab had taken for granted was safely his and to which he tacitly assumed he was on the verge of being officially appointed. I saw his shudder of choleric surprise when he heard my words. I stared right back at him.

Guess what happened. You hit the nail on the head.

My strategy worked and my stratagem backfired. Wouldn't you know it? Fucking Joab was the first one up the water shaft of the main well of the city, and stood sniggering insolently with his brawny arms folded after he had hewed apart the bolts and swung open the gates to allow the rest of us to charge in. Of course I did everything I could to break my word.

"Now I am legitimately the captain and the chief," he flaunted with no loss of time, as soon as the Jebusites had capitulated without resistance and the occupation of the city was complete. "I am commander of all your host for the rest of my life, right?"

I affected a breathless and displeased astonishment at so bald and unwarranted a proposal. "No way, Joab," I exclaimed. "What in the world are you prattling about?"

You should have seen the look on his face. I have to laugh to myself each time I recall it. We conducted our altercation in starlight amid a circle of subjugated Jebusite administrators looking on wide-eyed.

"What am *I* talking about?" It was an incredulous yelp Joab finally emitted when he was recovered from his initial jar. He went on in a voice made so shrill by distress that he sounded almost effeminate. "You promised, didn't you? Didn't you promise?"

"*I* promised?" I objected coolly. "Promised, you say? What did I promise, when did I promise? Who promised? Not me."

"You did so," he spluttered, fuming. "You gave your royal word."

"I gave my royal word?" I shook my head slowly and adamantly. "Not me."

"You said it, you said it," he insisted almost hysterically. "You said that whoever getteth up to the gutter first and smiteth the Jebusites and the lame and the blind would be chief and captain."

"I said all that? When?"

"Before."

"Before what?"

"Before now. Don't try to weasel out of it, David. You know you said it."

"I did no such thing," I informed him with majesty, lying in my teeth.

"You did so!" he screeched. "It's written down. Everyone knows it. In a proclamation. Your own proclamation. Where's the parchment? Who's got the fucking parchment?"

I watched my chances of pulling it off disintegrating when someone handed him the cylinder of papyrus from which I had read aloud. I thought for an instant of having slain on the spot the man who had passed him the scroll. Joab thrust the paper under my nose in a shaking fist, fumbling to unroll it.

"Here!" he boomed. "See? Read it."

I peered down my nose in silence, then turned away with an air of lofty distaste. "It's not my writing," I informed him in chilly reproof.

Again he responded as though he found it impossible to believe his ears. "Everyone heard you!" he screamed in a mixture of impotent wrath and fear, and seemed ready to dissolve in tears.

In the end I had to give up. This time he had the witnesses. And Joab has been captain over all my host ever since, withstanding every attempt of mine to dislodge him. Except for my personal palace guard of Cherethites and Pelethites, who are in service only to me and are commanded by Benaiah.

How strange it is that I have grown so old and Joab has not. We used to be the same age. I lie in bed with the chills, whining for love from my robust wife Bathsheba and shivering in passionless decrepitude with my shrunken arms hugging Abishag, and he sows barley, flax, and wheat and helps preserve the peace as a stalwart of Adonijah's. I have found him impossible to demote, even after his near-fatal blunder in Transjordan of plunging headlong with all his men into the empty area between the army of Ammonites outside the city of Rabbah and the army of Syrians of Zobah, Rehob, Ishtob, and Maccah hired by the Ammonites to come down to ally with them against us when the Ammonites saw they stank before me. Joab never could get into that obtuse military mind of his the obvious proposition that in war one side's salient is the other side's pincer. He plowed right into the middle and sent word to me cockily when he had established himself in that position.

"I have advanced unopposed and taken up my station between the two armies. What do you think of that?"

Strategy, on the other hand, has always been my middle name. "I think that you had better watch your ass," I responded at once, "because now you can be attacked from both sides, you moron, no matter which way you face. Divide your men."

Joab saw the light at once, deducing from my prompting that the battlefront was against him now both before and behind. He snatched victory from the jaws of defeat by doing at once what he does best: fighting. He picked the strongest men for himself and put them in array against the Syrians, and the rest he delivered to his brother Abishai to go against the children of Ammon. His directions to Abishai were uncomplicated:

"If the Syrians be too strong for me, then thou shalt help me. But if the children of Ammon be too strong for thee, then I will come and help thee. Be of good courage. We have nothing to fear but fear itself."

Lo and behold, the Syrians fled as Joab drew nigh into the battle against them. And when the children of Ammon saw that the Syrians were fled, they turned also and fled into the city. So Joab was able to withdraw intact from Ammon and return to Jerusalem, having achieved nothing for Israel from his mission into Jordan but the saving of his skin.

I took charge then, to show how it was done and to demonstrate the superiority of brains over brawn. I personally led my army north to Helam against Hadarezer and the other Syrian kings, boldly bearding these lions right in their den by striking them where they were enmassed on their home ground. What was the point in leaving them free to assemble and move south against me? I smote them there with a power that devastated them. Oh, what a field day I had. It was a picnic. We slew the men of seven hundred chariots of the Syrians, and forty thousand horsemen, and even smote Shobach, the captain of their host, who died there. They had nothing left. And when Hadarezer and all the kings that were servants to him saw that they were smitten before me, they made peace with Israel quickly and agreed to serve us, and they have been serving us meekly ever since. And they feared to help the children of Ammon anymore, leaving them at our mercy; but the summer was ended, the showers of autumn were falling back home, and it was time to return to our country to harvest our dates, olives, and grapes, and sow our wheat and our barley at the beginning of winter, and to change into fresh, dry clothes. For everything there is a season, you know.

So it came to pass after the year was expired and the almond trees were again coming into blossom, at that time when kings again made ready to go forth into battle, that the Ammonites were shutting themselves up once more inside their city of Rabbah, in anticipation of the siege they expected we would renew, and the stage was set for my meeting with Bathsheba and the nearly cataclysmic liaison that followed. By that time my reputation was large and glamorous and I could get just about every woman I wanted, simply by taking her. Joab arrived at my doorstep on hearing the first cuckoo of spring and enthusiastically unveiled his plans for invading both Europe and Asia. I thought them farfetched. I turned him down and watched him bare his teeth and growl at me in furious irritation again. That's some Joab I've got, isn't it? I have to shake my head and marvel every time I remember Absalom's setting fire to the barley field of this quick-tempered, heartless warrior and swearing he would put the torch to his other crops as well. That's some Absalom I had too. Who could help loving him, if only for that, and even for his unbelievable insolence in rising up to usurp my throne? The ambiguous pity is that he did not succeed. The one chance he had of conquering me he negligently threw away, thank God.

By the time of Absalom's insurrection, I had created, over the vociferous opposition of Joab, my personal palace guard of Cherethite and Pelethite mercenaries and given sole control of these soldiers to Benaiah the son of Jehoiada. The theory was originally Joab's that an élite corps of hired alien fighting men uninterested in domestic conflicts and immune to the influences of subversion would be a good thing for us to have. The idea to construct one and then put Benaiah at the head was entirely my own. Of course my nephew Joab was shocked.

Benaiah, a well-knit man with a deep chest and thick, bronzed neck, was one of my thirty mighty men of legend. Once, bearing just a staff, he had gone down to close with an armed Egyptian five cubits tall, wrested the spear from his grasp, and dispatched the fellow with his own weapon, he said. Another time, he related, he descended into a water pit to slay a lion. Why he elected to descend into a water pit to slay a lion is a question I have not bothered to put to him. Benaiah is a strong and simple man without a mind of his own, which was another factor recommending his selection: I wanted him responsive only to mine. It did not surprise me that Joab was apoplectic when I chose Benaiah to command my palace guard and made him responsible only to me.

"You're a lousy uncle!" he blurted out when he bulled his way in to see me. "I'm supposed to be chief and captain over all of the host. The head of the palace guard should be under me."

"The head of the palace guard," I replied temperately, "should be, I feel, under the head of the palace. Me."

"I am under you," he tried reasoning with me. "So Benaiah would still be under you if you put him under me."

I found that reasoning specious. "You're away too often," I said in opposition.

"What do you need him for anyway? You must tell him to rely on my authority whenever you're not near to instruct him."

"I will always be near to instruct him," I let Joab know in a level voice. "Benaiah will go wherever I go."

"Well, talk to him anyway." Joab gave up the argument with a pout. "Tell him he can always trust me. Remind him that I am the one who is commander over all the host, and not him."

There some concord was possible. "I will talk to him," I agreed laconically. "I will tell him how he can trust you."

I had already observed the deadly hatred with which my nephew Joab, through slitted, venomous eyes, was regarding Benaiah, and I judged it best to lose no more time in putting that sinewy young man of war on the alert.

"Joab. Joab?" I began with Benaiah, speaking in a kind of hurried abbreviation, with a voice dropped low enough to approximate a furtive whisper which I hoped would not travel. Taking Benaiah's elbow in a compelling grip, I conducted him in a very brisk and hasty march from one side of this room in my palace to another, as a precaution against any eavesdropper treasonably concealed behind an arras or any of the walls. "My nephew Joab?"

"I hear you." Benaiah was waiting attentively.

"Should he ever give you orders, as though you were subordinate to him . . ."

"Yes?"

"Ignore them. Or carry instructions to you as though they were issued by me . . ."

"Disobey them?"

"Benaiah, Benaiah, you've got such a fine Jewish head on your shoulders. Your mother must love you. Now if you ever catch him looking at you strangely . . ."

"I think I often do see him looking at me strangely."

"Strangely in a much different way."

"I think he may be beginning to approve of me."

"That's the way I meant, the warning I want to give you. If you ever find him looking at you with unexpected warmth, if he starts to treat you with glad affection, as though you were the one dear friend in the world he wanted most at that moment to see, if he throws an arm upon you amiably as though to take you aside for a choice state secret or the newest dirty joke . . ."

"Joab?"

"Yes, don't be fooled. Especially the one about the traveling knight in armor and the wife of Bath. Or greets you suddenly like a long-lost favorite cousin—"

"Joab and I are indeed distant cousins, through his second wife's first husband's mother's father's side, the son of—"

"Like his nearest and dearest cousin, with an overflow of warmth that leads you to believe he would make you his heir, that impels him to embrace you in one or both arms. If he inquires with greatest solicitude about the state of your health and takes your beard in his hand as though to kiss you, even if he does it with his right hand . . ."

"Yes? You're pausing. I'm holding my breath."

"Leap for your life! Jump back from him as quickly as you're able and as far from him as you possibly can get. As though he were poison. Give the biggest damned jump you ever took, by God, and go for your sword as though facing your end. Don't wait to see if you're mistaken, don't give him that chance. It's curtains if you try to play fair. Never take your eyes from his hands whenever he's with you, never. Watch both as though each were an adder. Joab can strike with the left as swiftly as the right. Strive not with an angry man and go not with him to a solitary place. Remember Abner? Remember what happened?"

"He killed him. In the gate of the city."

"Under the fifth rib he got him. With Joab, you must always make certain to guard your fifth rib."

He killed Amasa too, in exactly the way I described, when we had returned victorious after slaying my son and my enemy Absalom and I found myself with new trouble on my hands in the form of another defection, by that Israeli Benjamite rebel Sheba. In placating Israel with the honors owed Judah, I had come near alienating both, and if it was not one half of my country that was repudiating me, it was likely to be the other. It's sometimes hard figuring out the high reputation as a ruler I enjoy today. Sheba blew a trumpet to call the tribes of Israel to renounce me and depart from me. To put an end to this Sheba, I delegated a large body of men and appointed to command them my nephew Amasa, who'd served so lately as captain of mutinous Judah on the side of my slain son Absalom. He proved a poor choice, even as an act of appeasement. I gave him three days to set out. He was late getting started. Elevating Amasa was the first step in a scheme I'd devised for placating Judah and, simultaneously, superseding Joab for having violated orders and killed my son Absalom. There was never to be a second step. I might have foreseen that Joab would take exception to my plan. I might have foreseen that Joab would await him along the way and register his disapproval in a method impossible to overrule.

He waylaid Amasa at the great stone which is in Gibeon, and he said to his tardy cousin, "Art thou in health, my brother?"

Amasa never suspected a thing when Joab grasped him by the beard with his right hand to kiss him. And he never knew what hit him when Joab ran him through the fifth rib with the sword in his left, shedding his bowels to the ground so that he did not have to strike him again. Amasa wallowed in blood in the midst of the highway. And all the people he commanded stood still, as though petrified, until one of Joab's men removed Amasa out of the highway into the field and cast a cloth upon him. Then, of course, Joab himself took over the leadership of the chase and ruthlessly tracked Sheba down and destroyed him.

Benaiah still has not ceased thanking me for alerting him to the danger of Joab. He was certainly grateful when reports of the murder of Amasa got back to us in Jerusalem. "I am indebted to you still one more time," taciturn Benaiah said. "Again and again I owe you my life."

"What can I do with that Joab?" I implored with a shrug.

To tell you the truth, I cared no more for Amasa than I had for Abner. If anything, I liked him less, for what was complacence in Abner was impertinence in the younger man. What galled me most about both these slayings was Joab's deliberately going against my will. He pays hardly any attention to my wishes when his wishes vary from them. That's what really still sticks in my craw: his independence. I always wanted to feel like a king, and Joab has never let me. I imagine that God Himself frequently wants to feel like a king. Why else would He create the world? He did us a favor? But if it's up to me, He won't feel like a king again soon, not until I get my apology. I would settle for that. What would it hurt Him to apologize: "David, I'm sorry. I don't know what I was thinking of when I murdered your baby. Forgive me."

Yes, *murdered* is the word. When the good Lord made my baby die in order to have me repent my sin, that was murder, wasn't it? God is a murderer, imagine that. I told you I had the best story in the Bible, didn't I? I have always known that He was. Sooner or later He murders us all, doesn't He, and back we go to the dust from which we came.

So I'm no longer scared to defy Him. All He can do is kill me.

What I did do with Joab from the day I made Jerusalem mine and found him ensconced irrevocably as captain over all my host was to put him to good use in all of my military exploits. In the field we worked well together; my expeditions came off in rapid succession. In war he would do anything for me, lay down his life for me, discreetly send out Uriah to the Ammonite wall to lay down his own. I was glad for the wars as well back then, when I still had the vigor to fight in them, before I waxed faint that day in a minor action against a wayward band of diehard Philistines and had to be saved by Abishai. Right then and there my men swore to me, saying, "Thou shalt go no more out with us to battle, that thou quench not the light of Israel."

They were telling me in tactful words that my right hand had lost its cunning. That was the beginning of the end. There comes a time in the affairs of men when you cease striving to ward off the encroaching and unavoidable truth that you are no longer merely aging but are growing old, and that you're already embarked on that downhill journey from which no traveler ever returns.

I was glad for the wars back then because I always had faith I could win them easily. I instigated almost all of them, including those decisive two against the Philistines on the plain of Rephaim. Wars took me away from home. They gave me someplace to go while my palace was under construction and something stimulating to do, for to tell you another truth, Jerusalem was not much of a city either when I first moved in.

It was a pigsty, a stable, a squalid, muggy dump. The Jebusites were constitutionally methodical about everything but cleanliness, and they went to bed early. It was a dingy, dull, and drab town, a godawful eyesore, small, walled in, boring, and claustrophobic. It was a jammed and smelly slum. Where could I live with all my wives and children? I couldn't wait to get away alone on weekends to my tent in the country, or to go off to war for whole summers, when heaven is shut up and there is no rain. It is not a blasphemy for me to talk this way about our sacred city, for Jerusalem was not a sacred city until, by my presence, I made it one, and not a holy city until I consecrated it by bringing in the ark of the covenant and setting it in its place in the midst of the tabernacle I had pitched to contain it. God forbade me to build a temple, but He raised no rumpus with me about the ark. I led that magnificent procession and split with Michal for good when she whirled upon me like a lynx to berate me for exposing myself in the street to every maidservant who wanted to see how a king was built. Even a maidservant can look at a king, and they would have chances to look at this one again, I informed her with blazing egalitarian fervor, and lay with her no more. By then, of course, Jerusalem was already the glittering showplace of the Western world. Jerusalem was not a showplace until I built my splendid palace and made it one.

The streets were narrow and dark when I got there, the low, muddy houses dripping with moisture and sagging in upon each other. Drainage was abominable, and the odors of the city were revolting and overpowering. Forget what you hear about clean mountain air—ours reeked of garbage, and still does; of livestock and human excretions. Why do you think we burn so much incense and lay on oceans of perfume? Even the acrid smell of punk and myrrh is preferable to our natural atmosphere. I've never been able to entice the interest of any of my sons to the problem of a sewer system. I've spoiled them all for honest labor. Not one can I picture who, to save himself or save God's world, would go into the clay, tread the mortar, and take hold of the brick mold. They grew tired of hearing me tell them I'd begun life as a shepherd.

"Oh, no," said Amnon.

"Not again," said Absalom.

There were no open spaces in the town proper when I arrived. I dwelt in the fort at first, and began building round about from Mello and inward. Everything was damp and rank all winter long. Wool would not dry. The days were miserably short. It was like living in the goddamn Middle Ages, and one of the first things I undertook was to contract with Hiram king of Tyre to do my building, for his people could work with wood, stone, and precious metals. Hiram sent messengers to me, and cedar trees, lots of cedar trees, and carpenters and masons and stone-squarers and workers in brass, to erect for me the finest house in Jerusalem, the palace which Michal deemed merited only by someone of her highborn station, with a place for a harem for her and my other women, and with a big roof to walk around upon at the end of the day, from which I could look down upon every other house in the city. The harem could have been bigger, as it turned out, with cloistered passages into some of the individual apartments, but who knew then that I was going to go on liking women as much as I did and want them even now? From that rooftop, you recall, I looked down on naked Bathsheba. After a minute or two, my breath stopped. After a minute or two, I was struck by the thunderbolt and fell deeply and suddenly in love. Give not your heart to women, I have written, give not your strength away. But that was only for appearances, in my wisdom literature, and no more meant to be taken as truth than my remarkable sonnet sequences about the pale rider and the dark lady. You want the real story? If the chance ever comes to you again to fall in love, grab it, every time. You might always live to regret it, but you won't find anything to beat it, and you won't know if it will ever come to you once more.

To Hiram king of Tyre, as one of the conditions of our contract, I sent workers to cut wood and hew stone. Forced labor? I wouldn't exactly call it forced labor. But that's what it was, forced labor. Yet nowhere on the scale that Solomon tells me he has in mind should he ever possess the power to build things of his own in my kingdom. A thousand wives seems a lot? Peacocks and apes sound pretentious? That's just for starters. Solomon is a man drearily attentive to truthful details, and I am sometimes in terror that he may mean what he's talking about. Thirty thousand men he would conscript to cut wood in Lebanon, maybe a hundred and fifty thousand more to bring stone from the mountains.

"That's a lot of wood," I point out delicately, "and a lot of stone. What will you do with it all?"

"Build."

"What?"

"Lots of things. A brand-new palace. A larger, better dwelling of costly stone with lots of beaten gold of Ophir. I'd have nothing but the finest beaten gold."

"For me? I'll soon be dead."

"For me. I'd build a huge harem, much bigger than yours, for all the wives I'd take."

"Really a thousand?"

"An even thousand, seven hundred wives and three hundred concubines, princesses all. I would try to marry the Pharaoh's daughter, if ever I was king. Imagine that—me, a Jew from Judah, married to the daughter of the Pharaoh."

"You really like women that much?"

"No. I don't like women a bit."

"And that's why you'd have so many?"

"I'd jazz them all. What did you ever do with those ten concubines you left behind that Absalom went into after you fled the city?"

"I put them in ward and fed them and shut them up until the day of their death, living in widowhood, and never went in unto any of them again."

"I would have jazzed them all."

"I was afraid of herpes."

"I would have trusted in God and taken my chances. I'll build storehouses for grain in cities like Hazor, Megiddo, and Beersheba, and stables with stalls for more than four hundred and fifty chariot horses each. They're not much good up here, those horses. I'll build me a temple with an altar of brass and with a molten sea ten cubits from the one brim to the other, set upon twelve oxen looking outward. I'll have gigantic carvings of cherubims with their wings outstretched, fifteen feet high, made of olive wood and overlaid with gold, and carved figures of palm trees and open flowers, and the walls and ceilings of my temple also will be overlaid entirely with gold. I'll put people to work building towers in the wilderness and hewing out cisterns."

"Why?"

"I've no idea."

"I once thought of building a temple," I recalled with a twinge of regret. "But God told Nathan He wouldn't let me. 'Have I ever asked for a house of cedar?' was the way Nathan told me God said no, but I think there was more to the refusal than that. All of us ask so many questions, don't we? Even God. 'Where is Abel thy brother?' said the Lord unto Cain after Cain had slain him. Didn't God know?"

"I bet He'll let me," boasted Solomon, ignoring my digression. "Nathan thinks so too. You know why you weren't allowed to build a temple? Nathan tells me it was because you shed blood abundantly and made great wars. I wouldn't have to fight any more wars, thanks to you, because you've already won them all. I'll use stones from the mountains for the walls and foundation of my temple and have them sawn and measured at the quarry before they are brought here, so there will be neither hammer nor axe nor any tool of iron heard in the house while the temple is in building. It will last forever."

All this talk was quite surprising from someone of miserly temperament who invested in amulets as a hedge against inflation, counted the number of lentils or grains of barley in a cup whenever he lent or borrowed any, and always ate and drank exactly as many mouthfuls as did whomever he dined with, never more but never any less, even when he dined with his mother.

"Isn't that all highly extravagant?" I couldn't forbear inquiring of this idiot son. "How will you pay for it?"

"I will tax and spend, tax and spend," he answered earnestly, visibly encouraged by my interest. "I'll cede twenty cities to Hiram king of Tyre if I have to, from far away in northern Israel in Naphtali, where they'd never be missed by anyone here. I'll raise a levy of workers out of all Israel of thirty thousand men to send into Lebanon, with ten thousand of them working one month of every three. A month they will be in Lebanon, and two months at home, and a hundred and fifty thousand more I will put in the mountains to hew stone and haul stone."

"Really?" I suppressed a smile. My eyes, I felt, were starting to pop from my head as I listened to his ravings.

"Yes," Solomon responded soberly. "Threescore and ten thousand to bear the burdens and fourscore thousand to do the hewing. That makes up my hundred and fifty thousand. I will also give Hiram twenty thousand measures of wheat for food to his household and twenty measures of pure oil, year by year. And I'll still eat better than you."

"You don't care for food."

"That has little to do with it."

"Then why would you want to?"

"I must live like a king. I'll divide up all Israel into twelve regions."

"For each of the tribes?"

"For each of the months, and I will put officers over them. I'll make each region provide victuals for me and my household for a whole month; each man his month in a year will make provision to me. Every day I'll want thirty measures of fine flour, and threescore measures of meal, ten fat oxen, and twenty oxen out of the pastures, and a hundred sheep, besides harts and roebucks, and fallow deer, and fatted fowl. Not wild, but fatted."

"That seems a great deal."

"I would rather waste than want."

"What will be done with the people who lack bread for themselves?"

"Let them eat cake," he said calmly. "Man does not live by bread alone."

"That is spoken," I comment acidly, "with the wisdom of Solomon."

"Thank you," he replies. "I got that from you."

"You're a very hard man, Shlomo."

"Thank you again. My heart will not bleed for my people. My finger will lade them with a heavy yoke, and I will chastise them with whips."

"Suppose they object?"

"You have unified the country, centralized the government, solidified control. You have the largest army in the world, garrisons and militia at every crossroad, trained forces of mercenaries, a formidable palace guard under Benaiah, spies everywhere, and can bequeath all to your successor. You are snug as a bug in a rug. Why would anyone object?"

"Now that I am snug as a bug in a rug," I observe with irony, "I find I am dying."

"Yes." He agrees mechanically. "And you have everything to live for." He then goes on with that annoying trait of his mother's to pay no attention to what I've said. "I would not sleep on a bed like yours of plain applewood. The patricians of Megiddo have better appointments. I would want for myself to lie on a fine bed inlaid with carved ivory, in a room with magnificent draperies of dark purple Tyrian cloth. The sumptuous curtains of Solomon would be coveted everywhere. My table vessels and utensils would be of bronze, silver, and gold. I wouldn't use clay."

He says this while watching me wet my palate with wine from a flask of burned clay. "Shlomo," I say to him, putting aside my clay flask a touch self-consciously, "do you ever understand why you've never been my favorite?"

"No. I have never understood why I've never been your favorite."

"And I guess you never will. Fools hate knowledge."

"Should I write that down?"

"Do what you want."

"What does it mean?"

"You won't learn from me."

"Would you tell Adonijah? Adonijah is your favorite, isn't he?"

"Adonijah wouldn't want to know. And he's not my favorite. I have no favorites."

"Absalom was your favorite. I could tell."

"And so was Amnon, before Absalom killed him. Solomon, don't be envious. Your mother tells me you're frugal."

"Yes," answers Solomon. "With my own money, I am very frugal. I invest conservatively and always hoard as much as I can. But with the wealth of nations, the sky is the limit to what I could spend."

"For the good of the country and the glorification of God?"

"For the good of myself. I care only about myself, Father. And, of course, about you."

"And your mother?"

"I would do just about anything for my mother. And for you."

"If you were king," I put it to him, "and your mother came to you with a request to permit Adonijah to marry Abishag, what would you do?"

"I would have him killed."

"I can see you've been thinking."

"I think a lot. I try to think at least one hour a day. And do you know what I think? I think that if God ever came to me in a dream and offered me any one thing I wanted, I think I would choose wisdom. Because then, if I were wise enough, I could get everything else I wanted. I've also been thinking about buildings."

"Children and the building of a city continue a man's name," I inform him.

"That's what I say also. Even though my name isn't David and yours is not Jesse. That's the reason I want to build a temple, to continue my name."

"It's the reason I wanted to build mine."

"I'll build and I'll build," vowed Solomon, getting, for him, rather worked up. "And everything I build will be famous and stand forever and be named after me. I'll make donations to hospitals."

"Man's erections are only temporary," I intone with mock seriousness, but he does not smile.

"Mine will last an eternity," he asserts instead, "a hundred years, till hell freezes over or the stars tumble from their courses, till the Messiah comes, till the Assyrians arise or the Babylonians grow strong enough to overthrow Judah. And you know what little chance there is of any of that happening."

"In Ammon once," I glumly have another crack at instructing him, "I met a traveler from an antique land who said two vast and trunkless legs of stone stand in the desert. I went to see them for myself. Near them, on the sand, half sunk, a shattered visage lies, whose frown, and wrinkled lip, and sneer of cold command, tell that its sculptor well those passions read which yet survive, stamped on those lifeless things. And on the pedestal these words appear: 'My name is Ozymandias, king of kings. Look on my works, ye Mighty, and despair.' Nothing beside remains. Round the decay of that colossal wreck, boundless and bare, the lone and level sands stretch far away."

"What's it mean?" asks Solomon.

"You see no moral?"

"I would build towers there and hew out cisterns."

"There is no rainfall."

"What difference would it make? There are no people either. Before I'm through, there'll be a temple of Solomon and a palace of Solomon, the stables of Solomon and the mines of Solomon. Don't worry, you'll be famous too. Everyone will remember that you were my father when they sing hosannas to me and my enduring works. And all of this time, while I am disciplining myself by thinking at least one hour a day, my older brother Adonijah squanders his money and himself on fifty chariots and men to run before him, just as Absalom did, and on wasteful banquets that are as ephemeral as chaff and bring you no honor. Will you attend his luncheon, Father? I am told that it will be a catered affair and that all of the food will be warmed over. Mother informed me of that and told me to ask if you will go."

It has always been difficult for me to think of saucy Bathsheba as somebody's mother. "I haven't been invited yet."

"Nor have I," says Solomon. "Neither has Mother been invited, nor Nathan, nor Benaiah. Doesn't it begin to look like a plot by Adonijah to take over your kingdom?"

"Adonijah wouldn't do that. He's much too lazy. Tell me, has anyone been invited? Has he sent out invitations yet? Has a date been set?"

"I don't know. I won't go if Mother is not invited. Unless, of course, you direct me to."

"I haven't even given Adonijah permission to have his party yet."

"Did you tell him not to?"

"Did Bathsheba tell you to ask me that?"

"Mother bade me tell you," he replies systematically, "that if you said what you just did say, I was to answer that if Adonijah can go about saying he will be king, there is no reason he can't also go around saying he will give a feast."

"That's what she bade you tell me?"

"That's what she bade me tell you."

"Solomon, my wise child, how in the world did you ever remember all that?"

"She wrote it down for me on my tablet. She also put this little bell around my neck. To remind me to look."

"Sooner or later I was going to have to ask you about that bell. I thought it might be in case you got lost. You and your mother are very close, aren't you?"

"I like to believe that we are," Solomon answers with a nod. "She sits at my right hand whenever we are together. We always think only the very best of each other. She thinks I'm a god, and I think she's a virgin. Tell me, Father," he inquires with enormous gravity, "is it possible that my mother can be a virgin?"

"There you have me."

"She's been married twice."

"I wouldn't jump to conclusions."

"I've been thinking hard about it."

"I thought I smelled wood burning."

"I've been thinking also that I would have forty thousand horses and twelve thousand horsemen. I want to speak three thousand proverbs, and my songs will be about a thousand and five. From Dan even to Beersheba, when I have my way, every man will dwell safely under his vine and his fig tree, if I leave him his vine and leave him his fig tree. I want to cut a baby in half."

"Good God! You do?"

"I do."

"Why?"

"To show how fair I can be. Everyone will think I was very fair."

"Everyone will think you're nuts," I feel I have to let him know. "I think you'll go down in history as the biggest damned imbecile who ever lived if you tried even a single one of the things you've mentioned today. I won't breathe a word of your stupidity to a soul, and you don't say anything to anyone about any of this either. We will keep it our secret."

"I want to build a navy."

"Oh, my God!"

"I can float timber of cedar and timber of fir down by sea on barges from—"

"Abishag!"

My own manifold transgressions with the liberty of others were as farts in a blizzard when stacked up beside the mountain of tyrannies contemplated by this stolid offspring of my torrid copulations with Bathsheba. We met in the spring and were married by fall, with Uriah dead and her belly just starting to swell with the child who would die. She and I could not bear being apart in that feverish and astonishing and vertiginous lewd beginning. We plucked without stop at each other's flesh, in stroking and pinching caresses of the waist, hips, arms, backside, and thighs. Our fingers snatched touches. We kept touching tenderly when we weren't in violent embrace. We were constantly hot for each other.

"I get so wet," she sighed so often.

We debauched without stop in our uncommon ecstasy of renewed discovery and fulfillment. Other women cloy the appetites they feed, but Bathsheba made hungry where most she satisfied. No wonder I tarried in Jerusalem much longer than I had planned and did not go forth into the sands of Ammon to join Joab at Rabbah until the city was ready to fall.

In the beginning I still had foreign foes galore. Something in man requires an enemy, something in mankind demands a hostile balance of power. Without one, things fall apart. Absalom struck in a time of peace when the causes of all national strife had been eliminated, and Sheba rose when Absalom was gone. I was fortunate in the possession of so many unifying alien enemies when my reign was new and insecure.

Victory in war was exhilarating too. I had God on my side. Want to bet? My conquests were achieved with so little struggle and so few setbacks that it was natural for the world to conclude I was loved by the Lord and that he was taking care to preserve me whithersoever I decided to expand. The Ammonites fell to me last, as a matter of fact, and were really not much trouble after I had helped pull Joab's chestnuts out of the fire in the campaign the year before and beaten back the few Syrian rulers left with the balls to oppose me by siding with the Ammonites. That just took time, the final siege—enough time for me to impregnate Bathsheba and liquidate her husband after he refused to play into my hands by lying with her. He preferred staying in my palace and getting drunk there to going home to his wife. I can't think how I would have coped with that burgeoning scandal otherwise and still retained my charisma as a legendary religious figure meriting the veneration I receive today. I had much less difficulty with the whole array of my foreign opponents than Zedekiah did later on with only Nebuchadnezzar and the Babylonians: they slaughtered the sons of Zedekiah before his eyes and then blinded him and bound him with fetters of brass. These are rough times we live in, very rough times. We play for keeps.

First on my schedule of military objectives, of course, came the Philistines, who were more and more ruffled by the progress and growth in strength of their erstwhile vassal and protégé, but delayed too long in taking steps to curb me. Philistines are cumbersome in making decisions. They were never a single community. And this time we were. I was better organized. And I knew I had to dispose of these people as overlords before I could set my sights realistically on any of the others. By the time they were ready to attempt to suppress me, I practically outnumbered them.

When you consider their long history of domination, the Philistines were vanquished by me more easily than you might guess. Seven years of civil war had not been wasted on us: I had my standing army now, and my militias in every community of size in the north and the south that could be mustered by a blast of the trumpet or ram's horn and be on the march by nightfall. The Philistines were content so long as Judah and Israel were separate and at odds, and so long as they enjoyed unhindered access to their bastions in the north through the valley of Jezreel, which divided the mountains of Galilee from Samaria, and to the cities in Judah they found it profitable to occupy. Even my home town of Bethlehem was presently under the rule of Philistine hoodlums who had moved in and taken over.

Now, however, the situation was considerably altered. We were one nation, indivisible. The Philistines had let me know they were very disturbed that I'd been anointed king over Israel too. They were further provoked when they saw me secure myself against easy retribution by taking the fortress city of Jerusalem and making it my capital. They sent up messengers bearing ultimatums of disapproval. I responded impenitently that this was the land promised by the Lord of my fathers Abraham, Isaac, and Jacob, and that they could all go back to Crete and the other Greek islands if they didn't like it.

Instead of accepting my suggestion that they return to the Aegean settlements from which their seafaring forefathers had migrated, they came up toward Jerusalem for war and spread themselves in the valley of Rephaim. This was peachy with me; Philistines never were much good on high ground. I went down to the stronghold for safety and issued a call to arms. My mood was one of unreserved confidence as I waited for the people to come and my forces to grow. I talked with God, just to make sure.

"Shall I go up to the Philistines?" I inquired of the Lord in a solitary place where no one could overhear. "Wilt Thou deliver them into my hand?"

"Will I deliver them into thy hand," the Lord repeated without the inflection of an interrogative, as though my question were both tedious and unnecessary.

"Will you?"

"Why do you even ask?" said the Lord unto me. "Go up, go up. For I will doubtless deliver the Philistines into thine hand."

So I went up, I went up, for the word of the Lord back then was good enough for me. The Philistines had come forth almost casually, as on a minor punitive expedition, and their size was not daunting. This time, in fact, we did outnumber them, and we confronted them head-on in a straightforward way and beat them badly—no sun stood still, no turbulent, heaven-sent hailstorms or thunderstorms to mire or discomfit them—the first such pitched battle in which we had triumphed since the beginning of the earth. Had we hats, we would have tossed them in the air in the first flush of victory. Instead, I gave commands regarding the images of worship left behind by the Philistines in the field from whence they had fled—icons of Dagon, the fish god, and of Astarte, the goddess with the bared breasts of a woman and the trousers of a man—and we burned them. We burned them with fire and cheered once more as they went up in smoke.

It was not long before the Philistines were back with a vengeance. This time they marched up with the fullest complements of regiments, battalions, and platoons they could assemble from all of their big cities, and the ranks in which they plodded upward toward Jerusalem from their settlements in the coastal plains and spread themselves a second time in the valley of Rephaim were greatly increased and very formidable to behold. Joab quivered with joy in anticipation as we watched them come. I have never seen a person so eager for the fray.

"They're all here!" He couldn't wait. He clapped his hands, and his nostrils were flaring like those of a war-horse breathing fire. "Let's run right down at them and make a score of them sorry for a while."

"Why don't we walk down," I mused, "and make all of them sorry for good?"

"What do you mean?"

"I want to mull it over." This was going to be the big one. I borrowed the ephod from Abiathar and walked off by myself into the woods to get my guarantee from God. And I inquired of the Lord, "Shall I go up to the Philistines just as I did the time before? Wilt thou deliver them into my hand?"

And the Lord said, "No."

For the moment I was shaken. "No?"

"No."

"What do You mean, no?" I was indignant. "You won't deliver them into my hand?"

And the Lord said, "Do not go up against the Philistines as thou did before."

"What then?"

"But fetch a compass behind them, and come upon them over against the mulberry trees."

"A compass?"

"A compass."

"What's a compass?"

"Encircle them. Ambush and aggravate them."

"You're not going to believe this, O Lord," I said, "but I had that same idea myself, of sneaking around them through the mulberry trees on the sides of the plains and pouncing upon them from there and aggravating them from the flanks."

"Sure, sure you did."

"What worries me, O Lord, is the noise we might make as we move closer to them in the woods and prepare to charge. Is it possible they won't hear us? Wilt Thou deliver them?"

"Didn't you already ask Me that?"

"Did You give me an honest answer? Tell me yes or tell me no."

"I'll deliver them, I'll deliver them," said God. "What more do you want from Me?"

"What about the noise?"

"Fetch a compass through the mulberry trees. I already told you the compass, didn't I? When you're all in place, wait."

"Wait?"

"For the wind. Without a whisper. When thou hearest the sound of a wind going in the top of the mulberry trees, only then shalt thou bestir thyself. Let the movement of the branches be thy cue. Come forward with the rustle of the woods. They will not know you are there until you are already well upon them. Thus will all be delivered into thy hand."

And that was the last time God ever spoke to me, I realize now. Time flies. Thirty years have passed, and it seems like only yesterday. And excepting those seven days of prayer when my baby was stricken with illness and I lay all night on the earth, I've spoken to Him only one more time, when He sent that pestilence upon all Israel for the Census I took that everybody disapproved of. Now He saves us, now He kills us. People were dropping like flies from His disease, despite the scent bags of camphire from the vineyards of Engedi worn about the neck in sachets of linen. Camphire is good with mumps, but worthless against bubonic plague. The country stank from camphire. Even Joab took issue with my registering humans who belonged to my God and not to my government.

"Moses did it," I argued. "Read Numbers."

"You're Moses?"

I went ahead anyway, for I needed the records to facilitate conscription and taxation. The Devil made me do it. And there died of the people from Dan even to Beersheba seventy thousand men and women, and children too. When I saw the angel that had smote the people stretch out his hand upon Jerusalem to destroy it, I repented myself of the evil and cried out in panic, "What are you doing, what are you doing? Lo, I have sinned, and I have done wickedly. But these sheep, what have they done? Let thine hand, I pray thee, be against me, and against my father's house. Stop! Stop! What the fuck is the matter with all of you, anyway?"

I was not certain whether I was talking to the angel or talking to God. Either way, God pointedly refrained from answering me, and blandly addressed the angel instead, saying, "It is enough. Stay now thy hand." The city of Jerusalem was saved by a hair. And through my prophet He told me: buy the threshing floor on which the angel had stood and rear an altar. That was all it took in the end to appease our angry Diety, another goddamned altar. He needed that altar? Like Gilead needs balm and Heshbon fish pools. What does He want with so many altars? It was a stupid thing to do, for both of us, God and me.

We were smarter together against the Philistines, operating hand in glove in the flawless execution of our plan for utilizing the cover of the mulberry trees in the second battle of Rephaim. It worked like a charm. When the daily breeze from the sea of the Philistines reached us after we had fetched our compass, we advanced beneath the rising, blustery commotion of the leaves of the mulberry trees. That was our signal. The noise of our footsteps was drowned in the natural commotion of forest murmurs, and almost all together we came flying out from the sides with maniacal, bloodcurdling war cries and threw ourselves upon ranks and ranks of lumbering men in heavy armor routinely arranged in rows of battle lines facing . . . nothing. They were taken completely unawares. What could you expect from people with no more brains than to come a second time and spread themselves the same way in the same field from which they had so recently been routed, instead of dividing themselves into separate columns and continuing directly upward to the city to besiege it? Caught without warning by these assaults on the flanks, they were not able to reform, and they could strike at nothing but each other. What could they do but turn and flee? We pursued without letup. I was not satisfied with their five major cities. We hounded and smote them from Geba all the way until thou come to Gezer, beating them all down finally into an unconditional surrender and making extinct forever what little they had that passed for their culture.

I put bailiffs in Gath. I took their iron. I took their fish. I had their swords beaten into plowshares and their spears into pruning hooks, and they could not make war anymore unless they did so for me. I took their blacksmiths and smelters and miners and bade them teach us the uses of metal, and I recruited Ittai the Gittite and six hundred other Philistines to serve me—that same Ittai who, bereft of homeland a second time, wrung my heart with his devotion on the flight from Jerusalem when he chose to stay loyal to me after I had released him from his oath of service to enable him to seek a safe position with my enemy Absalom. Almost overnight I had made a quantum leap into the modern world—I had taken my people of Israel and led them out of the Bronze Age and into the Iron Age, which, for us, proved a golden age.

Strengthened all the more now by Philistine iron and Philistine fighting men, I gained one success after another. It was hard to keep track. Moab fell to my might and became a tributary state. I put garrisons in Edom and in the land of the Amelekites. From Aqaba in Edom I extracted the copper and iron ore needed to nourish our thriving new metalworking industry, which soon was rivaling our excellent garment center in fame and productivity. Opportunities for further expansion and appropriation dropped into my lap like apples of gold from a tree of silver. I could not believe my good luck when travelers passing through in trade on the highway into Egypt reported that the Syrian Hadadezer, the son of Rehob king of Zobah, was going north against Toi of Hamath to recover his border at the river Euphrates, leaving the Golan heights and the rest of his southern border practically undefended. I was already fully mobilized and searching for new worlds to conquer. Here was tougher game. Fortune favors the brave.

"Bid the men gird on their swords," I commanded Joab as soon as I made up my mind to jump at the chance. "Tell them to come not at their wives."

"No shit?"

"And no shit either. I don't want the camp unclean."

"We're going to war?"

"Against Hadadezer."

"Who?"

"Hadadezer."

"Hadarezer?"

"Hadadezer."

"Oh."

Many people were burdened with exotic names like that back then, and often, in my speculations on the esoteric, I theorize that the singular reason men like Joseph, Moses, Abraham, Jacob, Samuel, and me were selected by the currents of destiny to stand out from the ordinary was that we all have solid English names that are recognizable and familiar. It's no big wonder to me that my recorder Jehoshaphat leaps a foot into the air each time he's called. I would jump too if my name were Jehoshaphat or Hadadezer.

Hadadezer jumped plenty once I gave him a *zetz*, for I went up on the double to smite him, and I took from him a thousand chariots, and seven hundred horsemen, and twenty thousand footmen. And I hocked all the chariot horses, except those for a hundred chariots I decided to keep. And when the foolhardy Syrians of Damascus came to succor Hadadezer, I moved right through them like shit through a goose and slew two and twenty thousand men. The Syrians became servants to me and brought gifts, and I took the shields of gold that were on the servants of Hadadezer and brought them to Jerusalem. From Betah and Berotthia, two cities of Hadadezer, I took exceeding much brass, for to the victor belong the spoils. And on the way back I got me a name from smiting more of the Syrians in the valley of salt, being another eighteen thousand men. I looked back into that valley, which was full of dry bones, and wondered, can these dry bones really live? All my trials, it seemed to me then, were just about over. I put garrisons in Damascus and in the Golan heights, and I knew that the Syrians would never again be a problem for the children of Israel. That was another very good year.

I certainly was riding high, for in between my battles with the Philistines and my reduction of Moab, I had also brought the ark of the covenant into Jerusalem. Michal was indeed an enduring tribulation, but even a king must sometimes take the rough with the smooth and the bitter with the sweet.

When I had rest from my enemies and time to draw a breath, I could look around me in leisure and measure all I had accomplished. I was impressed. It was no little thing I had wrought. From the Euphrates in the north to Egypt in the south, just about everything in existence on the face of the earth was mine, from the sea of the Philistines into the desert of the east, excepting the scattered settlements of the Ammonites, who had not yet begun to stink in my eyes. I could, if I wished, stand on a peak in Darien, look about me in each direction, and know I was master of all I surveyed. No wonder I was satisfied with myself. I felt slick as owl shit. Who wouldn't? I was proud as a peacock, for I had taken a kingdom the size of Vermont and created an empire as large as the state of Maine!

There was nowhere to go but down.

10

NAKED
WE WERE

So surprising a thing it is for a man who doesn't believe in love to find himself so deeply in it. Naked we both were, almost every day, sometimes three or four times a day, and we were not ashamed. It began when the almond trees were coming into blossom. I know this because I remember his saying they were. I waited to hear more. Joab is not a man with much poetry in his spirit, and he usually has more important things on his mind than the rhythm of the seasons and the renewal of spring. The earth was putting forth green leaves already, he notified me with a quiver. Before we could look around, the voice of the turtle would again be heard in the land.

"So what?" I confessed my perplexity.

There was no time to lose. Europe was wide open. Asia too. Now that we had iron, he argued, we should strike while it was hot.

"What's the hurry?" I asked, affected with lethargy by the balmy change in the weather. "Where's the need?"

"The English are coming down from the trees," he informed me as though menaced. "The Germans are coming out of their caves. We have to act now. Before you know it, there could be an industrial revolution. Progress can destroy the world. Someone might discover America. I'm not exaggerating. They'll invent democracy and degenerate into capitalism, fascism, and communism. They could find a use for petroleum someday. What would happen if they harness electricity, or invent the internal combustion machine, or the steam engine? You want automobiles? Choochoo trains? There could be concentration camps. There might even be Nazis. There'll be lots of *goys*. They might not like us. They'll take our religion and forget where it came from."

JOSEPH HELLER

I scratched my head. This was food for thought. "How would you go about it?"

"Here's my plan." Joab unfolded his maps. "Let me have Abishai and six hundred men who can be trusted not to put down their swords when we kneel by a pool to drink but will lap water with their faces like a dog. We will travel upward through the isthmus of Turkey into the soft underbelly of Europe, sweeping all in our path before us. Once there, Abishai will turn east to his right hand with three hundred men to conquer the Caucasus, India, Afghanistan, Nepal, Tibet, Siberia, Mongolia, China, Vietnam, Korea, Japan, and Formosa. While Abishai is prevailing there, I will turn westward to my left hand with the other three hundred men to vanquish the rest of southern Russia from the Caspian Sea even unto the Black Sea, the Ukraine, and the Balkans. I will take Rumania, Hungary, Yugoslavia, Greece, Albania, Italy, Austria, Germany, France, the Low Countries, then Spain and Portugal. I will overcome Poland too, if there is one. I will leave a garrison on Gibraltar to dominate the entrance into the sea of the Philistines forever. I know what you're thinking."

"It sounds grandiose."

"You're laughing at me, aren't you?"

"You might run into opposition."

"Haven't I thought of that? But if the people of Europe be too strong for me, then Abishai shall come and help me. And if the children of Asia be too strong for Abishai, then I will go and help him. What could be plainer? Did I not succeed that same way against both the children of Ammon and the Syrians? When Iberia and France have been reduced, I will cross over from Calais to Dover and conquer the English and the Welsh before departing from Liverpool to Dublin to subdue Ireland. With Ireland pacified, I will commence my return through Scotland. From the Firth of Forth I will go into the bottom of Norway, march upward along the coast to the top and come down through Sweden and Finland. How does it sound so far?"

"What will you do for kosher food?"

"We'll leave with goat cheese and barley bread, with clusters of raisins and cakes of figs. In Turkey and Greece we'll replenish our provisions with dates and honey. We'll bring lentils and flat beans for protein. In Scotland we'll have kippers and smoked salmon. In Scandinavia, Holland, and Denmark, we'll have all the herring and smoked fish we can eat. I'll bring some back if you want me to. In Russia there's sturgeon, caviar, and black bread."

"Russia? You're going to conquer Russia too?"

"On the way home. Coming back, I will level a siege against Leningrad. Then I will take Moscow, Stalingrad, Rostov, Kiev, and Odessa. Returning southward into Turkey, I will join again with Abishai, homeward bound from overwhelming the Orient and all of the rest of Asia, and together we will journey back into Israel, arriving in time for the harvests of our grapes and olives and for the sowing of the seed for our barley, wheat, and flax. Could anything be easier?"

"How will you get from Scotland to Norway?" I wondered.

"By boat," said Joab.

"We have no boats," I reminded. "And we wouldn't know how to use them if we did."

Joab wrinkled his brow. "Then how will I get from France to England?"

"Maybe you'd better just walk across the Jordan into Ammon instead and surround Rabbah again."

"You wait here."

The next thing I knew I was madly in love. It hit like a thunderbolt. I was gaping at this naked woman as though transfixed and communing with voices on my roof like a frenzied and licentious maniac, for I tarried still in Jerusalem after I sent Joab and my servants off on this campaign against Rabbah, and I had nothing much to do for excitement as I waited for the new summer wardrobe for which I had already been measured. So I went for a walk on my roof each evening and let my mind go wandering where it would. I was bored. A time before when I was bored in Jerusalem, I brought the ark of the covenant into the city. I could think of nothing better to do, so I settled on that and had my big row with Michal that at last put an end to our conjugal relationship and to any lenient impulses I might have felt for her thereafter. The fight with Michal turned out a blessing in disguise, for by that time we had both grown very sick of each other.

To tell you the honest truth, I had no clear idea what the ark of the covenant even was when I decided to move it up into the city from the house of Obededom the Gittite, with no one but yours truly, the king himself, starring at the head of the spectacular procession I was beginning to orchestrate. But holy people did; the ark was important to them, and I saw no harm in propitiating the religious in the effort I was making to solidify all factions in a country that was proving to be hopelessly pluralistic and refractory. You think God had His troubles with Moses and those people in the desert? I had my hands full too. The ark was of acacia, and inside this chest of acacia wood were said to be those two original tablets of stone from Mount Sinai on which the basic ten words to Moses had been written by the finger of God. No one was permitted to look inside, so we never could ascertain if this was so or not. No one was permitted even to touch it. We deduced this from the sorry fate betiding poor Uzzah on my first attempt to transfer the ark three months earlier. Acting on reflex, and with only the most pietistic intentions, poor Uzzah put forth his hand to take hold of the ark when it shook on the wagon after one of the oxen stumbled. And the anger of God was kindled against Uzzah for this innocent misjudgment and God smote him there, and there he died by the ark of God, right there on the spot. The road to hell, I've written, is paved with good intentions. Admittedly, this was a small statistical basis for the verification of the inviolability of the ark; I could think of no humane way to enlarge it. Whom could I ask in the interest of experimentation to volunteer to touch it again?

This second time, I supervised the entire enterprise myself and gave closer attention to the details. No wagons, I ordained. Oxen could not be depended upon. This time I had poles put through the rings of the ark, as Moses once had commanded be done according to the word of God, and I employed human beings as bearers, Levites all, who would not have to come within ten feet of the chest of acacia, with those splendid carved figures of the two cherubims on top with their heads bowed, facing each other, and their arching wings stretched upward and forward on high so expressively. Levite carriers made a more dramatic effect than cattle and enhanced the occasion with a good deal of pomp. What a stirring day that was! The event transformed the city of David into the city of God, and Jerusalem continues as a center of worship even now. Where the ark was, there was God. Where the ark is today, God knows.

Weeks in advance, the voice of the trumpet sounded long through the land with proclamations encouraging all in Israel to come observe me parade if they wished to avail themselves of the opportunity to do so. It was not an action I was going to perform every day. Tentatively and cautiously, with bated breath, we lifted the ark out of the house of Obededom the Gittite, where it had rested since Uzzah touched it with his hand and dropped dead on the spot; Obededom had prospered since, and this was interpreted by my priests as an auspicious signal from God to go forward with my plan. And it was so that when they that bare the ark on the poles had gone six paces without any of them falling down dead, we knew we were home free. I let out a huzzah and sacrificed seven bullocks and seven fatlings. And then the celebration began. All Israel played before the Lord that day. Even I was carried away and sang hallelujah more times than I can remember. We played before the Lord on all manner of instruments made of fir wood, even on harps, and on psalteries, and on timbrels, and on cornets, and on cymbals. You never heard so much music or saw so much rejoicing as there was on the day we brought the ark of the covenant up into the city with shouting, and with the sound of the trumpet. There was never such music and such song and such shouting for joy since the spirit of God first moved upon the face of the waters and He said: "Let there be light." And there was light. And there was I, right out in front, leading them all, dancing before the Lord. I danced before the Lord with all my might, clothed in a robe of fine linen and girded with a linen ephod.

I was having the time of my life. I knew I was exposing myself for the whole town to see while I danced with all my might. I did not know that Michal was looking at me through a window as I danced before the Lord, and that she was despising me in her heart as she saw me leaping and dancing that way. Or that she would lose all self-control and lash out at me before others the moment I set foot in my house.

"It had to be before others," she tried lamely to extenuate herself afterward. "You're never alone with me anymore."

She was damned right about that, too.

But first there were those overactive hours of exhilarating ceremonies outside. Amid great toasting and great roaring jubilation, the ark of the Lord was set in its place in the midst of the tabernacle I'd had the foresight to order pitched for it, and I offered burnt offerings and peace offerings before the Lord and blessed the people in His name. And then I dealt out among all the people, as well to the women as the men, to everyone a cake of bread, and a good piece of flesh, and a flagon of wine. This was a day I made sure no

Jew would ever forget. So all the people were gratified with me and departed everyone to his house.

Now it was time for me to retire to my own dwelling to bask in my accomplishments. Flushed with triumph, glistening in the sheen of sweat of the merry athlete, I turned in toward my palace to bless my own household, overflowing with good feeling for each and every one of us. My heart was beating gladly. This was a capital day's work well done, I was thinking, for me and for my God; and I was thinking this way until I stepped across the threshold with my retinue of devoted admirers, and Michal, that daughter of Saul, before I could utter the first in the train of benedictory words I had prepared, sprang out to attack me and to shriek and bay at me like a maddened animal with a countenance so deformed by malevolence that she was hardly recognizable. I tell you truthfully, for a moment I was terrified, frozen in place. I gaped with horror. All her beauty was departed. It has never returned. I see her always with that same inhuman and distorted face, her eyes feral, her teeth bared. I do not know if she saw what she looked like. I do not know if she ever regretted the intemperate outburst with which she hurt and affronted me unforgivably for the very last time, even though the rest of her life was a misery because of it.

"How glorious was the king of Israel today," were the sneering words with which she excoriated me, spewing into my face her bitterness and contempt, as though I were anyone but that king of Israel to whom she was alluding in her tirade, "who uncovered himself in the eyes of the handmaids of his servants, as one of the vain fellows shamelessly uncovereth himself."

And I came blazing right back at her, saying, "It was before the Lord that I played, which chose me before thy father, and before all his house to anoint me ruler over the people of the Lord, over Israel. Not before you. Therefore will I play before the Lord again. I shalt make myself naked if I want to. And of the maidservants of which thou hast spoken, of them shall I be had in honor. Go now to thy quarters. And never with thy shadow darken this door of mine again, except thou first hast permission."

Thus was she banished. I went no more to lie with her. Therefore Michal the daughter of Saul had no child unto the day of her death.

It was not, however, the last I heard from her, for she paid no more attention to my prohibition against harassing me than she had to. In painful fact, I heard from her daily. She sent messengers hourly with threatening agendas of what she would and would not put up with and unending manifestos of criticism and demand. She wanted an alabaster bathtub after I gave one to Bathsheba; she wanted queenly dressing tables, an antique cake-stand, and larger, more public rooms in which to hold court in the harem. I thought often of moving her into an apartment all the way in the back, where I might never have to run into her on my trips to the others. She wanted more maidservants, and she wanted me to provide them. She had fewer than the five beauties Abigail had brought with her into our marriage for her own domestic convenience and my lubricious diversion. They were darling little creatures, all five, and I had children by two or three. Michal's chronic bursts of outrage and invective would resound eerily through my palace like the denunciations of something supernatural and damned, and sometimes leave me longing to be deaf, or even dead. Don't think I can't hear her still. Don't think I still can't see that whited, sepulchral face solidified like stone into an expression of violent hatred and misanthropy. The honeymoon was over.

So it came to pass in an eveningtide after Joab had been dispatched into Ammon that I arose from off my bed to avoid another servant from her bearing another mortifying communication of discontent. I hastened upstairs to my roof for some peace and to escape the baking heat inside. And I saw this luscious woman washing herself on her roof less than a bowshot away and eyeing me without modesty as she saw me regarding her. She was as naked as a jaybird and not afraid. I was impressed by that. She was not ashamed of the female form she presented or of my arrogant scrutiny, and the woman was indeed very beautiful to look upon. In fact, she even turned herself toward me a bit more to allow me a better frontal view of her plump belly and thick mons veneris. I will not deny I was attracted. Deep was calling unto deep when our gazes met and remained resolutely locked.

"Do my eyes deceive me?" I mused aloud softly, "or is her bird truly ash blonde?"

"Your eyes," my faithful servant Benaiah responded with honesty, "do not deceive you."

I sent to inquire after the woman and, scarcely breathing, hardly moving, gawked as she continued to lather and rinse seductively the rounded hills and pleasant valleys of her body, where I was already thirsting to pasture and knew in the marrow of my bones I would soon be grazing. She was making my mouth water as she stood there bare-assed on the roof in her basin of fired clay. In a sidelong, challenging way, she watched me steadily all the while. No one had ever looked so beautiful to me; no one has ever looked so beautiful to me since, not even she. Before I knew it, my cock was hard. I stroked it firmly beneath the fine white linen of my summer skirt. I wanted to put it into this strange unblushing woman. Who was she? Who she was turned less and less important as we prolonged our salacious eye contact while I waited to find out.

Everything about Bathsheba then was provocative and odd. She was no less haunting physically when she was already my mistress and I scanned her close up. I had never seen such peculiar breasts: they were small, and tipped with pink rather than dead-leaf brown. She had the weirdest eyes: they were blue. I had never beheld so strange a skin: it was practically white. Her legs as well were most extraordinary: they were long, they were thin, they were shapely and fetching. She herself—I don't know how to describe so striking a phenomenon—was tall, as tall almost as I, and her pelvis was ample without appearing thick. She was not stocky, not the least bit eastern European. Her nose was small, precise and straight, and a trifle retroussé. Yet in spite of all these physical irregularities, she was not unpleasant to look at. In fact, she was rather pretty. The uneven and abnormal color of her hair was already as light as honey, the fairer strands as pale as hay, with here and there some streaks of yellow. When we were married and I came upon her one day experimenting diligently with brushes of hyssop twigs to turn herself blonde in the tincture of loosestrife and saffron she had blended, I fathomed with a gasp what Bathsheba was up to: Bathsheba was trying to turn herself into a WASP! Between Michal and Bathsheba I had married the entire range. I was missing a *schvartze,* although Ahinoam and Maccah were both almost dark enough to pass.

How Michal envied and hated her! Wrinkled ass and all, Bathsheba was something truly commanding to look at then and knew better than any other woman in the world how to make a man feel good. And doubtless she would know how to please one again if the spirit moved her to do so. She had stretch marks on her buttocks from using them so much.

How Michal resented and detested her, along with the plethora of others equally at home in my household who now had as much right as she to be there. The list of names of wives and concubines and maidservants had grown too long for either one of us to fling at the other in its entirety. This one was too noisy, that one unsociable, this one snored, that one didn't bathe enough, the other bathed too often and wasted water. What a plague she was. Michal, who scorned my elegant Abigail as provincial, barren, and middle class, was afflicted sorely each time I fathered another child by Bathsheba or by one of the winsome damsels Abigail had brought into my household as maidservants for both of us.

"It is better," was one of the maxims with which she lectured me repeatedly, "to spill your seed on the ground than in the belly of a whore."

That shows how much she knew.

Michal never tired of telling me she despised me for consorting with such trollops as my other wives, instead of spending more time with her. How she whined and fulminated for a child of her own! She slammed doors and stamped her foot and smashed mirrors and rouge pots and perfume flasks, as though the procreation of the species took place in tantrums of petulance and tempestuous discharges of irrational antipathies. Hell hath no fury, she taught me, like a woman scorned. What was the point in telling her over and over again that she no longer could bear one and, after childless marriages to two men, had possibly always been barren?

"Why can't I bear one?" she snapped. "I'm just as good as everyone else. I've been married to you longer than any of those others, haven't I? And I am the daughter of a king."

"You're too old now," I told her mildly, hoping once more, against the weight of all previous evidence to the contrary, to succeed in turning away somebody's wrath with a soft answer. "You should have thought more about that twenty and thirty years ago, when you wouldn't put out more than once a month."

"That has nothing to do with it," she flashed back at me. "I'll put out now."

"It's too late now. You're past the age."

"What about Sarah? Sarah was past ninety when she had one. I'm just as good as she was."

I was shaking my head slowly. "Sarah was beloved of God, and beloved of Abraham. You're beloved of nobody, Michal. No one likes you. You think I do?"

"I have as much right to be liked as she had. Was her father a king?"

"Sarah was full of spirit and liked to laugh," I began to argue. "She even laughed when she got the word from God. That's why she named her child Isaac—Isaac means 'he laughed and played.' She even made a joke about that. You never laughed and played. You never crack a smile."

"What's there to laugh about?" said Michal. "Why should I smile? Every time I look around, you're back with that whore again. Why does she make so many noises?"

"Not just with her."

"You're telling me?"

Michal would howl like a harpy and screech like an owl each time she spotted me in my harem once Uriah was dead and the widow Bathsheba had installed herself in my household and was openly my favorite wife. I tried as hard as I could to convince Bathsheba to remain outside as my mistress. She wasn't buying that.

"I'd rather be a queen."

"We don't have queens. And why do you want to be my wife? I've already got seven. Come in as a concubine."

"There's no honor in that."

"Why do you want to come in at all? It smells in here. Haven't you noticed? It's noisy and full of people. It's really a horrible place to live, even for me. You're better off outside."

"I want to be the mother of a king."

"There's no chance of that."

"I'll be your best wife. I'll want my own apartment, with an indoor bathtub and a large studio for my work."

"Stay where you are. I'll give you money to fix your place up. You'll have all the things you want."

"What about the child?"

"Have it outside. Let them think you're a whore."

"Nothing doing."

"Once you come in, you can never get out. Don't you know that? You'll never be able to fuck another man."

"Never?"

"Well, hardly ever."

"I'll take my chances," she resolved. "I don't like meeting you in secret. It's almost as though you're ashamed of your association with me. I want everyone to know who I am."

"But stolen waters are sweet, and bread eaten in—"

"Please don't tell me that one again!"

The intolerable indignity for Michal was that Bathsheba was already pregnant when she moved in, and got knocked up again soon after our first child had been delivered and died.

Activities in my harem did begin to take on an antic quality once Bathsheba was there and expansively making herself at home. Michal was perpetually livid. Now I can laugh about it. But what a hectic time I had between the two of them whenever I tried to slip by both for a sporting visit with one of my others. Going in, I would have to speed past Michal's rooms with my fingers in my ears if I hadn't been able to enter unobserved by her. Abigail and I would exchange friendly remarks and she would obligingly offer a cup of goat's milk with barley bread and honey. I would tell her I might prefer to refresh myself with her on the way out. Ahinoam still would not speak until she was spoken to, and Maccah of Geshur still did not know a word of Hebrew. Of the others, I never could keep in mind for long which one was Haggith and which Abital. Most of my wives were beginning to look alike. After I had made my way past all these, I would have to brave Bathsheba if I were on my way to someone else and hadn't been so fortunate as to arrive while she was napping or absorbed in dyeing her hair or in another in the series of ventures she called creative. She would stand in her doorway with her arms on her hips, so authoritative in demeanor that she did not have to bar my path.

"Where do you think you're going?" she would demand. "You get in here right now."

What the hell, I would always tell myself each time she waylaid me, knowing I could scarcely do better elsewhere, and the next thing that happened, we'd be riotously at it again, making that wholesome beast with two backs once more. I did have fun.

She was always libidinous, always ready, like the truest of pagans. No pause for her periods, no time out for pregnancies. Other than during her actual confinements, I don't think a day went by then that we didn't fall to it, till the time came to pass that we had Solomon and she decided she no longer wanted to. Who can tell what happened? She lost her lust when she embraced motherhood and settled on her true vocation, her life's work: to be a queen mother. Now, of course, it's to be a queen mother and save her life.

Going out, there would be no way to avoid the displeasure of Michal, who by that time would have heard our rumpus even if she hadn't seen me come in. "How glorious was the king of Israel today," I would get from her again. She would castigate me pitilessly, like the evil witch who hasn't been invited to the christening. "Humping and pumping away with that whore just now like a filthy vile beast of the field. Have you no shame? At long last, have you no shame left? You don't know how I despise you. Get away from me, leave me, you revolt me, you disgust me. Why don't you spend more time with me? Why don't you ever come into my rooms, instead of always going with the others?" She never thought of apologizing, inviting, or enticing.

"You're unpleasant, Michal," I instructed her, without acrimony. "Why should I want to be with you? You're a shrew. All you do is criticize, shout, demand, and complain. Nothing pleases you, nothing pleases you for long."

"I'm married to you," she answered self-righteously. "A wife has a right to complain when her husband does things she disapproves of, doesn't she?"

"Michal, Michal," I would attempt to explain patiently. "I've got thirteen, fourteen, maybe fifteen wives now. If every one were going to complain about every little thing she disapproves of, I'd have no time to be king."

Oh, the denunciations I heaped upon Hiram king of Tyre for providing me with this impractical layout for my harem—if curses were coals, I would have turned him to ashes. Where was his head when his architects showed him the design? Up his ass, that's where his head was. Didn't he have a harem of his own? Of course he knew better. You'd be surprised how far you have to walk for a toilet or a basin of clean water. Where was the privacy? Noises carried. My comings and goings were public. Too many times when making my way out, it was to a tittering chorus of embarrassing feminine whoops and catcalls from the concubines gathered at the grilled wooden gates fencing them in, sometimes to a round of their enthusiastic applause. I incurred a different kind of hazard if I brought Bathsheba to my own quarters for purposes of coitus. I discovered that about her right off the bat—she never wanted to leave. Bathsheba luxuriated shamelessly in the spaciousness of my rooms. She loved the king-sized bed.

"At least here I can stretch my legs out and roll around," she'd say, and purr languorously and scratch her ribs and the insides of her thighs. "Let me live in here with you. Make me your queen. You won't be sorry. I'll do such things to you—I know not what they are. They'll make you hum, they'll make you sing songs."

"Take her back," I directed. "I sing songs now."

I wasn't born yesterday.

Even at the start, when we were trysting clandestinely in my own part of the palace, she was asking for concessions and rewards that were unprecedented. She wanted open demonstrations of affection, a studio of her own in a building adjacent to the palace. I had never heard of an arrangement like that.

"Oh, David, you know very well what I'm talking about," she said with the impatience of reprimand. "Now that you know what great fucking is, you're not going to want to do without it."

"Great fucking?"

"It's what you're getting from me," she told me sternly, "and don't you forget it. You're going to want to see me every day. When you aren't with me, I'll be able to get on with my work."

This too was something new. What kind of work? In time, she tried just about everything in her futile pursuit of an independent income. She wanted to weave, she wanted to write, she wanted to paint.

"Paint what?" I pointed out quickly, certain that I'd tripped her up. "We're not allowed to paint."

"My toenails," she said, and showed me her foot. She wanted cosmetics without limit. "Buy me everything. Do you like this new color I mixed out of vermilion, magenta, cerise, scarlet, and maroon? I call it red."

I got her the studio, of course, and if she had stuck to her writing, I probably would have provided her, sooner or later, with the word processor she angled for as well. And when Uriah was dead and she came full sail into my palace as my newest wife—she refused to the end to come in as a concubine and resisted my persuasions that she stay outside as a consort—I promptly provided her with extra rooms she could use as studios, workshops, or both. She wished to conduct classes in handicraft, but none of the other women there were interested in learning. I bought her a potter's wheel and an indoor kiln when she developed successive enthusiasms for ceramics and cloisonné. I gave them as birthday presents. She wanted more: topaz and sapphire. I bought her equipment for polishing gemstones. Her commitments flagged when she couldn't sell what she produced or make anything distinctive, and when she saw that her hands were soiled all day long and that the work was destroying her fingernails. She began to toy with the idea of inventing underwear.

"What's underwear?"

"Let me invent it first."

She was dead right about that premarital studio, though, as a love nest for our secret, immoral meetings. Stolen waters are sweet, and bread eaten in secret is pleasant, as I frequently remarked to her. I can vouch for that from personal experience. I was often jealous of her work. I was in love. I could not keep away. Separation was jealousy, and love was strong as death, and jealousy as cruel as the grave.

She was right about one thing more: I did want to see her every day once I knew I was in love with her and once I had found out from her what great fucking was. I did not want to be without it. Those words were hers, not mine. She taught me how to speak and think obscenely. My alluring, flattering, sensual, amoral sweetheart was as natural as nature itself in the language and all the practices of love, many of which, to me, seemed innovations too extreme.

"Would you like to fuck me in the ass?" she astounded me by asking one day when I casually slid a leg over her while she was lying on her belly.

You can believe me when I tell you I was horrified. "That's a terrible thing to say!" I exploded at once, in stark disbelief.

"That's one thing I won't let you do," she notified me firmly. "I'm telling you now."

"Who would want to?" I demanded to know. "That's just about the dirtiest thing I've ever heard of!"

"I'm still not going to let you do it."

"Don't even mention such a thing. Where in the world did you even get such a foul and perverted idea?"

She was not in the least unsettled. "From a Canaanite girlfriend I used to know who worked as a harlot. We were friends when I was growing up."

"You should be ashamed of yourself for even thinking of something like that. It's absolutely awful. Awful! That one's so filthy we don't even have a law against it! The mere idea is depraved!"

"Have it your way," she murmured lackadaisically.

I did have her my way, many, many times, which mainly was in the missionary position. Furthermore, I was led to see myself as monumentally masculine, thanks to her remark, volunteered thoughtfully, that I had a large penis—was built, in fact, like an Egyptian, whose members are those of asses, and whose issue is like that of horses. When I finished congratulating myself, I had to learn more.

"Bathsheba, Bathsheba," I inquired with mock levity to cloak my misgivings, "where did you ever find out so much about Egyptian men?"

"I know you're going to find this hard to believe," she answered, "but I heard it from a different Canaanite girlfriend of mine, who was also a harlot."

"Again a harlot?" I exclaimed. "What were you doing with so many harlots for friends?"

"Learning," she replied. "Who better than harlots? And what's wrong with harlots? You know, David, you'd probably be much better off with a harlot than with someone like me. A harlot may be hired for a loaf of bread, but an adulteress stalks a man's very life."

I was impressed. "Where'd you find that piece of wisdom?"

"I made it up. I'm into proverbs now."

"No more psalms?"

"You told me I was rotten at them."

I was pleased at having chased her out of that field of creative endeavor in record time; it annoyed me that she thought she could toss them off with her left hand.

"Psalms don't even have to rhyme," she had told me.

"The Lord is my shepherd," I had scoffed when she showed me her first effort. "Are you crazy? How fantastic can you get? That's crap, Bathsheba, pure crap. Where's your sense of metaphor? You're turning God into a laborer and your audience into animals. That's practically blasphemy. Shall not want what? You're raising questions instead of answering them. At least change it to 'won't' and save a syllable. You think all of mine are much too long?"

"Some are masterpieces," she stated calmly, "but, like everything you write, they're flawed by excessive length."

That cheeky, patronizing bitch. " 'Won't want' is better." I kept my temper and remained objective. "He maketh no one to lie down in green pastures, either. Where did you ever get a grotesque idea like that?"

"Didn't you ever sleep outdoors?"

"Only when I had to. And I felt no kindness toward the people who made me do it."

"Sheep sleep outdoors."

"We're not sheep. That's what's wrong with the whole concept. And here's another big error. Either 'valley of death' or 'shadow of death,' not both. Not 'walk through the valley of the shadow of death.' Oh, give it up, Bathsheba, give it up. You don't have the head for it. You think writing psalms is a snap? Go back to macramé."

"Can I have that alabaster bathtub?"

"Would you like an alabaster bathtub too?" I inquired of Abigail when I stopped in to see her on my way out.

And I must confess that when Abigail gracefully demurred and articulated to me tenderly that her cup runneth over, phrases began to fall into place in my head, and I was soon transported by my muse to the ingenious proposition that if cows can be contented, sheep and goats can be too, and that perhaps the bud of a good idea might be found in the presumptuous and chaotic ramblings of my spouse Bathsheba. I have given thanks ever since for her being too scatterbrained to retain any specific recollection of our conversation relating to the Lord and shepherds.

So instead of psalms and proverbs, Bathsheba invented underwear. While I, in one of those stimulated outpourings of constructive energy that are often the intoxicating concomitants of love, threw myself into new creative endeavors of my own. Almost before you could look around, I had organized the temple musicians into guilds, and then I did even more: I set singers also before the altar, that by their voices they might make sweet melody, and daily sing praises in their songs. While she got busy devising underwear, I invented the choir. I don't know why someone didn't think of a choir sooner. And once I had my choir, I went to work feverishly to put it to use, and in hardly more than a fortnight, I composed my B-Minor Mass, Mozart's Requiem, and Handel's *Messiah*. I came dashing into her room one day to whistle for her ears only my newly minted, high-spirited "Hallelujah" Chorus, but I didn't get very far. I stopped and stared openmouthed when she discarded her robe to expose the article of apparel she was wearing underneath, next to her skin. It was a truncated, billowy, flesh-colored garment of rather filmy, sheer material that enclosed her waist and descended in two dangling cylinders around much of each of her thighs separately, looking kind of comical and ridiculous.

"Do you like it?" she asked, assuming a seductive posture and displaying herself.

"What is it?" I responded. "What do you mean, do I like it?"

"Underwear," she told me. "I invented it. It's clothing."

"For a man or a woman?"

"What difference does it make?"

"A big difference," I explained. "A man is never supposed to wear anything that pertaineth to a woman, and a woman is never supposed to wear anything that pertaineth to a man."

"Says who?"

"Deuteronomy, that's who."

"I don't care about any of that," she said tartly. "I'm going to make a million dollars on these. Every woman will want them. I'll need a thousand sewing machines."

"We don't have sewing machines."

"Invent them. If I can invent these, you can invent a sewing machine. Aren't they lovely? I call them bloomers."

"Bloomers?"

"Don't they make me bloom?"

"What are they for?"

"To make me sexier, to make women more attractive to men. I have these smaller ones with lace that I call panties. And these I call bikinis. Do they work?"

"How should I know if they work? Pull them down and let me get at you."

"They work."

She didn't make a dime and soon was demanding something else. But nothing material she ever requested was anything in comparison to what she began to press for the second time she was made pregnant from lying with me.

"Why can't we name him King?" she proposed again at the circumcision, with transparent duplicity.

We called him Solomon instead.

I ALMOST DIDN'T LIE with Bathsheba at all that first day on the roof when the intelligence was brought back to me that this woman for whom I had been lusting so avidly was Bathsheba the daughter of Eliam, the wife of Uriah the Hittite, my faithful servant who even that same day was at war in the field for me against the children of Ammon. Uriah the Hittite? What was I to do? I was not wholly without conscience, you know. My initiative weakened. But just in time, up spoke the Devil to rally my faltering spirit and give me the heart I needed to throw at least a little bit of caution to the wind and march to the insistent beat of this different drummer. Let me give the Devil his due.

"Go get her," I heard a voice edged with mirth and irony instruct. "Take her, you dope. Go on. Fuck her belly off. You want her, don't you? What are you waiting for, stupid? You're a king, ain't you?"

"Is that you, God?" I asked diffidently.

"Mephistopheles."

"Oh, shit," I said, groaning with disappointment. "Are you after my soul?"

"Do I need souls?" was the mocking answer. "I want mischief, not souls. I want laughs, fun. I want to watch. Bring her here. Hurry. Before she finishes drying and goes inside. Just look at those tits. Ooh, oooh, ooooh!"

"Will it be all right? Am I allowed?"

"Of course you're allowed. Ain't you the king?"

"Doesn't the law say no?"

"If the law says no to that, the law is an ass. Male and female He created you, didn't He?"

"What should I do?"

"What you want. Go ahead. Get her. Shove it in. Stick it in her ear."

Who was I to argue?

Who could resist such subtle persuasions?

So I sent messengers and they took her into a room in my palace through a side door; in compliance with their directives, she wore a veil and a mantle. And I lay with her that same day, for she was purified from her uncleanliness, and when I returned her unto her house I missed her, so I lay with her again the next day, and the next day, and the next, because each time she went away I missed her more strongly and wanted her back. We simply took it for granted each time she came to me that she was purified from her uncleanliness. Or else we didn't care. Clean, unclean, what did it matter? We were doing such things anyway. For seven days I lay with her, and then I lay with her for seven more. The fact is, I could not stop thinking about her or wanting to be with her, and wanting even to listen to her. I could not stop craving her. I could not get her out of my mind. At all hours, during all kinds of other activities, she was spinning and glittering in my brain. I could concentrate on nothing else for long.

"I have never felt this way before," I was candid enough to admit with a sigh of surrender.

So I had her brought to me each morning and again in the afternoon, for I found I wanted always to have her in my hands, and have her wet lips on my mouth, and her warm breath on my neck, and in almost no time at all, as it happened, she was asking for myriads of things no woman had ever requested from me before.

"Now, David," she was addressing me strictly by the end of the first week, "what are we going to do? You have to decide."

"About what?" We were standing face to face, and I hadn't the dimmest idea what she meant.

"About us. You're not going to want to do without me, you know. No man ever has."

Until Uriah, as it turned out to my extreme chagrin.

"I'll make you a concubine."

"I won't be a concubine. You're forgetting I'm married. What will you do when Uriah is back?"

"I'll make him a captain of a million and send him away again."

"And another thing I don't like is the way you try to pretend we're strangers whenever they bring me here. You never touch me or kiss me when anyone else is around. You never say you love me except when we're alone."

"Are you crazy?" I exclaimed, virtually unable to believe my ears. "I'm a married man! I don't want Michal, Abigail, Ahinoam, Maccah, Haggith, Abital, or Eglah to find out about us."

"What difference would it make?" she argued crossly. "Don't you think all the rest of your people know why you bring me here?"

JOSEPH HELLER

"You could be stoned, for adultery."

"So could you."

"I'm a man. And I'm also the king. And I don't want a word of scandal about this."

"Then give me my own place and you come there. You'll be surprised how often you'll want to be with me."

I wanted to be with her more often than either of us could have imagined. Occasionally, she chided me for barging in without notice and interfering with her work. I think it's true—I liked my women very much more than they liked me, and I enjoyed lying with them more than they enjoyed having me with them, until Bathsheba. She was a hot one. She wanted it at least as much as I did, and I soon discovered something else eccentric about her: if I didn't come as swiftly as I hoped I would, she herself would eventually go off like a string of firecrackers hung from the tail of a vixen, exploding in a climax of her own with those marvelous and shocking tumults that are incomparably titillating and began causing talk through the whole neighborhood. Who'd ever heard of a thing like that? She called it her orgasm. She awarded me points for giving her multiples.

"I make such noises when I'm with you," she'd frequently observe in a kind of puzzled and contented exhaustion, her fair and tawny face flushed pink still. "Whew!"

She had the knack of making me feel good. This is a priceless quality in a woman and added another extra dimension to our heady sexual commerce, as did her precious accolade that I was built like an Egyptian with a member as large as that of an ass and had an issue like the issue of horses. It isn't every day a man is treated to an exaggeration like that.

"I first saw it," she confessed, to my considerable surprise, "the day you played before the Lord and were dancing with all your might at the head of that parade and showing yourself to the whole world. I took a good look. I had to believe that your wife was a lucky woman. I envied her. I couldn't get over how well hung you were. It was then that I made up my mind to meet you. A king and all that too—who could resist? So I began bathing on my roof every evening to attract you." Hers was undoubtedly the best rinsed body in Israel by the time I laid eyes on her.

We broke so many laws in those first happy days of sinful, thrusting frenzy. So many hours so often we drenched ourselves to

312

the waist in perspiration. Our hair was lank and tangled and thickly matted with oil, sweat, and perfume. Her belly was as bright ivory overlaid with sapphires, her cheeks like a bed of spices, as sweet flowers, her lips like lilies, dropping sweet-smelling myrrh. This was my beloved, who introduced me to so much and filled my soul with such ineffable sweetness—she taught me to say "I love you" and mean it, and to put my hand upon her delicately, though others were looking on. I was insatiable. When it was almost time for us to be with one another again, I would go into a frenetic state of anticipation and could not wait to come into her garden once more and eat her pleasant fruits, to gorge myself and never surfeit. She, more than I, was astounded to discover that she soon became the person more likely to ask, "When will I see you again? Will it be soon?"

It was mainly always soon in the beginning. I enjoyed her more than any other woman I had ever known. She clearly thought she was in love with me then, and does not deny that even now. And I was in love with her. And I felt so splendidly good about myself for knowing that I was. Her skin alone, that porous, luminous membrane delineating her unique identity for me, was for me the most beautiful of miracles. Here and there was a mark—a mole, a scratch, a pimple—unlike my perfect Abishag, who is utterly without spot. That did not matter. I idolized the fact of her. I cherished touching her. I gazed and gazed; and she in turn gazed back, drank me in with her eyes. Even the bones of her knees were thrilling, as was the curvature of her shins and her large feet, as though she alone on earth possessed such ungainly queer-shaped features. I liked to stare at her naked. I loved to study her engrossed in embroidery in her nightgown or bloomers, with her spectacles on and the hoop of wood steady in her fingers. Most of all, I loved to peer into her small face, into her mischievous, plotting blue eyes, to lose myself in the decoding of the shimmering nuances of calculation in her unconscious half smile. I treasured that weight and arousing rotundity of her ass. I could not believe or get used to the tenderness of the emotions I experienced for her. I was suffused with reveries of her. My first desire upon awaking each dawn was to telephone my adored one and leave messages of worship and lewd endearment on her answering machine, but, of course, we had no telephones back then, nor had we recording machines. For hours and hours at a stretch, I embraced her and just took it for granted that I would lie with her at will every day of my life that I chose, until that fateful day broke when the sickness of women was already upon her and I began to apostrophize aloud to the fates in despair at the necessity to abstain. She was mildly surprised at first by the attitude of aversion to her condition that I unconsciously evinced; then she treated me, as she heard me go on, to that look of humoring derision one normally reserves for an oafish prig.

"Whatever you want," she said.

So lofty was her depreciatory manner that I felt myself gauche and was put on the defensive. "You'll be unwell," I protested lamely.

"So what?" she said.

"We're really allowed?"

"Who's to stop us?"

"We'd be cut off from the people if anyone found out. For seven days."

"Who would find out? And we'd have more time together if anyone did."

"It's really possible?" I asked naïvely. "During your period?"

"Would there be a law against it if it weren't?"

"It isn't gross?"

"It isn't gross."

"You've done it before?"

"Is everyone squeamish?"

"Suppose your flowers be upon me?"

"You'll wash."

"I'd be unclean for seven days."

"Don't noise it around."

"And all of the bed on which I lay would be unclean."

"Don't noise that around either."

"I'm not sure I want to."

"Have it your way." She turned from me torpidly and left me feeling foolish.

This time I had it her way, in the missionary position again, of course, and exulted so greatly in the mere knowledge of what I was doing—*mirabile dictu*, I was not struck dead, nor was I cut off from the people—that I could not wait for her menstrual cycle to come around the next time so I could do it her way again. Alas, it was not to be, for the best laid schemes of mice and men gang aft a-gley. Passover came and went without observance, believe it or not, and then, instead of her period appearing on schedule, there arrived from her instead those four little words that rarely fail to incite a melodramatic reaction in even the blandest of extramarital affairs. Bathsheba sent to me and said:

"I am with child."

"Holy shit!" was the fashion in which I gave screaming utterance to mine.

There I was with a pregnant girlfriend on my hands. Well, abortion was illegal then, of course, and Bathsheba was not the self-sacrificing kind to put her safety at risk for mine. She had not lain with her husband for nearly three months. This could prove a bigger embarrassment for me than the killing of Abner. What was I to do?

"This time," I warned her, "they may really stone you. You committed adultery."

"They'll stone you too," she answered. "You committed adultery also, and you even coveted your neighbor's wife."

"I'm a man. They don't stone men for that."

"You think that will help? It's written that a man that committeth adultery with another man's wife, the adulterer and the adulteress shall surely both be put to death. That means you."

"How come you know so much about it?"

"Don't you think I looked it up? I like to know my rights. You're in just as much trouble as I am. If a man be found lying with a woman married to a husband, then they shall both of them die. You'll find that written too. You'd better think of something fast."

"Well, I'm also the king, and I decide who's stoned and who isn't."

"You think you'll survive?"

"You wouldn't name me."

"Don't bet on it!"

"Get me Uriah!" I have to admit I believe it was I who let out that shout.

And thereby ensued that grisly contretemps of a Restoration farce that deteriorated inexorably into pathos, and then into a tragedy in which I was stricken with unbearable grief and made prostrate with that most awful knowledge that my newborn baby was sick and doomed to early death because of me. So said Nathan. The poor little thing was burning with fever and perishing of thirst and starvation. He was drying up and withering away and I could not watch, just as Hagar a millennium earlier could not watch, and set the boy Ishmael beneath one of the shrubs and sat herself down a good bowshot away, because she could not look on and see him die. And Ishmael was already past thirteen, old enough to scorn and endanger Isaac. My baby boy was just tiny and red. His unopened eyes were like useless gills. A thousand times in seven days there echoed in my head those ancient, touching words of that Egyptian servant girl Hagar, expelled with her young son out of Abraham's bosom into the wilderness of Beersheba with just some bread and a bottle of water that soon was spent.

"Let me not see the death of the child."

But God answered Hagar with the gift of survival.

"Arise, lift up the lad, and hold him in thine hand," He called to Hagar out of heaven. "For I will make him a great nation."

A great nation, God promised, whose hand would always be against every man.

To me He would not give the time of day. He made my baby die. He was working again in one of His mysterious ways. How could I ever forget? Nathan told me He would. I still have not forgiven Him for that, although I feel I need my God now more than ever before, and miss Him more than I would care to let Him know. And I do not believe that He has forgotten me.

It was not with harmful intentions that I sent to Joab to return Uriah the Hittite from the battlefields of Ammon on the pretext of filling me in on what was going on. All I wanted Uriah to do was sleep with Bathsheba. If I could do it, why couldn't he? My plan was to award him a hero's welcome, fire him up with a little wine, and turn him loose atop his wife, my exciting mistress. What could be more benign than that? In this way did I plot to conceal our embarrassing indiscretions from anyone left in the city who was still not cognizant of the true state of our affair. It was a peach of an idea—for someone other than Uriah. The fallacy in my inspiration was the self-deceptive notion, not uncommon among men newly in love, that every other breathing male was as sex-starved as I was for the object of my passion. Uriah was not. Go figure.

It was hard to look him straight in the eye when he was brought before me. "Come in, my friend, come in, my boy," I hailed him with an effusive cordiality with which I wanted to put him entirely at ease. "Come in, my good Uriah, and wash thy feet. I could not tell you how pleased I am to have you here." That much was true. "Tell me all, tell me what is happening at Rabbah in Ammon. Am I needed?" I could not have cared less about what I requested he relate, and barely listened as he zealously told me how well my people did and how our fortunes, though slowly, were prospering. Couriers with news ran back and forth several times a day, even on the Sabbath. "Good, good, good," I urged him on to finish more rapidly, as eager to cast him into bed with Bathsheba as I so often was to be with her myself. "Have some wine now. You have brought me the reports I wanted to hear and have made me happy. Now rest, take a load off thy feet. Soak them some more?"

"I think they're clean enough."

"So do I. Go down to thy house now and rest. Have some fun. I'm sending a mess of meat from my kitchen for you and your wife to feast on."

"Not me," said Uriah emphatically, giving me quite a fright.

"Why not?" I cried.

"Not while I'm on duty in your service."

"Consider yourself relieved for this night of duty in my service," I said, with an uneasy laugh. "You like the wine? Drink more. Take the whole flask. I'll send more bottles when I send the meat. Go home now, Uriah. They tell me you have a lovely wife. Go down to thy house now and *shtupp* her. Give her a good boff or two. You've earned the right. Leave me now and go home to your wife."

You think he leaped at the chance? Out of my presence he finally plodded after drinking some more, tilting heavily to leeward as though drunk and footsore. I heaved a sigh when he was gone and took a good belt of wine from a flask myself. But instead of quitting the palace as I expected, the contrary son of a bitch settled himself for the night on the floor near one of the portals with the rest of my soldiers on station there. I sped right to him when I found that out, no longer congratulating myself so extravagantly.

"Uriah, get up, go home." I began to harangue him, in a magisterial tone of command that degenerated wholly on the second or third word into a pathetic shambles of abject pleading. "Why be uncomfortable here?"

He was reeking of wine and puffed out his chest when he answered. "Not while my comrades from Israel and Judah abide in tents," he declared, to my amazement.

"What good does it do them for you to abide here?" I reasoned with him. "Go to your home, to a good soft bed. To a plump, warm wife. I've already sent victuals and bottles of strong wine. Why be a *schmuck?*"

"Not," Uriah declared blearily, "while my lord Joab, and the servants of my lord, are encamped in the open fields. Shall I then go into mine house—"

"Yes, go into thy house," I answered.

"—to eat and drink, and to lie with my wife? As thou livest," he vowed, "and as thy soul livest, I will not do this thing."

"Do this thing, please do this thing," I begged, withholding myself only with a gigantic effort of self-discipline from grabbing him by the throat and shaking him to death, or taking my own thick hair in my hands and pulling it all out in a seizure of helpless frustration. "Uriah, please go home," I whimpered. "Your comrades-in-arms would want you to have a good time. For there is no better thing a man can do with himself than to eat and to drink and be merry. Don't you know that? Have more wine," I threw in at the end when he did not move to comply.

Getting him drunk proved a huge mistake. I should have remembered that in matters of sex, liquor quickens desire but weakens performance. My mind went reeling as he took a herculean draught and smacked his lips noisily. After a second big swig, he let out a jolly cheer, and propelled himself into a lurching sailor's hornpipe, emitting hilarious cries as he danced, until he tripped himself up and almost toppled over on his noodle. I was going mad. He took another huge drink, and then I beheld the sodden blockhead lose touch with everything concerning me. With sinking heart, I could only stand by as he lowered himself exhaustedly to the floor midway through a ribald ballad he was rendering off key about a girl somewhere who once had let him play with her ring-dang-doo.

"A ring-dang-doo? Pray what is that?"

But he'd already passed out, leaving me not a whit the wiser.

Bathsheba was put in very bad humor by this reversal in our fortunes. How else should a flamboyant sexpot feel when faced with the fact of a husband who did not want to lie with her after a deprivation of some three months?

"Shicka is a goy," was the tight-lipped snub of vindication she proposed, while I looked her over circumspectly for any flaws in

her person that could have eluded my attention, and of which Uriah the Hittite, through longer familiarity with her body, was aware. "Do you think he could have another woman with him out there in Ammon? I'll bet he does."

"You may be right," I answered brightly. "He was singing something about a girl he'd met once who let him play with her ring-dang-doo."

"That was me," she said tersely.

We decided together to keep him longer in Jerusalem for at least one more crack at him, but the day that followed was even more of a trial. We made a propitious beginning when he awoke with a hangover in the dazed state of an amnesiac.

"Oh, boy, I must have been terrible." He made a sheepish and grinning apology to me. "I can't remember a thing I did last night, not a single thing."

At once my hopes soared. "You remember nothing?"

"That's right, nothing at all," Uriah the Hittite assured me. "I can't remember a single thing that happened to me last night, not a single thing, once I made up my mind to lie down on the floor of your palace and spend the night right here with your guards instead of going to my house."

And now I felt my hopes die. "You remember that, though, don't you?" You drunken prick, I added to myself. I cannot recall ever having felt so disheartened with anyone.

"May I please have a hair of the dog that bit me?"

"Uriah, go home now," I directed paternally, then took him by the shoulder, affecting, with great strain, to appear to him as benevolent a despot as ever existed on God's earth. "There is plenty of wine at your house that I sent to you yesterday. So go down to thy house, go right now, this minute, and wash thy feet. They are dirty again. Look at them. It's been a long campaign, for the two of us. Indulge yourself, with my permission. Yes, you have my permission. The things I've sent for your pleasure—the victuals, the mess of meat—all will spoil if you don't enjoy them today." He was obdurate to my entreaties and stood there motionless, as stolid as a wooden post. "Your wife is comely, they tell me, comely," I began on a different approach, "and awaits you passionately at home in a revealing tunic with a very short miniskirt that hangs inches and inches above her sexy knees. She sent to inquire about you while you slept, many times she sent to inquire about you.

Amorously, they tell me, amorously, she awaits you, oh so amorously. Don't you like her?"

"I love my wife."

"Then go home and fuck her."

You lousy, thickheaded, stubborn son of a bitch, I ran on to myself. Why are you putting me through all this?

"Not on your life," he declared loudly and proudly, his chest thrown out like a man consecrated to the glory of a life of deprivation and honor. "Not while Israel and Judah abide in tents and are encamped in the open fields of Ammon. I am leaving at once to rejoin them."

Like hell you are! You're doing no such thing! "No, my good and faithful Uriah," is how I did reply. "You can't go back now. I have dispatches to return with you that will not be completed until tomorrow. You must stay another day. And another night. Consider yourself on furlough. Your comrades-in-arms would expect you to relax, and to pleasure yourself with your wife while you have the opportunity. Don't let them down. They will be rooting for you. How will you face them if you do not? You will shame them if you do not perform the work of a virile man with so charming a woman as I hear your wife is. They tell me she is pretty, they tell me she is vibrant, they say she looks passionate. Ooh, oooooh, ooooooh, you bastard! So go home, Uriah, go home right now, run! Do as I tell you. Go home to your wife now. And to her ring-dang-doo."

"I will be unclean if I lie with her."

"So you'll be unclean."

"I would not be able to go back into battle for three more days."

"Why not? You're a gentile, you're not even Jewish," I reminded him harshly.

"Some of my best friends are Jewish."

"Go home and fuck your wife!" I shouted.

"As thou livest," he vowed adamantly, shaking his head, "and as thy soul liveth—"

"I will absolve you," I promised, regaining control of my temper and beaming at him. You rotten bastard, I swore at him to myself. "I will allow you back into battle right away." You dirty son of a bitch. "So please go home." I moved closer to him with a knowing wink and continued directly into his ear. "Oh, I can just picture the wife that lies there awaiting you expectantly, sighing and breathing in sweet anticipation of the love she desires to give you after so long an absence from her felicity. Oh, Uriah, Uriah, how I envy you, how I wish I were in your shoes," I cajoled him truthfully. No hissing serpent ever whispered temptations more subtly, no Iago ever labored more sinisterly. "I bet her lips are like a thread of scarlet. I can just picture her. Her belly is like a heap of wheat set about with lilies. The joints of her thighs are like the work of the hands of a cunning workman, and her breasts like to clusters of grapes on the vine. She is fair, your love, behold, she is fair. I bet there is no spot on her." I knew there were plenty. "Her eyes are as the eyes of doves by the rivers of waters, washed with milk, and fitly set. Her teeth are like a flock of sheep that are even shorn. Make haste, Uriah, make haste, for thy beloved will be to thee like to a roe or to a young hart upon the mountains of spices."

"Can I have another hair of the dog that bit me?"

That took the wind out of my sails. I handed him the bottle. I was giving up, although I went on trying with him all day. It was no lark. I even did eat with him and drink with him, repeating, "Uriah, go home," with every mouthful—his company was as wearisome as Solomon's—and when all words proved to no avail, I even did make him drunk again. "Uriah, go home," I importuned the unyielding blockhead until I was hoarse from the effort and sick from repeating, "Uriah, Uriah, go home and fuck your wife." But when evening came, he parted from me unchanged, to make his bed in my palace again with the servants of the guard, and went not down to his house. And I sat drinking, glumly, until all of the wine in my chamber was finished.

What else could I do with Uriah but what I did do? Wasn't it better for the unity of the nation to cover up this government scandal if I could? Who could blame me for wishing to try? God could blame me, as it turned out, if Nathan was telling me the truth. Nathan dreams about everything all of the time, therefore has to be right about some things some of the time. Nathan is the only person I know of who dreams of God. The rest of us have more pressing matters weighing on us when we sleep.

I don't know whose idea it was to send Uriah back to the wars in Ammon to be destroyed. Let us call it the work of the Devil, although Nathan was not impressed with that defense when he brought me the bad news of the disasters to come. But I was the one who returned Uriah with the letter to Joab, saying, "Set ye

Uriah the Hittite in the forefront of the hottest battle, and retire ye from him, that he may be smitten and die." Joab complied by assigning Uriah unto a place where valiant men were fighting, where there fell some of the people of my servants, and Uriah the Hittite died also.

So Uriah the Hittite was another in the long history of warfare who laid down his life patriotically for his king and his country.

And as soon as the mourning was past, his fertile widow became my wife and moved into my palace, appropriating for herself the largest set of rooms in the women's quarter, knocking down walls to double their size, and requisitioning a custom-made bathtub immediately upon learning that I recently had acquired alabaster stones in great quantity.

My troubles were over.

They had only just begun.

For this thing that I had done displeased the Lord, and I can't say that I blame Him, although I will never excuse Him for killing the baby in retribution. That was an act of God that was warped and inhuman.

I have given up as hopeless trying to keep track of all of the laws I had violated in this single experience with Bathsheba and her late husband. There were a few in Leviticus I'd broken that I hoped neither Nathan nor God knew I'd violated, and more than once, I'm afraid, in the inconceivable rapture I enjoyed with Bathsheba, I had taken the Lord's name in vain. Boy, did we have laws—laws governing everything. Before I gave up, I counted six hundred and thirteen commandments, which I found a rather remarkably large number for a society with a language that had no written vowels and a total vocabulary of only eighty-eight words, of which seventeen can be defined as synonyms for God.

I was skeptical but not altogether surprised when Nathan showed up to denounce me for having incited the Lord's displeasure and to acquaint me with the schedule of punishments in store. I had disappointed Him bitterly. It was nothing to the way God shortly was going to disappoint me.

"How did He find out?" I wanted to know.

"He has His ways."

"He didn't know where Abel was after Cain killed him, or where Adam hid after they ate the apple."

"Those were trick questions."

"In what language," I asked, "did God address you?" This was a trick question of my own.

"In Yiddish of course," said Nathan. "In what other language would a Jewish God speak?"

Had Nathan said Latin, I would have known he was fabricating. He began with that parable—is it any wonder I detest them?— about the poor owner of a single ewe lamb that is taken away by the rich owner of a large herd to make a lavish meal for a traveler come to visit. And when I delivered the predictable verdict against the man with plenty, Nathan gleefully pounced:

"Thou art the man!"

"What will it be?" I asked fatalistically. "Breach for breach, I guess. An eye for an eye, and a tooth for a tooth?"

"Loosely," said Nathan. "He will let the punishment fit the crime."

"Can't He turn the other cheek?"

"You're making me laugh." Like my son Solomon, with whom he now is united in an improbable alliance, Nathan has always been impervious to the ironic wit in my more elliptical sallies. "Hast thou not despised the commandment of the Lord to do evil in His sight?" he went on with a shake of his head, speaking in a hortatory and didactic way, and pronouncing his words as though he'd been educated at Oxford. "Thou hast taken the wife of Uriah the Hittite to be thy wife, and hast slain him with the sword of the children of Ammon. Now, therefore, the sword shall never depart from thine house. This saith the Lord, behold, I will raise up evil against thee out of thine own house, and I will take thy wives before thine eyes, and give them unto thy neighbor, and he shall lie with thy wives in the sight of this sun. For thou didst it secretly, but I will do this thing before all Israel, and before the sun. Howbeit, because by this deed thou hast given great occasion to the enemies of the Lord to blaspheme."

I did not dream he was talking of Absalom, and would not have believed it if I'd been told that he was. To shorten the discourse, I made admission of sin.

"But don't worry, don't worry," Nathan made haste to comfort me. "Nothing will happen to you. The Lord also hath put away thy sin."

That was a comfort. I would survive. But my blood turned to ice when he said that the son Bathsheba was going to bear me would surely die.

Now where in God's world was the justice in that? He could not have pained me more had He struck me down dead. To avenge the guilty with the life of an innocent? I would not allow myself to truly believe it until I saw it begin to happen.

"Is it well with the child?" I asked when Bathsheba was delivered of him.

"It is well with the child," was the knowledge they gave me.

"Is it well with the child?" I asked each morn and each even.

Until that day shortly came when it was no longer well, and the child was very sick. As water to a thirsty soul, I wanted mercy for the infant boy. "Let me not see the death of the child," I therefore besought God in those plaintive words of Hagar. I could not bear to be guilty witness, so I fasted and went into a room, and I lay all night upon the earth. And the elders of my house arose and came to me, to raise me up from the earth, but I would not let them, neither did I eat bread with them, or eat anything with anyone when they came to succor me. My sighs were many and my heart was faint. For seven days I lay all night upon the earth and besought God for the life of the child, knowing in my heart that my prayers were hopeless and that I was losing both my baby and my God with each moment that passed. And on the seventh day the child died.

I had a hunch before they told me. I could guess from the flurries of lowered voices I heard outside my room. My servants feared to tell me, afraid of the fatal effect the information might have upon me. They had seen how I mourned while the child yet lived. I lay on the earth a few minutes longer, weeping in silence into the dirt, then surrendered all hope and began pulling myself together. To make things easier for all of us, I put a brave face on the matter.

"Is the child dead?" I inquired bluntly.

And my servants, relieved of the burden of bringing me such news, said, "He is dead."

When the vigil was ended and the child had died, I washed alone and changed from soiled clothes to clean, and then, to the astonishment of my servants, I said I was hungry and asked to have prepared for me a filling meal that was fit for a king.

I was angry at God and angry at man. I could not make sense of the quiet in the universe. I wanted the entire world to be heartbroken, to be choked with sorrow and outrage at so heartless an event. In helpless wrath, I longed to shake my fists on the highest mountain and shriek, "Howl, howl, ye shepherds, and cry!" How could any sentient being of conscience go about unaffected as though nothing so monstrous and universally perfidious as the death of my child had not just taken place. "Oh, ye are men of stone!"

For the violent death of Absalom later, I knew I would have to mourn by myself. I was not incensed; there justice had to be done. But this was a newborn child. Rachel weeping for her children was as apathy itself compared to the misery I suffered at the death of these two of mine, for Rachel weeping for her children was but a figure of speech.

I said not a word of these feelings while I arose from the earth, and washed, and anointed myself, and changed my apparel, and came out of the room and went into the house of the Lord, and worshipped. You can guess how reverent and forgiving I really was in my heart.

The behavior I displayed has now become the substance of legend. I went back into my own house, and my people set bread before me, and meat, and the fruits of the field, and I ate ravenously. By then I really was famished. The silence surrounding me was stupefying. My pliant servants stared as though struck dumb, alarmed and astounded by the fearful peculiarity of my rugged character and by my resilient recovery and appetite. I had fasted a day at Abner's death. I was dining at my baby's. At last, one finally found the nerve to inquire, saying, "What thing is this that thou hast done? Thou didst fast and weep for the child whilst it was alive. But when the child was dead, thou didst rise and eat bread."

Until I explained, they thought I was possessed. I answered softly. I did not want to break down in their sight.

"While the child was yet alive," I said, and managed to keep my voice steady, "I fasted and wept, for I said, 'Who can tell whether God will be gracious to me, that the child may live?' But now that he is dead, wherefore should I fast? Can I bring him back again? All go into one place, all are of the dust, and all turn to dust again. He'll come no more, never, never, never. I shall go to him, but he shall not return to me."

"The Lord gave, and the Lord hath taken away," Nathan intoned unctuously, and I wanted to sock him in the eye.

"Amen," chorused his acolytes. "Blessed be the name of the Lord."

I cursed the lot of them under my breath. Miserable comforters were they all, with their self-righteous "blessed be the name of the Lord's," and I wanted the day to perish wherein they were born. Had they all forgotten that the Lord would not even let us know His name?

In solitude, I was raging at the Lord, seething with scornful belligerence toward the Lord, and spoiling for a fight with Him. I really could not keep my temper. I wanted to have it out with Him. I was ready to curse God and die. But He would not take me on. I never did get from Him the justification I wanted for the death of the child. I received instead the answer I least expected.

Silence.

It is the only answer I have got from Him since.

I would have welcomed His roar. I wanted to hear Him thunder majestically at me out of the whirlwind, I hungered to let me see Him react, I challenged and goaded Him to let me hear, instead of that vast and impenetrable silence, His all-powerful voice command me from on high:

"Who is this that darkeneth counsel by words without knowledge? Gird up now thy loins like a man."

I'd just love to hear Him try that kind of shit with me. I would not answer with the patience of Job.

"Who do you have to be?" I would snarl at Him in reply.

I dare Him to answer, "I will demand of thee, and declare thou unto Me. Where wast thou when I laid the foundations of the earth? Declare, if thou hast understanding."

"What difference does that make?" I can hear myself replying in disparagement of His irrelevance.

Then let Him answer me out of the whirlwind and say, "Who hath laid the measures thereof, if thou knowest, or who hath stretched the line upon it? Or who shut up the sea with doors, when it broke forth, as if it had issued out of the womb? Hast thou commanded the morning since thy days? Hast thou perceived the breadth of the earth? Hast thou entered into the treasures of the snow, or hast thou seen the treasures of the hail? Out of whose womb came the ice? And the hoary frost of heaven, who hath gendered it? Canst thou bind the sweet influences of Pleiades, or loose the bands of Orion? Doth the hawk fly by thy wisdom, and stretch her wings toward the south, or the eagle mount up at thy command, and make her nest on high? Canst thou draw out leviathan with a hook, or his tongue with a cord which thou lettest down? Who created the heaven and the earth? Who hath divided a watercourse for the overflowing of waters, or a way for the lightning of thunder to cause it to rain on the earth? Answer thou Me, if thou has understanding."

"But that doesn't matter anymore," I would contend with my Almighty God and instruct Him in biting reply. "Can't You see? That no longer matters at all."

I GOT FURTHER WITH Bathsheba than I was able to get with God. Bathsheba and I said hardly anything, anything at all, in the tender meeting we had following the death of the child, and those few words we did exchange were half-heard murmurs and fell like wistful eulogies between our long and heartfelt silences. I went to her room when our baby was dead, to comfort her as she lay in her bed, and I held her hand while she lay in her bed, and she cried quietly for more than an hour. Her tears flowed slowly.

11

SO IT CAME TO PASS

Sweet is her voice and comely her countenance, and it came to pass that Bathsheba bore me another son after I went in unto her and lay with her again. We called his name Solomon, and the Lord loved him, according to her, although it's still impossible for me to figure out why.

"How come?" I had asked before and was compelled to wonder again, "you never had children with Uriah? Or with any of the many other men who went in unto you before him?"

"I took precautions," she told me, intently working an ointment of malachite around her eyes to shade them green. "I was on the pill."

"So how come you keep having children with me?"

"Someday I want to be the mother of a king. That's one of the reasons I moved in here."

"You made a mistake," I told her. "You can't be the mother of a king."

"Solomon?"

"Right now he's just about last in line."

"Move him up front."

"It's out of the question, my love, my dove—"

"Then keep your hands to yourself."

"—my sister, my undefiled."

"I don't want there to be any more sex between us until we settle this matter once and for all."

"Thou art fair, my love, thou art fair."

"Give up, David. That isn't going to work today. You know what I want, and I want you to give it to me. I want to be a queen."

"We don't have queens. Must I tell you again?"

"Then make me the first," she persisted. "You can do whatever

331

you want to. I'd like to be famous. I want to be in the Bible someday. Even your own mother isn't in the Bible by name."

Here I had to laugh. "Do you really think you're ever going to be forgotten after what you and I did to Uriah?" I laughed again. "Don't worry, you'll be in the Bible. You might not like what it says, but you'll be in there."

"Uriah will be more famous than I am," Bathsheba forecast ruefully. "He'll get more space as my husband than I'll get as his wife, or yours, or as the mother of Solomon."

"You are not going to be known much longer as the mother of Solomon if you continue to instigate so blatantly. The child will be in danger the minute I die, and so will you. Amnon is selfish and Absalom proud. People have murdered for less."

"Then promise me now that you will name him your heir. You're going to do it for me anyway, sooner or later, so you might as well promise me now."

Her effrontery was dazzling, and I grinned. "Why would I ever do that?"

"Because I suck your cock, that's why. And I'm giving you the greatest fucking you ever had."

"Give me some now."

"Give me my promise. Just keep back. I said no. Don't touch me there. Don't you dare scratch me like that. I mean it, David, David. I do."

Much of which she had boasted was true, I conceded, but not quite to the point. "There is not a chance in a million that your little Solomon will ever be king," I advised her, "so you might just as well stop thinking about it now, and you must stop talking about it too. There's Amnon and Absalom ahead of him already, and then Adonijah, and that's only the *A*'s. So lie down, my love, let me come into thy garden and eat thy pleasant fruits. Thou hast doves' eyes within thy locks. Thy navel is like a round goblet which wanteth not liquor, thy belly is like a heap of wheat set about with lilies. Thy teeth are like a flock of sheep that are even shorn."

"Oh, David. No, David."

"Thy breasts like to clusters of grapes on the vine. The joints of thy thighs are like jewels, the work of the hands of a cunning workman, thy neck is as a tower of ivory. Let my banner over thee be love. Let me stick it in your ear."

"No, David. Oh, David. Oh, David, David—no, David." And,

saying she would ne'er consent, consented, and was not sorry afterward. "David," she sighed with bliss when we rested. "That was divine. Where do you get such beautiful words?"

"I make them up out of whole cloth," I told her, feeling pretty good about them myself. "I could easily have forced you, my darling, you know."

"And what would you get?" she replied with a snicker. "You might just as well force Ahinoam or Abigail or Abital, for all the pleasure that would give you, and that's only the *A*'s."

"Abigail's not bad," I felt obliged to put in loyally.

"But can she compare?" said Bathsheba with reason. "Listen, David, about the succession. You weren't exactly the oldest when Samuel picked you, were you?"

"Samuel didn't pick me," I revealed to her, "and would have greatly preferred any one of my brothers. Samuel was not exactly crazy about me. God was. If God speaks to me, of course I would have to do what He says."

"Then you speak to Him," she demanded. "He owes you a favor, doesn't He?"

"He owes me an apology," I corrected. "Can't you see the difference?"

"I don't want to."

"He doesn't have to atone to me; He just has to apologize. And I'm not going to talk to Him again until He does. He'll speak up Himself when He feels He has something to say, don't worry about that. Amnon comes first, and Absalom right behind him, if both live. And whichever one I do name will get rid of the other promptly, if he has any brains."

"If both don't live?"

"Then next comes Adonijah. But why shouldn't they live? What are you thinking of, you little fox?"

"I'll stick needles into images."

"Don't you dare!"

And both my sons were swept away with such stunning and monstrous finality that I have to check myself, even now, from concluding that perhaps they did. Amnon sent word he was sick. People, I'd heard, have power to bring about such failures in health in others through pins and needles, insect powders, and other varieties of black magic, and, of course, through poison. But Amnon was faking, as it turned out—so Bathsheba was exculpated—and

333

setting me up as the credulous dupe to deliver my innocent daughter Tamar, his half sister, into his house and into his fell clutches. Not even Bathsheba, with all her duplicity and all the pins and needles in the world, could have worked up that scenario. I have to exonerate her, tempting as it is to grasp at any explanation for the train of events leading to the disintegration of my family that would leave me blameless. The fault lay elsewhere, because each of us—Amnon, Absalom, and I—was aggressive contributor to the brutal climaxes betiding us, and Amnon and Absalom died by the sword.

Only Tamar was innocent.

Because Tamar, the sister of Absalom, was very fair and a virgin, Amnon thought it would be hard for him to do anything with her through legitimate wooing. Yet he fancied himself sick with love for her and was vexed. Handsome, idle, and overprivileged, Amnon, my first born, was one of those vain youths to whom the merest caprice is an imperative demand and the slightest denial a crushing misfortune too agonizing to be borne. So he concocted his unconscionable plot to rape her, and I went for the fiction of his illness hook, line, and sinker. By sparing the rod, I had spoiled this child; by sparing him again, I set the stage for much worse. Perhaps I deserved it. I had never had a quarrel with Absalom over anything before this thing of Amnon's to Tamar. Thereafter, I never found end to my quarrel with Absalom until Joab put three darts into his heart while he hung from the tree by his head and then had him cut down and cast into a filthy pit in the woods like an animal unfit for orthodox human burial. There was death in the pot.

"I pray thee," Amnon asked me when I came to call on my son, who had sent word he was ailing, "let Tamar my sister come to take care of me." He had laid himself down like a man who was ill.

"It's probably a virus."

He nodded, looking faint and depressed. "Let her make me a couple of cakes in my sight, that I may eat at her hand and be more cheerful."

What parent would have said no? They had played together as children. He had servants in his house; they would not be alone.

"Go now to thy brother Amnon's house," I said to Tamar when I was back in my own home, "and dress him meat. He is sick and in bed and has asked you to be with him."

So Tamar went to her brother Amnon's house, and she had a garment of divers colors upon her that was as luminous and gay and gaudy as the rich, resplendent robes worn daily by my winsome servant Abishag. It was that pretty virgin's robe, perhaps, that made her irresistibly desirable to Amnon, for there's no making sense otherwise of the way he treated her afterward.

Amnon had made sure he was laid down and looking pathetic when Tamar arrived. She rolled up her sleeves and went to work like a trooper with the things she had come to do. She took flour and kneaded it, and made cakes in his sight, and did bake the cakes where he could watch. And she took a pan when they were finished and poured them out before him; but Amnon shook his head and refused to eat.

"You aren't hungry?" the girl inquired shyly, solicitous.

"I am hungry," he answered listlessly, "but so fatigued. Have everyone else out from me. Please. I feel so weak. They make me crazy." And when all had gone out, he said unto Tamar, "Bring the meat in my chamber, where I have more room, that I may eat of thine hand. Help me up, my sister. I think I can walk, but please help me up."

So Tamar took the cakes that she had made and brought them into the chamber, where Amnon had laid himself down on his larger bed. He left room for Tamar to sit at his side with the pan and feed him. But when she offered to give him the cakes from the pan, he took hold of her then with strength and roughness she did not expect and said, "Come lie with me, my sister."

The startled girl attempted to pull back. He held her fast.

"Nay, my brother," Tamar pleaded with him in fright. "Do not do this thing."

"Please," he commanded her gruffly. "I must have you."

"Do not force me," she sued, "for no such thing ought to be done in Israel."

"You won't be sorry."

"Do not thou this folly."

"I won't let you say no."

"And I?" she tried timidly, desperately, to convince him. "Whither shall I cause my shame to go? And as for thee, thou shalt be as one of the fools in Israel. Now therefore, I pray thee, speak unto the king to have me, for he will not withhold me from thee."

Her guess was a good one. Since Leviticus, a man is forbidden to lie with the daughter of his father's wife, but I would have said yes had his intentions been reputable and he'd asked to marry her. Such laws often are more honored in the breach than in the observance, and I would have looked the other way and danced at their wedding. But marriage was not what Amnon had in mind. By then he was no longer hearkening to her voice, but crushing her down beneath him.

"Don't cry out," he threatened. "Or my servants will know about us too."

And being stronger than she, he forced her down to the bed. He pulled up her skirt. And then he raped her.

Oh, the harm he caused, the ruin he brought about. To himself as well, for Tamar was not the only victim. Because of him, I was fleeing for my life from my city of Jerusalem seven years later. Time goes so swiftly when we look back, doesn't it? It seemed more like seven seconds. Because of this, and what came after, for Amnon did not love her any longer when he was through. Instead, he hated her exceedingly, so that the hatred wherewith he hated her was greater than the love wherewith he had loved her. He did not know or question the cause. What in hell did he expect from a virgin?

"Arise and be gone," he ordered her with cruelty, scorn, and revulsion. He shoved her from him.

The bewildered, violated girl was close to collapse. "There is no cause," she said unto him tearfully. "This evil in sending me away is greater than the other that thou didst unto me."

But he would not hearken unto her now either, and he debased her further by calling back inside the servant that ministered unto him and, while she cringed at his words as though they were whips, giving orders to the man: "Put now this woman out from me, and bolt the door after her. Do not admit her if she comes seeking me more."

Then the man, his servant, with a leer and a snigger, brought her out of the house without a word and bolted the door after her.

Amnon threw her out. Why? So much is hidden from the seeing eye and the hearing ear.

And Tamar, ejected so rudely, put ashes on her head, and rent her garment that was on her, that festive robe of divers colors, and she did as she would do when she mourned for someone who was dead. She laid her hand on her head and went on crying till she came to Absalom her brother, who guessed the whole from her distraught beginning, so she did not have to speak it then. "Hath Amnon thy brother been with thee? Hold now thy peace and tell it to no one else," he instructed her, "because he is thy brother." She remained desolate in her brother Absalom's house and would not come out.

"That was good, Absalom," I complimented him when the event was laid before me. The dread that weighed heaviest upon me was that I was now in very deep trouble again and would find myself with ticklish decisions to make. My darkest and most demoralizing regret at first was that my eldest son had made a fool of me. "That was a good thing for you to tell her to do."

"And what will you do?" Absalom asked, and watched me intently as he awaited my answer.

"To Amnon?"

"To punish him."

"He is my son."

"My sister is your daughter."

"She's only a girl. And she didn't cry out, did she?"

"Who would have come? Amnon is the king's son."

"That makes no difference. A damsel taken in the city who does not cry out is as much to blame as the man."

"Really?" said Absalom, almost apathetically. But he raised his eyebrows.

"Yes, it's in the Bible. You can look it up."

"Can the Devil cite Scripture for his purpose?"

"I am not the Devil, Absalom. And your sister Tamar is not even betrothed. There is really no law against raping a woman who is not betrothed. Did you know that?"

"Pass one," said Absalom. "Maybe my brother Amnon will impose a law against rape when he becomes king."

I had not known he possessed this gift for enigmatic sarcasm. I was concerned. I could not guess what he was thinking.

"Have you spoken to Amnon?" I was anxious to find out.

"I have said nothing unto Amnon, either good or bad."

"That's a good boy," I commended him.

"What would be the point?" His face remained inscrutable, but his penetrating dark eyes did not waver from studying me. "I am only trying to learn."

"There would be no point. Amnon is your brother."

"And Tamar is just my sister." I could not tell if he was being ironic.

"Yes."

"Will you speak to Amnon?" Absalom wanted to know.

"I will be very wroth with him," I replied. "I can promise you that."

"Do you want to see her?"

"Who?"

"Tamar."

"Why?"

"To speak with her."

"About what?"

"She is in my house and won't come out. She is not the same. She does not want to talk to anybody. Ever again."

"Then why should I want to talk to her? What can I tell her to help her?"

"You sent her to him."

"He said he was sick."

"He lied to you."

"I'll tax him with that."

"She is desolate in my home. She weeps continually."

"Can I console her?"

"She feels there is nowhere in Israel she can hide her shame."

"We can hush it up. Who has to know?"

"Can she hide it from herself? He had her cast out from his house, by a servant, as though she were something obscene."

"I'll put this question to you," I said to him. "What can I say to her? That I'll make Amnon marry her?"

"She doesn't want that now," Absalom answered.

"What does she want?"

"She does not want to be seen in Israel again."

"Where shall I send her?"

"May I send her to Geshur to the house of the king, our mother's father?"

"I like that idea," I consented immediately. "Bring her there yourself."

"And what will you do?"

"To Amnon?" It was a hard question. "Heed the words of your father, my son." I tried to avoid answering it; my manner was professorial.

"I am listening," declared Absalom, waiting. "I am trying my best to learn."

"Then heed these words of thy father. She is only your sister, Absalom. It is not as though she were your wife, or your concubine, or your daughter."

"Tamar is your daughter."

"Should I avenge a daughter or save a son? You tell me that, if you think it's so easy."

"Which will you do?"

"Would you really expect me to have him killed?"

In the end I did nothing, of course, except attempt without success to bully my son Amnon into some sense of contrition. It is sometimes so much easier to look the other way. And Absalom never forgave me. I understand that now. I would not let myself understand then that he even blamed me. But how did he expect me to punish Amnon? How in the world could I have punished Absalom himself if Joab had not done it for me? Kept him in chains?

I indeed was very wroth with Amnon—or tried to be—when I spoke with him alone, for all the good that did. He was languid and bored and could not have cared less when I upbraided him for this deed he had done. He pretended to humor me with a detached and superior smile, taking for granted that I would impose no penalty. He combed his curls in the midst of my reprimand. His locks were freshly oiled and he wore more arm bracelets than I care to see on a man. He no more repented his violation of Tamar than he did his irreverent offense in so deceitfully reducing me, his king and father, to his procurer. I let him have it for that one too, and made no deeper impression on him for that transgression than for the other.

"You should not have used me in your scheme," I reproved him. "Why did you have to make such a dunce of me?"

My objection amused him. "I wanted to see if I could. Can't you take a joke? You're wroth with me, aren't you? I can tell."

"I am very wroth."

"I can tell you're wroth. I really can't see what you're so angry about. I loved Tamar, and was so vexed with love for her that I couldn't eat, and made myself lean from day to day. After I had her, I no longer loved her. Is that really so hard to understand? Or so unusual? She's really very much to blame, you know. Wouldn't you say she led me on? She should not have come to my house if she didn't want me to force her."

I regarded him for a moment with my mouth agape. "I sent her to you."

"You ought not to have done that," he admonished me gently.

"You told me to."

"And she certainly should not have allowed herself to be alone with me in my chamber."

"You sent away your servants."

"She did not cry out, did she? We were in the city, weren't we? She has to cry out. Otherwise she is just as much to blame as I am and can be stoned to death."

"Who would have come to aid her? You're the king's son."

"That makes no difference," he rejoined. "In the city she has to cry out."

"It's all her fault?"

"Why are you getting so upset?" Amnon said placidly. "Someday I'll be king, and none of this will make any difference, will it?"

"The girl is shamed, Amnon," I tried to impress upon him, "and won't stop weeping. She won't come out of the house."

Amnon shrugged. "If I'm going to have to worry about every girl who's shamed, I might never rape another one."

"Did you have to throw her out afterward?"

"She disgusted me, Father. What else was I to do? The hatred with which I hated her afterward was much greater than the love with which I had loved her, so I wanted her out of my presence as quickly as possible. I could not bear her an instant longer. Don't you often feel that way about women after you've lain with them?"

"Never," I told him and, reflecting, added, "except sometimes when they want to talk a lot."

"With me it's more than that," he admitted introspectively. "I almost always do. That's the only part of this whole thing that really troubles me. I may have a problem. I tend to feel revulsion for women as soon as I finish having sex with them. Why are you staring at me like that?"

"I feel you may be in for a headache when you do become king," I was obliged to inform him. "I'm going to leave you a very big harem. You may not be able to make it there. You'll have a house full of women who will think of themselves as your wives and sweethearts and who, you tell me, will fill you with disgust. How will you stand it? It's like living inside a cage full of birds. Your harem will be hell. It's never much good at best. Yours will be a nightmare."

"I worry about that," he confided pensively. "I wonder if maybe deep down inside me there isn't something wrong with me, something mysterious, as with you and Jonathan."

I stared at him coldly. "And just what in hell do you mean by that?"

"Well, you know," he said with a trace of impatience. "I don't see why you're so touchy about it. I'm not the only one who talks about it, you know."

"About what?" I demanded. I was quivering with outrage.

"About that friendship you had with Jonathan," he answered, unruffled. "It's not exactly a secret, you know. Even you come right out and talk about it in that poem of yours. Don't you say that you enjoyed his love more than you did the love of women?"

"I say no such thing," I disagreed violently. It was thoroughly upsetting to find that all of a sudden *I* was the one on the defensive. "What I do say," I explained with precision, "is that his love to me was *passing* the love of women, not more enjoyable, which is a different thing entirely."

Says you, is what he seemed to be signifying as he regarded me with a look of skepticism. "Where's the difference?"

"I was exalting friendship," I labored on to elucidate. "And when you take into account that the only women I'd known up till then were Michal, Abigail, and Ahinoam, it's not such a tall claim, is it?"

"You've heard the stories, haven't you?"

"They're apocryphal. Read it again, read it more closely. All I was trying to say was that Jonathan had been a good friend and was as close to me as a brother. That's all."

"Like Absalom to me?" asked Amnon with a smirk, smoothing the sleeves of his tunic as though he were restless to leave.

"Exactly." I felt on a firmer footing now that we were back on the primary subject of our discussion. Jonathan and me—the very idea that this son of mine should throw it up to me now! "Yes, just like Absalom and you. Has thy brother Absalom spoken to you?"

"My brother Absalom?" It seemed to me he was toying with me in his affected lassitude. "About what?"

"His sister Tamar."

"Why should he? My brother Absalom has spoken nothing to me either good or bad."

"He does not seem wroth?"

"Why should he seem wroth?" said Amnon. "Who cares so much about a sister?"

Simeon and Levi, was an answer I might have given had I thought of it, those two ferocious headstrong sons of Jacob and Leah, who avenged the defilement of their sister Dinah by killing the lovesick prince of Shechem and all the other males in his city. Simeon and Levi fell upon the city boldly with their swords when the time was ripe, while the men of Shechem were still sore from the acts of group circumcision to which they had submitted as part of the spurious nuptial agreement the two had proposed in order to render the men there unfit to defend themselves. They slew them all and spared neither the prince nor his father. And poor old patriarch Jacob was anything but pleased by the dangers they had wrought. "Ye have troubled me to make me stink among the inhabitants of the land," he berated Simeon and Levi furiously, and ordered the tents struck and the cattle gathered and the earrings that were in their ears and their idols of strange gods buried under the oak that is in Shechem in preparation for the flight he foresaw would now be necessary. "I being few in number, they shall gather themselves together against me, and slay me. And I shall be destroyed, I and my house."

So it happened that Jacob, my respected, complicated, overburdened ancestor, was forced again to flee for his life, but not, as I was, from a son, although he'd fled much earlier from his brother Esau, whose blessing he'd filched and whose birthright he'd bought for a mess of red pottage when Esau was back from hunting and so faint from hunger he thought he might die.

Absalom bided his time. No doubt I should have been more severe with Amnon. Because sentence against an evil work is not executed speedily, the heart of the sons of men is fully set in them to do evil. At least that was true of Absalom. With a patience, guile, and self-discipline for which no one who knew him would have given him credit, he smiled and smiled for two full years and still was a villain. He did nothing. But in his heart Absalom hated Amnon, because he had forced his sister Tamar. And now I know he also hated me. He knew I loved him. He must have known I loved him, and he must have detested me all the more because he saw I doted on him slavishly. He must have known from the way I finally welcomed him into my presence after his long banishment. Maybe I'd kept him away too long: three years in Geshur, two here in Jerusalem, without letting him see my face. Maybe five years apart was much too long.

I wonder what he really had in mind by asking me, along with all his brothers, to the sheepshearing celebration to which he lured Amnon into fatal ambush. I quail from thinking about the contingency plans he might have put into operation had I not declined. The first reports of slaughter that came howling into the city were horrifying: voices screeched hysterically of Absalom's having butchered all my princes, all of his brothers, all of my sons. My senses failed me. I could not breathe. People swooned in the streets of the city. Then my other sons began arriving in a disorderly rush with the grisly tidings that the enormous enmity of my son Absalom had centered only upon Amnon. Believe it or not, in contrast to those first overwhelming and incredible rumors of mass fratricide, that was good news.

It was only for Amnon that Absalom had laid so carefully his plans for reprisal, and had commanded his servants in stealth, saying, "Mark ye now when Amnon's heart is merry with wine, and when I say unto you, 'Smite Amnon,' then kill him. Fear not. Be courageous, and be valiant. Have I not commanded you?"

And at the opportune moment, Absalom commanded them, "Smite Amnon!" And they smote Amnon.

So Amnon died in his cups and did not have the time even to attempt to know why. And Absalom fled to Geshur, where his grandfather was king, and was there three years. I did not pursue, and I did not send to have this fugitive returned. A request for his extradition would undoubtedly have been honored, for Geshur is in Syria and all Syria was in vassalage to me. I let him stay, I let him live. But in one fell swoop I had lost them both, in one ghastly moment at a normal sheepshearing party. For Amnon I was soon comforted, seeing he was dead, but my soul longed to go forth unto Absalom. Joab knew. Every day, I mourned this loss of my handsome, surviving, splendid boy of whom I had always been so irrepressibly admiring. I worried about him. I lived in morbid dread I might never see him again.

Joab perceived that my heart was toward Absalom, and eventually he took the bull by the horns. I did not try to hide that I wanted him near. But the law, I fretted—the law. How could I pardon the one of my sons who had murdered another, bring back as my successor the youth who had killed the older brother standing before him as heir? Trust in Joab to demonstrate how easily it could be done.

He began with the aid of the wise woman of Tekoah, sending her in first to break the ice and pave the way for the action he himself wished to advocate. He had her come to me as a widow costumed in mourning apparel. The wise woman of Tekoah fell on her face on the ground when she entered and did obeisance, then besought me with a convincing, woeful story purporting to be true which turned out in the end to be but another irritating parable.

"Help, O king," she said.

And I said unto her sympathetically, "What aileth thee?"

And she commenced her sober charade by answering, "I am indeed a widow woman, and mine husband is dead. And thy handmaid had two sons, and they two strove together in the field, and the one smote the other and slew him. And behold, the whole family is risen against me. They want me to deliver the one that lives, that they may kill him, for the life of his brother whom he slew and is already dead. And so they shall quench my one coal which is left, and shall not leave to my husband neither name nor remainder upon the earth. Will that bring my slain one back to life?"

I saw the rightness on her side and was disposed to be compassionate. "Go to thine house," I said, "and I will give charge concerning thee. Whosoever saith aught unto thee, bring him to me, and he shall not touch thee anymore."

Then said she, "The people have made me afraid. I pray thee, let the king remember the Lord thy God, that thou wouldest not suffer the revengers of blood to destroy anymore, lest they destroy my son."

And I promised, "As the Lord liveth, there shall not one hair of thy son fall to the earth."

Then the woman continued resolutely, as though bent on obtaining more. "Let thy handmaid, I pray thee, speak further unto my lord the king."

How could I refuse? "Say on."

And the woman said, "The king doth speak this thing as one which is faulty. Wherefore then doth the king not fetch home again his own banished son?" There was a momentary flicker of fear on her face when she heard my startled gasp. "For we must needs die," she went on hastily, as though to forestall any anger I might show at this incredible presumption, "and are as water spilt upon the ground. Neither doth God owe respect to any person. Yet see, as with me, how He doth devise means, that a father's banished son be not expelled from him forevermore." And the woman concluded, "Let my lord the king now speak."

"Who put you up to this?" were the words with which I finally responded, and that she not be afraid, assured her I intended no harm. "Hide not from me, I pray thee, the thing that I shall ask thee. Is not the hand of Joab with thee in all this?"

And the wise woman of Tekoah, who indeed was wise enough to use flattery skillfully, replied as follows, "As thy soul liveth, my lord the king is wise, according to the wisdom of an angel of God, to know all things that are in the earth. For thy servant Joab, he bade me, and he put all these words in the mouth of thine handmaid."

"Behold now," I said as I released her, "tell Joab you have done this thing, and bring him to me. By the way, just for my personal curiosity, you don't really have a son who slew another, do you?"

"No, my lord, I do not. And I am no widow."

"I'm beginning to catch on."

With Joab himself I succumbed willingly to arguments from him that I hoped from the start would prove unanswerable. I was more grateful than I can describe for his realistic universal precept that no laws are legitimate and that, in consequence, there is no such thing as crime. And I could dispute with him no further after he propounded for me the celebrated golden rule upon which the civilized world turns to this day:

"Always do unto others what is best for you."

Any possible further resistance by me was swept away. "Go therefore," I yielded magnanimously, as though I were the one doing *him* the favor, "bring the young man Absalom home again."

And then Joab did a most surprising thing, which I have never forgotten and for which, perhaps, he has never forgiven himself. He fell to the ground on his face, and bowed himself and thanked me, even unto calling himself my servant and me his lord and king. All this from Joab? To this day I don't know what came over him.

I was so astonished by such open and reverential submission from him that I came near weeping. We did a lot of weeping back then.

"Today," Joab professed, in this most unlikely outpouring of emotion, "thy servant knoweth that I have found grace in thy sight, my lord, O king, in that the king hath fulfilled the request of his servant."

It took me a minute to recover from my surprise. "But let him," I directed, "turn to his own house and let him not see my face. And let him know to take care, for he will be abhorred by the people."

So Joab arose and went to Geshur, and brought Absalom to Jerusalem. Only later, when I was slouching in flight from Jerusalem toward the Jordan, did it cross my mind that Joab's motives in making this supplication were something other than humane. Suspicions, once born, are never put to rest, and I am inclined to doubt him still. Absalom may have blown it all with the barley field.

So after three years in exile, Absalom returned to his own house and did not see my face for two more. And to my amazement, he was anything but abhorred for having smitten his brother. In all Israel, in fact, there was soon none to be so much praised as Absalom. He was acclaimed for his beauty. I had joy from him. And unto Absalom there were born three sons—my grandsons, naturally—and one daughter, whom he had named Tamar, after her ruined dishonored aunt, my daughter. And she was a girl of a fair countenance, but that did not help her, for she soon lost her father in war anyway. Women named Tamar do not fare well in the Bible, do they? The first was that Canaanite woman who was widowed twice, the second time by her husband Onan, who sooner spilled his seed on the ground lest he give child to the former wife of his deceased brother and continue his brother's line, wherefore the Lord slew him. She had to adopt the attire of a prostitute, with her face covered with a veil, to seduce Judah, her father-in-law, into performing the levirate marriage to which she was entitled and into getting her with the child due her by a member of her dead husband's family. The second Tamar was my Tamar, who had the ill fortune to be raped by her half brother Amnon. And this little Tamar lost her father in the battle of the wood of Ephraim and was never heard from again.

So Absalom, her father, dwelt in Jerusalem two full years and saw not my face or came into the king's palace even once. I basked in the reflected popularity I heard he was enjoying. I wanted so much to see his face, and his beautiful head of hair that was the wonder of all who beheld him, so long and full and luxuriant it was and as black and shiny as tar. I felt deliciously and maliciously vindicated each time I was told that he desired to come to me. Perversely and self-righteously, I forbade it, and felt oddly virtuous in frustrating us both. Quick-tempered Absalom was intractable at the end of those two years and ready to explode. Therefore, he sent for Joab to have him come to me to obtain full amnesty on his behalf. But Joab ignored his summons. When Absalom sent a second time, Joab still would not come. Therefore, Absalom said unto his servants, "See, Joab's field is near mine, and he hath barley there. Go and set it on fire."

Then Joab arose and came to Absalom unto his house and said, "Wherefore have thy servants set my field on fire?"

And plucky Absalom, without batting an eye, replied unto my general, "Behold, I sent unto thee, saying, 'Come hither,' and you would not come. Behold, I will set all your fields on fire if you do not come when I call you."

"What is it that you want?" Joab was stymied. He knew his hands were tied.

"Go to the king, my father," Absalom ordered him, "and speak for me that he therefore may allow me to see his face. Am I a stranger to him? Say to him wherefore am I come from Geshur if I am not to be his son again? Better it would have been for me to be there still. And tell him if there be any iniquity in me, let him kill me. Otherwise let me see his face."

By now it was beginning to appear that my son Absalom as desperately wanted to see my face as I did to see his, and would do everything in his power to effect that desired reunion. I listened with a great warm glow as I heard Joab indignantly recount what had taken place. It was good to see my eminent general fuming. I had never beheld him so balked, overwrought, and exasperated.

"He vows to set fire to all my fields," announced my captain and chief over all my host. I had to grin and laugh out loud. "Wherefore did you bring him home from Geshur if you won't let him see your face? I pray, let there be peace between him and thee. What's the point? It had been better for all of us for him to have been there still rather than have strife now between us three."

Now, as you know, I did say yes.

Absalom did not toady when I had him brought to me. He strode in with a swagger, as though *he* were the injured party, and, with no sound or look of gratitude or apology, bowed himself on his face to the ground before me. I relished his air of confidence and pride. I held his shoulders when he arose and I enfolded him in my arms with a sob. And I kissed him. I was in tears again. He did not kiss me.

12

SNAKE IN THE GRASS

In the months that followed, I showered honors and presents upon him, and it came to pass shortly after we were reconciled that Absalom prepared him chariots and horses, and fifty men to run before him. Adonijah does that now. Absalom was the talk of the city. He was like a brilliant young god in whom the people rejoiced. And I took shameless vicarious pleasure in the adulation he received and in the energy he displayed with such graceful self-assurance. He justified my self-conceit by the dedication with which he pitched in to help with the tedious business of government, applying himself with an industry and a civic zeal never exerted by any of my other sons, before or since. He was, I honored us both, a chip off the old block.

Absalom quickly discovered within himself a genius and liking for governing that I myself have never inherently possessed. He took to politics like a duck to water. I beamed when I observed him so willing and conscientious. I was naïve. Joab did not dare tell me then that Absalom was doing to me with the people what I had done to Saul so long ago in the past: currying their favor and kindling their love. He rose up early each day and made it his duty to stand beside the way of the gate into the city. And it was so that when any man that had a controversy or grievance was coming with the hope of seeing the king for judgment, then Absalom called unto him, "Of what city art thou?" And if the man answered, "Thy servant is of one of the tribes of Israel," then Absalom would butter him up, saying unto him, "See, thy matters are good and right. But there is no man deputed of the king to hear thee, no man but me, and I have taken it upon myself."

The fact of the matter is that, like so many great leaders in history, I was easily bored by the repetitive minutiae of administering power. War, not reigning, was my real work. Like a fish out

JOSEPH HELLER

of water is a man of war in time of peace; I hardly knew what to do
with myself most of the time. Oh, I was a paragon at delegating
responsibility. Just about anyone who wanted it could have it. Joab
was over all the host, Benaiah was over my palace guard of Cherethites and Pelethites, Adoram was over the tribute, jumping
Jehoshaphat was my recorder, Zadok and Abiathar were priests,
and my sons were chief rulers, and never much good at it. Among
the legion of institutions I had neglected to formalize was an effective judiciary system. I blessed the enterprise of Absalom when I
learned he was handling complaints in my stead and relieving me
of the need to do so.

"Oh that I were made judge in the land," I was pleased to be
told my son Absalom was saying to console all those with wrongs
who journeyed by the way of the gate of Jerusalem in the hope of
obtaining an audience with me, "that every man with any suit or
cause might come unto me, and I would do him justice! What a
pity that there is no man deputed of the king to hear thee. I will
take the time to judge."

He wanted to judge? So I let him judge. I was all too willing to
see my son representing me with such ingratiating success. I did
not know that in this fashion he was deliberately and systematically undermining me. And I couldn't have seen, even had I been
cautioned, why he should want to. He was next in line, wasn't he?
So it was with doting and uncritical spirit that I allowed him to
flourish. To this day I find it hard to believe that someone as
worldly and astute as myself could be misguided by paternal fondness into imitating the action of the ostrich, that ungainly bird
which stands with its head sunk in the earth because it does not
wish to see that which is good in the sight of the sun and that
which is evil.

It was that way with me in the matter of my son Absalom. I saw
nothing dangerous to me in that when any man came nigh to him
to do him obeisance, he put forth his hand, and took him, and
kissed him. And in this manner did Absalom to all Israel that came
to the king for judgment: so Absalom stole the hearts of the men of
Israel. Tacitly I cheered him on. I crowed with fatherly pleasure
and cherished the deeds and graces of my matchless pride and joy.
It did my own heart good that he stole the hearts of the men of
Israel, that this son of mine who was the apple of my eye was my

principal heir, and that my heir, who would succeed me as king, was so revered, applauded, and adored.

How could I know he would not wait? I did not dream he would not wait. If indeed he had been obedient enough to wait, he would be waiting still, and would not be so youthful and charismatic anymore, for I have lived a long time. Even a man of such hollow character as Adonijah is already chafing at the delay in the fulfillment of his royal patrimony and grows progressively less disposed to wait passively to inherit it. Or to wait for Abishag my Shunammite either.

"Haven't you seen the way he eyes her," Bathsheba continues to insinuate, "the lascivious way he looks her over each time he comes here to see you? Are you blind?"

And he is moving ahead with his plans for the lavish outdoor feast at which he will exalt himself by the sheer expense and by saying once again that he will be king. He no longer seems to feel he needs my permission to proceed. The site he has chosen is in an open field outside the city, where the number of guests he can accommodate will be great and the spectators from the city and the surrounding countryside without limit. Joab and he are at work on the guest list. He invites me to attend. There are no plans yet for inviting Solomon or Bathsheba. Why not? He doesn't like them, which is reasonable enough if he is willing to incur the risk of such calculated affronts. Zadok? He already has a priest. He has chosen Abiathar? Abiathar has chosen him, he replies with a simper.

It is hard to be pleased with someone so pleased with himself: a man's attire and excessive laughter and gait show what he is, and I did not like his. I have neither the vitality nor the wish ever to go out of my palace again. Adonijah proposes to transport me to the place on a comfortable litter borne on a wagon drawn by oxen. We can sit side by side at the banquet table, even if I don't eat much. He will laud me in a toast. I will talk and he will clap his hands and whistle.

"I'd freeze my nuts off," I say, declining, which brings to his mind another request.

"Can I have Abishag," Adonijah surprises me by asking, "to take as a wife?"

"Don't you know," I reply, looking him squarely in the eye, "that in asking for Abishag, you are asking for the kingdom also? Didn't Joab tell you that?"

"Thou knowest that the kingdom is mine anyway, isn't it?"

"If ever it isn't," I respond to him dryly, "just ask for Abishag again, and see what happens. Can't you wait at least until I have given up the ghost, breathed my last, and gone to sleep with my fathers?"

"Joab thought it would be a good idea to ask for her now."

"You rely much on Joab?"

"He helps keep the peace."

"Are you inviting Benaiah?"

"Joab doesn't see the need."

From the street below my windows when he goes, I hear the hullabaloo from his chariot as he mounts and departs and the stagy clamor of the voices of the fifty men he has retained to run before him when he rides.

"He thinks he's Absalom," Bathsheba derides, without smiling.

He is emulating Absalom, coveting the glamour that emanated like an undimmed phosphorescence from my favorite, black-haired prince, and overlooking the sad and sordid end to which it carried him, to a putrefying pit in the wood beneath a heap of stones.

What I don't want now is another *putsch*. Absalom initiated his in a way that seemed harmless enough, an ordinary request to go to Hebron to repay a vow he told me he'd made while abiding in Geshur in Syria, saying: "I vowed that if the Lord should bring me home again, then I would serve the Lord with sacrifice."

"There are no priests in Jerusalem?" I wondered aloud, humoring him.

"In Hebron they are dissatisfied with us because we live in Jerusalem." Absalom was normally not so perspicacious, and I wonder now if he was already being coached by Ahitophel, or perhaps by Joab. "They will be less disposed to argue that we have forsaken Judah if we show ourselves before them. My mission has a diplomatic value as well as a sacramental one."

"Go in good health," I said, giving in.

So Absalom arose and went to Hebron, but went with secret, treasonable plans. He went to make war, against me.

Who would have guessed it? Against me, a king and father more sinned against than sinning, who loved him more than I did my own soul. Who would have guessed that a young man of such fiery, open pride and such passionate temperament would speak with such an oily tongue, that a character so volatile and reckless could be so sly? I should have kept in mind the obsidian reserve with which my beautiful dark-eyed son delayed for two whole years to slay Amnon, without once betraying a hint of the determination for murderous revenge festering inside him. I should have consulted about him more with my adviser Ahitophel the Gilonite while the shrewd wisdom of Ahitophel was still available to me, that same Ahitophel the Gilonite who never made a mistake—even when he rode home on his ass, put his family affairs in order, and hanged himself. Thereafter, it became a proverb, "That Ahitophel, he died young. He was never wrong."

Except for his assumption that my son would heed his sound advice. That was vanity, for both of them. Ahitophel the infallible did underestimate the egoism of the dashing, freebooting prince for whose service he had deserted mine, and the role conceit might play when Absalom, in that first heady flush of triumph, began esteeming himself immune from the possibility of error.

Absalom instituted his attack against me with a clandestine network of spies dispersed throughout all the tribes of Israel to spread the word to others potentially in league with him, saying, "As soon as ye hear the sound of the trumpet, then ye shall say for all to hear, 'Absalom reigneth in Hebron.' "

And with Absalom, when he'd packed and left for Hebron, coincidentally went two hundred unsuspecting religious travelers out of Jerusalem who felt the call to worship at this same fete to which Absalom pretended to be going. They went with him in their simplicity and they knew not anything. But they came into the city following Absalom and soon found themselves counted among the imposing numbers thought to favor his uprising against me. Absalom then blew his trumpet and proclaimed himself king. And Absalom then sent at once for Ahitophel the Gilonite, my chief counselor, to come from his city, even from Giloh, to join with him in his insurrection, and Absalom offered holy sacrifices while he waited to hear, and while his spies broadcast word of his coup throughout all the tribes of Israel. When Ahitophel the Gilonite came over to his side, the conspiracy mushroomed and became strong. Rebellion spread like wildfire. To my dismay and bewilderment, the people increased continually with Absalom.

Who would have thought I had dissatisfied so many? I was outnumbered and overthrown before I even knew what was happening. Joyous partisans had taken up arms in mobs and were trooping toward the city from the north, south, and west. That simplified my choice of direction for my getaway. I had to go east into the plain of the wilderness to attain sanctuary somewhere on the other side of the Jordan. From Judah and even unto Israel, they were siding with him.

"The hearts of the men of Israel are after Absalom," there came messengers saying, and all reports that followed brought more ominous confirmation.

I lost no time getting out.

"Arise, and let us flee," were the orders I gave to those that were with me at Jerusalem when I saw how the land lay, "for we shall not else escape from Absalom. Make speed to depart, lest he overtake us suddenly, and bring evil upon us, and smite the city with the edge of the sword."

I had distrust for everyone. Who would follow and who would stay? My servants seemed ready to oblige me in any way I could appoint.

I packed quickly to beat a hasty retreat. From my palace I went forth toward brook Kidron at the eastern boundary of the city, and all my household and all my servants after me. And what a stupendous household mine had by that time become, with all those wives and fucking unnecessary concubines I had accumulated and was already tired of, and all those squalling children. I left those ten of my women behind, all of them concubines, to keep the house, with strict instructions to ventilate the rooms and to air the bedding on the roof daily, regardless of who slept there, in the event it came to pass that I did return. I fled while I could because my chances of emerging victorious from any battle were greater in an open field than inside a city in which I could not deploy my forces to best advantage and in which I did not know who was loyal to me and who was not. I had lost Ahitophel already. My nephew Amasa, child of my favorite sister, Abigail, had gone over to Absalom and was captain of his host. There was no sign of Joab.

Once again, I commiserated with myself as I started out eastward toward brook Kidron, I had no place to safely lay my head.

At the stream, I tarried to take stock. Certainly, I could see, I was not alone. My spirits improved. Benaiah and all the Cherethites and all the Perethites were true blue and passed on beside me and crossed brook Kidron. At least I knew I would not be taken by surprise and stabbed under the fifth rib, as Saul could

356

have been by me had that ever been my objective. Then came Ittai and his Gittites, all six hundred men of war who had come up after me from Gath to serve in my forces following my victory over the Philistines, and they passed on before me also. I had part of an army. I'm afraid my heart broke with gratitude at the welcome sight of Ittai and his Gittites, and I turned maudlin for a minute. I may have overidentified. I was feeling sorry for myself in feeling sorry for him.

"Wherefore goest thou also with us?" I blurted out with feeling. "Return to thy place and abide with the new king, for thou art a stranger and also an exile. I know what it is to be without a home. Whereas thou camest but yesterday, should I this day make thee go up and down and back and forth with us? Seeing I will have to go whither I may, return thou, and take back thy brethren. Mercy and truth be with thee."

And Ittai answered me and said, "As the Lord liveth, and as my lord the king liveth, surely in what place my lord the king shall be, whether in death or life, even there also will thy servant be."

"Go and pass over," I said to Ittai the Gittite, and almost wept again. I don't know what I would have done had he accepted my suggestion. Wept a good deal more.

And Ittai the Gittite passed over the brook, and all his men, and all the wives and the little ones that were with him. And it seemed as though all the city and all the country wept with a loud voice as all the people passed over, and then as I myself passed over brook Kidron toward the way of the wilderness between the city in the mountains and the valley of the Jordan. Then Abishai too was there, looking tough and wiry, with another large contingent of experienced warriors from my regular army. No, I was far from alone.

"Thy brother Joab," I inquired of Abishai. "Where is he?"

"Am I my brother's keeper?" he answered cryptically. "I did not see him in the city."

Saying nothing, Benaiah unobtrusively set men between me and Abishai to guard me. And lo, Zadok also, my priest, and all the Levites with him, everyone in the priesthood, to my amazement, came out of the city also, bearing the ark of the covenant of God, and they set down the ark of God while they waited for me to resume my woeful journey. And then Abiathar, my other priest, was there with them too. This was turning into much more of an evacuation than I had bargained for, a swelling exodus. Fortunately, I kept my head. I asked them to carry back the ark of God into the city. It was heartening to know that the priests were loyal, but they could serve more usefully professing fealty to Absalom in the city than trudging along outward as an encumbrance to me. They would have to be fed, they could not fight. This was not the time for ceremonial demonstrations.

"I am David, not Moses," I made certain to let them know, "and I shall return. If I shall find favor in the eyes of the Lord, He will bring me again, and show me both His ark and His habitation. But if He thus say He hath no delight in me, behold, here am I, let Him do to me as seemeth good unto Him. But let the ark remain in the city that is holy. Besides," I then put in to Zadok and to Abiathar, "art thou not each of you a seer? Return into the city in peace, and your two sons with you, and see what thou canst see for me. I will tarry in the plain of the wilderness, until there come word from you to certify me what to do."

Ahimaaz the son of Zadok and Jonathan the son of Abiathar could serve as runners. Zadok therefore and Abiathar carried the ark of God again to Jerusalem, and they tarried there in manners that were pious and innocuous while they waited to see what they could see for me.

And I, when they turned and left, went up by the ascent of Mount Olivet, and wept as I went up, and had my head covered, and went barefoot. What a lot of water, I reminisced dejectedly, had gone under the bridge since I first had blazed forth as a star from little Bethlehem. All was over, I was inclined to feel; I had been forsaken by the world and left naked to mine enemies. Until I lifted my eyes and took notice that all of the people with me covered every man his head and came up the Mount of Olives too, all of them weeping as they went up behind me.

And there, on the mount, one verified to me that Ahitophel was indeed among the conspirators with Absalom, and I trembled when I heard, and I said, gazing upward into the heavens toward God: "O Lord, I pray Thee, turn the counsel of Ahitophel into foolishness."

I was not going to bank on that. Although it did come to pass when I was at the top of the mountain and worshipping God, that I beheld Hushai the Archite coming up to meet me, with his coat rent, and earth upon his head. He too was already in mourning.

And he might have been coming in answer to my prayer, for things began to click the instant I saw him and I hit upon a bold idea. Hushai the Archite was another senior figure in my cabinet—one with practical sagacity, to whom I could speak frankly.

I drew him aside and confided to him with a lowered voice: "If thou passest on with me, then thou shall be a burden to me. Thou canst not fight. But if thou return to the city and say unto Absalom, 'O king, as I have been thy father's servant hitherto, so will I now also be thy servant,' then mayest thou defeat the counsel of Ahitophel for me. What thing soever thou shalt hear out of the king's house, thou shalt tell it to Zadok and Abiathar the priests. Behold, they have there with them their two sons. And by them you shall send unto me everything that ye can hear."

So Hushai went back into the city, and was there in wait when Absalom my son came into Jerusalem.

Moving on past the top of the hill of Mount Olivet, downward I then proceeded on the opposite side along the winding way to the plain of the wilderness. All hope of allegiance from the people of Israel against this revolt from Judah disintegrated quickly when I moved past Bahurim and was assailed by that nauseating worm Shimei. The house of Saul was in opposition to me also. Shimei came out to curse me, and cursed me still as closer he came. Even in my most tortured nightmares I could not have invented so ugly an image as Shimei. He cast stones at me and at the people with me, and all of the people on my right hand and all of the mighty men on my left hand bunched closer to shield me from the things he threw. And Shimei said thus to me when he cursed:

"Come out, come out, thou bloody man, and thou man of Belial. The Lord hath returned upon thee all the blood of the house of Saul, in whose stead thou hast reigned. And the Lord hath delivered the kingdom into the hand of Absalom thy son. And behold, thou art taken in thy mischief, because thou art a bloody man."

You think I understood everything he was talking about? Blame it on those translators of King James the First. Abishai the son of Zeruiah was incensed by these gloating jeers and loudly said to me:

"Why should this dead dog curse my lord the king? Let me go over, I pray thee, and take off his head."

I firmly refused. And I said unto Abishai, "Every time you speak, Abishai, you want to take off somebody's head. Tell me this: where is your brother Joab?"

"Do I know?"

"Let Shimei curse," I said resignedly, in full awareness of my fallen condition, "because the Lord hath said unto him to curse David. Who therefore shall say to him why he hath done so? Let him live. And it may be that the Lord will look on my affliction, and that the Lord will requite me good for his cursing this day."

And as I and my men continued downward on our heartsick and tortuous way, Shimei went along on the hill's side with me, and cursed as he went, and threw stones at me, and even cast dust. Until we had gone a good distance and he had fallen behind. We were weary. We rested when we had traveled in our labored descent to the level land of the plain, and we refreshed ourselves there while Absalom and the people strode triumphantly into the city I had abandoned, and Ahitophel, that turncoat, with him. As I sat upon the ground, my thoughts returned to my early patron Saul, dispossessed by God and Samuel in his final days. Of the death of kings I longed to wax poetic, but my servants were too tired to listen. Of the wrath of Achilles I wanted to sing once more, but I didn't feel up to it.

And in Jerusalem, meanwhile, my secret agent, Hushai the Archite, had stationed himself along the king's way to hail Absalom as he passed into the city and greet him loudly, saying, "God save the king, God save the king."

Absalom halted when he recognized him. "Is this thy kindness to thy friend?" he inquired acidly. "Why wentest thou not with my father?"

And Hushai, who was wily, said, "Nay, but whom the Lord and His people, all the men of Israel, choose, his will I be, and with him shall I abide." Hushai did not stop there. "And again, whom should I serve if thou art now the king? As I have served in thy father's presence, so I will be in the presence of his son."

Absalom was won over by this tribute and took him into his council, aware of what indispensable value he had been to me in the past, and Hushai kept silent and remained courteous when Absalom sought guidance for what next to do. He uttered no protest when crafty Ahitophel recommended, "Go in unto thy father's concubines, which he hath left to keep the house."

"All ten?"

"Each and every one."

"They're his worst ones."

"But all Israel shall hear then that thou art abhorred of thy father," explained Ahitophel, "and the hands of all that are with thee shall be strong, knowing what fate will betide them shalt thou fail. The women are the property of the king, and the people will know that all that pertained to thy father belongs now to you."

"God save the king," said Hushai the Archite.

So they spread for Absalom a tent upon the top of the palace, and Absalom went in unto his father's concubines before all Israel in the sight of the sun, somewhat in the manner that Nathan had prophesied. The crowd below was applauding wildly after the seventh and egging him onward toward each of the rest with a mounting roar. There were girls who were cheerleaders.

"Let's give him an *A!*" they choroused.

It came as no shock to anyone that he was fairly winded when he had done with the ten, and therein lay the seeds of my salvation, in that post-orgasmic fatigue in which he allowed himself to languish.

"What next?" he inquired sleepily, mainly of Ahitophel, whose history of unerring counsel in those days was as that of a man who had inquired at the oracle of God. "I think I'm pooped."

Ahitophel was quick with another sensible proposal. "Then let me be the one to choose out twelve thousand men," he offered unto Absalom. "And I myself will arise and pursue after David this night. The men are here. We can depart right now." Hushai the Archite told me later that he felt his heartbeat grow fainter when he heard this advice and understood the wisdom behind it. Ahitophel went on, saying, "And I will come upon him while he is still weary and weakhanded, and will make him afraid. And the people that are with him shall flee in the confusion, and I will smite the king only. Thus will the others be brought over to you, there then being no other king to serve. So will I bring back all the people unto thee, and all the people shall be in peace."

The strategy seemed as wise to Absalom and those others around him as it did to Hushai the Archite, who now was gravely anxious that it might be immediately put into play. This was the moment of truth. He did not let me down.

"The counsel that Ahitophel hath given is not good at this time, I am sorry to have to say." Hushai spoke very carefully, making sure to nod profoundly as he dissented, after Absalom had called unto him for a second opinion. Tactfully, with a guise of most somber concern, Hushai elucidated why, blending reason and soft soap as delicately as an apothecary mixing balm. "Thou knowest thy father and his men, that they be mighty men, and that thy father is a man of war. He will not lodge with the people"—which is exactly what I *was* doing—"but is hid right now in ambush in some pit, or in some other place, awaiting thee. And it will come to pass when some of your men be downed at the first, that whosoever heareth it will say, 'There is a slaughter among the people that follow Absalom,' and he will be filled with fright. And he also that is valiant, whose heart is as the heart of a lion, shall utterly melt, for all Israel knoweth that thy father is a mighty man, and they which be with him are valiant men. Therefore I counsel thee to wait, that all Israel be generally gathered unto thee, from Dan even to Beersheba, as the sand that is by the sea for multitude. And that thou then go to battle in thine own person. Who can withstand thee then, when all Israel has been gathered unto thee? So shall we come upon him in some place where he shall be found, and we will light upon him as the dew falleth on the ground. And of him and of all the men that are with him there shall not be left so much as one. Moreover, if he be gotten into a city, then shall all Israel bring ropes to that city, and we will draw it into the river, until there be not one small stone left there."

And Absalom, savoring the picture of himself at the head of that magnificent army Hushai had conjured up for his delectation, and the men of Israel all with him, decided that the counsel of Hushai the Archite was better than the counsel of Ahitophel the Gilonite. But Hushai, who'd been taking no chances, had already sent to Zadok and Abiathar to dispatch couriers quickly, their sons Ahimaaz and Jonathan, to warn me that my enemies meant business and to spur me to go rapidly as far from Jerusalem that night as I was able to travel. The youths were spotted by the watchmen of Absalom as soon as they set out, and they themselves quickly became the quarry of another hunt. It was touch and go with them until they sheered off the main road and came to the house of a man in Bahurim who sided with me and who had a well in his court, and they hid themselves inside it. The woman of the house spread a covering over the well's mouth and put ground corn upon it to deceive the searching party, which, misdirected by the women about the path the two young runners had taken, found no trace where they were sent and returned empty-handed to Jerusalem.

Ahimaaz and this young man Jonathan came up out of the well when the coast was clear and continued on their way through the starlit night until at last they came to the place where I had made my stop.

"Watchman, what of the night?" I inquired when alerted by a stir I heard at one of the outposts of my encampment. I had staked out sentries everywhere. Not like Saul was I ever going to be caught napping on the ground by someone like me.

"Two messengers," my guard reported. "Ahimaaz is here, and Jonathan too."

Both were hot from sprinting and covered with sweat. Ahimaaz the son of Zadok I recognized first, and I solemnly made inquiry of him.

"How doth the city sit solitary that was full of people?"

"It is full of people again," Ahimaaz disappointed me with his reply, and filled me in on the events following my hurried exit. He delivered the insistent, dire message from Hushai to arise and pass quickly over the water, saying, in the words of Hushai, "Lodge not this night in the plains of the wilderness, but speedily pass over, lest you be swallowed up, and all the people that are with thee."

Who is on my side, who? I had a momentary impulse to cry out in my melancholy and despair, emulating Saul in the depths of his haggard madness. It would have been folly. For all about me were people on my side, and Joab was soon with me too, bringing with him additional cohorts of soldiers he had mustered. I was growing stronger with each hour: I soon would have time to organize. Whereas when traitorous Ahitophel saw that his counsel was not followed, he saddled his ass, and arose, and got him home to his house, to his city of Giloh, and put his household in order, and hanged himself and died. Wise Ahitophel knew before I could what the outcome would be. And he saw he had no future. I lumbered onward to the river in response to the warning from Hushai, and by morning light there lacked not one of my people that had not gone over Jordan.

We were spared. My danger past, I felt no elation. My heart was heavy, my head was bowed with the knowledge of impending tragedy. I knew that Absalom would come after me, and I knew he would die. He had sown the wind. He would reap the whirlwind.

I'll tell you now what wounds me still. "I will smite the king only," he listened to Ahitophel advise. While the order I gave was

"Deal gently for my sake with the young man Absalom." Is it right, I ask you, that a child should so much seek the death of his father, and that a father should so much seek to protect the life of his son? They told me how his face lit up when Ahitophel spoke of smiting me, and when Hushai talked of lighting upon me as the dew falleth on the ground, and of drawing the whole city that had sheltered me into the river until there did not remain even one small stone. When he was small, my son, he wouldn't let me sleep. Now he wouldn't let me live.

IN THE MORNING, we arose with the voice of the first bird and traveled north until we came to Mahanaim in Gilead, that same city in which Abner had based himself with Ishbosheth when he was at war against me. And it was in that distant part of Gilead that I was succored with the kindness and loyalty which I would have better enjoyed receiving from my subjects closer to home in Judah and Israel.

While we rested and bathed and ate and drank, Absalom passed over Jordan with his overhastily recruited citizen army of celebrants, who came to war as though to a festival and flocked to his banner to do battle against me in Gilead like dancers attending a beheading and a coronation. Absalom had Amasa as captain of his host, while I, thank God, had Joab. Inexperience was evident from the start, when they pitched in the land of Gilead with their backs to the wall of the wood of Ephraim, into which they could not withdraw in adroit maneuver if they wished to or retreat in an orderly fashion if they had to. Their numbers were large; they could have pitched on two sides of us. We wondered why they did close themselves in just there, before the wood of Ephraim, which still remains a trackless jungle affording no certainty of escape. And it did come to pass that when their lines broke, as many of their men were devoured by the wood as were devoured by the sword. They withheld no one in reserve to divert us on the flank. I watched their obvious mistakes with ambivalent feelings. They did not know what they were doing. I did not want to see my son lose. I did not want to see my countrymen who were with him routed. I divided my army in three, and the enemy was dumbfounded. They had no idea how to cope with us, how to attack or defend. Even before they had arrived in place, I had numbered the people with me and separated them into equal forces, a third part under the hand of Joab, a third part under the hand of Abishai, and a third part under the hand of Ittai the Gittite. I planned to set forth with Joab, as in yore. But my leaders did not want me out there at all that day, insisting I was worth ten thousand to the enemy, who could destroy the whole by destroying the one and would ignore all else to fall on me. I agreed to remain by the two gates of the city and wait for word. I stood by the gate as my people went forth in their groups into the field against Absalom. The tension I suffered was terrible. I felt my heart in my mouth.

"Deal gently for my sake with the young man, even with Absalom," I gave orders, begging, first to Joab, then to Abishai, and to Ittai. "Beware that none touch the young man Absalom."

Prayerfully, I repeated these words a thousand times, to make absolutely certain that all of the people taking the field that day were familiar with the charge I had given the captains concerning Absalom; and that unknown soldier who came upon Absalom first with his head caught in the oak tree remembered my wish and braved the ire of Joab by refusing to put forth his hand against the king's son while he hanged there.

"You saw Absalom and you did not smite him?" Joab had much more mopping up to do and was furiously brief. "I would have given thee ten shekels of silver, and a girdle, hadst thou smitten him to the ground."

And this man, who had backbone, replied unto Joab, "Not for a thousand shekels would I put forth my hand against the king's son. For in our hearing the king charged thee and Abishai and Ittai, saying, 'Beware that none touch the young man Absalom.' Otherwise I should have wrought falsehood against mine own life. For there is no matter hid from the king, and thou thyself would have set thyself against me." I've many times wished that Joab had recorded this man's name.

"Take me to him," Joab demanded. "I haven't time to argue."

The man brought him there to that tree from which Absalom was hanging by his head. Joab tarried not but made short shrift of the matter with the three darts in his hand. He thrust them through the heart of Absalom, while he was yet alive in the midst of the oak. Joab did not withhold from me any of the gory details when he came to my chamber later to rebuke me in contempt and to help me pull myself together after I had gone all to pieces with the shattering news that my son Absalom was dead.

"Then," said Joab when I had ended my weeping and sat staring at him in numb exhaustion, "I had the ten young men that bear my armor surround him, and smite him, and slay him, just to make sure."

"Joab—spare me." I put my hand up weakly.

"Then I had him cut down and cast into a great pit in the wood."

"Please—I pray you."

"And laid a very great heap of stones upon him."

"My son, my son."

"Don't start that again."

"No burial? No prayer?"

"He had lifted his hand in revolt against God's anointed."

"No more, I beg you, no more."

But that was after the minor mix-up with the messengers from the field that gave me the first false hope that all the news was going to be wondrously good. Joab showed judgment in selecting someone other than Ahimaaz to tell me the worst.

The fighting itself was almost perfunctory. The people of Absalom were quickly slain and routed and scattered over the face of all the country about the wood of Ephraim. And Absalom also fled when he met my servants. He rode away in flight on a mule, and the mule went under the thick boughs of a great oak, and his head caught hold of the oak, and he was taken up between the heaven and the earth, and the mule that was under him continued away, leaving him hanged in that oak, helplessly alive, until Joab strode to that spot and finished him off with those three darts he took in his hand. The war was over. And Absalom was dead. But I didn't know.

Then Ahimaaz the son of Zadok spoke up eagerly, saying to Joab, "Let me now run and bear the king tidings, how that the Lord hath avenged him of his enemies."

Here Joab was sensitive and instinctively guessed that the young man should not be the one to be sent to bear me the whole truth. "Thou shalt not bear tidings this day," Joab said unto him soberly, "but thou shalt bear tidings another day. But this day thou shalt bear no tidings, because the king's son is dead, and thou shalt not want to be the one to go to him with that."

He sent Cushi the Ethiopian instead to run to me and tell me what he had seen. But Ahimaaz could not stand still and begged leave a new time, to run after Cushi and give his report too.

And Joab said, "Wherefore wilt thou run, my son, seeing that thou hast now no new tidings ready?"

"But howsoever," the excited youth pleaded in his dither of freshness and enthusiasm, "let me also run. I came to the king with sorry news when he was departed out of Jerusalem. Let me go to the king now with good."

Then Joab relented. "Run," he permitted, positive that the Ethiopian Cushi would reach me first with the horrible news to be broken.

But Ahimaaz was faster and ran by the shorter way of the plain, and he overtook Cushi, and was coming with his tidings first.

I was sitting on a bench between the two gates when the watchman on the roof over the gate called down to the porter that he beheld a man running alone toward us. I almost fell down when I sprang up from my seat to see the sooner, for one of my legs was asleep and the joints of both knees were stiff. I was no longer young. But I was not as old as our revered Judge fat Eli, of whom I could not help thinking during those long hours when I sat on my bench and waited—old fat Eli, penultimate Judge of Israel and mentor to Samuel, no ancestor of mine, thank God. Fat Eli too, I remembered, had sat on a bench at the gate of a city, awaiting news from the field, and fell off his seat backward and broke his neck and died when told of a loss to the Philistines in which the ark of God had been captured and every man of Israel had fled into his tent. Eli was ninety and eight years old when that happened and very heavy, and his eyes were dim. I was younger and had better reason to expect a triumph. My agitation was for something more.

"If he be alone," I reasoned out loud about the messenger hastening to us, "there is tidings in his mouth." Then the watchman called down that he saw a second man. There was tidings in his mouth too, I guessed, and it could not be tidings of defeat or they would be coming in droves. Next the watchman called down that he thought the running of the foremost was like the running of Ahimaaz the son of Zadok, and I let out a great cry of relief when I heard that.

"Then the news must be good!" I exclaimed with joy. "For

Ahimaaz is a good man, and would cometh to me only with good tidings."

And even as I saw him approach, his jubilant manner seemed to confirm my optimistic expectations, for Ahimaaz was calling out to me, with his head thrown back and his slender leaf-brown chest heaving, saying, "All is well, all is well."

"All is well?"

To me that seemed the most blessed of miracles: there *was* a God, and He answered prayers. All I'd wished for from the depths of my being had somehow come to pass: victory was mine and Absalom was yet alive! My limbs were quivering, my eyes overflowed with tears. I was laughing in an incoherence of hysteria. I wanted to catch this very dear boy by the cheeks and embrace him even as he came stumbling to a halt where I stood and threw himself to his knees to the earth on his face to bow before me.

"Blessed be the Lord thy God," Ahimaaz proclaimed, gulping air, when I had bid him arise, "which hath delivered up the men that lifted up their hand against my lord the king. They are dead and they are scattered."

"Is the young man Absalom safe?" I wanted to know. That was *all* I wanted to know.

I saw his jaw drop. I watched him turn white as a ghost, and I felt my breath catch. He glanced off to the right with an expression of guilt, then began with a stammer, and I knew intuitively that whatever reply he was going to give me would not be a candid one. "When Joab sent me," he said, "I saw a great tumult, but I knew not what it was."

I ordered him aside with uncontrollable dread, to clear a path for the next runner, who was just then pounding up to the gate, and hurried forward to hear him. I almost could not restrain myself from speaking first, from interrupting him even before he began.

"Tidings, my lord the king," the runner Cushi cried out to me breathlessly, his lungs wheezing, "for the Lord hath avenged thee this day of all them that rose up against thee."

And I screamed into his face, "Is the young man Absalom safe?" I wanted to seize him in my fists and shake the reply out of him faster.

And this foreigner from Ethiopia, who was not too familiar with our incomprehensible, sentimental ways, responded heartily, "The enemies of my lord the king, and all that rise against thee to do thee hurt, be as that young man is."

I was too much moved to say more. I turned away, already sobbing, and went up to the chamber over the gate and wept, and even as I went up, I heard myself weeping more and more loudly, and soon I was crying out at the top of my voice, and I heard myself wailing, "O my son Absalom, my son, my son Absalom! Would God I had died for thee, O Absalom, my son, my son!"

And I did not stop.

I wept inconsolably. I could not stop. I did not want to stop. I did not care if I never stopped. It felt so much easier to continue weeping than even to think about ever, ever doing anything else.

I was oblivious to everything else, and had forgotten in my grief that by the fact of my grief I was demeaning those who had fought for me and that I was turning our victory of that day into an occasion of tragic sorrow. All in the city heard how I lamented for the death of my son in that unlit chamber above the gate and would not stop.

"O my son, my son Absalom! O Absalom, my son, my son!"

And my soldiers, streaming back from the battle, got themselves by stealth into the city, as though returning in ignominy, as people being ashamed steal away when they flee in battle. All passing through the way of the gate could hear me while they were not yet near, for it was with a raised voice that I wept, that I held my head with my hands and cried, "O my son Absalom! O Absalom, my son, my son!"

And I wept and I wailed all the louder each time I felt the pain of my sorrow abate and the desire to cease weeping begin to take hold in me. I was deaf and unmindful of all but my misery until from below, hours later, I heard someone say clearly:

"He's still at it?"

And I recognized the voice of Joab.

"He will not stop."

They had sent into the field to Joab to tell him how I was weeping and mourning for Absalom. To those at the door I had given instructions to bar everyone. Joab shouldered right in anyway, and, without a syllable of condolence or a second of silence for compassion, said to me brusquely, "David, it's enough already. Cut it out."

"My son, Joab. My son Absalom, O my son—"

"You're making a spectacle of yourself."

"You don't understand." I tried to explain. "I lost my son, my son Absalom."

"*You* don't understand," he cut me off without pity. "You're losing an army. Your men are ashamed." He thrust his face very close to mine. "Yes, you are making your men ashamed, ashamed of themselves and ashamed of you."

"Ashamed?"

"This day thou hast shamed the faces of all thy servants," he reprimanded me roughly, his mouth twisted into a sneer, "who this day have saved thy life, and the lives of thy sons and daughters, and the lives of thy wives, and the lives of thy concubines. And now you do insult them. You treat them as one treats people who are foul, and guilty of deeds that are evil."

His harsh manner and fantastic allegation brought me up short. I didn't know what he was talking about and stopped my sniveling long enough to find out. I wiped my grimy tears from my eyes and cheeks and the snot from my nose.

"How," I addressed him weakly, "have I done that?"

"In that this day," said Joab, at no loss for a reply, "thou hast shown that thou lovest thine enemies and hatest thy friends, that thou hast no regard for thy princes or servants. For this day I perceive that if Absalom had lived and all of us had died this day, then it had pleased thee more. You would not have carried on for any or all of us as you do for him, would you?"

In craven admission I answered him weepily. "No."

"Let's keep that our secret," said Joab, speaking in a more moderate voice.

"He was my son, Joab. He is dead."

"He would have killed us both, David. Have you forgotten? Didn't they tell you how his face grew bright and how ready he was to agree when Ahitophel talked of smiting you?"

"How did it happen? I didn't ask before. Tell me how it happened." I was more in control of myself now.

"Following your strategy, we slowly advanced in three parts, with a large space between, and waited to see how they would choose to attack."

"How he died, I mean," I broke in. "Tell me how he died."

No sooner did he begin than I regretted I'd asked and was imploring him to stop. But he proceeded with a sadistic relish he made no effort to disguise or temper, telling me in painstaking particulars of the death of my son, of the mule and the oak and the darts from his hand, and of the pit in the wood and the very great heap of stones piled upon the hacked and mangled remains, until I was squeezing my eyes shut and was near to whimpering.

"Yes, ten young men bearing my armor compassed about and smote Absalom and slew him and took him down from the oak and cast him into that great pit in the wood."

"Please," I begged. "No more, no more. Have a heart. Show mercy. Take pity."

"When you wash," said Joab, "and dress and go outside and congratulate the men who fought for you, and who were ready to die. Was this a bad thing that they did for you this day that you will not let them see your face? Give them the reward they've earned, of allowing them to cheer you and celebrate."

"Celebrate?" I said ruefully.

"Oh, David, David, you *schvantz—*"

"The death of my son?"

"—you selfish *teivel,* you *naar.* When will you learn to be a king? Have you forgotten you won a battle today, that you have a country to rule? We aren't popular, David, not as much as we are tempted to believe. Doesn't this rebellion show you? We've never been popular in the north, and it turns out Absalom was better liked in Judah too. Oh, David, David—Uncle, Uncle—why were you too blind to see in him the same cunning deceptions you used for yourself when you were trying to win the hearts of the people from Saul? Sending him out to mollify malcontents—all he had to do was wring his hands and cluck his tongue, and he had another adherent against you. He didn't even have to kill a Philistine."

"Why didn't you warn me?"

"Would you have listened?"

"Joab, tell me this. I have wondered. Why didn't you turn to Absalom's side?"

"He was going to lose."

"How could you know?"

"We had the experience."

"You would have given him experience."

"I am loyal to you."

"Why were you loyal?"

"I'm used to you. We know each other."

"That's all?"

"With Absalom there would have been arguments. He had respect for nobody. There is room for only one ruler."

"Who will be ruler in Jerusalem now?"

"You can be ruler," said Joab. "But I am the straw that stirs the drink. You can make the laws, as long as I am the one with the authority and strength to enforce them. Absalom would have wanted both—he had too much youthful energy—and then there would have been no need for laws."

"Joab, why did you kill him?" Like a dog returning to his vomit, I steeled myself. I had to ask. "We had already won. Why did you have to kill my son?"

"Did *you* want to be the one to do it?" he answered.

"Was there no other punishment?"

"Give me an example."

"It's a hard dilemma, isn't it?" I reflected.

"Uneasy lies the head that wears a crown," Joab replied phlegmatically.

"Saul used to say that a lot."

"That's one of the reasons I'm content to let you wear it," said Joab, and smiled. "David, David, wake up. This was a war we had today, not a family quarrel."

"To me," I told him honestly, "it was a family quarrel."

"Then keep that our secret too," Joab said. "Or rebellions will sprout everywhere, and you won't have a soldier left to help you put them down."

"Joab, my son, my son Absalom—"

"Don't start that again."

"Have you no feeling?"

"Let me tell you a story," he answered. "I swear by the Lord that if you do not get up now, and wash, and put on a clean robe, and go forth with a cheerful countenance for the people to see you, there will not tarry a single one with thee this night. You will have no army left. And what will follow will be an evil worse to thee than all the evil that befell thee from thy youth until now."

"Worse than the day of the death of my son? At the hands of my own soldiers?"

"It's only a life," said Joab almost idly. "What in the world are you making such a fuss about?"

"My son's too?"

"What then? From that bowl, millions of bubbles like us He has poured, and will pour."

"Can we still be friends?" To his perfect and inimitable logic, I could find no better response at that moment, and I confess I have not been able to find one since.

"If you arise now, go forth, and speak comfortably to those who have served you," Joab dickered.

The rest was silence. I did as he enjoined me, washing, combing, dressing in clean clothes, and sitting in the gate for all the people to behold and come before me, and it was all so much easier to go through than I had feared. Is it any wonder I hated him? And hate him still?

At sundown, with the lugubrious dirge from the ram's horn, we conducted our small private services for the dead. The priest said Kaddish. Nathan put his pontifical two cents in by mentioning, not for the first time, that we are all us of the dust and all things that are of the earth shall turn to the earth again and that which is of the waters doth return to the sea, and he would have discoursed longer on these matters of dust and water had not Joab, with whom he was squabbling even back then, cut him short. In the minute of silent prayer that followed, I lowered my head and prayed for my son Absalom to be brought back to life. I knew he wouldn't be. And then I prayed to God for another Joab to help me get rid of this one.

I thought I recognized him in my nephew Amasa and commissioned him to hunt down and destroy the rebel Sheba. I knew I was mistaken when Amasa started out late. By the time that floundering *schmuck* showed up, Abishai was already on the road with the brigade I had assigned and Joab had made plans to waylay and slaughter Amasa at the great stone which is in Gibeon.

Otherwise everything went smoothly after the war was won, and my restoration to the throne was a breeze. I thought I masked my feelings of agonized grief over Absalom well. Abigail would have seen into the window of my soul and known the truth, but Abigail had gone to eternal sleep with her fathers. Bathsheba, who was into astrology now, and palmistry too, asked to come to me daily, ravenous to begin making political hay now that only Adonijah stood in the way of her Solomon. It was not a subject I wanted to touch on then. I kept her away in her distant place in the caravan. I had no yen for pussy. Abishag the Shunammite was one year old.

There was the forbidding prospect of chaos in the fragmented political situation I now had to piece together. I deliberately took my time decamping in order to give the people back home time for the realization to sink in that I was returning to Jerusalem as their king, whether I was wanted there or not. With Absalom dead, they had no other.

The people of the north, those of the tribes of Israel, were the quickest to perceive the wisdom in soliciting my reinstatement, saying one to another, reported my envoys, that I had saved them out of the hand of their enemies, and delivered them out of the hand of the Philistines, and that now, with Absalom, whom they had anointed, dead in battle, why was each speaking not a word of bringing me back as their king? That was good. I was glad when they told me.

"And not Judah too?"

There was not yet word from Judah of reconciliation. I was beginning to get an acrid taste of the aggravation God had complained of in the past from having to deal with such a stiff-necked people. I sent strong sentiments to Jerusalem to my priests Zadok and Abiathar to speak to the elders and demand why the peoples of Judah were last behind Israel in petitioning to have me come back as their ruler. Was I not near in kin to them?

"Say to them," I gave stern orders, "that they are my brethren, they are my bones and my flesh. And say ye also to Amasa that he is of my bone and my flesh, and that God do so to me, and more also, if he be not captain of the host before me continually in the room of Joab, and more, if he but declare for me now. Say all that."

This last proviso, I knew, was rash. But what had I to lose? Amasa's life, as it turned out.

I had made to Amasa an offer he could not refuse. He accepted with alacrity, and Israel and Judah were soon at cross-purposes and quarreling like cats and dogs for the servile honor of submitting to me most slavishly and soonest, the elders of Israel advancing the claim that they had the stronger right because they had ten parts of me through ten tribes. Somewhere along the line, we had lost a tribe, but I didn't miss it. The men of Judah answered the men of Israel that they were nearer to me in kin. I was glad they were competing.

My confidence in my control of my realm was complete as I

made my leisurely way homeward back down through Gilead toward the fording points of the Jordan over which I had fled so recently. My emotional state was a different matter. I was not always clear whether it was a triumphal or a funeral procession I was leading. My mind was most at peace in the pleasant company of ancient Barzillai the Gileadite, no fair-weather friend he—one of those who had come to my assistance freely and fearlessly in Mahanaim. Like good wine, he was rare, an affable old bird of advanced age who was neither garrulous, repetitious, nor forgetful, and he could hear distinctly as well. After the battle, he came down from Rogelim and offered himself to accompany me over the Jordan until he saw I was received in safety. I invited him to continue with me into Jerusalem, to come there to live: I promised him the run of the palace, he would live like a king. He shook his grizzled head, chuckling.

"Take my servant Chimham," he said, declining amiably, "and do to him what shall seem good unto thee, for him to enjoy the very good things in life."

"And why not thee?"

His rheumy, yellowed eyes twinkled. "How long have I to live," he answered with composure, "that I should go up with the king unto Jerusalem? I am this day fourscore years old. And can thy servant taste what I eat or what I drink? Can I hear anymore the voice of singing men and singing women?"

"You hear better than you think."

"And wherefore then should thy servant be yet another burden unto my lord the king? Let thy servant go a little way over Jordan with the king until the others greet thee and receive thee in safety. Then let thy servant, I pray thee, turn back again, that I may die in my own city, and be buried by the grave of my father and of my mother."

There is no wine like old wine, and no friend like an old friend. "Whatsoever thou shalt require of me, that will I do for thee."

And I knew that he would never require anything of me, for Barzillai the Gileadite was eighty years old and going home in peace to die in his own city and be buried by the grave of his father and of his mother. What better could a man aspire to when his days were fulfilled? We said farewell when we were come over Jordan. I kissed my countryman Barzillai and blessed him, and released him to return unto his own place.

"May you soon be comforted for the death of your son," he consoled me in parting.

"Let thy garments be always white," I extolled him in reply, "and let thy head lack no ointment."

He was not there to witness his odious opposite, that fawning hypocrite Shimei, come bursting through the restraining line of my guards to be the first of the penitents to seek my forgiveness. The crowds at the river were enormous and devout. By the time I arrived there, Judah had come to Gilgal to go to meet me and conduct me back over the Jordan. And a thousand men of Benjamin had come to escort me too. And at the river there went back and forth a ferryboat to carry over all in my household and to do whatever else I thought good. And then, on the other side, all of a sudden there came lunging toward me that sputtering indignity of a cretin, Shimei the son of Gera, who came with an animal cry and hurled himself down at my feet in a drooling, frenzied quest for pardon for the abuse he had heaped upon my head when my fortunes were at an ebb and I was coming out from Jerusalem in abdication and disgrace. I shuddered with revulsion the instant I recognized the scrawny, loathsome, bandy-legged runt and despaired he might touch me.

"Let not my lord impute iniquity unto me," the groveling, mean-spirited bastard blubbered again, flinching and squirming upon the ground on which he had flung himself. What the fuck did he expect me to impute to him if not iniquity? "Neither do thou remember that which thy servant did perversely the day that my lord the king went out of Jerusalem, that the king should take it to his heart. For thy servant doth now know that I have sinned. Therefore, behold, I am come the first this day of all the house of Joseph to go down to meet my lord the king."

Big deal, I said to myself, frowning, and chewed on the inside of my lip as I wondered what best to do with the knave. But trust to the extreme behavior of those sons of my sister Zeruiah to help me make up my mind! This time it was Abishai, with his hand already on the hilt of his sword.

"Shall not this dead dog Shimei be put to death for this, because he cursed the Lord's anointed? Let me take off his head."

"Again his head?" I answered reproachfully. And I realized in answering him that I needed grateful subjects more than I needed headless corpses.

"Shall he be allowed to live?"

"Shall there be any man put to death this day in Israel?" said I sanctimoniously, transfigured on the spot into the very epitome of benevolence. "Oh, Abishai, Abishai," I mocked, "what am I to do with you, ye sons of my sister Zeruiah, that ye should this day be adversaries unto me? This day will I pardon the whole world. For do not I know that this day I am king again in all Israel?"

And Shimei chimed in eagerly, "Blessed be my lord and king."

"Shimei," I said to him in judgment, "thou shalt not die this day." I paused in thought a moment, then added craftily, "I swear to you by the Lord that I will not put thee to death by the sword."

The sly loophole left in that pledge I made eludes the perception of Solomon still, although I have attempted to point him toward it a dozen times, and railed at his mother an equal number for his stupidity in failing to observe it. I would break my vow if I gave the order explicitly.

"I know what I meant," I complain to Bathsheba yet again, "you know what I meant, Abishag knows what I meant. Why doesn't he?"

"I will tell him."

"Out of the mouths of very babes and sucklings comes ordained strength in true words of wisdom," I observe.

"Oh, David, David," she exclaims. "That's so beautiful. I could listen forever."

"Is it getting you horny?"

"But go on anyway."

"Why can't I get one fucking word of common sense out of him!"

"I will tell him," she promised, "if you will say he will be king."

"A dozen times I've tried to explain to him. Hold Shimei not guiltless, but his hoar head bring down to the grave with blood. He can't even keep in mind what a hoar head is."

"I will sit at his right hand and explain."

"Would he know what to do?"

"And Benaiah will do it. I'll make you that promise if you make Solomon king. But make him king now. Adonijah is busy and the city is tense."

"The people of the city couldn't care less."

"They talk of nothing else but Adonijah and his feast. And I am afraid. Ask Nathan, ask Zadok your priest, ask even Benaiah. We are all afraid!"

Afraid of Adonijah, and the more so of Joab, who would know in a second what I want for Shimei and execute my wish without hesitating, if I gave him the high sign. But Joab is another of the survivors I would like to have slain, and I hardly can count on Joab to get rid of himself too, can I? It's a real dilemma, I say to myself, and I hardly care, for soon I will die and leave nothing behind me but my children and my kingdom. A temple might have been nice, but Nathan said no, and a star named after me is not much to boast of. It would be vanity to add that I have no more vanity left. The dilemma I'm faced with is one I might enjoy talking over with God if I ever condescended to seek divine guidance again, for I can hear in my fancy the judgments I'd receive.

"Should I promise Adonijah that the kingdom will be his?" I would inquire of God.

And He would say unto me, "Promise Adonijah."

"But should I not promise Solomon also that I will let him be king?"

"Why not?" God would answer. "Say unto Solomon also that you will let him be king."

Here I would find myself lost in thought for a moment and would scratch reflectively at my head. "But if I promise Adonijah that I will let him be king, and if I promise Solomon also that I will let him be king, won't I have to break my promise to one or the other?"

"So?" saith the Lord. "You'll break your promise."

We got along fine like that back then, He and I.

The trouble is, despite my success in battle, I wasn't truly in a strong enough position to do everything I wanted when I made my return to Jerusalem, and I have not been a very strong ruler since. I have the feeling that the kingdom is going to fall apart not long after I let it go.

Take that new rebellion that almost arose even as I was returning to my throne in glory, and in full military strength. From the Jordan I was conducted on to Gilgal by all the people of Judah, and also half the people of Israel, each group vying with the other to be nearer me. Both had rejected me for Absalom; now they were jostling in rivalry to make amends. An equal division of influence was pleasing to neither, and I could think of no workable solution then for neutralizing their differences. Besides, my mind dwelt obsessively on the betrayal and death of Absalom more than on anything else, even as the controversy between my subjects deepened and grew more rancorous. The words of the men of Judah were fiercer than the words of the men of Israel—they were behaving as badly as Benjamites—and I was hardly back in my palace before Sheba the son of Bichri, himself a Benjamite, was brazenly blowing his trumpet to call all the people of Israel up from following me, saying: "We have no part in David, neither have we inheritance in the son of Jesse. Every man to his tents, O Israel."

And O, the people of Israel started moving up from following me to follow him. That did awaken me out of my doldrums. And I pounced at the opportunity I spied to advance Amasa ahead of Joab. I allotted him three days to assemble the men of Judah and set out with them after Sheba. There was no sign of him on the fourth. Where the fuck was he?

"They say he is coming," said my recorder Jehoshaphat.

"So is Christmas!" I retorted, and directed Abishai to set forth immediately. "Otherwise shall Sheba the son of Bichri do us more harm than did Absalom. Take thou my men, and pursue after him, lest he get him fenced cities, and escape us."

And then I sent Joab out behind him to oversee and report back to me on any greater adverse effects we might not have foreseen. When my clumsy nephew Amasa finally did come bungling back into the city, he had forgotten a suitable robe and had forgotten his sword. I began to have discouraging premonitions of misjudgment about him. I let him take a robe and a sword from those belonging to Joab. Both were too large and too heavy for him—he looked like a buffoon when he went stumbling away—and I charged him to overtake Joab and Abishai and assume command. I even supplied him with a written authorization.

My sleep was fitful. In the dead of night, I came bolt upright on my bed with a shock of vivid clairvoyance and emitted my characteristic yawp of surprise: "Holy shit!"

My servants stormed in with their swords drawn and their bodkins bared. I called for my recorder, I called for my scribe. I could see beyond doubt what inadvertently I had done. "Send a wire!" I shouted.

"We have no wires," Jehoshaphat recalled for me.

JOSEPH HELLER

By noon the next day it was already too late, as my intuition had ominously foretold.

"Art thou in health, my brother?" double-dealing Joab said to Amasa with a fraternal smile, taking him by the beard to kiss him when they met at the great rock which is in Gibeon, where he had been biding his time like fate itself to ensnare him.

"I'm sure glad to find you here, cousin," Amasa replied in a hurrying manner. "Which way did they go?"

"Let me give you a hand," offered Joab sociably, and ran him through the fifth rib, shedding his bowels to the ground in the midst of the highway, so that he did not have to strike him again.

"What can I do with him?" I expostulated back home with Benaiah when they brought me the report.

Nothing then. For Joab was the lion of Judah after the people of Abel in Bethmaachah had cut off the head of Sheba and cast it out to him, and when he had returned to Jerusalem after putting down opposition in all of the territories of Israel. I was the king, but he was the prevailing hero, indeed the straw that stirred the drink, and I did not feel much like a king. I had known what it was like to feel like a hero, and I did not care to feel that way again.

I have really not felt much of anything since my wife Abigail died and my son Absalom betrayed me and was killed. I still do not know which of these two facts about Absalom has been more unhappy for me. I know I didn't feel like a victor when I started back from Mahanaim after that distressing triumph. I felt instead like a fugitive, and I feel like one now, a fugitive long pursued by invisible demons that can no longer be held at bay. In my intervals of broken sleep I feel like exhausted prey at the end of a fatal chase. As the days draw nigh when I am going to die, I remember with envy Barzillai the Gileadite. I do not have that serene sense of natural completion that he enjoyed as his end came near and his days were fulfilled. I call for Abishag when I desire her close, and she comes each time. But I get no heat from her, and I am just as desolate when she is gone as I was before. Yet I know I love her. I have a monkey on my back that I cannot shake off, and now I know who that monkey is: His name is God. I have seen His face and lived: He wears thick eyeglasses and leads us not only into temptation but into many mistakes. Conquering the land of Canaan He had promised to Abraham was not my biggest victory. Nor was delivering the people of Israel out of the hand of their

380

enemies, either, although I may have thought so at the time. No. Defeating my son in battle was much more important to me, for that kind of victory is a loss, and I feel it still. God knows what I mean. I feel nearer to God when I am deepest in anguish. That's when I know He is closing in again, and I yearn to call out to Him now what I have longed to say to Him before, to address my Almighty God with those words of Ahab to Elijah in the vineyard of Naboth, "Hast thou found me, O mine enemy?"

But Ahab built altars to Baal and slew true believers of Jehovah, and he and Jezebel were hated by God for these and the multitude of other evils performed by himself and his wife. All I did was fuck another woman.

"And send her husband to his death," I can hear God correcting me if we were on speaking terms again as we have been in the past.

"The Devil made me do it," I would remind Him in my defense.

"There's no such thing," He would argue in reply.

"The Garden of Eden?"

And He'd say unto me, "That was a snake. You can look it up."

The fault, I know, was not in my stars but in myself. I've learned so many things that have not been much use to me. The human brain has a mind of its own.

13

IN THE
CAVE OF
MACHPELAH

But try telling anything complex to Bathsheba. "There's a divinity that shapes our ends," I explain altruistically, to cushion her for the disappointment I know is inevitable, "rough-hew them how we will, and all our yesterdays have lighted fools the way to dusty death."

She pretends I'm talking gibberish and persists in another futile attempt to persuade me in favor of Solomon. "Two down and one to go," is the way she blithely assessed the situation after my return to Jerusalem from Mahanaim.

"I want you," she requests of me now, "to pass over Adonijah and name Solomon your heir. And I want you to do it before Adonijah's feast, while people still pay some attention to you, so there'll be no argument about it after you die."

"Bathsheba, Bathsheba," I cajole, "now why in the world would I agree to that?"

She is honest in reply. "Because I want you to."

"No better reason?"

"Please don't make me think."

Irresponsible certainty on her part has given way to fear as she has seen me sink into a more extreme desuetude and observed Adonijah ballooning out boldly to fill up the area in which I am shrinking. I hear more and more people talking about that outdoor feast he's planned at the foot of a hill not far outside the city. The hour has been set. I'm told he'll serve meat, and I'm almost sorry I said no. It's going to be a barbecue. Long tables of wood are being built in the shape of a square, and tents with stripes of yellow and white will be raised, in case there's rain. More and more often I hear criers in the street cheer, "Long live Adonijah." They sound like the voices of the fifty men he has hired to run before his chariot. What's wrong with that? What do I care how long he lives after I am no longer among the quick and have gone to sleep with my fathers? I find myself wondering if they will esteem me enough to bury me in the cave of Machpelah at Mamre before Hebron, to rest with my ancestors Abraham and Sarah, Isaac and Rebekah, and Jacob and Leah. That would be nice, wouldn't it—another signal honor to which I would be insensible. A lot I would enjoy it.

For a good while, Bathsheba openly sought to enlist the influence of Abishag until she realized the charming young servant girl doesn't have any.

"Solomon cannot be king," I announce once more, for what I hope will be the last time. Solomon would function much better as one of those apes he covets. Adonijah could be a peacock. "He's dumb, Bathsheba, dumb. He wouldn't last a minute."

"I would sit by his right hand and advise him."

"Do you know what he told me when I spoke to him last? You won't believe it!"

"He told me you didn't give him a chance to explain."

"He wants to build a navy."

"What's wrong with a navy?"

"You're as smart as he is when it comes to ruling a country. He has no brains at all."

"What difference does that make," she asks, "when it comes to ruling a country?"

And there, of course, she has me, but I stick to our point. "Salute Adonijah," I counsel and forewarn her. "Hail him and serve him."

"I'd rather scrub floors."

"He'll be king when I die."

"Then you might as well live!"

That made me laugh.

Things happened so quickly when I finally took charge that I had no time for second thoughts.

14

KINGS

W ell, it's all over, isn't it?" I say, and Abishag the Shunammite hears me in silence with a face that is serious, composed, and noncommittal. She gives off the scent of jasmine and
soap; her fingers convey a pleasing hint of coriander. She grooms
me for the night, combing my white hair with very delicate strokes
and cleaning the corners of my eyes with a solution of glycerine
and water on a damp, warm cloth of white wool. Her passion to
serve me is serene and fulfilled. She will cover me with clothes
when I lie down on my bed. And then, after she washes and
anoints and perfumes herself anew, she will stand before me un-
clothed for a few moments, that we may cherish each other with
our gazes before she curls in beside me to lie in my bosom. It
doesn't sound bad, does it? But I will get no heat. And I will not
know her in marriage. And again I will wish for Bathsheba, who
refuses me still.

"After all I've done for you?"

"I have my hands full."

Bathsheba is queen mother now and sits upon the right hand of
her son, and she submits in her defense the added excuse that it
would not be seemly. Solomon has won, and Adonijah has lost.
Indecision no longer hangs in the air. Solomon sits upon my throne
in my stead, and Adonijah has pledged himself to be a good boy,
after catching hold on the horns of the altar for sanctuary and
begging that he not be slain with the sword. If he showed himself
worthy he would not be slain, Solomon sent to him entirely on his
own, surprising me. The people are heartened that there will not be
civil war, and again they go about the street rejoicing, saying this
time, "Long live the king. God save King Solomon." That doesn't
upset me either, although the words sound somewhat queer to me,
as though I will never grow used to them. Why it has all turned out

389

this way remains something of a mystery, even to me. I do know that reason had not much to do with it. I did not pick one son over the other, the useless frugal one over the useless, shallow rakish one with the manners of a dance master and the morals of a whore. To tell you the truth, I had preference for neither. To tell you the truth, I did it in pique and I did it for love. I decided for Bathsheba, because once, for a few years of my life, she had made me happy, and no one but Abigail had ever done that.

I did not like to see her looking so frightened.

And for once in her life she came in with the truth, egged on by Nathan, who was indeed in terror when he perceived the crisis that was materializing on the day of Adonijah's feast.

All who'd been summoned by Adonijah were there to attend, and he slew sheep and oxen and fat cattle in abundance by the stone of Zoheleth which is by Enrogel. The long tables were in place, with coverings of purple and cloths of blue, and the tents with stripes of gold and white had been raised. It sounded quite nifty, but you couldn't tell that from Bathsheba's distress. Adonijah had conferred with Joab the son of Zeruiah, and with Abiathar my old priest, both of whom had followed him from the start and were helping him now. But Zadok my young priest, and Nathan the prophet, and Benaiah the son of Jehoiada had not turned to the party of Adonijah, and they had not been invited, nor had any of the mighty men who still belonged to me, for they were not with Adonijah. It was beginning to look like the old guard against the new, with Nathan blackballed because he hadn't jumped aboard. And Adonijah called all his other brethren, all the king's other sons, out to his feast. But Solomon his brother he called not, and this deliberate and portentous omission began to bode grave evil to many. Wherefore Nathan spoke up to Bathsheba that she might save her own life and the life of her son Solomon, and sent her in to see me, instructing her to bow and do obeisance to me and acquaint me with the particulars of the event.

He rehearsed her to say: "Didst not thou, my lord, O king, swear unto thine handmaid, saying assuredly that Solomon thy son would reign after you and sit upon your throne?"

To which I replied, saying, "Don't start nagging me about that again. I promised no such thing, ever."

"No, but did thou promise," she attacks sharply, with a kind of tense and angry emotion, "that thy son Adonijah would reign in thy stead while thou yet were alive?"

"I never promised anything like that either. Why are you trembling? What are you so upset about?"

"You did not promise Adonijah?" she scoffs, and only with a visible effort at suppressing tension is she able to sustain her scornful expression of exaggerated surprise. "Why then doth Adonijah reign?"

"What are you talking about?" I demand, with consternation of my own.

"Hast thou not heard?" she mocks.

"That Adonijah reigns?"

"That Adonijah the son of Haggith doth reign in Jerusalem this day?"

"Bullshit! Is this true?"

"And David our lord knoweth it not? Ask Nathan your prophet, who awaits outside. Send Benaiah to inquire if you think it's not so."

Benaiah, my trustworthy, is nodding. He has heard rumors that it is.

"He hath slain oxen and fat cattle and sheep in abundance," Bathsheba my wife races on. I am moved by the fact that she looks such a worried mess. "He hath called all the sons of the king to his party, and Abiathar the priest, and Joab the captain of the host. For myself I don't care—he is calling no women. But Solomon thy servant hath he not called, the only son of the king not there. And Zadok thy priest he hath not called. And Nathan thy prophet, and Benaiah thy servant." What she is saying is starting to add up. "And thou, my lord, O king, the eyes of all Israel are upon thee, that thou shouldst tell them, this day, who shall sit on the throne of my lord the king after him. Otherwise I dread it shall certainly come to pass, when my lord the king shall sleep with his fathers, that I and my son Solomon shall be counted offenders, in that we remained with thee."

"I don't believe you," I exclaim with confusion.

"Ask Nathan. Send out Benaiah."

"Go out. Send in Nathan. No fucking parables!" I bark in warning at my jittery prophet the instant he hurries in.

Nathan is grim and, for him, almost laconic, for he comes straight to the subject. "My lord, O king," he begins, "hast thou said already that Adonijah shall reign after you and sit upon your throne, and hast thou done this thing, my lord, and not showed it to thy servant, or to thy priest Zadok, or even to Benaiah and to the mighty men that still belong to thee, that we should know to serve him now?"

"Of course not!" I answer with a cry of reproof. "Why in the hell would you suppose that I did?"

"For he is gone down this day," Nathan answers in the same state of alarm, "and hath slain oxen and fat cattle and sheep in abundance, and hath called all the king's sons, and the captains of the host, and Abiathar the priest. But me, even me thy servant, and Zadok thy priest, and Benaiah the son of Jehoiada, and thy servant Solomon, hath he not called. Doesn't that tell us something? Ask Benaiah. Call up a ghost. Do you need a prophet to tell you what's happening? Wherefore, the celebration grows. And behold, they eat and drink before him even now, and say, 'God save the king!' "

"What's wrong with that?"

"They say, 'God save King Adonijah!' "

I come alive with a jolt. "King who?"

"King Adonijah."

"There is no King Adonijah!" I shout.

"Yes, there is, my lord, O king, unless you announce there is not. And if you do not say so now, there is left this day in Israel no more King David. Let me tell you a story."

"Never mind your story. Send back Benaiah."

By this time Benaiah has all the facts. I am being deposed, smoothly superannuated, without objection, discussion, consent. I am being moved aside. I am supporting Adonijah by keeping neutral. I don't like the idea. Bathsheba will be imprisoned and isolated. I like that less. From there it does not take me long to spring, so to speak, into action.

"Call me back Bathsheba," I command. "And wait—tell her that now I remember the promise I swore unto her." She kneels when she enters, still in a fright, and does obeisance to me again. "I remember clearly now the promise I gave you," I continue without even a wink, and I am holding her face in my hands to comfort her. "And assuredly Solomon thy son shall reign after me, and he shall sit upon my throne in my stead, and even so will I certainly do this day." And I kiss her so courteously with the kisses of my mouth.

"As the Lord liveth," she begins thanking me, and her voice chokes—only for the second time in my life did I see my wife Bathsheba cry, and this time the tears she shed were those of happiness—"as the Lord liveth, thou hath redeemed my soul out of all distress."

And now I am truly in control. King Adonijah? That bastard! I'll give him King Adonijah, that pipsqueak, that punk!

"Call me Zadok the priest in too," I commanded, "that he, with Nathan, and with Benaiah and his mighty men, shall all go forth together."

And Bathsheba was already her old self, saying, "Call in Solomon too."

"Do no such thing!" was my strict response. "Not yet, not yet." The plans I had in mind didn't require my seeing him so soon. "Cause Solomon my son to ride upon my own mule, and bring him down to Gihon. And let Zadok the priest and Nathan the prophet anoint him there king over Israel. And blow ye loud with the trumpet, and say, 'God save King Solomon.' And do this in a place in Gihon where the guests of Adonijah can hear." And that, I thought, was a very deft touch. "And then," I went on, "ye shall come up after him, that he may come and sit upon my throne, for he shall be king in my stead, and I have appointed him to be ruler over Israel and over Judah."

At which Benaiah the son of Jehoiada, typically so stoic and taciturn, heaved a sigh and said, "Amen. As the Lord hath been with my lord the king, even so be He with Solomon, and make his throne greater than the throne of my lord King David."

I concluded, after a moment of reflection, that I had no real quarrel with that.

So Zadok the priest, and Nathan the prophet, and Benaiah the son of Jehoiada, and the Cherethites and the Pelethites went down, and caused Solomon to ride upon my own mule, and brought him to Gihon. And Zadok the priest took a horn of oil out of the tabernacle and anointed Solomon. And they blew the trumpet. And the voice of the trumpet sounded long, and all the people said, "God save King Solomon." And all the people came back up into the city after him, and the people piped with pipes, and rejoiced with great joy, so that the earth rent with the sound of them.

And Adonijah and all the guests that were with him heard it as they made an end of eating, and Joab spoke up when he heard the sound of the trumpet and again when he heard the city being in an uproar.

"Wherefore is such noise in the city?"

And even while he yet spoke, Jonathan the speedy son of Abiathar the priest came running up to Adonijah to give the news, saying, "Verily our lord King David hath made Solomon king!"

Needless to say, Adonijah could not have been more amazed. "Solomon? My younger brother Solomon? That same Solomon who wants to build a navy?"

"Solomon sitteth on the throne of the kingdom," answered this Jonathan. "This is the noise that ye have heard. They are come up from Gihon rejoicing, so that the city rang again. And moreover, the king's servants came to bless our lord King David, saying, 'God make the name of Solomon better than thy name, and make his throne greater than thy throne.' And to this, they are saying, the king rose up on his knees and bowed himself upon the bed."

You can bet the party broke up quickly. All the guests that were with Adonijah were afraid, Joab too, and rose up and went every man his way in haste. Adonijah feared for his life because of Solomon and bolted up and caught hold on the horns of the altar and vowed he would not let go until he had a guarantee of life from the new king. Benaiah's squads were everywhere by this time and told us of Adonijah's saying, "Let King Solomon swear unto me today that he will not slay his servant with the sword."

And Solomon answered, "If he will show himself a worthy man, there shall not a hair of him fall to the earth. But if wickedness shall be found in him, he shall die." And even as the armed couriers of Benaiah were dashing out of my room with his reply, he turned to me and inquired, "Did I say that well?"

"Do you really want a navy?"

"Can a navy hurt?"

"Spoken," said Bathsheba approvingly, "with the wisdom of Solomon."

My farewell address was a much better one than Jacob's on his deathbed, which was inappropriate as a blessing and almost incomprehensible in content and objective. What was the reason for it, the twelve sons in attendance must have asked themselves more than once as they listened to him run on, primitive in intellect though several of them doubtless were. The speech I gave at least was functional.

"Here's what I want you to do," I said. "Thou hast with thee Shimei the son of Gera, that Benjamite of Bahurim, which cursed me with a grievous curse that day when I went to Mahanaim. You know I'm not one to bear a grudge. But I want my revenge. I swore to the Lord I would not put him to death by the sword."

"I think I know now what a hoar head is," Solomon broke in eagerly, consulting notes.

I paid no attention. "You must not slay him for what he did to me, for I vowed to God he would be spared. Therefore, you must slay him for something else. Set him about with restrictions that he will have to violate, and slay him for his failure to obey you there. You do understand now? Your mother will explain. To Abiathar the priest show mercy, though he turned to Adonijah, for he hast been afflicted with me in all wherein I was afflicted. Allow him to return in peace to Anathoth, unto his own fields, for he is a worthy man. Show kindness unto the sons of Barzillai the Gileadite, and let them be of those that eat at thy table, for so they came to me when I fled because of Absalom thy brother. And now, last but not least, we come to my nephew Joab, that son of Zeruiah." I cough to clear my throat, then moisten my mouth with water from an earthen cup Abishag thoughtfully extends when she hears my voice going dry. The girl is beautiful to the extreme and excellent at everything. Bathsheba, in the seat we have caused to be set for her on Solomon's right hand, bends forward in rapt suspense. "Thou knowest also what Joab the son of Zeruiah did to me," I state very somberly, and pause to make certain that all of my meaning will sink in.

"I will explain to you later," Bathsheba puts in hurriedly to Solomon.

"And also thou knowest what he did to the two captains of the host of Israel, unto Abner the son of Ner, and unto Amasa the son of Jether, whom he slew, and shed the blood of war in peace, and put the blood of war upon his girdle that was about his loins, and in his shoes that were on his feet. For what he did to them but not for what he did to me," I stress to signify unequivocally that I desire just the obverse, "do therefore to Joab according to thy wisdom."

"I think you are trying to tell me," conjectures Solomon with a furrowed brow, "not to let the hoar head of Joab go down to the grave in peace."

"Forget the hoar head!" I answer at the end of my patience, lifting my voice almost to a shout. "I want you to kill Joab. Don't you understand? Blow the bastard away!"

"He wants," Bathsheba translates for him, with a very sweet smile and with inexhaustible maternal tolerance, "you to blow the bastard away."

"I'm pretty sure I understand him now."

"And I want you to do it today."

He does not yet see that I want this done for his sake too.

Bad news travels quickly, even to Joab, and when the first hint of the tidings came to him, he rose and fled for refuge into the tabernacle of the Lord and caught hold on the horns of the altar. Benaiah demanded he come forth. Joab said nay but would sooner die than come out. Solomon looked to me for decision.

"Do as he hath said," I recommended with a smile, "and fall upon him there."

"Do as he hath said, and fall upon him there," Solomon parroted to Benaiah, and began to acquire that reputation for intellect and trenchant humor that really derives from me.

From Bathsheba I got no more than a cursory blessing, and a chaste kiss on the forehead. "Let my lord King David live forever," was the way she thanked me.

"That's very easy for you to say now," was my caustic response. "Lie here with me tonight," I asked her. "Make me happy once more."

"Use Abishag for that."

"I am asking for you. As God is my judge, I have sworn to lie with you at least one more time before I die."

"David, David," she says, losing interest in me and starting to inspect herself, "you're talking like a child."

"I remember thy love more than wine," I tell her in earnest. "Thou art beautiful, O my Bathsheba. A garden enclosed, a spring shut up, a fountain sealed. Please stay with me again until the day breaks and the shadows flee away. Thou hast doves' eyes within thy locks."

"I think I must have put on thirty pounds in just the past few weeks," she answers with a pout, and turns partway around to show me. "I don't know where it's come from, but you can see where it's gone. And I used to have such a magnificent ass, didn't I?"

I give her up sullenly. She bestows her kiss and goes away. God has let me down again. "Easy come, easy go," is the sardonic philosophy of resignation with which I try to console and amuse myself as I watch her leave. It is almost time for bed, and I will try to sleep.

Abishag the Shunammite washes and dries herself when she has finished with me and begins to anoint and perfume herself as she makes ready to join me. My lamps are lit. Her lips drip as the honeycomb, and I know that the smell of her nose is like apples. Honey and milk are under her tongue, and the roof of her mouth is like wine. The fragrant, sensuous vapors of the best incense suffuse my rooms, of incense compounded of stacte, onycha, galbanum, and frankincense. I would personally prefer a bit more frankincense in the mixture, but my powers of smell are not what they used to be, and what is pungent to me is acrid to others. Abishag the Shunammite sits without comment on the indigo folds of her robe, which has slipped from her shoulders and settled in lush and gleaming ripples about her waist and thighs. She reaches out her arms to lave them in liquid myrrh and then applies the unguent lotion to her chest as well and to her purple-nippled breasts. Her tiny feet are perfectly formed. There is still no spot on her. I am very old, and fortunate that someone so lovely and faultless as Abishag the Shunammite ministers to me every day. In another minute or two, she will be completed with her preparations and come to my bed. I will treasure the warmth and sweetness of her. You think that makes me happy? You think I'm at peace now with my Maker? Anything but. I am thinking of God now, and I am thinking of Saul. I think of Saul in his wordless gloom and torment every time I came to his chamber to play for him, and I realize as I remember that I never saw a sadder face on human being until a little while ago, when Abishag the Shunammite held a mirror up for me to see and I looked at mine.

It is almost night again. The skies of the desert are turning brown. In the pools of lamplight smoldering in the shadows in the far corner of my room I watch a vision slowly take shape. I see an eager, bright-eyed youth there on a low wooden stool; then one bare knee of his is bent to the ground, and he is holding in his lap a lyre with eight strings. The apparition has come to play for me. He is ruddy, and withal of a goodly countenance, and very pleasant to look at. His neck is as a tower of ivory. His locks are bushy, and black as a raven, and his head is as most fine gold. I know him, of course, and thrill at the instant of recognition, at the sight of such healthy, vibrant, expectant beauty in a face that is mine. I can hardly wait for more. He starts with a song I used to know, in a clear, pure voice too sweet for a girl's and too young for a man's. His music is soothing, almost divine. I have never been so happy as when I hear him begin. And then I look around me for a javelin to hurl at his head. Abishag my angel has risen from her chair and approaches without noise, wearing only a vivid scarf. Her eyes are as dark as the tents of Kedar. I want my God back; and they send me a girl.